The Immortal's Secret

The Immortal's Secret

Alexandra Edmiston

The Immortal's Secret

© 2024 by Y. Alexandra Edmiston Arpin

All rights reserved. No part of this book, covered by the above copyright, may be used or reproduced in any manner without the written permission of the publisher. Reviewers are invited to include brief quotations in a review of the book. For permission requests, write to the publisher, at the address below.

Scripture verses are from the King James Version of the Bible: biblegateway.com/

First Paperback edition: October 2024

The Publishing Prose
15 Malvern Avenue, Toronto, ON, M4E 3E2, CANADA
www.theimmortalssecret.com

First edition.

Paperback: 978-0-96800058-4-2
E-book: 978-0-9680058-3-5

This is a work of fiction. Names, characters, places, and incidents are the product of the author's imagination. Any resemblance to actual persons, living or dead, events, or locales is entirely coincidental.

Editor: Lorna Stuber - lornastuber.com
Illustrations: Cover & map: Marlena Temporao -marlenatemporao.com
Cover Design: Miblart - miblart.com

Also by Alexandra Edmiston

Confessions from the Cubicle: Women Talk about Surviving in Today's Work Force (non-fiction)

Unable are the loved to die. For love is immortality.
— Emily Dickinson

For my husband, Robert

> *To hear me? Let me go: take back thy gift:*
> *Why should a man desire in any way*
> *To vary from the kindly race of men*
> *Or pass beyond the goal of ordinance*
> *Where all should pause, as is most meet for all?*
> — "Tithonus," Alfred Lord Tennyson

Contents

Preface and Acknowledgements	1
Characters	3
Map	5
Chapter 1 In Search of The Immortal	7
Chapter 2 The Arrival of Annacletica	15
Chapter 3 Letter from Rocco Benedetti, Procurator of St. Mark's Basilica, to His Sister Lucia	23
Chapter 4 The Golden Find	27
Chapter 5 The Arrival of Cle	37
Chapter 6 Tom Cruise of the Louvre	43
Chapter 7 Examining the Plate	49
Chapter 8 Crossing the Boundary Between Light and Darkness	61
Chapter 9 Making the Pledge	75
Chapter 10 The Mysterious Empress	81
Chapter 11 Be not Faithless but Believing	95
Chapter 12 His Nightingale	99
Chapter 13 St. Mark's Basilica	115
Chapter 14 The Arrival of Grace	137
Chapter 15 The Return of Jenna or Paeon	143
Chapter 16 Isola di Speranza	147
Chapter 17 Meeting Annacletica	167
Chapter 18 Reckoning	181
Chapter 19 Moment of Truth	185
Chapter 20 Settling the Score	195

Chapter 21 The Chapel of Hope	201
Chapter 22 Reaching The Chapel of Hope	221
Chapter 23 The Chasm	227
Chapter 24 Finding Josiah	235
Chapter 25 The Funeral	246
Chapter 26 Returning Home	253
About The Author	261
Notes	263

Preface and Acknowledgements

One of my favourite paintings in the Louvre is Titian's *Man with a Glove*, created in 1520. The identity of its subject remains a mystery. He may have been a member of the Gonzaga family of Florence, but his name is lost to time.

This portrait was my inspiration for *The Immortal's Secret*. The mystery of the subject's identity, his faraway gaze, and the way he seems to defy mortality through Titian's brushstrokes inspired me to explore the themes of immortality and the supernatural against the evocative backdrop of the art world.

In its timelessness, art has the unique power to immortalize moments, emotions, and individuals. From a young age, I was captured by the mysterious allure of gothic fiction—notably *Dracula* and *The Picture of Dorian Gray*. I was intrigued by this genre's focus on immortality, inner conflict, moral struggle, and isolation. These themes inspired my writing, creating a rich tapestry from which to explore.

My characters wrestle with the essence of our existence: the challenge of being mortal and vulnerable, the pursuit of a meaningful life, and the quest to find one person who will offer unconditional love. They are presented the opportunity to slip off the usual path of life that leads to a final destination and join one that is beautiful, circular, and endless. Some accept this Faustian bargain, and their choices and struggles are at the heart of this story.

Writing this book has been a lifelong dream and one of the biggest challenges of my life. Through it all, I've had the love and support of so many. Writing can be lonely. On many nights, I would sit alone for hours, sometimes producing nothing. Yet, the next day, I was back at it, driven by something—I'm not sure what. I'm thrilled I can now hold up a completed book.

I am so grateful to my family. To my husband, Robert, your unwavering love, support, patience, guidance, and inspiration have been a constant source of strength through all my pursuits. My mother, Margaret and my late father, Alexander always made me believe I could achieve anything. My sister Carolyn passed away unexpectedly while I was writing this book. The grief and sadness were crippling. I will never get over how she never had the chance to share her gifts with the world.

Greg Ioannou, President of Iguana Books, you were the first to read my work. Your kindness and talent shone through in your feedback, encouraging me to continue. Christopher Tradowsky, thank you for working your magic on my second draft and showing me that everyone loves a villain.

Lorna Stuber, I knew I was hiring an extraordinary editor, but I didn't realize the breadth of your talents: expert on the publishing industry, successful author, fount of creative ideas, and a charming and funny collaborator. Marlena Temporao, I am still amazed I put out an appeal for a cover illustrator and a huge talent just landed in my lap.

To my many friends who read various versions and provided commentary, I thank you from the bottom of my heart. Special shoutouts to Vicki Bradley, Maggie Fairs, Kellie Garrett, Ezri Carlebach, and Maria Arpin. Your feedback and encouragement were invaluable. Shaun O'Neill, thank you for reviewing almost everything I've written over the years.

Thank you to everyone who reads *The Immortal's Secret* and becomes part of this journey. I hope *The Immortal's Secret* sparks your imagination and leaves a lasting impression, much like the art and literature that inspired me.

Characters

Annacletica/The Immortal: An ancient Egyptian beauty who creates a book of golden plates infused with supernatural properties that unlock the secret to immortality. This becomes a curse, forcing her to seek redemption and endure centuries of isolation and sorrow.

Dr. Benjamin Mann: A curator at the Louvre who is being treated for cancer. When he lapses into a coma and almost dies, his beloved grandfather, Josiah disappears. When Benjamin recovers, he embarks on a journey to find Josiah and ends up uncovering family secrets that will change his life forever.

Josiah Mann: Art collector, charming kook, and the former CEO of Mannfield Gold Corporation. Suffering from dementia, he vanishes, and his family fears he is dead. His eccentricities and deep knowledge of the golden book's history drive much of the plot's intrigue.

Cle: A quirky friend of Josiah with a sketchy background. She becomes Benjamin's assistant and helps him navigate the magical secrets surrounding *The Immortal* and the golden book.

Andrea Sartore: A Renaissance master who painted *The Immortal* and was committed to helping Annacletica devote her life to helping those who are suffering.

Grace Parker: Childhood friend of Benjamin who suffered a brutal attack in elementary school that left her physically scarred and emotionally wounded. Grace's reappearance in Benjamin's life triggers events that propel the narrative forward.

Jenna Parrish: The love of Benjamin's life, who left him abruptly. Intense connection and deep betrayal mark their passionate relationship.

Duncan Mann: Benjamin's father and CEO of Mannfield Gold Corporation. He tried to find his father, Josiah, but gave up hope after the trail went cold.

Father Roberto Sartore: His love for Annacletica and his role in the history of the book add mystical and historical elements to the story.

Mai: Annacletica's lover, he was a gifted alchemist who died shortly after helping create the golden book. Both his relationship and collaboration with Annacletica are pivotal to the story's supernatural elements.

Paeon: A mysterious character from Istanbul who may have been granted immortality. She may possess a critical piece of the golden book, and her knowledge is crucial to solving the book's mystery.

Sera Sartore: Josiah's wife and the grandmother Benjamin never knew. A descendant of Andrea Sartore, she discovered plates from the golden book in her Venetian palazzo. When she was on her deathbed, Josiah promised her he would find the golden book.

Map

Chapter 1

In Search of The Immortal

February 22, 2017
The Louvre, Paris, France

Benjamin Mann's head is tilted against the taxicab's window, his eyes closed tightly behind dark glasses. Clad in clothes he grabbed from his bedroom floor, he is oblivious to the joyful energy and "spring has sprung" postcard views streaking by his window. He's leaning down as far as his long legs will oblige, hiding himself from life outside the car and the nosy driver, who keeps peering at him in the rearview mirror.

"You okay, mister?" the driver says as he strains his head over the rearview mirror and watches Benjamin stroking his backpack.

Benjamin can see the driver's eyes darting in a triangle between him, the road, and the top of the baseball bat Benjamin saw peeking out from under the front seat. The driver cranks up reggae on the radio—Daddy Mory's *Seigneurs de Guerre*—drowning out Benjamin's deep breathing.

Since graduating with his PhD in art history from Oxford in 2008, Benjamin has been working as a curator at the Louvre. Before his colon cancer diagnosis in 2016, he was determined to excel, pushing himself to exhaustion as he obsessed about every detail in his job description.

Hurry up, he thinks, as he watches his foot tapping the floor. He notices his shoes are both black but don't match.

Alexandra Edmiston

A few hours ago, he spontaneously committed to tonight's unspeakable act. He was rolling a joint while leaning over the terrace in his luxurious apartment on the fifth floor of Ave. Montaigne, the most sought-after address in the Golden Triangle off the Champs-Elysées in Paris. He decided he had to call a taxi to get to the Louvre and confront *The Immortal*. The decision was triggered by an act of lust, sex, and the carnal enjoyment happening under his terrace as he was sprinkling his weed in the rolling paper.

A young couple was French kissing like two reptiles devouring each other's tongues. The man's hands were roaming up and down the woman's body, and she was moving in sync, stroking his face before pushing her hands down. Zippers were unzipped, garments were savagely pushed downward, genitals were exposed. Then the typical upward thrust, thrust, moan, thrust, moan, and the anticipated climax. The man's head collapsed into the woman's magnificent red hair—hair like a model in a Botticelli portrait.

This last-tango-in-Paris public display of lust and the stench of her perfume infuriated Benjamin. Colon cancer has ruined his life, and he simply could not endure this couple flaunting their youth, health, vitality, and sexuality. He didn't want to be reminded of his former life. He used to have a high-functioning cock, one that was out of his pants more than it was in, generating a lot of pleasure. Perhaps too much. And he used to have a grandfather who he cherished.

He wanted to fight back against the universe or whatever invisible foe transformed his life into his current hell. He wanted to blast out a string of expletives to the heavens, through the clouds, through the galaxy, finally deafening the ears of the Almighty himself…if He existed.

Instead, the universe threw its own sucker punch.

Benjamin's head and upper body dropped over the side of the terrace as if he was a marionette whose strings had been suddenly snipped.

Did I slip on something?

He wasn't sure, but he was stunned that his muscles had the strength to push his body upright and anchor his feet on the safe side of the terrace. The slip wasted some good pot leaves that were now covering his T-shirt,

The Immortal's Secret

his face, and his eyelids.

Staggering back through the glass door into his apartment, he groped his way to the sofa, flopped onto it, and dropped his head between his knees trying to get air into his lungs from his diaphragm and back out again. As soon as his breathing was steady and he could stand, he returned to the terrace and whipped the cordless phone off the terrace wall.

Back inside, he grabbed the first items of clothing not covered in dust bunnies on the floor of his bedroom closet, mentally prepared for this mission, and called a cab.

If people are starting to fuck in the street in this neighbourhood, if cancer can reduce my forty-year-old body to skin barely clinging to bones, it's time to act like the beast the disease has created.

His desire for destruction is motivated by one thing and one thing only: the disappearance of his grandfather. While Benjamin was fighting for his life in a Toronto hospital, Josiah was a constant fixture beside his hospital bed until one night he took off. The next day the family received an email from Josiah saying he was going on a journey with *The Immortal* to find the truth about what they didn't know. The complete absence of clues about what happened to Josiah is making Benjamin crazy.

The Immortal is in Benjamin's office at the Louvre. It mysteriously appeared there a month ago and his assistant secured it in a locked cabinet.

Before Benjamin left Toronto for Paris, he received a package from The Sacred Sinai Desert Monastery at the foot of Mount Sinai. It was from a woman named Cle, Josiah's friend for years. Although Benjamin met her a few times, he can't remember much about her. Cle sent a smattering of Josiah's belongings to Benjamin: a Rolex watch, a book about the Desert Fathers by a Father Roberto Sartore, a rosary, a Bible (New Testament) filled with Post-it Notes, and a child's composition notebook with scribblings in many different languages.

No clues as to his grandfather's disappearance were in that odd assortment of objects. *The Immortal*, the venerated golden icon, is his only potential clue.

Alexandra Edmiston

Now he just needs this taxi driver to boot it to scene of his crime so he can exit this cab and rid himself of the noxious mindfuck of sharp turns and the French reggae boom-booming in his ears. The feel of the outline of his green kidney-shaped vomit dish in his backpack comforts him. He can't stop caressing it. This parting gift from one of the countless, nameless hospitals has been a constant companion over the past year.

The taxi swings in front of the Louvre on the Quai des Tuileries.

"You can let me off at the Porte des Lions. Just over there," he shouts, fighting to be heard in between each booming bass note of the reggae.

He exits the cab and leans on the side of the car, pulling the fresh air into his lungs. The warm February weather is like giant oxygen mask. He stretches his arm out the open window on the passenger side and gives the driver a 20 Euro note.

Clutching his waistband, he wobbles through the arches of the Porte des Lions.

Why didn't I grab a belt? He's a weight loss poster child in these jeans. He was a healthy 180-pound man when he put on the first hospital gown. Now, he's an ashen bald head balanced on a popsicle stick.

Snaking slowly through the ground floor hallways of the Louvre, he tries not to waste the little energy he has; he'll need it upstairs. He brought a strawberry Ensure in case the pot he smoked brings on the desire to eat.

He pauses and stares at the majestic Daru marble staircase in front of him. It is framed by the fading light of the day streaming in from the giant cupolas that illuminate *The Winged Victory of Samothrace* at the top.

Pressing his sweater firmly into his jeans, he joins the hoard of visitors who've chosen to visit when the Louvre is open late. Clutching the handrail, he pulls himself slowly up the stairs. He almost tips over when he reaches the winged Nike at the top. There was a time when he flew up the stairs two at a time. But now, this bit of exertion makes his lungs feel like they're going to collapse. He bends down and grabs onto the side of the statue, gagging as his body tries to expel something that just isn't there.

Being untethered from the expensive oncology equipment and intravenous drugs that have been keeping him alive for the past year feels foreign to Ben. He could use a bag of saline in his blood right now, but he doesn't miss the constant needles. This sickness has created a relentless urge to embrace a toilet bowl. At least it's now his own toilet bowl and not the relic in the hospital bathroom. He's almost forgotten what a normal life is even though his life before cancer had been far from normal.

The Immortal's Secret

His focus is on his task and the tools that are in his office: a scalpel, infrared camera, various screwdrivers, and custom computer programs. For years, he's wanted to do this for pure fun, to discover more about *The Immortal*, but he would never dare. She's always been exquisite mystery in a frame. Placing his bare hands on her was out of the question, like touching a first folio of Shakespeare's without gloves.

Way back when, he believed each brush stroke, each shadow, and every nuanced colour of a great work of art was like a line of scripture. Art was his religion then.

He no longer worships the beauty of art. Fighting death is now his focus so he can find out what happened to Josiah in the time he has left.

Josiah never had *The Immortal* appraised but insisted she was worth millions. She's now temporarily under Benjamin's care. At first, Benjamin was excited she was back and he was praying Josiah may not be far behind. As each day goes by, he can't stop his mind from focusing on frightening scenarios about Josiah's whereabouts. *The Immortal* is his Pandora's box. He's so mad at her and would throw her down the Daru staircase if she weren't a precious piece of evidence that he's anxious to analyze.

He fumbles with the key to his office. Once inside, he turns the doorknob tight to make sure it's locked. He does not want to be disturbed.

As he slides into one of the leather chairs, he sucks in air and focuses on controlling his breathing. This is his first time stepping foot in his office in a year. He's missed it: the wall-to-wall-bookshelves, his Roman statues, his large picture window with a view of the Cour Napoleon, the leather sofa that doubled as a bed, especially when he was too absorbed in his work to make the short trip home.

He gets up and unlocks the cabinet. There she is. A Renaissance love poem shaped out of the most luxurious gold. A mixture of cloisonné gold, enamel, and oil paint. The gold of *The Immortal*'s face is beaming.

Another one of his prized possessions is a portrait of Marie Antoinette painted when she was a child and still the Austrian Archduchess. It hangs over his seventeenth-century black marble fireplace. He used to live like Marie Antoinette. Now he's a desperate, unkempt revolutionary, fighting phantom enemies. He walks over to the fireplace, carefully lifts Marie Antoinette up and over her hook on the wall, and replaces her with *The Immortal*. It's a feat of strength for such a weak man but he accomplishes his task with only a couple of pauses to take a few deeps breaths.

He is finally going to release *The Immortal* from her ornate six-inch-thick frame of golden Corinthian columns. He may be dead soon, either naturally or deliberately. If the latter, it will happen with the gun he plans on procuring if he discovers Josiah is dead.

But first, he needs to vent his fury on this stunning woman whose face has penetrated his soul since he was a child.

Andrea Sartore's *The Immortal* was owned by Josiah's wife Sera, the Venetian grandmother Benjamin never met. Not long ago it had been in Josiah's home. After he started getting disturbing letters from a woman who wanted to buy her, Josiah hid *The Immortal* in his secret room that he loftily called his studiolo. Josiah never shared the mysterious woman's name with Benjamin. As a CEO, Josiah was no stranger to disturbing mail but the correspondence and continual phone calls from the woman were aggressive. She became so unhinged, Josiah had to threaten legal action.

Sartore's legacy is *The Immortal*. Benjamin has searched for other examples of his work. Many are described in grand detail in ornate prose in the Venetian archives but he's hasn't been able to track them down.

Staring at her had been his favourite childhood pastime, but until now, he hadn't seen her in at least five years. He'd forgotten how beautiful she is. Her features so delicate, as if the gold had been poured onto her face, creating a divine death mask, then buffed meticulously by angels' hands. Each side of her face is a mirror of the other: oval-shaped with a tiny nose, smooth jaw, eyebrows like an exquisite frame around a masterpiece. Her full lips are sculpted out of rubies, slightly open like they're awaiting a soft kiss or pondering her deep secrets. She's a perfect woman.

He glides his finger over her hair—a luscious wavy mane of black enamel that cascades down her shoulders giving her the look of a Greek goddess—resting on a lavish purple gown. A mosaic of gold glass is fashioned into a commanding scepter, entwined with two serpents crowned with delicate wings. The Rod of Caduceus. The symbol of health and magic and alchemy.

Her elegant hands clutch a small gold book to her heart. Her only flaw, if it could be called one, are her eyes: two deep golden almonds, elevated from wooden panel, with round pupils punched deeply into the gold, and polished. They look like bullets.

The pupils aren't symmetrical; the left gazes up over a flawless arched brow and the right stares off to the side. She doesn't want to look at anyone...yet she doesn't want to miss anything with her mysterious gaze.

The Immortal's Secret

Benjamin has always been sure the positioning of her eyes was intentional but doesn't know why.

This golden goddess is surrounded by a dark and eerie desert oil paint landscape. The landscape is not unlike da Vinci's *Madonna of the Rocks*.

Over her shoulder is the gloomy entrance to a cave, a foreboding hollow framed by dark brown rocks of various sizes. The portrait's background looks like Mount Sinai has been smashed into pieces and formed into a mishmash of granite beasts out of the mismatched rocks. Since childhood, Benjamin has been trying to uncover meaning in the way the rocks were arranged, how the hues of brown were created.

Beyond the rocks, the landscape opens towards the golden light of day and a blurry object, perhaps a building. He walks closer and studies the portrait like he has done so many times. As he stares at the object in the distance, the portrait starts falling towards him, twenty pounds that just misses pounding his face. He reaches to catch it, but it slides through his hands and hits his head. He can feel himself falling towards the conference table. He breaks his fall by grabbing the back of one of the leather conference chairs.

The Immortal crashes to the floor, landing face up. She stares at him with an intense, unwavering gaze.

How on earth did she fall to the floor? I checked the hook. Everything was secure.

He moves to his desk and retrieves a flashlight from one of the drawers. As he slowly circles the room, he shines the flashlight in all directions. He is definitely alone.

Benjamin is not easily spooked but this is peculiar. If he still had any hair on his arms, it would be standing up. For a moment, he considers contacting someone for help to place *The Immortal* back on the wall before bolting home.

No, he can't go home. He must discover what lies within her.

He focuses the flashlight back on the painting to examine the damage. Strangely, she's intact—including the glass in the frame—except for some damage at the top of the frame. One of the brackets has come apart. Moving in closer he examines two pieces of wood that have separated to see if the frame can easily be fixed. Benjamin rubs his hands over the severed edge and notices something poking out.

He realizes the protrusion isn't a metal clamp to keep edges of the frame together as he had assumed. Something is lodged inside the corner of the frame. He puts his reading glasses on to examine it more closely

and notices it is gold. He gives it a few gentle tugs, freeing it from the frame, and brings it to his eyes to have a closer look.
    "Holy shit."

Chapter 2

The Arrival of Annacletica

AD July, 590
Near the Foot of Mount Sinai, Egypt

Annacletica is unrecognizable as human. Her emaciated body is barely alive and is splayed under a blanket of sand, a gruesome sight baking in the blazing afternoon sun of the Sinai Peninsula. All that is visible of her are her right arm and the side of her head, covered by her lush black hair, which is mangled into a grey mixture of dried sand and debris.

Her face, once the envy of all women in Alexandria, with her pouty lips and exquisite bone structure, is puffed to twice its normal size. The skin on her arm looks like it has been turned inside out, revealing the tender layers below: an angry, fried, and blistered mess of blood and puss after weeks of exposure to the relentless sun and winds. She could easily be mistaken for a half-eaten animal.

She is in agony. The to-and-froing on the hump of Sobek for over a week has left her tailbone screaming for relief.

Sobek is the young camel she bartered for in Cairo in exchange for a treasured turquoise necklace made by her grandmother. It was one of the only items she had left of any value.

Sobek had easily negotiated the deep sand and jagged rocks until they arrived in this spot after the blinding haze and fury of yet another vicious windstorm. He started limping in his left leg, his breathing became more and more laboured, and his hump began to shrink beneath her. She found it difficult to balance on top of him.

As Mount Sinai came into sight, she was touched that his last gallant act was to sit, ever so slowly while favouring his injured leg, allowing her to dismount. Her loyal and gentle creature had served her well. She stroked his face and placed her last drops of water on his dried-out lips. He moaned weakly, finally dropping his head in her lap, then rolled over into the sand for the last time.

"Take this beautiful soul and deliver him to the Gods, who are waiting to guide him in the next journey." Her mother had recited those words over everyone she ever loved when they died. Annacletica repeated them over Sobek and placed a tender kiss on his cheek before she collapsed beside him.

She had done her best to take care of him, feeding and watering him regularly even though she had been told he needed very little. But even the strongest animal built for this terrain could not last this journey.

Yet, she is still breathing life into her frame of protruding bones and bleeding flesh. She envies Sobek because death has welcomed him. He was as gentle and loyal as her beloved Mai, her companion on her first journey to this terrifyingly beautiful and barren spot over 500 years before.

That memory is guiding her on this new journey—one she has undertaken to undo the mistake they both made on his hallowed ground all those years ago. That mistake has forced her to roam the earth for centuries as a human who cannot die.

Lover, mentor, clown, and collaborator in redefining life, that was Mai. Annacletica's world with him had always been full of pagans and magical Egyptian Gods. An idealist then, she was so anxious to marry and live with him forever, to achieve immortality in a world where she found beauty in everything. She would not accept immortality from Osiris in the afterlife. Toiling day and night with Mai, her gifted alchemist and magician, Annacletica knew mortality would be unlocked in this life. They created the gold from instructions they discovered in an ancient document in the Library of Alexandria, and they were driven to discover how to infuse the gift of immortality into the book she now clutches to her chest.

Renowned worldwide for their wisdom and for helping the needy, The Gods of the Desert have a beautiful, magical pagan sanctuary not far from this spot where Annacletica is lying. They call it The Gods of the Desert Sanctuary. It is like Delphi in Greece, a sacred place that attracts pilgrims from around the world eager to consult The Gods of the Desert about cures for sickness or advice on major decisions. Prompted by their

The Immortal's Secret

families, Annacletica and Mai travelled to The Gods of the Desert Sanctuary to uncover the quintessence that would unlock the secret to immortality.

The details of that day are so vivid in her mind. She was waiting in line to consult the Pythia, who translated the sacred oracles of The Gods of the Desert. The outside of the sanctuary pulsed with life, a vibrant bustle of people from every corner of the globe, a kaleidoscope of colours and nations. Voices blended into a symphony of languages; fragments of conversations mingled together.

The air was thick with anticipation, each person eager to consult the Pythia. Exotic animals added to the sensory overload, from majestic camels to brightly-plumed birds. Monkeys chattered in the trees overhead, their mischievous antics a playful backdrop to the serious business of this sacred place. Sweet incense blended with the aroma of spices and the perfume of flowers.

Annacletica and Mai stood nervously with their arms around one another awaiting their turn, taking in the scene, feeling the weight of history in this ancient place.

As they inched closer to the entrance, each step forward felt so heavy. The secrets of the ancients lay beyond. What would they say? Annacletica buried her face in Mai's shoulder and couldn't shake the feeling that this moment, this meeting with the Pythia, would alter the course of their lives forever.

When they entered The Gods of the Desert Sanctuary, they saw the large chasm, its air thick with sulfur and laurel fumes. Mai was standing beside her clutching their golden book. They peered down into the chasm, where The Gods of the Desert were said to reside under the protective fog of intoxicating vapours. The Pythia, an older woman with wise eyes, was before Annacletica and Mai on her tripod perched over the chasm. The Pythia stared forward at no one; she gyrated, and the fumes of barley rose as she fell deeper and deeper into her trance. Annacletica was afraid to pose her question.

Mai nudged her in the side, and she said, "How do I infuse this golden book with the quintessence to become immortal and live a life that is beautiful, circular, endless?"

The Pythia extended her arm and said, "Please hand me the book." Pushing it to her chest, the Pythia twirled her head and rocked her body. "Make the pledge. Carve your image in your golden book in a holy place, light the candles, burn incense, and make a pledge to gain immortality. This is the quintessence that will grant your wish."

Annacletica and Mai were numb thinking of the possibilities. And so began her transformation into a pagan version of Tithonus turning from mortal to immortal, standing still as the earth revolves, unlocking herself from the time and the rhythm of life, becoming a sun that rises but no longer sets. Unlike Tithonus who continued to age, she was granted eternal youth.

Today's journey, hundreds of years after that extraordinary day in The Gods of the Desert Sanctuary with the Pythia, is one of desperation: to undo what was done, to seek redemption not from a pagan God but from the Christian God, the one they say came before Moses in the burning bush on this hallowed ground. He is her only hope, her only escape from her purgatory of perpetual youth and life everlasting.

The long journey here is over. She has practiced her prayer and her plea for help before this Christian God. She had wanted to be at the foot of Mount Sinai but she is going to make her appeal here, beside Sobek.

Taking a deep painful breath, she pushes down forcefully on her hands to pull herself out of the sand, slide onto her knees, and lift her swollen body up. She fights back against the pain shooting from every nerve. The rush of blood to her head is like an explosion that pushes her body forward, plunging her face and chest in the sand. She gasps and wheezes and grunts and coughs as her body's reflexes struggle to expel the sand blocking her throat.

As she rolls over in her bed in the sand, she notices, through the painful slits in her eyes, a cloud over Mount Sinai. It is shaped like an eye. The image reminds her of the Eye of Horus, an amulet her lover Mai once gave her for protection against evil spirits. Before Mai died, he promised he'd always watch over her. Is this him? She lies motionless, staring at it until the other clouds creep in and erase it.

Smacking one cheek, and then the other, she flips over onto her stomach and begins to crawl on her elbows while focusing on Mount Sinai. Taking deep painful breaths, she slides her body slowly over the sand, never taking her eyes off the mountain. The heat of the sand turns her hands into burning coals. She cannot endure the pain. Her elbows collapse and her chest falls back onto the sand.

Lifting her head up, she again rolls onto her side and gently slides her golden book out from the secret pocket she created in her white robe to protect it. After flicking off the sand embedded in the engravings on the cover, she rolls onto her back, holds the book between her hands, and stretches her arms as far as she can.

Directing the cover of the book towards the mountain, she cries out, "Lord of the Christians. I do not know you. I am told you are a merciful God, a God without judgment who welcomes all. I did something unholy over 500 years ago. I came here, to this desert, to a place near here called The Gods of the Desert Sanctuary, and infused this golden book with the quintessence. It has transmuted my soul and brought me the torment of immortality. My soul cannot survive in this constant loop of perpetual darkness. Please release me and redeem my soul so I can carry on the sacred and natural journey of all mortals."

The book tumbles from her hands onto her chest. She wraps her hands tightly around it, closes her eyes, moans, then weeps and wails, bathing her face in tears, sand, and blood.

Tiny grains of sand begin to swirl around her head, dropping on her tears, dancing around her body like a balmy summer breeze. The sand twirls faster and faster. Her eyes open fully without pain, and she stares at the twinkling sand as the rhythm of the small sandstorm picks up and comes together as a hypnotic golden vortex of sand, dust, and sun. It's like a force carrying an energy of peace and strength that travels over her limbs, infusing them with life.

She struggles to her feet, holds out her arms, and spins around in the centre of the vortex as the energy swirls up and down her body until she collapses with exhaustion.

When she awakens, the sun is cresting over the mountain like a starburst framed by orange and yellow streaks. She can still feel the slight presence of the energy. There are no pangs of hunger, no thirst, no pain. Only peace.

In the centre of the energy, she heard a voice scream out, "You have two choices: take the book back to The Gods of the Desert Sanctuary, let the fumes of the chasm destroy it, and pray for your soul. Or return to The Gods of the Desert Sanctuary and cleanse your soul by placing the golden book at the altar of their chapel to transform it from a book offering immortality into something holy. It will have the power to offer those who suffer one wish: their heart's desire to give them hope."

These were her instructions. But who spoke to her?

She isn't sure but she's praying it's the Christian God.

Did she imagine all of this in the mysterious energy, or were the words spoken to her while she was sleeping?

She isn't sure, but she knows she must go back to the chapel at The Gods of the Desert Sanctuary and place the book at the altar to help others. This is her mission.

A gentle tap on her shoulder startles her. She turns her head tentatively, not sure what she is going to find.

A young man is crouched down, gazing at her through the gentlest eyes framed by the hood of a dingy black robe. He would look frightening to her if he didn't have the face of a God with such chiselled features. She loves the way his patient brown eyes gaze at her, so gentle and kind.

"My child, are you okay?" He smiles and raises a goatskin bag filled with water.

She doesn't move.

He continues staring at her, his eyes moving from the suppurating skin on her arm over to Sobek's twisted face lying peacefully on the sand. The animal's blood is pooling into the ripples of sand.

"You are travelling out here with no supplies and an injured animal?" She silently takes the bag from him and holds it to her lips, gorging on the water until she starts spitting it up. It soaks the front of her robe right into her pocket, where her golden book is hidden.

"I'm so sorry, I drank it all."

The man laughs, shakes the sand off his hand, extends it towards her, and says, "I am Father Roberto."

He points over near the mountain. "I live with the other Desert Fathers in the humble monastery over there. You should come with me. You need help."

He picks her up gently, like she's a twig, and carries her to a scraggly black donkey standing quietly with his head down, almost touching the sand. He looks like he's sleeping. Father Roberto places her on top of the donkey with such a gentle touch that she feels no pain.

The donkey ambles forward with Father Roberto guiding him. She looks back at Sobek. The sand is blowing over his body and parts of him are already buried. From her position, she has a good view of where something sliced his leg open from his foot to the top of his thigh. She blows him a kiss.

The donkey stumbles a little but quickly composes himself, getting his scrawny legs moving again. His ribs dig into her legs. Despite his smelling like dung, she feels like she is on the top of a luxurious chariot. He is guiding her to a future defined by hope where she will help others.

As the mountain grows bigger in front of them, she stares ahead at the back of Father Roberto's hood, her eyes fixed on a golden object on a chain swinging back and forth. The wind must have blown it behind him. It's a large cross.

Redemption is within in her reach. She will go back to The Gods of the Desert Sanctuary and find the chapel. After more than 500 years, Annacletica finally has a plan to save her soul.

Chapter 3

Letter from Rocco Benedetti, Procurator of St. Mark's Basilica, to His Sister Lucia

May, 1580
Venice, Italy

My dearest sister,

I must share something before I am taken by the great Almighty. Some of this I saw with my own eyes, some I was told by those whom I felt were most trustworthy.

You remember the plague that fell on the most serene citizens of Venice in the year AD 1576. I am still haunted by the bodies of such good people heaped on carts and the smell of disease that clung in the air, homes, and on garments. Citizens were afraid to touch others' hands for fear they would be next. It was as if we all had transformed from humans to savages. Men and women wore gloves and carried sticks to move objects out of their way.

Then one day hope arrived. A magical golden book appeared at our most holy St. Mark's Basilica, in front of the altar of the baptistery. This book promised one wish to those suffering—their heart's desire. The Venetians turned to the book to heal disease. They touched the gold cover and prayed in front of an icon of a woman known only as The Immortal. It was thought she had been an Egyptian nun called

Alexandra Edmiston

Annacletica, a beautiful young woman, mysterious, other worldly, and with a gentle touch for those suffering and their families. Others insisted she was Empress of the Eastern Roman Empire, wife of Emperor Massimo, and sister of Emperor Theodosius I. When word spread about the book, desperate Venetians flocked to our basilica waiting in line for days to touch and pray on the book. Hundreds of sacred souls were miraculously spared.

I heard from a trusted source that a young mother, Giulia Bruno, brought her dying baby to the basilica and the child was cured. One of the plague doctors stayed by the book day and night, often accompanied by the gentlest of men: Andrea Sartore of the oldest noble family of Venice and relative of the Doge Alvise Satore. It was said that Andrea had known the immortal woman and created the portrait of her above the altar. It was venerated by all those who saw it. Everyone knew he had created other great works of art, although I have never seen them.

During the horrific time of the plague, the basilica became a refuge because of the book. There was a beautiful chapel in the basilica that we called the Cappella della Speranza. It was the only place left where civility, dignity, and hope reigned. I witnessed with my own eyes the healing that made visitors feel that God was shining his light on this sacred place, one miracle after another. Then it all ended.

One morning on the 12th of July, an ox of a man arrived in the basilica to publicly proclaim the book blasphemous. He stood at the altar and screamed that the subject of The Immortal *was an Egyptian pagan, a woman who promoted witchcraft. Everyone panicked and thought he was possessed. We stopped the line at the door and cleared the altar for safety. There was so much confusion. The brute had to be removed by myself and some of my fellow procurators. We were badly beaten in the brawl that ensued. We were finally able to drag him out and clear the basilica. When we went back to secure the golden book and portrait, they were both gone. They had been stolen in the confusion.*

A deep darkness fell over the chapel and the people of Venice. Hope was gone. The chapel was closed. Vittoria Sartore, Andrea's mother, was implicated by many. Witnesses saw the ox of a man and a smaller man at the chapel that day. They worked for Vittoria. She always claimed she was innocent and appealed to the police to search her Sartore

The Immortal's Secret

Palace on Isola di Speranza. They did, but to no avail. They arrested her but she eventually escaped to destinations unknown.

Citizens wanted an audience with Doge Satore, but he could not be found. It was said that he was hiding in a secret room off one of the courtyards of his palace and that he refused to move from a constant fire he burnt to ward off the plague.

Not only did The Immortal *disappear that day, but Andrea Sartore and the plague doctor were never seen again. Legend has it that they were both locked in a secret room in the basilica, a room no one was ever able to locate. I knew every corner of our sacred basilica but even I could not locate this secret room.*

No one understood why Vittoria would take The Immortal *and the golden book. There were many theories. One was that she was a sorceress. She most likely took, or will take, her secret to her grave—to hell, which will surely be her last resting place. Andrea, the golden book, the portrait, and all his other portraits were never seen again. He was a man of outstanding character and was missed by all who knew him.*

Please share this with everyone, my beautiful sister. It could help in locating the book from its hiding place. It's a story of hope and faith, one that inspires others to never give up. I hope to meet you in heaven, where disease and suffering do not exist.

Chapter 4

The Golden Find

February 22, 2017
The Louvre, Paris, France

Benjamin stares at an exquisite gold antique book. He recalls that Josiah had been searching for a golden book since his Sera died. It was an obsession. Josiah promised Sera he would never stop searching for the book and its truth. Benjamin is certain he is on the path to uncovering the book's secret for his grandmother.

The book is six inches by six inches with edges encrusted in green twinkling jewels. Holding the book up to his eyes, he's guessing it's worth a fortune. Engraved into this square, quarter-inch-thick slab of stunning gold—24 karats for sure—is an image of a small church, a chapel, with the most delicate details: a tiny spire with a Latin cross on top.

Benjamin examines the inside plates. They are half the thickness of the cover. Each has two tiny holes at the top, and they are fastened together with a circular ring, a golden rope crowned by the Rod of Caduceus. A little lock at the top of the rod keeps pages secure. The lock appears to have been pried open, based on the way the gold has been crushed at the lock's opening.

He carefully flips the cover up over the ring to examine the first plate. In the middle of the plate are words carved in both Greek, a language Benjamin loves, and hieroglyphs.

Benjamin slowly translates the Greek in his head and is amazed by what it says…or what he thinks it says.

> *The contents shared in the seven plates of this secret golden book are for those who believe in the ancient practice of alchemy. The gold is infused with the quintessence. It grants wishes to those who hold it tightly and pray. It offers the gift of healing to the devout or the gateway to immortality.*

Benjamin reads it again to ensure he translated it properly.

The carving is raised from the gold creating an almost 3D effect. He slides his fingers over the raised letters. They feel warm, as if the book is a living thing. Benjamin is nervous to continue touching them.

As a curator, there's nothing he loves more than discovering a rare piece of art. He loves the process: he gets a clue that something rare and special is out there, something fascinating located somewhere in the world. His passion drives him to find rare pieces and the stories behind them. He loves a good mystery hiding right before his eyes, anything that he cannot understand. If he's presented with a giant problem, he can barely sleep or eat until he solves it. Those who work in museums secretly hope the portraits will give them a sign, a twinkle, something only they can see. A curator longs for their favourite art to share what brought the subject of the painting or sculpture to the moment when they were immortalized by the artist. True art aficionados will the subjects of the pieces to come alive. At the same time, Benjamin is nervous that he is not equipped to deal with this book without Josiah, his partner in maneuvering through the world of all things mystical, esoteric, and downright freakish. He pauses and stares down at the book again.

Everyone in his family is convinced Josiah must be dead. Benjamin's father, Duncan, had unleashed an army of private eyes into the world—to the various places around the world Josiah loved to frequent. They produced no real clues or leads. Benjamin is the only one who's willing to consider another option.

It would be easy for him to dismiss this book as some esoterica created by Sartore, or perhaps something hidden years later by an admirer.

No, this is a significant artifact.

Benjamin slides his fingers over the furrows in the gold. He's certain he has stumbled upon something very significant. The book is a massive clue to something.

He turns to the second plate. Its heading is Emerald Tablet.
He reads the text slowly, translating it into English in his head.

That which is above is from that which is below, and that which is below is from that which is above, working the miracles of one.

As all things were from one.

Its father is the Sun and its mother the Moon.

The Earth carried it in her belly, and the Wind nourished it in her belly,

as Earth which shall become Fire.

Feed the Earth from that which is subtle, with the greatest power.

It ascends from the earth to the heaven and becomes ruler over that which is above and that which is below.[1]

These words are familiar to Benjamin. This direct quote is pulled from the *Emerald Tablet of Hermes*, an ancient text attributed to Hermes Trismegistus containing hermetic wisdom and principles. The passage was in an ornate gold frame inside Josiah's executive office on the forty-fourth floor of Mannfield Gold Corporation, or MGC, one of the largest private gold mining companies in Canada. Twelve active mines on three continents, headquartered in the heart of downtown Toronto. Before he disappeared, Josiah was the chairman, in name only, a titular head really. Duncan had been running the company for years.

Benjamin has heard Josiah recite this passage so many times. The idea behind the quote was to illustrate the mystery of gold. The media always called Josiah an eccentric mixture of captain of industry, billionaire, devout Catholic, devoted family man, philanthropist, and bushman. They never guessed alchemist/magician belonged on that list. Benjamin is one of a select few who know of his grandfather's other interests. And he's the only one who knows the location of the secret studiolo in Josiah's home. Gold defined Josiah's life.

The third plate is also in the two languages and has a carved title at the top.

The Oracle

Death is not the end but the beginning of something profoundly beautiful. A journey that rivals the miracle of birth. This golden book is for the devout. It will heal the sick. If you dare, it offers the gateway to immortality on Earth, an open and endless passage through time, a blurring of the borders that fuse your soul to life everlasting.

Carve your name and a true likeness of yourself in one of the plates of gold, representing the glorious elements of matter, and warm your image over candlelight burning the subtle essence of frankincense. Your gold will be blessed with the fifth element, the quintessence, to embed your spirit into this matter, giving you the gift of immortality. Your spirit will become one with nature.

Now Benjamin is intrigued.
The key to immortality? What is this?
The painting that had mysteriously shown up at his office is called *The Immortal* and this book promises immortality.

He tentatively lifts the next plate, the fourth one. It's an exceptional work of art, a splash of white, black, yellow, and red that brings to life the image of a woman who could decorate the wall of an Egyptian cave. Her eyes are brown and intense, framed by deep kohl eyeliner and highlighted with a fierce bolt of malachite eyeshadow. He feels her knows her.

Could she be the subject of The Immortal?
Her name appears to be carved deeply into the plate at the bottom in hieroglyphics with no Greek translation. He knows little of this ancient language, but he knows the vulture is an A, and there are several of them. The lion is a L and there is just one. It's an ancient Wheel of Fortune puzzle, and as he struggles towards solving it letter by letter, he thinks it spells out "Annacletica".

He places the golden book on the mantle of the fireplace and traces his fingers over the carvings. This is the most incredible artifact he has ever touched.

Pulling *The Immortal* towards him, he places her on the conference table. He retrieves his tools from the top drawer of his desk and places them down like surgical instruments. Soon he's looking down at her with his scalpel in his hand, like Jack the Ripper.

After flipping her over, he slices the thick paper at the back of the portrait with the wild abandon of an energetic four-year-old opening a Christmas gift. Each of the layers of paper on top of the mahogany stretchers is glued tighter than the last. This unwrapping is a brutal artistic rape, but Benjamin joyfully rips and rips.

He's crossing lines he would never have dared cross before. There is no shame deep enough to make his behaviour stop. He'd turn the blade on himself if he had the guts, but he doesn't.

He whips his foot like a machete into the tower of paper, sending it flying through the air.

The damage incurred from releasing the panel from the back of the stretchers is surprisingly minimal. *The Immortal* is free, stripped down naked to her canvas mounted on a thin piece of wood. He places *The Immortal* beside the golden book.

He flicks on the light over the mantle and illuminates *The Immortal*. The light bounces off the gold, exposing her as if she were the brightest star in the galaxy. He moves closer, inches away from her face, and stares, gently stroking her golden cheeks.

Is she warm? Am I imagining this?

He is finally looking straight at Sartore's masterpiece, his nose full of the oil paint, glaze, and gesso the great artist had used. Experiencing the portrait like Sartore did. Staring deeply into the chasm of the soul of whoever this woman was.

The smell is alive, pungent yet familiar. It's steeped in Sartore's beloved Venice, like the muddy, stagnant waters of the Grand Canal, mingled with the thick smell of incense from St Mark's Basilica, with just a whisk of musk from the dyed-in-urine blonde hair of one of the city's famous courtesans.

This treasure he is touching, something Sartore touched, is a work of art over 500 years old. A face embalmed in gold and trapped in her macabre, dark oil backdrop—one moment in *The Immortal*'s life in Renaissance Venice, which Sartore sealed in time.

He rubs his fingers over the paint of the rocks. They're almost painful to touch. Who knew there could be so many different shades of brown? The browns used here are so deep and vibrant, intensely morose and disturbing. The rocks come together like monsters who are poised, waiting, ready to reach out, take hold of those who view the piece of art, and suck them deep into the crevasses.

As he prepares his high-resolution infrared reflectography camera, Benjamin hopes this step will expose what lies below her layers of background oil paint. He had meticulously researched and chosen this camera. He bought it for other art studies and now it's the specialized technology he needs to solve his mystery. When infrared radiation hits the paint layers, it lifts them up like a curtain revealing everything that was painted or drawn on the canvas. He's hoping a different background is concealed below the paint like a ghost, or maybe some alchemical breadcrumb that will lead him to Josiah. He's especially excited to see any preliminary sketches Sartore may have placed on the canvas before beginning to paint.

He lines up his camera, holding the long handle tightly with his long gaunt fingers, pointing at the top right of the portrait, where the blurry structure is located. He stares through the viewfinder taking care not to photograph her golden face. It's a light hand-held camera with a large screen, perfect for a convalescing weakling who couldn't maneuver, let alone move, the bulky infrared photographic equipment of the past.

He snaps and the camera flashes.

Her golden face lights up like an explosion of golden shards directly into his eyes. Her eyes are like two light sabers in the middle of the fiery chaos. Two floating blazing circles.

He almost drops the camera as his fingers rush to soothe his eyes.

"Ow, ow, ow!"

His pupils feel like they've been scorched, and he rubs and rubs wildly, creating a light show in his head. The eruption of the gold is not something he was expecting, not something he thought logically possible.

He gropes his way to his desk and settles into his chair, leaning back and cradling his head against the headrest. The fireworks in his head are like a psychedelic drug, pushing his mind into fast forward, with images melting down into pieces, floating in front of his eyes like a lava lamp.

Then it stops. Just stops. Everything is suddenly clearly visible in his office again, particularly *The Immortal*, smirking at him in her schizophrenic way like has nothing happened.

There's no explanation for what he does next. Maybe it's the lack of food, fitful nights of sleep that masquerade as rest, or a mind pickled by endless drug therapies. Or maybe she is willing him.

He places the camera on the desk and lights a beeswax taper and some frankincense that he found tucked away in his desk drawer. With one flick, the chandelier is off. The room is lit only by the soft glow of the taper as he walks slowly over to *The Immortal*. He raises the candlelight directly to her face to examine her like Sartore would have in his atelier somewhere in Venice, in one of the exquisite palazzos along the Grand Canal.

The Immortal's Secret

Benjamin knows that Sartore learned to paint by examining and sketching the mosaics in St. Mark's Basilica alone at night, illuminated by candlelight. He feels the connection to the great artist as he examines *The Immortal*'s right eye, then her left, moving the candlelight in between her eyes to irradiate the two bullet holes with the faraway gaze.

A gentle whisk of frankincense travels up his nose and reminds him of church, Catholic mass, and hymns.

He slides the golden book over to him, clutching it to his chest. He closes his eyes, focusing his other senses on the memory, the scent, the stillness, and the heat of the candle as he sings, "How Great Thou Art."

When he opens his eyes, both of hers are staring at him and shimmering like she has been infused with life. It's an energy that radiates from his toes to his scalp, tingling and setting off sparks in his body.

"Whoa," he says grabbing the side of the mantle. The candle tilts and he moves his fingers to avoid the dripping wax. Every nerve in his body is on fire.

Looking back at her is like looking deep into the sun. She's hypnotizing him and pulling him forward in a swirl of positive energy, enveloping him in a gentle embrace. The swirl of energy surrounding his body is fascinating, like it has taken on a form and is caressing him in all of his most tender places. She possesses an innate understanding of his deepest vulnerabilities, offering only pure goodness to embrace his battered body.

After placing the candle beside her, he moves over to the sofa to sit down. He feels like every part of his body has been caressed. Such a sensual feeling. He almost feels a tinge of movement in his penis. He sits and stares at her, feeling like she is human. Matter has come to life. His body and soul are locked to her in a mystic way. A gold image come to life: mystical, sensual, and deeply mysterious. It's like all the energy in the world is embodied in her eyes, communicating with him behind a layer of gold. His connection to her is impossible to comprehend. He wants to lean in, kiss her, and fuse his energy with hers.

His desire for *The Immortal* to lead him to something strange—to something profound—terrifies and energizes him in equal measure. He wants to teeter on the edge of her world, float out to somewhere he may not be able to return from. Benjamin read somewhere that the Byzantines were trying to embed spirit into their icons. They wanted to design a spiritual gateway in their churches to make believers feel that they were communing with something divine. When they peered into the face of the icon, they were looking into the face of The Virgin Mary or Christ himself. They couldn't just rely on faith. God had to be felt. They had to stimulate all their senses to create a mind-expanding experience. To deepen the connection with God by showing that he is real. Benjamin always felt this concept was a deception passed down from pagan times. Until now. What he is feeling is real.

As he rises from the sofa and approaches her, he moves his finger in to touch her again. The candlelight flickers rapidly over the ghoulish background of the painting. Then, all of the energy suddenly dissolves.

Benjamin moves forward but her eyes are no longer staring. They have returned to their focus on the beyond, the place only she can see. She is no longer warm. Whatever had happened is gone.

"Don't go," he pleads into the silence and lightly rubs his finger over her cheek.

As he stands at the mantle beside her, he places his hand on the golden book. An image of Josiah flashes in his mind: in bed, weak but breathing. Benjamin is walking over to touch him. The illusion is so real he can smell Josiah's favourite cologne. He keeps his hand on the book, squeezing it tightly, but the image disappears.

Remembering his camera, he staggers up and flicks on the chandelier, then returns to sit at his desk. Specialized software on his computer may reveal clues as to what he had just experienced.

At his laptop, he begins the download process to attempt to create a digital composite of the infrared image. He watches patiently as an image appears on the screen, building up from the bottom, exposing an infrared green blob of texture where *The Immortal*'s face is. Once the background builds on the screen to complete the portrait, he realizes there is no sketching underneath. There appears to be nothing in the infrared reflectogram but the current background in the painting reversed like a negative. This is not what he was hoping. He zooms in.

Beyond the rocks, there does appear to be something odd embedded in the background. A detailed sketch perhaps that never became part of the portrait. Is the portrait he's stared at countless times over the years revealing a secret? He can make out a small structure, like a building. Benjamin uploads the infrared into his reconstruction software to see if it will colourize the negative and deliver a more three-dimensional image.

Five minutes later, the program creates the image and Benjamin moves his mouse around on the screen anxiously. The cursor suddenly stops and refuses to move.

"Shit." He moves the mouse in circles but still nothing happens.

"C'mon," he says as he punches the escape button on the keyboard.

Just when he's convinced the huge file may have crashed his laptop, an image begins to emerge slowly on the screen with the pixels forming from the bottom. *The Immortal* appears, her beauty shining in the dark and brooding background.

Beyond the oily blackened rocks that lead out into a magnificent sunrise is a sketch of the small object. Benjamin's tired eyes home in. He zooms in on the screen to make the image as large as he can. The structure is a small golden chapel with a delicate spire anchoring a huge cross. Unmistakably, a chapel is hidden beyond this chaotic rock formation. A chapel in the desert near what looks like a chasm. This is the image he's wanted to make out his whole life. He places his finger on the screen and traces the chapel. There are words above the door than he can't make out.

"He hath compassed the waters with bounds, until the day and night come to an end." He whispers his favourite passage from the Book of Job. He's not sure why it pops into his head.

Josiah, did you go there? Did you retreat to this chapel to find a clue? Is this where you went? Is this my first solid clue? A chapel in the desert…a very large desert?

As he continues examining the image, a sudden wave of exhaustion hits him, draining any energy left in his withering frame. His eyes drop slowly like the lids are turning to stone and his body slides off the chair onto the floor.

A surge of vicious nausea thrusts its way up his throat, and he bends over. All he can think of is getting to his green vomit dish, but the feeling passes. The evening's adventure was an ambitious undertaking, and he is forced to admit that he has pushed himself too far physically.

As he rests on the floor, he watches *The Immortal* for as long as his eyes will allow, until they close like the lids are made of lead. His head drops and he falls into a deep sleep bathed in candlelight.

Chapter 5

The Arrival of Cle

February 23, 2017
The Louvre, Paris, France

"Ben."

Denis Favreau, one of the Louvre's assistant curators, is standing over Benjamin.

"Ben...est-ce que tu vas bien?" Denis is jingling coins in his pocket, clearly annoyed.

Benjamin looks up from the rubble created by the rape of *The Immortal*. Lying on his side with his head propped up on the mound of paper, he stares at Denis as if he's never seen a human before.

He's trying to process his surroundings. Where is he? He scans the room and sees *The Immortal* propped up on his mantle between two copper book ends with the golden book beside it. He swears he can smell incense. The faint smell of the sweet fragrance that burnt in his church back home in Toronto. It's tickling his nose like it always did in church. Everything comes back to him slowly.

Looking up at Denis, he says, "En anglais s'il vous plaît."

He rubs his nose and thinks he might sneeze. Then he becomes aware of the pain. A corner of the paper is digging into his eyelid.

As his mind focuses on whether he has any Visine in his backpack, Denis continues. "Très bien. Nous pouvons parler anglais. We need to get you home. You are not fit to be here. Has any of this been cleared by your doctors?"

"Yes, of course," Benjamin appeals as he attempts to roll over onto his knees. He could have sworn Denis had been fired just before Benjamin left on sick leave, but maybe the sneaky fuck found a way to get reinstated.

Benjamin's arms are asleep, forcing him to do strange gyrations on the floor to attempt to elevate himself. Denis is not a welcome sight first thing in the morning or anytime of the day.

Benjamin finally sits up and rocks back and forth, trying to find a comfortable position for his bony bottom on the hard floor. Standing behind Denis is a woman with a shock of long, thick, fire-engine red hair, looking towards the sunlight streaming in through the window. Her head is twitching slightly.

Denis motions to the doll-like creature, who looks like she would squeak if you poked her.

"Ben, this is Cle Bernice. She delivered *The Immortal* from the South Sinai. I think you know her."

Benjamin missed her name and doesn't ask Favreau to repeat. He cannot stop examining her face, but his eyes aren't focusing. Her face looks like it was painted with crayons.

"She has kindly volunteered to accompany you home."

Benjamin looks up at Denis.

"I was just planning on heading out. Can you give me a minute?"

Denis turns to the woman and asks, "Would you mind waiting outside, Cle? We'll just be a moment."

Benjamin knows what's coming next. He figures he'll let Denis lecture for five minutes for the entertainment value. Then he'll let him have it, a full-on, take-no-prisoners, spit-infused dressing down, two intimidating inches away from his face. Just to remind him who has the fucking PhD in art history from Oxford and a grandfather who's a billionaire art patron.

Denis bends his knees and wraps his chubby arm around Benjamin, filling Benjamin's nose with the aroma from his morning smoke break. It brings Benjamin's stomach to full attention.

"I am very worried about you. Look at the state of this portrait. Why would you do something so horrific? You, who worship art and lecture all of us on the correct protocol for handling it."

Benjamin digs his nose into his slacks to protect his sensitive nasal membranes and avert any quick liquid expulsions from his stomach.

"I was checking out the portrait because the frame appeared to be damaged," he says, examining the debris. "I was fine when I got to work,

The Immortal's Secret

but I must have had one of my spells that I've been getting post chemo. It's crazy shit, you know."

"You need to get to the comfort of your home," Denis says, looking at the exquisite frame in mangled pieces on the mantle. "Come."

Denis grabs Benjamin under the arms and gently hoists him onto his feet, pausing to make sure he's steady before he removes his hands.

"Ben, everyone here is so upset about the colon cancer and is waiting for you to return to work full time. We miss your expertise and mentorship. But you must admit, this is not the right time. Let's get you out of here and back home to rest."

"Can you give me a moment to collect my stuff?" Benjamin says, ambling towards his desk to move Denis away from the precious book. "You can tell that woman I'll be fine," he says while pushing the cover down on his laptop.

Denis moves over to *The Immortal* and stares at her face. He blows out the last candle on the candelabra and turns to Benjamin.

"I'd be more comfortable if Cle accompanies you." He tries to pick up the golden book. Benjamin leans over and grabs it.

"I never thought I'd say this but I'm not in the mood to go home with a woman." He winks and dramatically holds his expression for a second or two longer than normal, a move to get under Denis's skin.

Denis ignores the taunting and instead, walks out the door and shuts it with a bang. Benjamin can hear Denis's voice giving orders to the woman in the hallway just outside the office.

"Make sure you stay with Mr. Mann so he doesn't hurt himself. He's not himself. He almost died. He looks like he is still quite ill."

I look ill?

Benjamin is surprised he's offended; he knows he looks like shit.

That android Denis should clean the filthy grease off his mirror to examine his own dead face.

He finds some bottled water in his desk. While staring at *The Immortal* and the golden book on the mantle, he swallows a blood thinner along with a Percodan and a bonus Gravol that was in the Percodan bottle for some reason. This is the cocktail of pills he's been taking every morning. They're self-prescribed since he's no longer under a doctor's care after slipping out of the cancer unit in Toronto.

A knock on the door makes Benjamin jump.

"Ben, are you coming?"

He wants to tell Favreau to fuck off but instead he says calmly, "I'll be out in a sec." Benjamin enjoys keeping others waiting. Not everyone. Just the idiots.

Walking over to *The Immortal*, he looks at her again. He moves the book towards the centre of the painting beside her left hand.

Is she holding the book I'm holding?

He closely examines the book in her hands. It could be the same carvings, chapel, etc. He'll have to check his digital image.

He is deep in thought as Denis screams, "Ben, Cle ordered a cab. It'll be here any minute."

A bang on the door. Benjamin turns around to look.

"Cle is waiting, Ben."

Who is Cle? Oh yes, the woman. Why did Denis allow her to see me in that state? Why do I even care if some subordinate sees me like that? For some reason, I do.

He gathers his things, carefully placing the golden book in his backpack and securing *The Immortal* tightly under his arm. As he walks out of his office, his embarrassment turns to anger when he faces Cle and Denis standing against the wall across from his office door.

"Let me help you with that, Ben," Favreau says, leaping towards him.

"No need. I'm good. Thanks."

Denis glances at Ben's office door, then at Benjamin and says, "You need to get out of here." He storms down the hall.

Cle is waiting next to a Roman statue, twirling a thick strand of her long red hair and watching him behind black-rimmed, Coke-bottle glasses. He notices she has a Mickey Mouse T-shirt underneath her ill-fitting blazer. It all looks like stuff you would find in the Louvre lost and found or you could buy at the gift shop. He's not sure why he's being so judgmental given he's slept in his clothes and can't remember the last time they were laundered.

"Good morning, pardon me," he says firmly as he passes her and moves as quickly as he can down the hall, praying she won't follow him. She's familiar in a way he can't place.

"Benjamin. Wait, please," she says as he opens the door to exit the executive offices and enter the museum. He doesn't want company and wants to dodge her in the crowd of morning visitors that should be circling the Mollien staircase by now.

He stops and pivots towards her.

"I'm okay, really."

"I'm not following you. I want to make sure you get home safely."

He points at her tiny little nose, the one that looks like it belongs on a squeaky toy.

"I've forgotten your name."

She looks oddly familiar for some reason.

"Cle." Her poorly-applied red lipstick on her caramel-coloured skin reminds him of a Raggedy Ann doll with Harry Potter glasses. "You know me. I am a friend of Josiah."

His head suddenly becomes heavy like it's made of marble, like one of the Louvre's famous statues. It pushes his body down, and his butt smacks on the stairs.

Rushing over to him, she gently holds his arms and pulls him to his feet. He hangs over the edge of the stairs trying to compose himself and focus on whether all his bones are intact. He's not sure if the strange fall is the result of some mysterious cancer-related reaction. He places his hand in his backpack and is relieved when he feels the outline of the golden book.

"Wait here and I'll get the taxi."

He watches her scurry away as he drops his head on the edge of the railing and closes his eyes.

Chapter 6

Tom Cruise of the Louvre

February 23, 2017
Benjamin's Apartment, Paris, France

As the taxi moves down the Rue de Rivoli on the way to Benjamin's apartment on Ave. Montaigne, he is in his own world. His arm is caressing the outline of golden book tucked in his backpack. He's trying to remember the name of the woman in the front seat. She introduced herself when he was feeling light-headed.

Cle, or was it Anna? She was a friend of Josiah's. I'm not going to ask. Peace is what I need right now, not conversation.

He's focusing on how he'd like to exit his body. He wants to be a soul floating homeless and painless until his good health finally returns. Energy is what he desires, and a full, uninterrupted night of sleep. They are what he needs so he can have the strength to solve this mystery for Josiah.

Tapping his phone, he looks for any texts from Jenna. He's been doing his every day in vain since she left him and broke his heart.

Parisians are going to work along the Rue de Rivoli near the Place des Pyramides. The packs of tourists are clucking merrily, studying maps in front of the tour office. When his cab stops at a red light, he stares at a tall young woman wearing a white coat and red beret. She's flanked by her attractive friends. She returns his gaze and waves at him with two fingers. This anonymous human connection makes him want to cry.

He's not invisible, which is how people often unintentionally make cancer patients feel. When his hair disappeared and his skin turned a sickly mélange of white-grey-puke, his presence elicited an instant turn of the head in the other direction from most people. He misses his athletic limbs sculpted from years of running and his lush hair, which always magically fell into place, with a cowlick that pushed a huge swath of hair over one of his eyes.

Tom Cruise of the Louvre. He was dubbed this years ago by a reporter, and the moniker stuck. It's been used in every article written about him since. Benjamin loved it but Josiah rejected the comparison, preferring the phrase "classically handsome." He felt Benjamin had been blessed with the good looks that he lacked: eyes shaped like Sera's, magnificent, healthy, chestnut hair, and a cleft chin that Josiah felt was the ultimate mark of masculinity.

His hand and arm continue caressing the golden book, and the frankincense he burnt last night is still tickling his nose. It brings him back to his hospital room in Toronto, where he fought away tears, drooped over a hospital chair while being infused with chemotherapy. It was his last cycle (number eight) of chemo, and it was scorching through his abused veins like Drano. Someone had carved "Get me out of here" in blue pen on the beige vinyl chair. He focused on the words, moving his eyes up and down the curves of the letters, willing them to transport him to a reality a bit less brutal.

When the treatment was over, his mother, Janet, pushed him in a wheelchair, with his body almost at a 45-degree angle, to her car. He spent the journey from the hospital to his mother's home in the fetal position in the back seat, drooling on her white leather seats, emitting moaning noises produced from deep in his diaphragm. That night he suffered from a combination of agitation and a strange feeling like he was wading in Jell-O. He took a bath and hung his head over the side of the tub. Half conscious and feeling half human, he spit up a vile concoction of something solid mixed with blood. He remembers his mother on the other side of the door saying, "Benji, I have some toast here with some tea." When the innocuous smell of the toast reached his nose, he stood up, got out of the bath, slipped on the blood, and toppled over sideways, thumping his head into the side of the tub.

All he remembers after that night was lying in a hospital bed in intensive care hooked up to so much stuff. It was like he was looking through the wrong side of binoculars where everyone appears so far away. Someone, probably Josiah, had wrapped a rosary around his fingers. If

The Immortal's Secret

Benjamin could have spoken, he would have told Josiah the rosary felt like sandpaper. At some point, everyone got smaller and smaller and he was gone—he lapsed into a coma.

Many neurologists insist people in comas don't dream, yet Benjamin kept dreaming of a girl named Grace Parker—continually seeing her head thump against the side of a swing set like a wrecking ball. The vision kept going back and forth. She was attacked by a group of twelve-year-olds, and their cruel actions raged in and out of his dreams.

The last image he saw before he woke from the coma was of Grace holding out her two tiny hands to help him out of the hospital bed. She moved the covers. He sat up and paused before putting one foot on the floor. This action alone was dizzying.

"We thought we were going to lose you." His mother kept screaming amidst sobs as medical professionals surrounded him with more equipment. "The priest gave you last rites," she said as she rubbed his brow and she struggled to breathe.

The doctors kept insisting he was a medical miracle. A stream of white coats visited his bedside probing for information he couldn't provide. All he could remember was Grace. But he wasn't going to share her memory with strangers. The person he longed to see was Josiah.

Benjamin's father, Duncan, kept insisting Josiah wasn't feeling well and would visit soon. After a week, Benjamin grew impatient and called Josiah's home. The housekeeper, Angelina, said he was missing.

The next call was to his dad.

"What is this shit about my grandfather being missing?"

"He disappeared. Before that, he kidnapped you from the hospital. He could have killed you. Assisted by who knows who, he led a stealth mission to sneak you out of the hospital and take you to his home."

Josiah was certain the hospital was going to kill Benjamin. The doctors said that when the police raided Josiah's home, Benjamin was mere hours from death.

Josiah fought, but the police overpowered him. After they took Benjamin back to the hospital, they attempted to take Josiah to the police station, but he jumped out of the car, staggering into the darkness. Now he's a ghost that cannot be traced by the regular credit card or CCTV trail. He's alluded all modern technology. No one knows where he is.

"The police are investigating. I got an email from him that said, 'Benji is gone. I can't live without him. The blood is on all your hands. I've gone to find the truth.' When I responded to tell him you were okay, the email bounced. He seemed certain you had passed away. We were hoping he just went off on one of his confused states, off to examine some gold mine somewhere. I've hired people to find him, a company he's used in the past."

"What did they say?" Benjamin asked.

"His credit card showed he bought a plane ticket to Istanbul but he was nowhere to be found. No activity on his card once he arrived."

Benjamin said, "He must be using cash."

Josiah loved to use cash and steadfastly never trusted anything digital, saying it was too easy to press a few buttons and see cash pop out.

"Yes, that's an option, I suppose. The night we found you at his home, he was in his own world, setting things up on the table: candles and incense. He was waving a gold plate over your head. His maid said he left with a few items of clothing and that painting, the one of the golden woman, the one your grandmother loved, the one he was infatuated with: *The Immortal.*"

There was a long pause on the phone and Benjamin was sure they'd lost their connection.

Finally, he heard Duncan breathing.

When Duncan shared this story, his tone was serious, deep, and baritone, like the voice he reserved for meetings with his senior managers.

"There is one thing you need to know about your grandfather," Duncan said as he cleared his throat. "He likes disappearing, going off somewhere you'll never find him. He prides himself on leaving no clues and even throwing you off his trail. He's been like that since I was a child. Some find it charming. I call it a sickness."

"Okay," said Benjamin. He didn't feel like he should ask Duncan to elaborate.

"Do you remember anything about being at his house?" Duncan said.

"No, nothing. However, I am haunted by dreams I had."

"What were they about?"

"Do you remember the young girl who was attacked when I was twelve—Grace Parker? She was guiding me. Giving me strength to go on."

"It was tragic, what happened to her back then. A beautiful young life cut short by evil."

"She was so alive in my dreams."

"Maybe she's a guardian angel. I feel my mother is my angel, looking over us, despite Josiah feeling my birth killed her."

"Are you okay?" Cle asks from the front seat of the cab, snapping him back to his current reality. She cranes her neck to have a good look at his pathetic form leaning onto his backpack.

"I'm fine," he says, wishing he were home so he could say goodbye and she would exit his life. He closes his eyes to signal he wants no conversation.

The driver stops in front of his apartment. Cle takes care of the payment before Benjamin has a chance to wonder about the location of his wallet. He remembers it was in the grey Armani overcoat he is not wearing anymore.

Benjamin stands in front of his apartment door waiting for Cle. His eyes wander over to the laneways between his building and the restaurant next door.

"The key…for the door? Do you have it?" Cle asks. He is surprised, relieved is more like it, to find his key in a pocket in his jeans. After a number of false starts, he's able to place it in the keyhole. As he's attempting to turn it, Cle moves in like a little elfin doorman and pushes the door open for him.

"Nice place," she says as they walk into the marbled foyer. He had purchased the apartment furnished, sight unseen. His mother checked it out and proclaimed it looked like a museum. It was located in what she called her spiritual home, the most luxurious address in Paris across from Yves Saint Laurent. He couldn't care less about trendy neighbourhoods. Janet knew he would live in the Louvre Palace curled up in the corner of one of the spectacular rooms if they'd let him. She wanted her son to have a "fabulous" (her favourite word) place to live for when she visited, which was supposed to be often but turned out to be maybe once a year.

Cle swirls her head around taking in the scenery.

"I love this street. I can't believe I'm standing inside one of the residences. I honestly never thought people lived in them. It's like the whole street is a fantasy."

She glances around the apartment, taking in the cathedral ceilings. The grand window at the side of Benjamin's winding marble staircase is a replica of the Rose Window at the Sainte-Chapelle in the heart of Paris on the Île de la Cité.

Benjamin whips off his shoes and walks past her, grabbing the top of the golden banister. He sits down on the bottom stair and rubs his brow.

"You introduced yourself. My apologies, I've forgotten your name."

"I want to help and to take care of you. You're recovering? Yes? You don't know who I am?"

He stares at her.

"We know one another? How?" He pushes his fists into his eyes.

"I am Josiah's assistant. My name is Cle Bernice. I met you in Istanbul years ago. You don't remember?"

Benjamin rubs his eyes with his sleeve.

"Josiah asked me to deliver *The Immortal* to your office. He said you had passed away."

"Yes, that's what he thought. My father sent him an email to let him know I was okay. It bounced."

She turns towards the door and starts walking.

"Get some sleep. Keep the portrait and golden book close to you at all times. They will lead you to Josiah. Do not trust that man Denis. There are others like him."

He jumps up and rushes over as she's halfway out the door.

"Wait, Cle, please don't go. Is Josiah alive?"

He stands at the front door and watches her racing down the street. She calls back at him, "I will come back tomorrow."

He considers chasing her, but he has no energy. Instead, he watches her disappear behind one of the street's beautifully manicured trees. When he loses sight of her, he walks inside, pulling the giant wooden door behind him.

Chapter 7

Examining the Plate

February 24, 2017
Benjamin's Apartment, Paris, France

Benjamin is sitting on his bed leaning over, draped in his silk bedspread. He felt like shit when Cle left and went straight to bed, but the eight-hour sleep has done wonders for his energy. With his pillows propped cozily on the bed, he feels comfortable and is caressing the golden book.

He thinks about Venice. Sera, Josiah's wife, was from the Sartore family, one of the oldest families in Venice, who predated the founding the city. There wasn't a day Josiah didn't think about their first date sitting on the terrace of the Hotel Danieli.

"I memorized everything about her," he often said to Benjamin. Sera had died of a heart condition shortly after Duncan was born. Neither Duncan nor Benjamin knew her.

Josiah and Sera were obsessed with a golden book. Benjamin didn't know a lot of details. Josiah never shared, saying he couldn't bear to talk about it. He had only mentioned to Benjamin that he seemed to think the golden book was stolen the day of Sartore's death on July 12, 1576, when Sartore was barely thirty.

Josiah also told Benjamin the Sartore family had a secret chapel in St. Mark's Basilica. But that's all he disclosed. He promised Benjamin they would travel to Venice together so he could show him everything. He called it their "future pilgrimage".

Alexandra Edmiston

One week after being discharged from the hospital, Benjamin travelled back home to Paris, claiming he was feeling great and wanted to go back to work. Before flying home, Benjamin made one stop: Josiah's home in North Toronto. He stood outside for such a long time, waiting for the OxyContin he threw at the back of his throat to reduce his various pains. He wished there was a drug he could take to numb the love he felt for Josiah. He wasn't sure what hurt more: the physical pain of the cancer or the emotional turmoil of not knowing where Josiah was.

When Josiah's housekeeper Angelina saw him at the door, she swung it open and ran up to him.

"Mr. Benji, we missed you. We're so glad you are better. Come in."

"I just need to pick up a few things."

"Please go ahead," she said. "The police examined all of Josiah's belongings, along with other experts like private detectives on TV. They still have no clues. That's what they told us. We think he'll be back."

"I think he'll be back. I'm optimistic," he said, trying to be convincing.

Josiah lived alone in a massive house. Except for the living room and a few others, most rooms were never used. Angelina spent hours dusting every week.

Benjamin burrowed himself in Josiah's favourite Italian leather chair in his giant living room, surrounded by ridiculously expensive antique furniture: a Goddard and Townsend secretary desk, a Ming Dynasty vase, and a chandelier that (apparently) was owned by Napoleon. He smoked a joint (his "medical" marijuana that wasn't procured by prescription) and stared at the empty space above the mantle where *The Immortal* used to hang years ago. Now, it was a lonely square of faded gold paint with a hole where the hook had been. The void reminded him of the chalk outline of a body on a TV police show.

That spot above the mantle had been her home as long as he can remember. Ten years ago, Josiah took her into his studiolo. He said he had been receiving inquiries from people interested in buying her. They were aggressive and he was concerned. These offers coincided with the onset of Josiah's dementia. Benjamin spent the summer investigating Josiah's claim there was interest in buying *The Immortal* but couldn't substantiate anything.

He could feel the imprint of Josiah's body in his grandfather's favourite chair as he burrowed his body into the leather, staring ahead like he was willing Josiah and *The Immortal* to return. Before Josiah disappeared, she was his first love after Sera: the perfect companion, always there when he needed company, like a friend who listened unconditionally during every one of life's messy moments.

Benjamin's eyes turned to the rich carved oak bookcase on the widest wall. It was built with shelves that stretched from floor to ceiling, like a fixture in an old English bookshop in a Charles Dickens novel.

Josiah's secret room was behind the bookshelf. That was his real home, his spiritual home. He called it his studiolo.

It wasn't like any other room in the house. A hidden button activated an opening in the bookshelf that cut through his books on the history of Venice. The shelves moved towards the inside of the room, revealing another hidden door that opened to the inner sanctum. Benjamin had been invited in a few times to examine the results of Josiah's intricate alchemy experiments. As far as Benjamin knew, he was the only person ever granted access.

There were clues there. He was certain of this.

The keys were usually hidden on a hook in the closet in Josiah's massive bedroom, which looked out onto his man-made canal and stunning gardens. He spent a lot of money to maintain gardens that only a few people enjoyed.

Benjamin went right to the hook. No keys. He then opened every drawer and every nook and cranny where Josiah might keep a key: under his mattress, in suit coat jackets, in his sock drawer.

After an hour of scouring, he discovered the keys in the washroom in the master suite. They were in the glass where Josiah kept his toothbrush and hairbrush.

Benjamin walked back into the library towards the bookshelf and pushed a button. The wall moved towards him, revealing the other door in the middle of a back wall constructed of a strong metal.

He placed one key in a steel latch, moved it to the side, and placed the other key in the hole hidden by the latch. The door moved slowly towards him. Walking in through the opening, he moved his hand along the wall to find the light switch, then walked up a narrow golden staircase guided by a stream of soft light into an exquisite narrow room. The inner sanctum was guarded by two bronze statues at each side of the staircase: one of a towering man holding a lyre, the other of a woman with an angel draped around her and placing a crown of flowers on her head.

This was Josiah's life, where he moved with ease between two worlds: one where he was a respected business titan, and another where he was a medieval wizard. His love of all things magical was refined in Venice just after meeting Sera.

Benjamin turned on another light to illuminate the whole space, revealing a barrel-vaulted golden ceiling, a stunning masterpiece of stucco with walls adorned with frescoed panels.

The frescos on one wall displayed a beautiful sunrise with Aurora, goddess of the dawn, looking down, her fiery hair framing a saffron sky and her rosy fingers luring the dawn to break and reveal another glorious day. Another wall displayed a moonlit night with Diana, the winged goddess of the night, deep in the sky over towering mountains and framed by a magnificent shower of shooting stars.

At the back of the studiolo was a huge oven. It sat in front of two large picture windows that opened onto a balcony with the most magnificent view of the backyard with its outstanding gardens of peonies, roses, and hydrangeas. The balcony was completely hidden from nosy eyes by a giant row of evergreens that blended in perfectly with ivy climbing down the brick. Josiah spent a lot of time contemplating, looking up at the sky, listening to the oven contents crackle and burn.

The materials for his experiments were stored in a series of cabinets with inlaid carvings trimmed in gold. On a beautiful table in the middle of the room was a message on the front of a notepad in bold black magic marker: FOR BENJI: TO SEEK THE TRUTH. THIS IS OUR PLAN. The message was dated March 24, 2016:

1. Travel to Istanbul to the church
2. Visit Venice
3. Travel to the South Sinai Desert
4. Find the golden book and destroy it

Spread out on the table were items related to *The Immortal* and Sera. Items he'd never seen before: stunning sepia photos of Josiah twirling Sera in Venice in St. Mark's Square in front of the basilica, the two of them snuggling in a gondola on the canal, Josiah and Sera sitting on the beach at the Lido. There were other photos positioned in a neat pile in the corner of the table. One he couldn't put down was of Sera as at small child holding the hand of what must have been her father. They were in front of a palazzo that looked like a building for squatters with its crumbling façade. There was a Post-it on top with a message in Josiah's handwriting:

"For Benji: This is The Sartore Palace, built in the thirteenth century on the Isola di Speranza. Sera is with her father, Giovanni, who looks like you. I've signed the deed of the palace over to you. It's in the pile of papers on the right."

Benjamin studied the photo, so badly wanting to make out Giovanni's face. The photo was cracked from age but he was certain he could fix it with reconstruction software.

He's always felt like an orphan who reminded his parents of a big mistake. His conception happened in one of two places: in the ladies' loo at a Queen concert at the Hammersmith Odeon in London, or later in the evening in the bathtub of his father's suite at the Savoy. Either way, he was conceived in a bathroom.

His parents met that evening. Janet got massively drunk on snakebites. After the second pint, she shoved her tongue down Duncan's throat and dragged him with her to the loo.

No child should know this, but Benjamin was subjected to this during so many of his mother's martini-infused rants about how his father ruined her life that night and that was the first and last time he got in her panties. When Benjamin was three, Duncan and Janet had enough of their sham union and created lives that rarely included the other.

This photo included family history that he was desperate to learn more about—from the man in the picture to The Sartore Palace's existence. He had checked the Venetian archives and discovered there was a demolished Sartore Palace on the Grand Canal but nothing on Isola di Speranza.

He stared at the photo for several minutes before placing it down gently to pick up a napkin from the Hotel Danieli imprinted with someone's bright red lipstick, probably Sera's. There was also a very old bottle of Chanel No 5 perfume, a pair of lace gloves, and an alarming photo of Sera in a beautiful room lying in a bed with Josiah beside her. She looked like a shrunken doll with bulging eyes.

He walked to the picture window, opened it, went out onto the balcony, and gazed at the clouds that seemed to touch the top of the house. He was separated from Josiah, but he never felt closer to him than when standing in the secret world his grandfather created.

Benjamin sat down on a chaise lounge on the balcony and fell asleep. When he woke, it was morning.

Through the trees, he could see the sun was rising and glistening over the little canal. He had to catch his flight to Paris that night. He carefully gathered up the contents on the table and placed them in his backpack. This remained on his knee during the eight-hour flight.

sNow that we are wed, we are preparing grand restorations on my family's Sartore Palace, which will be our first home together. It is going to be a shrine to The Immortal *and the tragic love of Andrea and Annacletica.*

There is an envelope. When he opens the flap and peers in, he sees something delicate. At first he assumes it is a piece of cloth. Upon closer examination, he discovers a worn and crumbling piece of parchment. It's a letter from someone telling the story of an event in Venice during the bubonic plague of 1576. It's written in Latin. A snippet of a letter from Rocco Benedetti, a procurator of St. Mark's Basilica, to his sister Lucia, dated May 1580. He studies it and translates it in his head:

> *I must share something before I am taken by the great Almighty. Some of this I saw with my own eyes, some I was told by those whom I felt were most trustworthy. You remember the plague fell on the most serene citizens of Venice in the year AD 1576. I am still haunted by the bodies of such good people heaped on carts and the smell of disease that clung in the air, your home, your clothes...*

Also inside the envelope is a piece of paper, not dated, with notes written by Sera:

> *The subject of* The Immortal *was an Egyptian called Annacletica. She was from the Sinai Peninsula and arrived in Venice with Father Roberto Sartore in [Benjamin can't read the year], and a woman with her name was seen again in 1576. Perhaps this was one of her descendants who was given the same name. This woman had a magical golden book and met Andrea Sartore.*

There is an entry ripped out of a diary dated June 24, 1946:

> *I went to St. Mark's and entered the secret room in The Secret Sartore Chapel by pushing the head of The Blessed Virgin Mary on the altar. I pushed myself in through the narrow opening. I brought a flashlight,*

but I didn't need it. The room was flooded by light. I was so captivated by the beauty and the pure peace. I found a sarcophagus and moved the top and looked inside. I fell asleep and when I awoke a woman appeared before me. She looked alive and then she didn't, like she was a person who bridged both worlds.

And lastly, an undated email from Josiah to Benjamin:

Dear Benji,

There is something so mysterious about love and so destructive about loss. I should have died with your grandmother. It would have been easier. I faked most of my life. I couldn't cope. I went to the Sinai when she died. But I couldn't stay there. I was a father and I had to raise my baby somehow. Yet, I could barely to get out of bed.

When my father, Noah, died, your father was two. I had to face reality, come home, and run the family company. The situation was crippling. Here I was, this outwardly strong man who was crippled by the grief of losing my wife and father, and I could barely function, barely hold a razor to shave my face.

After recruiting the best talent for the senior team, I entrusted them to run my company. I was always the face of the company, but the meaningful work of building the company into what it is today was done by others. I chose to shun business and to live a life of service to others. I had one moment with Sera and I knew I could never recreate it. She wanted me to find the elusive golden book. That was the mission of love that I had to fulfill.

I hid in my lab. I toiled. I was trying to hide from reality, focus on this mission, and it was pushing me mentally and physically. This singular focus on finding the book was making me feel like my sanity was hanging by a thread. I was looking for the answer—looking everywhere—but I just couldn't find the golden book; in desperation, I tried to recreate it. When I finally created a replica, or thought I did, Annacletica tested it and proclaimed it didn't work. It wasn't her book. It had no power to do anything and we couldn't change that. We were back to where we started and had to find the original. The endless search almost destroyed me emotionally. At one point, your father hospitalized me for exhaustion—against my will, almost at gunpoint.

Alexandra Edmiston

My life was defined by searching. Why was I always searching? I don't know. I lost my mother tragically when I was seven. I remember watching her in our kitchen preparing my breakfast of bacon and scrambled eggs. I ate half of it and flew out the house to get to the playground to tear around with my friends. She ran after me calling, "Jos, your baseball cap!" I grabbed it and said nothing. My last words were silence.

At second period, the principal came into our class and escorted me to a cab. He said, "You have to get home." I asked why and he was silent. When the cab pulled up at my house, a woman ran up to the car. I can't remember who. It doesn't matter. All that matters were the words she uttered. "Your mother is gone." When I asked where she'd gone, the person hesitated and again said, "She's gone."

So frustrated by this person, I remember saying, "Shut up."

The explanation shared with me: "They couldn't save her." That was what I was told, nothing more. I spent a month with my grandparents until my father was capable of looking after me. Years later, I bribed someone to make a copy of the police report for me. My mother had fallen down the stairs in our basement just after I left and hit her head. It appeared that she had tried to crawl to the top before bleeding to death. She was thirty-five. To this day I cannot eat bacon and eggs. The sight of them produces the gag reflex.

For some reason, the police thought her death was suspicious and investigated my father, who had been away on a business trip at the time.

Our church became a big blanket I could wrap around myself and hide inside—the only place I could find true solace from the pain of the nightmares and images that constantly gripped my young mind. I tried to push them away by playing "St. Matthew's Passion" on my father's turntable at full blast. Bach's masterpiece that explores what defines life for me—joy, evil, betrayal, punishment, and salvation. I was convinced the music provided clues—a giant treasure map of black marks on white paper that would show me the way. If I listened to it carefully, studied the score, and analyzed each note, I was sure the clue would rise from the record's grooves.

The Immortal's Secret

I committed to a life of faith and earned a theology degree. The next step was the path to priesthood and the seminary.

Enter a small detour to Venice to manage a restoration project for my father in the baptistery in St. Mark's Basilica. It was a project for which I was totally unqualified. One morning I was in St. Mark's Square drinking an espresso when your grandmother flew by me—a streak of red, a goddess in a sleeveless dress. Her scent lingered in my nose like fresh hand-picked roses. She took my breath away. She smelled exactly like my mother, like the rose perfume my father always bought.

We were meant for one another; ours was a perfect love story, and then she died. I was lost on a deep level. The grief destroyed me. I couldn't let it go and tried so hard to move past it.

I paid for expensive therapy, sought out psychics, hosted seances, talked to her when I was alone, and searched for women who looked like her—someone to replace her. Nothing. Years passed and the depth of my pain was like a hurricane on the ocean that just kept gaining strength.

Then a strange fluke changed my life. A drunken one-night stand was my saviour. The two parties: your mother and father. There would be no abortion. I had to insist under threat of disinheritance. I had to step in to do the right thing, to make sure you were born. I secretly hoped you would have qualities that would bring to life a little bit of Sera. Your crazy, immature parents were more concerned about looking good and drinking the best booze money could buy.

I was there when your mother went into labour. I waited with your father. We barely spoke. I never wanted him. I'm ashamed to say that. He was too much like me. I didn't want a clone of me in this life. I am not a perfect man. But I wanted you. I wanted another chance and prayed for that.

When I looked into your eyes, I saw my second chance at life, at love. It was my second chance at making amends for everything, mostly for rejecting my own child.

You had the same twinkle in your eye as Sera, her wonderful smile, her personality. Her gentle nature. I could get up in the morning again. I just wanted to care for you.

You were my miracle and I thank you for being the blessing that allowed me to come back to life. It was always me and Sera. Then, it was me and you. You are a good man and I want you to live the happy and fulfilled life you deserve.

In addition to the envelope, there is a red satin pouch. Inside is something protected with a silk scarf that must have belonged to his grandmother. Unfolding the scarf, he discovers it's a golden plate, the same size as the ones in his golden book.

Benjamin puts on his strongest reading glasses and places the plate directly under the light on his night table. The carving on the image is faint, but he can make out a woman's face. The name at the bottom is hard to decipher, too.

He buffs the plate gently with a tissue he's been using to dab the constant perspiration on his brow. The image is no clearer, but the tissue is unusually warm to the touch. He clicks the plate into the golden book. It's a perfect fit.

He picks up his phone, snaps a photo of the plate, and downloads it into his photo editing software on his laptop. The image takes a while to appear on the screen but when it does, the name becomes a bit clearer.

Zooming in and out with his fingers, he examines the plate in detail. In zoom mode he can read the name. It's very clear, unmistakably clear. It shocks and frightens him.

Sera Sartore. Oh my God, what does this mean?

As he rubs his finger over and over the outline of the features, he stares down, looking deeply into Sera's face.

Benjamin recalls that Jenna always kept incense candles in bedside table drawer to burn while she prayed by the side of their bed. She was convinced the fragrance and smoke helped raise her prayers to heaven.

He finds the incense and lights one of the sticks. The room fills with swirls of frankincense and laurel leaves, which she loved. The flame illuminates the image in the golden book, making it appear like it's floating on top of the gold.

Benjamin picks up the book and peers deep into this new plate. Sera's eyes are beaming. He locks his gaze with hers to create a bond of energy that makes the nerve endings on his head tingle like the little hand-held firework sparklers he loved as a child.

He is stunned by the image.

The Immortal's Secret

Guide me to Josiah. Please help me find out what happened to him.

Warmth radiates like crashing waves over his skin, and he feels the soft touch he felt as a child when he would twirl around until he felt dizzy and forgot where he was. The sensation feels so real. He's elated.

Falling back onto his bed still holding the book, Benjamin feels energy sweep over him, drifting off into that halfway state, teetering on the boundary of sleep and consciousness.

He feels like he's falling. His body glides above a chasm like he's a feather, free flowing up and down. He is reunited with his body at the bottom of the chasm, surrounded by ghastly rocks that jut out all around him like those in the background of *The Immortal*. On one side of the chasm, the rocks smooth out to form a slate staircase that rises towards a little chapel poking out of a veil of mist. He feels calm filtering into his pores as he climbs the stairs that are being washed by the warm mist.

The chapel is a small exquisite building, no larger than a garden shed. It's made of pink granite stones, each one carefully cut as if by the most talented artisan's hands. The walls rise towards a pointed roof. The roof is levelled out at the base to support a crown with a tiny steeple and a gold cross on the spire. A small arched door in the centre of the chapel is framed by golden hieroglyphs fashioned out of emeralds. They form three words that Benjamin is easily able to decipher. He's not sure how he is able to do this because he has never seriously studied hieroglyphs. The three words are "Chapel of Hope."

Light streams out of the door and he walks towards it. Inside the chapel, he can no longer see. He can only smell the mist, which strangely resembles the scent of the oleander bushes in his family garden back home. He rubs his eyes frantically, attempting to see something. His eyes slowly focus to reveal the back of a young man and a woman whose face is partly obscured by a scarf, sitting by what looks like an altar. Their skin is brown and glowing like they've been kissed by the sun for days. The woman's lips are painted a luscious dark red. They are holding hands and praying softly. The man is caressing an animal that looks like it could be a baby goat. The woman is clutching something, and Benjamin moves closer to get a better look. It's glistening under the lights. It could be his golden book. He tries to move his legs but they are no longer functioning. He holds up his hands and tries to touch the object.

A bright light appears like a rising sun and he looks up at a pot light shining on his face. It's blinding him. He grabs the covers on the bed and places them over his head.

When his vision returns, he lowers the covers and looks ahead. The book is still in his hands, warming the tips of his fingers like it is alive. Was he dreaming? The scene felt like a dream but he doesn't think it was.

He lies back on his pillow and stares at the ceiling. He is shaking from his head to toes. It's not a reaction to fear. It's exhilarating. It's adrenalin. He runs his fingers over the image carved in one of the plates.

Sera Sartore. Was her wish immortality? Is that what she asked for? Did she carve her name to choose immortality? I certainly hope she didn't.

A normal man would be frightened. Benjamin is anything but normal, and he is not afraid of death or the unknown. "A brave man is always intrigued by fear." That's what Josiah always said. Truth is what intrigues Benjamin. He has always sought it through art. Art as always been a mirror that exposes the truth about the world. Truth is what he thought was going to guide him in living a life bigger than himself, a life that would elevate the truth and immortality of art and bring beauty to those who don't understand art.

The Immortal is drawing him into her world, and he is ready to follow her. She is a lost soul like him and she needs him.

He opens the book and counts the plates. There are five. The book says there are seven plates.

Where are the other two?

Chapter 8

Crossing the Boundary Between Light and Darkness

February 25, 2017
Benjamin's Apartment, Paris, France

Benjamin wraps a blanket around himself and creeps out onto the terrace with the golden book under his arm. The illusion makes him hopeful. Is *The Immortal* guiding him?

He places the golden book on the rattan bench beside him and stares at it while weaving his grandmother's silk scarf through his fingers. It's heaven to touch something that belonged to her.

His memory takes him back to the times he stayed overnight at Josiah's home. Such precious moments. His grandfather would read the Bible to Benjamin while squeezing his rosary and stroking Benjamin's chestnut hair, appealing to God to shroud his grandson with strength and allow him time to live out his dreams and fall deeply in love. If Josiah had only one wish for his grandson, it would be this: find true love. That was his definition of a successful life.

"If a thing loves, it is infinite" was a William Blake quote Josiah loved.

Somehow Benjamin never tired of hearing Josiah say he would take Benjamin to Venice and reveal more about Sera.

"I am Dante, and she inspired me like Beatrice."

Josiah would constantly coax Benjamin to read up on the astonishing beauty of Venice to prepare.

"It will be a great adventure." That's all he would say. When Benjamin asked when they were going, he always replied, "Not yet. I will let you know when."

Josiah's love for his grandson was the most beautiful thing in his life. Benjamin was damaged and tortured. He recoiled from deep human interactions except for those with Josiah, the only kindred soul who could penetrate the wall.

Now, he's on a surreal journey. This is not like his regular curator detective work to find outstanding works of art owned by mysterious people around the world. He needs to map out his search for his grandfather. His first stop is going to be Istanbul.

I'll call that Cle woman at the Louvre tomorrow.

He needs to find out any useful information she may have about Josiah. He could use an assistant. He also might be too weak to achieve what he needs to do.

He pushes his fists into his eyes.

Josiah, you have to be alive. I cannot live without you. I have no plan B if you're gone forever.

His phone beeps and he slides it out of his pocket. It's a text message. A Venice number he doesn't recognize. He reads the first visible lines:

<Benjamin, I know where Josiah is. He's with Grace Parker. She didn't die.>

What is this?

He clicks on the message to read the rest.

<Get 2 Venice next week. Will disclose more later. Will text u time and place 2 meet.>

He stands up and reads the message again. Then he dials the number and pushes the phone to his ear. It rings and rings without going to voicemail.

He types the number into Google. Nothing.

Another message pops up on his screen.

<In case u need proof.>

He clicks on a picture of a Josiah and a woman locking arms. They're in front of the Riva degli Schiavoni in Venice, steps from The Danieli Hotel. It's not a romantic pose. He appears to be leaning on her.

What the heck?

He pushes on the screen to zoom in and sees that Josiah is looking down, pushing his face into a scarf. It looks like the one Benjamin gave him a few Christmases ago. He has on his trademark Daniel Boone hat and baggy chinos. If this is real, he could be alive. Yet, he's wearing nothing Benjamin feels was purchased over the past six months. Josiah is a public figure and Benjamin has been following the news coverage on his disappearance. It's been scant. This message could be a bad joke.

The reference to Grace Parker is also unsettling. It couldn't be Grace. Few people know about his relationship with her other than his family. He's never gotten over what happened to her, and the dreams in the hospital that centred on her still haunt him.

Josiah believed in living life heroically. He was focused on helping those in need, not out of guilt for his vast fortune. His motivation was pure kindness. He launched a philanthropic initiative through Mannfield called Break the Cycle. Its mission was to fund the education and living expenses of hundreds of exceptional students living below the poverty line. Fifty of the children who benefited from the program went to Benjamin's grade school. Initially, Benjamin was so proud of this initiative until he started to witness the enduring abuse directed towards the "projects", as they were called. It mostly came from a band of boys Benjamin and his best friend Jeff dubbed the Ewoks in Reeboks. They took pride in terrorizing the projects by tripping them, stealing their lunches, and taping rude messages on their backs.

One evening when he was alone with Josiah, Benjamin plucked up the courage to describe how stressful it was to watch the abuse directed at the projects. He shared how the Ewoks had taken to calling him The Patrician, a word Benjamin had to look up in his Funk & Wagnall's encyclopedia.

"Why would they call me that? Because we are rich? They're well off too. That's why we all go to Elderberry."

"It's a misdirected slight, meant for me."

"Why do they treat those kids like they don't belong? They're just as smart as we are."

"The prejudice comes from their parents. This must stop. I will speak with your principal in private. A threat to cut off my donations to your school will get his attention. They understand cold hard cash. Remember one thing Benji: never cave to pressure and stop doing what's right. Stand your ground."

Then Josiah said something that Benjamin didn't understand at all. Benjamin asked him to write it in his notebook. At Josiah's request, he carried the notebook with him in his pants pocket. Josiah wanted Benjamin to write down important information and advice Josiah gave him so he wouldn't forget it.

"I have to make tough decisions at Mannfield and many have torn me up inside. I've tried not to ever compromise my integrity but sometimes I've had to forget I was my father's son. The way I live with myself is to make sure the compromises are worth it. And I give back something good. Helping these children is one of the things that makes me proud."

Benjamin pushes the golden book to his chest and thinks about Grace. The book seems to meld into his skin.

That day destroyed him, and he's never recovered from the evil that was directed at Grace—and by default at him for choosing to help her. He stopped praying that day and he's never expected anything from God since.

It was September 20, 1989, during morning recess, and he was watching his classmates from the back door of his school in Toronto's exclusive Forest Hill neighbourhood. He was eating the strawberry Fruit Roll-Up that his mother packed in his lunch. It was a beautiful day and he was wearing the new sunglasses he got for his birthday that he thought (hoped) made him look like Tom Cruise in *Risky Business*. He was alone. His best friend, Jeff, was sick again, suffering from what he called a projectile-vomit flu. One of the kids, a girl, was on the swing set at the back of the playground. One of the boys was either watching her or pushing her; Benjamin wasn't sure. The maple trees that framed the swing set were preventing a clear view.

At first Benjamin thought the kids were watching a contest to see how high the girl could fly on the swing. As the undisputed champion of the swing set, Benjamin started walking over to get a closer look at this potential new challenger. To the astonishment of his classmates, during the last school year he had pushed himself so high on the swing set that his legs were parallel with the top bar. In a move that was one part showing off and one part validation, he topped off the feat by jumping off and landing on his feet. The stunt has never been repeated.

The Immortal's Secret

The Ewoks in Reeboks had formed a human shield around the swing and were bouncing up and down cheering and caterwauling. As Benjamin got closer, he was able to peek through the heads of some of the Ewoks. The girl on the swing was little Grace Parker and the boy pushing the swing was Kyle Jenkins, the big-headed, small-bodied, mutant chief of the Ewoks. He was thrusting her forward with such force that her tiny body was pushed back in the leather seat, precariously flying so very close to the top post of the swing set.

A curious cross between a scraggly red-haired cabbage patch doll and Little Orphan Annie was how Benjamin remembered Grace. She was one of the project kids who was bussed in from Regent Park, a place Benjamin's mother always threatened to send him if he misbehaved. Grace was supported through Break the Cycle.

He liked how she was always smiling, a wide warm smile that exposed perfect teeth. When she answered questions in class, her answers were so intelligent; she had clearly done her homework. When she put her hand up, she did it with such grace. Her school supplies were always placed neatly at the top of her desk and she always obliged if someone wanted to borrow anything. At lunch she ate alone under a tree, absorbed in a book.

Her bookmark with a small tassel was always poking out of whatever she was reading. It had a quote from Aesop: "No act of kindness, no matter how small, is ever wasted." She was a bright little light in this horrible school. Benjamin had a secret crush on her and subtly looked out for her. Jeff wasn't a fan of the projects so Benjamin never confessed his crush to Jeff.

When they had their class picture taken, most kids dressed up. The Ewoks all dressed in Star Trek uniforms but were forced to go home to change. Grace was dressed in a pink frilly dress. Her beauty was free from the odd clothes. She was so tiny and was placed in the centre of the front row. Benjamin was standing right behind her. One of the Ewoks screamed out, "You look like a big pink meringue, Grace." Benjamin turned around to the boy who said it, made sure the teacher wasn't looking, and said, "Fuck off."

Benjamin had read up on natural selection and was certain the Ewoks would have sent Darwin back to the drawing board. The kids from the projects were a bull's eye in the constant line of fire for Ewok name-calling, lunch-bag-stealing, and recess-line wedgies. Most of the time they clung together, but Grace was alone at the swing sets that day.

A quick glance was all Benjamin needed to determine disaster was seconds away. He was racing over to push Kyle away when the swing began twisting back and forth violently. Grace had morphed into a little demolition ball. The look of terror in her bulging eyes is still scorched in his memory. He tried to grab Grace but her head smashed into the side bar of the swing set, making a sound like a hammer on a coconut. His stomach dropped like he was tumbling on the steepest track of a roller coaster. The Ewoks cheered. When her head ricocheted off the side bar again, creating an even more horrific bang, they cheered even louder.

When her body was thrust from the swing, she looked like an exploding ball of red wool. The full weight of her body landed face down on the gravel with a horrible thud. She didn't move. Benjamin raced over and bent down to help her. Her tiny face was covered in blood, and she was moaning quietly, making animal sounds. She was clutching a lace handkerchief. He slid it out of her tiny hands and used it to soak up the blood on her face.

"Whoa, what a crash landing," one of the boys howled.

"You are evil, all of you!" Benjamin screamed. "This is not a video game. She's a little girl." At twelve years of age, he was much larger than the Ewoks and could probably snap most of them in two. No one dared challenge him. To this day, he wishes he'd ordered one of them to help.

He gently picked up Grace and raced her over to Miss Riley, their art teacher, the only teacher on recess supervision that day. The kindergarten girls were playing hopscotch, and Miss Riley was helping one of them tie her shoe.

"Miss Riley! Miss Riley! We have an emergency!"

The teacher craned her head around and instantly jumped to her feet.

"Benjamin, oh my goodness!" she screamed through her shaky voice. "We need to get an ambulance."

The teacher called 911. The emergency crew arrived within minutes.

"Sweetie, can you hear me? What's your name?" said the female EMS attendant. Grace whimpered and babbled sounds that made no sense, and she was moving in and out of consciousness.

"Her name is Grace Parker," Benjamin yelled, trying to return some dignity to this tiny little abused human. Miss Riley stood beside him crying with her hands cupped over her face. Other teachers surrounded them in a semi-circle. The male EMS attendant helped Miss Riley into the ambulance so she could accompany Grace to the hospital.

The Immortal's Secret

As the ambulance raced away and the teachers slowly filed back into the school, Benjamin closed his eyes and drifted into a dream. Grace's bloodied face was floating behind the darkness of his eyelids. When he moved his hand up to rub his tears, he realized he was holding Grace's handkerchief and his hand was covered in her blood.

He gently placed the handkerchief in the pocket of his new grey cargo pants, another present for his birthday. It suddenly hit him that he may have witnessed a murder, one planned by Kyle and those Ewoks for their sick amusement.

Grace was going to die. He was sure of it. He never dreamt a twelve-year-old could die but he was going to be the witness to a murder. The thought terrified him and he fell on the pavement making noises he'd never made in his life. He never wondered about the whereabouts of the Ewoks as his youthful innocence disappeared on that that sidewalk.

Principal Jenkins came out to comfort him. He guided Benjamin inside and to the teachers' lounge, where he placed him in one of their comfy chairs.

Benjamin can't remember what happened after that. Perhaps the police came; he's not sure. He does remember this vividly: he was the only witness to the accident other than the boys who had caused the tragedy. The Ewoks would stick together. Grace was incapable of speaking. It was going to be his word against theirs.

After school, he went home and immediately called The Hospital for Sick Children and asked for the number of Grace's room. The trip to the hospital was his first ride on the subway alone, and he tried not to think how angry his mother would be if she knew of this adventure. When he arrived, he slipped in among the grown-ups, attracting no attention. He made his way to the men's room to clean Grace's handkerchief to remove any frightening traces of blood. While he was drying it under the machine, he noticed two initials subtly monogramed in light pink: GP. As he was placing it in his backpack, he noticed money in an envelope that he was going to use to buy a Raleigh bike.

When he found the trauma unit, he checked the names on every room until he found Grace's name written in blue magic marker on a white door sign at the end of the corridor.

There were tons of huge machines and tubes attached to her tiny body. A woman who looked like an older version of Grace, with the same soft features, was sitting on a chair beside the bed holding Grace's tiny hand. He walked up to her and said, "I am Grace's friend. Is she going to be alright?" He startled the lady, and she dropped the rosary dangling in her other hand.

"I'm sorry," Benjamin said and picked it up for her.

She stood up and looked down at him with glassy blue eyes.

"You're a friend of my Grace? She never mentioned any friends." Looking over at Grace she said, "She has severe head injuries among several other things."

"She fell off the swings and I carried her to the ambulance."

"She hates the swings," she said while looking at her rosary. "You helped her?"

"I did."

"God bless you. Thank you so much."

"You are very welcome."

"The principal said they were still piecing together what happened. Do you know?"

"I ran up to help when she fell. I was standing near the door of the school, quite far from the swings. I didn't see what happened before that. I carried her to safety to get her in the ambulance."

Benjamin knew lying was a sin but felt exceptions had to be made when you wanted to protect someone. This is a rule he made up while sitting in Sunday School listening to the choir sing "Jesus Loves Me". He didn't want to elaborate with Grace's mother. This gentle Christian woman didn't need to know the specifics of how her child was tortured by classmates in full view of anyone who had cared to pay attention. He was going to discuss next steps with Josiah, who always knew what to do.

"Thank you so much for helping my dear child," she said in a voice heavy with emotion. She stood up and he could smell Irish Spring soap. Their housekeeper used it to bathe his dog. As Grace's mother leaned in to hug him, his stomach growled loudly over the din of medical buzzing.

"Oh my, you are hungry. Did you have dinner?"

"No, I couldn't eat. It's been a really difficult day. I was so worried about Grace."

She looked at Grace and rubbed her daughter's forehead, the only visible skin on her face.

"I'm waiting for the doctors to provide an update. Let me see if I can find something for you. Do you like juice?"

"Yes."

The Immortal's Secret

When she left the room to find some juice, he slipped an envelope into the side of her worn black patent leather handbag. It was leaning against the arm of the chair where she had been sitting. Every Saturday Josiah gave Benjamin $20 to buy Star Wars action figures. He had collected all his favourites and had started stockpiling the rest of the money to buy a Raleigh bike. He had planned to deposit the money at his bank at the end of the school year. That evening he decided Grace and her mother needed the $500 more.

The main compartment of her purse was open and he could see a pile of papers balanced on top of the other contents. There was a to-do list written on a piece of note paper framed in roses. It had today's date on it. The first item on the list: Pick up Duncan Hines mixes and frozen pizza for Grace's birthday.

He stared at Grace's petite face enclosed in a bandage that made her look like a miniature invisible man. Her eyes were tightly closed and tiny specks of blood covered her lids. He thought of kneeling at her bed, but he couldn't bring himself to do it. No way could he appeal to a God who had allowed such savages to do this to her on her birthday. He kissed her forehead softly and whispered, "Happy Birthday."

"I got some apple juice," Grace's mother said as she walked towards him, "along with a chocolate bar, which I thought you'd like."

As she handed him the juice, he realized how hungry he was.

"Grace is going to be fine," he said, telling another lie, proving you can never tell just one. That was one of his mother's favourite sayings.

Taking his hand in hers, Grace's mother said, "Thank you so much. She is my only child." Her hands were so soft. There was no wedding ring on her finger.

"You are welcome," he said while taking the handkerchief from his pocket. "This is Grace's. She was holding this and I used it to clean her face. I washed it for her." As soon as he said those words out loud, he realized the handkerchief could have been evidence.

She stroked his cheek and Benjamin thought he might cry.

"Thank you. Her grandmother made this for Grace and asked her to always keep it with her…to remember her. She died last year."

After leaving her, he sat outside the hospital on a bench, watching the rush hour traffic on University Avenue, trying to hold back tears. When a passerby stopped to inquire if he was alright, he asked if she had a phone. She rummaged inside her large tote and handed him a cell phone. It looked like his dad's. He called Josiah but it immediately bounced to his voice mail.

While Grace was in the hospital in a coma, classes continued. The Ewoks looked for new targets among the projects. Every time Benjamin walked past Mr. Jenkins's open door, the principal was speaking in hushed tones to someone in a suit or a uniform.

One day during recess, he noticed his parents walking up to the school's main entrance. His father was looking straight ahead, walking with a strong sense of purpose clutching the side of his mother's arm, something Benjamin had never seen him do. When everyone was comfortably back in class, his name was called over the loudspeaker.

Uh-oh, kept going through his mind. He knew this wasn't good.

He was ushered into Mr. Jenkins's office, where his parents were sitting on a sofa dressed in business attire. His mother, so indifferent to any form of human contact, always showed her affection by blowing him kisses and saying "hug hug" instead of actually hugging him. Now, for the first time ever, she took his hand. The sensation was electrifying, an overwhelming mix of warmth and wonder. His entire world seemed to narrow down to the simple, profound connection of their fingers being locked. The unfamiliar gesture filled him with a blend of joy, relief, and a hint of disbelief, making this moment unforgettable.

Mr. Jenkins was behind his steel desk. Two police officers—a woman and a man—were standing by the big picture window with a perfect view of the swing sets.

The female police officer had brunette hair tied into a messy bun. She said they had spoken to all the Ewoks in Reeboks, Miss Riley, other teachers (who Benjamin knew weren't even in the schoolyard when the accident happened), and a random man riding by on a bike. They were trying to piece together what happened that morning.

"We wanted to get your side of the story, Benjamin."

"My side of the story?" he said as his mother's fingers squeezed deeper over his as if she were trying to transfer her strength to him.

"You've never really told it."

"That's not true," his mother said. "He told his teachers and us. We shared the details with everyone who needed to know. We have been very co-operative." She stood up without letting go of his hand. "Can I remind you that you are speaking to a child?"

Benjamin pulled her back towards the sofa. He sat up straight and tried to drop his voice a few octaves to appear older.

"My mother is right. I told many people—teachers, my parents, and my grandfather."

"We just want to hear your side of the story," the female officer said slowly, enunciating each word as if she thought English wasn't Benjamin's native language.

His mother crossed her legs and whispered under her breath, "This is ridiculous." She coldly stared ahead at the female officer. Benjamin was more focused on his parents' uncompromising support. He had never felt such love shrouding him. It took this event to see this side of his parents. It had never surfaced until then.

Whatever was happening that day was an attempted cover-up. His parents were just tolerating the participants in the meeting, allowing them to share their side of the story. They were waiting to bring down the influence and integrity of the Mann name like it was a tsunami that would wash all this away. This puffed up Benjamin with confidence and he proclaimed, "There is only one side of the story and it's the truth."

He knew he was innocent and was so shocked that others didn't see it too. It was the first and last time he would ever make that mistake.

"We told you what our son said," his dad said in loud and controlled tones, perfectly pronouncing each word to underscore that he knew what the police officers were trying to do. "He is the most trustworthy child in this school. There is no teacher who doesn't have enormous respect for him. They tell us this in each report card. He goes out of his way to help others; he doesn't bully and mistreat other children."

Benjamin had never heard his dad raise his voice. He looked at him and said, "It's okay, Dad." Turning to the female officer again, he remembered how in control of the situation he was, channeling the adult he would become.

"What have the others said?"

There was silence and the officer paused. She rubbed her arms, looked at her colleague for approval, and then said, "We were told you were pushing Grace in the swing to see how high she would go."

That day, in that room, with a view through the window of the swing set far off in the playground, with Mr. Jenkins slumped in his chair playing with his polyester tie, with the nameless duo of police officers staring at him, with his defiant parents enveloping him like a warm blanket, Benjamin discovered the true meaning of evil. It had always been an abstract concept—something mentioned many times in parables in Sunday School and highlighted in movies to scare him while devouring too much candy. Evil had never visited him, touched him, or breathed too close. That day it ceased to be something abstract and turned into something that delivered pain to every area of his life. He was shocked that children could cause such suffering.

Benjamin realized that he and his parents, like Job, were standing on the boundary between light and darkness. The police believed Kyle and the Ewoks. Those boys were the embodiment of weak souls whose energy can be easily drawn to evil.

It was a moment he would never forget, a defining lesson in what life was really about. Josiah always said a truly blessed man would find maybe five people during his lifetime to truly trust and love. From that moment on, Benjamin would bring very few people into his confidence.

As he was about to open his mouth to respond to the officer's allegation, the door burst wide open like it was going to fly off its hinges. Benjamin and his parents jumped in synch. In came Josiah, trailed by Mr. Jenkins' assistant, her face wet with perspiration.

"My apologies, Mr. Jenkins," the assistant said. She then turned and went back to her desk.

"This meeting is over," Josiah said. "Benji, Duncan, Janet, let's go. My family will be speaking through our lawyers."

None of the others moved while Josiah held the door open and Benjamin and his parents filed out. Benjamin turned around and looked at the other three's blank faces. It was like Josiah had become kryptonite and blown up in their faces.

There was no more talk of Benjamin being charged with anything. The situation lay in limbo while he counted the days until the end of the school year. He worried about Grace but was instructed not to visit her.

Word got around quickly about what had happened in the office. Benjamin ceased to have any joy in life. No one associated with him in the schoolyard except Jeff, who never faltered in his support. He told Benjamin, "You are the strongest and kindest kid in this school. My dad says nice guys finish last, but I know he's wrong."

The Ewoks directed their crusade of cruelty towards him in surreptitious, indirect, cowardly ways. They wrote insults like "Killer" and "Liar" and "Project People Lover" on his locker in giant letters, placed Elmer glue on his chair, and smeared mud on his jacket.

The Immortal's Secret

Benjamin started having trouble sleeping. He no longer took pleasure in his Star Wars collectibles and his mystery books; he lost his appetite for everything including his favourite foods like french fries and chocolate cheesecake. There were no more prayers before he went to bed, and he announced to his parents that he no longer wanted to be an altar boy. When his parents insisted he give it one more try, he couldn't do it and collapsed in the sacristy, crying on top of a pile of Bibles.

His mother developed strange rashes on her skin with a funny name (psoriasis), and his father stopped tinkering in his lab in his basement, his favourite activity. There were daily calls from Josiah to check in.

By May, Benjamin refused to go to school anymore and his mother arranged a tutor to guide him through the remainder of the year. She encouraged him to swim in their pool, which used to be one of his favourite activities. One afternoon when his mother wasn't watching him with her eagle eyes at the window, he dove to the bottom and held his breathe. Lights appeared before his eyes and water filled up his lungs. His mother dove in, still wearing her housecoat, and pulled him to the surface. They sat on a chaise lounge beside the pool as she hugged him and pushed her face into his hair and wept. The phone kept ringing on the table beside them. When she finally answered it, she listened for a moment, looked at Benjamin and said, "Your grandfather is with Grace. She woke up."

The girl whose skull he thought was bashed like a pumpkin on Devil's Night woke up. Her nurse and her mother were in her room with Josiah when she opened her eyes, smiled at them, and said, "I'm so hungry." After she ate some ice cream with chocolate syrup and peanuts she said, "I have an angel. I've been thinking about him while I was sleeping."

"An angel? Who is it?" her mother asked.

"His name is Benji Mann. He saved me from those evil boys. He carried me to the ambulance. He told them my name was Grace."

Benjamin and his parents wanted to visit Grace after she was released from the hospital but they were told she left to convalesce with relatives in a community in BC. He never heard anything else, and numerous private detectives and constant Google searches throughout the years revealed nothing.

On the day Grace woke up, Benjamin received another call from a man who lived across from the school. He was a techie guy named Dan who travelled constantly and installed cameras after a burglary. There was some suspicious activity at his home the day Grace was attacked so he saved the tape. It included footage of the entire incident with the Ewoks.

Benjamin was finally exonerated but with no apology. Kyle and the Ewoks found themselves in reform school, where evil knew no bounds. Mr. Jenkins took forced retirement and filled his days placing bets at Woodbine Racetrack and eating burgers at Harvey's.

Was justice served? The Ewoks were punished but Benjamin knew he'd never forget the evil.

Benjamin pushes his head to his knees to catch his breath. Ruminating on that day is so stressful. With the golden book tucked into his pajama bottoms, he staggers back into his bedroom. When he reaches his bed, he tips over like a tree onto the hardwood floor.

As he pushes himself up on his elbows to attempt to get to his feet, something pops into his head. There are few people who know the whole story of Grace. One of them is Jenna.

Chapter 9

Making the Pledge

February 26, 2017
Benjamin's Apartment, Paris, France

"You're such a reckless soul, intent on killing yourself," Cle says while walking over to the ornate electric fireplace in Benjamin's bedroom. "How does this thing work?"

She examines it from all angles, and he finally says, "You turn it on with the button on the side, the red one."

Giving the button a hard push, she turns it on, then walks back over to him and rubs his back as he looks up at her through bleary eyes.

"How did you get in?" he asks tentatively, his eyebrows slightly raised.

"You're stone cold," she says while rubbing his hands. "I knocked. You didn't close the door properly. I hope it was you that left it open."

Benjamin is shivering. She places another blanket around him from a pile stacked on the floor.

He stares at her with his tired eyes. Her hands are like ice.

"I can't stress enough that there are weird people out there." She keeps piling blankets on him.

He sits up in bed, still trembling.

She moves away from the bed to the ornate chair his mother bought for his bedroom. Sitting up straight, she clasps her hands in front of her and says without looking at him, "That man. The one who barged into your office?"

"Yes."

"I've been helping out in your office. I arrived to work early, around 7 a.m. I was drinking herbal tea when he walked past me. I followed him and I saw him place the key in the door of your office. I called out to him and said, 'Please don't go into the office. It's not to be disturbed.' He swore at me and told me to mind my own business.

"I followed him inside and saw you on the floor. He was on his way towards the portrait when you woke up. All that stuff he was saying about me accompanying you home was to get rid of both of us."

"How do we know one another?"

She blinks at him.

"I know your grandfather and I know you. I was at The Church of the Holy Mary when Josiah was looking for the golden book. You don't remember?"

Benjamin stares at the floor.

"Yes, it's coming back."

"When Josiah was lucid, he said if anything happened to him, I was to bring *The Immortal* to the Louvre. He wanted you to have it. He gave me the money for the trip years ago. When I contacted your department, your assistant said you hadn't…died. It was very confusing but the best of news. She said you were coming back to Paris in a few days and she would place it in a cabinet in your office where you secured art."

"I need to know…please. Is he still alive? Do you know?"

"I don't. I think this was the journey he took after he left you in Toronto. He went to Istanbul, then Venice, to meet with a few people he didn't identify. I just went along with what he said, because of his dementia, as he tried to piece together a mystery with limited information. He was frantic, almost crazed, and wasn't making much sense after you died—or, pardon me—almost died. Some of what he said made sense, some didn't."

Flipping open her pink furry purse, she takes out a white folded sheet of paper and hands it to him.

"This letter is recent. Written after he thought you died."

He unfolds it slowly and notices the familiar stationery from Mannfield. The perfect script is Josiah's. So proud of his penmanship, Josiah loved writing letters with a fountain pen. Writing in his own hand helped him maintain a connection to the analogue world. A world he loved.

The Immortal's Secret

Cle,

I must leave. I can no longer stay here. The Immortal *is not safe anymore, anywhere. We will never find the golden book and Benjamin is no longer here to help in our search. We must save you. You need to destroy it. Throw* The Immortal *in the chasm by The Chapel of Hope. Please do this for me. I am leaving and I will contact you when I am settled. Thank you for caring for me and being a dear friend.*

It's signed "Jos", a name reserved for close friends.

"What does the note mean? You needing to be saved?"

"It's truth mixed with delusion. You know his dementia was becoming debilitating."

Benjamin stares at Cle.

Was it all delusion? I have a book with a chapel on the front. I have dreamt of a chasm. Don't disclose anything until you know more.

"Let me help you like Josiah helped me. It's very dangerous to have the portrait…and the book. You know what Josiah's mission is."

Josiah always cautioned him to watch out for strangers taking too much of an interest in *The Immortal.*

Does this apply to this woman who just appeared in my bedroom?

Cle walks over, wraps the pile of blankets over Benjamin's shoulder, and rubs his skin.

"His mission? Which one? He had so many," says Benjamin.

"He was looking for the golden book. He's had people searching for it for years. Someone in Venice called Tomas Allegeni. A friend of his. You have the golden book. May I see it?"

He slides it from under the pillow and holds it up. She stares at it.

"Where did you find it?" She stretches out her arm. "May I?"

"Inside the frame of *The Immortal,*" he reveals.

"Inside the frame?"

"I don't know how it got there. It must've been there for many years."

"Close to five hundred years," she says, barely audible. She falls to the ground hugging it tightly.

"Are you okay?" he says. He puts his feet on the floor, getting ready to walk over to help her.

She sees him and puts her hand up and says, "I'm fine." She strokes the book and says something softly in another language Benjamin can't quite make out.

"Five hundred years. Why do you think that?" he asks.

"That's when it was stolen from St. Mark's in Venice."

Without looking at him she says, "This is a magic book. It performs miracles, for some. It could lead us to Josiah." She cradles it like a baby and kisses it.

"How so?"

"The book is alive. If you hold it, you may see things. It will show you things, particularly if you are the owner."

"What kind of things?"

"It's hard to explain. It doesn't work for everyone. It might show you things you might want to experience or those you might not, like reading your mind."

"Please show me," Benjamin says.

She joins him at the side of the bed, puts his hands on the book, and places her tiny hands on top of his.

"Think of Josiah. Think of him holding *The Immortal*."

They do this for ten minutes while he keeps one eye closed and one on her. Both eyelids feel warm as a vision appears: it's Josiah. He's sleeping, and it's dark. He has a beard, a silver beard.

The vision excites Benjamin. The pit of his stomach feels like it does during the click-click-click when riding in the car of a roller coaster during its climb.

The image feels so real that he takes his hand off the book to try to touch Josiah. The image disappears.

Cle opens her eyes halfway and looks up at him.

"Did you see anything?"

Benjamin catches a tear and rubs it into his cheek before Cle notices.

"I saw him. He was sleeping, breathing, just slightly. I am not sure where he was."

"You saw him sleeping and he was breathing. Are you positive?"

"I just miss him so much," says Benjamin. "I can't believe what I just saw. There was a thick grey blanket on the bed. He always had it with him. His family used it to cover him when he was born."

Perhaps I should pray on the book and heal myself. My grandmother did. Maybe I should take a leap of faith for the first time in my life.

"Could you excuse me?" He gets up and walks slowly in the direction of the washroom.

"Do you need my help?" she says.

"No, I'm good. I can walk."

Once he's behind the washroom door, he takes a few deeps breaths and sits on the side of the tub. Memories come flooding back of the last time he was sitting beside the tub in excruciating pain.

I've come a long way. That was an image of Josiah. He starts to laugh for the first time in a year. *He might be alive. Could he still be alive? This book will guide me, but I need my health.*

He walks back into the bedroom.

"Cle, if I pray on the book, can you guide me?"

She is looking out the window onto the street below. She is silent.

"I don't know if Josiah would want this. He never wanted it for my grandmother, Sera. My family told me he was waving a golden plate around my head in the hospital room while I was in a coma."

"Really, I'm not sure about that. He was probably trying to heal you and you appear to be still ill?"

"Yes. Whatever he did, or didn't do, didn't cure me."

She walks back to the ornate chair, places her hands together as she sits, and starts to quietly pray. After five minutes, she opens her eyes and looks at him.

"Could you come over and sit with me? Please hand me the book?"

He places it in her hands and she puts his hands on top of hers. Her hands are still cold but strangely soothing on top of his.

"Please recite this: 'I appeal to the power of this golden book to heal me. To bring me back to health. To cure my cancer.'" She looks at him. He's fixated on a blanket on the floor. "Do you understand?"

Benjamin doesn't move and he says nothing.

"When Josiah and I were in the desert, he would talk about your faith. You lost it. He felt responsible," she continued.

"It wasn't his fault. It's hard to maintain your faith with so much suffering. There are evil people in the world."

"Yes, there are. We have to be careful. We need to trust one another."

He walks over to light his candle again, burning the laurel leaves and frankincense. He returns to Cle, takes the book tightly in his hands, and holds it against his heart. He concentrates, closes his eyes, and says, "I appeal to the power of this golden book to heal me. To bring me back to health. To cure my cancer." He continues to squeeze the book to his chest and he starts to weep. Tears stream down his face. The salty moisture on his cheeks is always a foreign feeling.

Alexandra Edmiston

Taking a deep breath, he says the words again, slowly and carefully, and then waits. He enjoys the silence. It seems to envelope him like it's taken on a form. He starts to feel dizzy, like he is falling back down into that chasm with the chapel at the bottom.

He sees a vision of a woman standing in front of the chapel. A vision in a lavish purple flowing gown, she floats over to him, takes his left hand, pushes it to her lips, and slowly kisses him. He knows her face and her scent and is certain he's met her before. In Istanbul.

Chapter 10

The Mysterious Empress

February 27, 2017
The Louvre, Paris, France

Benjamin flicks the flashlight off and on, focusing on the man's face. With one flash, he looks at the man and then turns away. Another flash reflects the furrowed lines on the man's forehead, bulging like deep dirt tire tracks. The next flash highlights the man's nose, dark red like a smushed candy apple, turned down like a hawk. Two more flashes on his eye reveal the fixed lifeless gaze of a cadaver.

The sun is going down. It's a quiet evening in Paris. Benjamin is thrilled to be in his office at the Louvre taking time to reflect.

The portrait he is sitting in front of is *The Incredulity of Saint Thomas* by Caravaggio. He's seen the original in the Sanssouci Picture Gallery in Potsdam. This is a beautiful print he bought in Istanbul in an antique store in Beyoğlu. He framed it because it's the one religious portrait that makes him want to believe in something. "Reach hither thy finger, and behold my hands; and reach hither thy hand, and thrust [it] into my side: and be not faithless but believing."[2] He's always been moved by that line of scripture. Thomas had to see the resurrected Christ and place his finger in the painful wound to believe the miracle had happened.

Benjamin finds Thomas's image deeply comforting, as if the paint is fusing with some part of his soul, like a fast-acting, soothing narcotic shooting directly into his largest vein.

Still holding the flashlight to the eyes, Benjamin grips his other hand around a bottle of red wine, which has been precariously balancing on the cushioned bench where he's sitting.

He can't believe what's happened to him since he prayed on the golden book. This morning at 8:30 he jumped out from under his warm covers, made his way to the shower, and stood under his expensive shower head with the six settings on the brushed copper nozzle. He stood still under the water, not moving for several minutes, letting the water cascade over his shrunken body. As it caressed and warmed his muscles, he closed his eyes and dissolved into the serene moment.

Then something suddenly occurred to Benjamin, hitting him so strongly: he was standing in the shower, doing what he used to do before this bitch of a disease hit him. It was as if he had instantly reverted to his former self.

After he got out of the shower, he stood at the side of the bed shaking the water off his head. His stomach was making a noise, an annoying, loud noise. It was grumbling.

My stomach is grumbling!

Everyone's stomach does that in the morning. But his hadn't since he started his treatment. He was also steady on his feet, not wobbly and in danger of toppling over.

He stood still again and concentrated on how his damp bare feet were holding him up. He couldn't believe this transformation. Any small glimpse of normalcy had long been gone from his life, yet here he was— experiencing the morning routine that he had always taken for granted until he got sick.

The golden book was lying on the sheets. He grazed his hands over it and wondered, *Is the book healing me?*

Now, in his office, he's pondering what's next now that he's made a covenant with the unknown. He's never been one to believe in that which can't be seen. Yet he feels great—healthy, for the first time in a year.

Benjamin, like Thomas, is a doubter. He has to see and feel things to believe in them. Benjamin's faith is like a tiny ember and can be stoked a little when he sits on this bench.

He sits staring at Saint Thomas's side profile, taking in the saint's expression as he struggles to comprehend the truth in placing his finger up against the open wound. The sheer impact of forging his index finger deep into the wound of a man he thought dead. It's horrific, brutal to behold, but beautiful. It physically hurts Benjamin to look at Thomas's finger in the wound.

Reflecting on the painting calms him and helps him think clearly. The arrival of Cle twigged a memory that might be a huge clue to Josiah's whereabouts. He now remembers that he and Cle met and encountered something profound together years ago. The events of that time were disturbing and he had clearly pushed the memory to the back of his mind.

It was May 15, 1999. He was twenty-two and was set to leave in a few days for Istanbul with Josiah. This would be Benjamin's first trip there. The two men were in Josiah's den watching *The X-Files* when Josiah pressed mute and said, "I've been talking to *The Immortal*. She has the answers. I am trying to decipher them. I'm convinced she could have saved your grandmother."

Benjamin almost choked on the pretzels he was eating.

One moment Josiah was lucid; the next he was talking of empresses, Isaac Newton, antimony, ancient elixirs, and miracles that would bring his wife back from the grave.

"All of the world's problems can be solved by alchemy," he said while getting off the sofa, turning off the TV, and asking Benjamin if he wanted a beer. With his head inside the beer fridge beside the sofa he said, "I'm close to discovering the philosopher's stone. Would you like to see?"

After three beers, he invited Benjamin into his elaborate studiolo. Benjamin always knew of the room but thought it was a wine cellar, and he was shocked when he was guided into a lab packed with tools and equipment. Josiah said he inherited everything from his father, Noah. The room was pristine but with no evidence of any attempt to uncover the philosopher's stone.

No one had noticed the lapses at this point. Josiah's dementia was in its beginning stages. Benjamin decided he was going to protect his grandfather and stay by his side no matter the outcome.

May 18 that year was a surreal day beginning with the Mannfield annual general meeting. Benjamin had expressed an interest in pursuing an MBA. Josiah was delighted and had told him, "You need to come to our AGM. I'll teach you everything I know."

Sitting in the ballroom at the Fairmont Royal York hotel, Benjamin felt like a dog wearing clothes in the new suit he bought at The Bay's clearance sale. The price tag was still hanging inside the collar, scraping his neck. He meant to snip it off before he left the house, but he had slept in and all of his energy was focused on eating a quick breakfast and getting to the hotel on time.

As the board chair, Josiah called the meeting to order and breezed through the agenda quite expeditiously, explaining the consolidated financial statements, electing new members to the board, welcoming them warmly, and then reappointing the auditor for the upcoming year.

Then came the "Other Business", which Benjamin thought was code for adjournment and lunch. Everyone sat in silence as Josiah's executive assistant hurriedly set up a PowerPoint presentation.

"A surprise," Josiah told the audience.

Duncan walked over to him and Josiah waved his hands, ignoring any attempt for Duncan to whisper in his ear.

Finally, Josiah stopped, looked at Duncan, and cut him off with a loud shout. It was just three words.

"No, no, and no!"

In his dramatic fashion, Josiah started out with a story about the alchemist Hermes Trismegistus and his book *Hermetica*, which contained spells, recipes, and answers to life's mysteries. Then a photo of Isaac Newton popped onto the screen and Josiah proclaimed they were going to start creating their own gold.

"It a new project—innovation at its best."

Duncan raced over and flicked off the LCD projector. Josiah pushed him away with his long muscular arms and continued talking about setting up alchemy labs in the UK. His mic was switched off but he continued speaking to the crowd in his booming baritone. People in the audience looked at each other puzzled; some Mannfield employees sat on the edge of their chairs, some chuckled, and most kept their eyes glued to the agenda. The reporters scribbled wildly and camera flashes went off like a laser show. A woman dropped hot coffee on her suit, taking some of the attention from Josiah with her curdling shrieks. Duncan calmly took a hand-held mic and announced the adjournment. Josiah lunged at him and gripped him by the knot in his new paisley tie.

The Immortal's Secret

Josiah was shouting swear words Benjamin had never heard him use. Benjamin rushed over to his father and grandfather. His mother stayed seated, looking shocked, squeezing the agenda between her fingers.

Benjamin stayed close to Josiah as a security guard ushered Josiah into a side room. Refreshments were rushed in. Josiah refused everything with a violent wave of his hand as he engaged in a few hushed phone calls on the white phone on the wall. A doctor arrived.

"What's your name?" the doctor asked Josiah.

While walking to the door, Josiah said, "First name Fuck, last name You. Your services won't be needed. Nothing to see here."

That afternoon Josiah and Benjamin boarded a direct flight to Istanbul. *The Immortal* was beside them on her own seat. How she got there, Benjamin didn't know.

"Why Istanbul?" Benjamin asked while he was enjoying his steak and frites dinner in first class.

"It holds the answers. The empress was there."

"What empress?"

"Empress Paeon of the Eastern Roman Empire."

"What information does she have?" Benjamin said, deciding to go along with this story.

Taking Benjamin's hand in his huge hands, Josiah squeezed hard before saying, "I am hoping she knows the whereabouts of the golden book. I love you Benji."

"I love you too."

Early the next morning when they arrived at their five-star hotel overlooking the Bosphorus, Benjamin's thoughts were on his dad, his dad's health, and how Duncan was stick-handling the damage control back home.

Josiah paid in full for one month's stay. When they got to Benjamin's room, Josiah's gave him a fistful of money along with a platinum credit card with his name on it.

"I want you to explore this majestic city and enjoy yourself. Don't worry about anything. We are on a mission. I will let you know if we are able to open the tomb to see if the golden book is in her crypt."

"You're opening a crypt?"

"Yes. She may have stolen the book."

There was nothing Benjamin loved more than a mission, but he was old enough to know opening a crypt was illegal. All he wanted to do was call home. He knew it wasn't wise to do this in front of Josiah, who hadn't budged from his position at the window. Josiah stared out at the view of Hagia Sophia, her dome and minarets beaming under the morning sun. Benjamin stood behind him.

"You're scaring me," Benjamin finally blurted out and instantly regretted it.

Josiah turned around and looked at Benjamin with the gentlest of eyes. He walked over and hugged his grandson, squeezing him so tightly that Benjamin struggled to breathe.

"I love you more than anything on this earth. I have to be here right now, to do this, and I need you here with me. I must find her and that golden book." Josiah kissed him on the forehead and walked towards the door. Before closing it, he said, "I have my phone. Call if you need me."

As the door clicked shut, Benjamin rushed to the phone.

As each day began in Istanbul, they slipped into the same routine: Josiah disappeared during the day and returned late, just in time to do the head bobs through a quiet dinner. Benjamin's routine was that of tourist, indulging in everything the city had to offer.

At first, Benjamin was enthralled by the haunting calls to prayer, going for jogs on the Bosphorus, enjoying the simit with feta cheese and strong tea, touring the mosques and Ottoman palaces, sampling the spices at Istanbul's Grand Bazaar, gorging on meze, and getting woozy on the raki. He was captivated. Benjamin loved hanging out at the Atatürk Library doing research on the Byzantine era.

One night he heard a key in the door of his hotel room. It was Josiah. Like a robot, the old man walked to the bed, collapsing onto the luxurious comforter, his eyes lost in the ceiling's patterns.

Benjamin, slouched in a chair, looked up from a Turkish-dubbed episode of *Hogan's Heroes*.

"Grandad, are you alright? How was your day?"

No response.

Benjamin slid onto the bed and rested his head on Josiah's shoulder.

"If you're willing to share, I'm here. I'm starting to run out of solo adventures as a tourist anyway. Perhaps I could join you during the day."

Josiah kissed Benjamin's head and said he would "engage him" when they were both ready.

After two more weeks, when Benjamin had enough of his own company, they were eating breakfast when Josiah said it was time.

his plate of scrambled eggs to the side, Benjamin said, "Really, seriously? I get to come? I've been waiting for this for so long. I love to go on adventures with you."

"Get ready," Josiah said. "This is one that is going to blow you away."

Benjamin's knees were shaking with excitement as they left the hotel in a taxi. They ventured into the historic centre, following the Golden Horn through the ancient gates and down neighbourhood streets until they reached an area known in Byzantine times as Blachernae. It was where the Fourth Crusaders scaled the magnificent city bulwarks in 1204 and began the vicious rape of the city and its citizens during the sack of Constantinople before it was conquered by Mehmed II.

The driver negotiated a narrow road, and at the bottom of a steep hill tucked between two tall buildings, Benjamin saw the stained-glass windows of a church.

"Welcome to The Church of the Holy Mary," said Josiah as they exited the taxi. "Come and see this beautiful crumbling jewel."

The sun was shining down on the small building with a spire and a delicate cross on top. Josiah held the door open for Benjamin as he walked in through the carved majestic golden doors.

A young woman was waiting inside the door. Benjamin now remembers the familiar red hair and eclectic clothing procured from a garage sale or a grandma's basement. At the time, he thought those clothes had to be a disguise.

Who's she hiding from? Me?

He wrote her off as eccentric, but she was also so poised and elegant. She moved with such grace, like she was always balancing a plate on her head. The memory is so vivid to him now that he and Cle have reacquainted.

Her rose perfume mingled with the sweet incense that filled the air. The light streamed in through the stained glass, warming up the stunning purple and green marble floor. Josiah motioned for Benjamin to sit beside him in one of the pews near the back. It was cushioned and Benjamin sank into the leather. Josiah pulled the bench down and started to pray. Cle slid in beside Josiah and joined him. Benjamin refused to pray and Josiah knew not to ask him to.

Benjamin was overwhelmed by a golden iconostasis burning like a fiery sun under the security spotlights. It stretched out across the altar, a twelve-foot screen of gold climbing almost to the ceiling. Benjamin had learned this from his tour of a Hagia Sophia: to create a gate to heaven on earth, the Byzantines divided the altar from the nave with an iconostasis. Using the pillars as a guide, Benjamin walked up to the nave.

The centrepiece of the iconostasis was a seven-foot carved iron gate framed by golden hearts fashioned out of the purest gold. Above the gate was an icon of The Virgin Mary, and towering over her was an icon of a solemn Christ, his features blended to perfection in tempera with a golden background muddled in with pieces of white plaster.

There was one icon on each side of The Virgin that he couldn't identify: one was a handsome nobleman in a military uniform and the other a woman, or he thought it was a woman. Her image was almost completely faded—covered in plaster except for her eyes and elements of her purple gown. He moved in and looked up, staring deeply into her intense dark pupils. He felt flushed as he connected with this piece of painted wood.

Inside the church was peaceful and quiet with the odd soft muffled voice scattered about. They were coming from outside or in the direction of the altar, breaking the silence.

Then he heard the most deafening sound right underneath his feet, like an army of jackhammers.

Josiah stopped praying.

"I think they're ready for us," he said and motioned towards a rickety wooden door at the side of altar. The three of them walked slowly down the stairs.

When they reached the bottom, Benjamin could see a massive stone wall. A huge hole was pounded out in the middle.

"Keep walking," Josiah said. "The crypt is beyond the hole."

Benjamin walked towards the opening, where he was amazed at a stunning sarcophagus that dominated the room: a black marble behemoth sitting atop three white slabs that acted as stairs. A statue graced the top—a woman and man standing beside one another tightly holding hands. The woman was wearing a long gown and the man was dressed in a Roman miliary uniform. Two names were intertwined on a heart: "Paeon" and "Marcian".

Three huge men were trying to slide the marble top with massive tools. Josiah, who was over sixty, hurried over in an attempt to help. Ever the bushman from Northern Ontario, he felt he was strong as a bear. The four of them couldn't get the marble top to budge.

The Immortal's Secret

There were quiet discussions with Josiah and then one of the men said loudly, "We will bring new tools in the morning."

They shook Josiah's hand, walked towards the column where Benjamin was standing, moved past him, and then sprinted up the stairs.

"No show today," said Josiah. "Let's stay here tonight, keep an eye on this place. I have a room upstairs beside the altar. Come, join me."

It was like a luxury hotel room, not like the crumbling walls beyond its doors. There was a beautiful king-size bed, plush rugs, and a mini-bar.

In the middle of the night, Josiah's snoring was intolerable and Benjamin couldn't close his eyes. He sat down beside the mini-bar and pushed his head inside. One mini bottle of Scotch led to two, then a small bottle of Freixenet, followed by two cans of Heineken. The booze fest was not successful in drowning out the snoring so he staggered out into the nave and collapsed into a pew. His body was exhausted but his mind, wanting action, was pulling him onto a crazy, drunken roller coaster. He twisted his back up against one of the pews, trying to get into a comfortable position and take control over his thoughts. He considered going back to the hotel but this was precious private time with Josiah. Just as he was finally drifting off, he thought he heard footsteps but was too drunk to open an eye.

A few moments later, he felt something graze his forehead. Thinking it was an insect, he groggily slid his hand over his hair, hoping to flick the intruder off. He grazed skin but not his skin.

He opened his eyes to see a woman standing above him, bathed in a romantic glow from the security lighting.

His mouth dropped open but he was unable to speak.

She stared into the darkness in the church as if she were in a trance and continued to stroke his hair softly. She was so exotic looking with long black hair held back from her face by a jewelled antique Alice band.

Where did she come from? The doors are locked.

He had watched Cle close them. They had laughed about how every day it gets harder because everything in the church is so ancient.

The woman was stirring sensual feelings throughout his body. The feeling was overwhelming. He had never felt a connection like this with a girl, woman, or any human. It was like his sexuality was coming to life.

Benjamin remained still as she stroked his hair and then grazed her fingers down the side of his face. His skin felt like it was on fire.

Moving in ever so slowly, she placed her lips on his and pushed down. The connection opened him up to a world he didn't know existed. It was passion, chemistry, magic. As he kissed her back, the kiss seemed to last forever. He didn't want it to end, but she gently pivoted and began walking towards the door.

A vision in her purple satin gown with a three-foot velvet train trimmed in ermine. He was so stunned by her face—so angular, soft, and tanned. She looked ethereal, like someone from a different time, a different universe. She kept motioning for him to come, curling her middle and index finger.

Before she disappeared, he snapped a picture on his phone. The image was a streak of purple and he couldn't make out her face.

Her fragrance remained, swirling around him. A haze of verbena and roses. He wanted to run after her and ask her name, but the shock and alcohol rendered him helpless.

How did she open the door to leave the church?

The key was difficult to get in the keyhole, let along move the lock. Only Cle had the special touch.

"Who was that woman?"

Benjamin turned around but he knew it was Josiah speaking. He saw his grandfather standing above him in the pew. Josiah was wearing his housecoat and standing barefoot on the ancient tiles. He was pushing his hand into the wood of the pew.

"Who was she? She looked like a ghost. She touched you," Josiah said. He grazed Benjamin's cheek. "Do you feel alright?"

Josiah sat down in the pew in front of Benjamin and leaned his head on the top of it.

Benjamin said, "That woman was human…but not human if you know what I mean. You were watching? You got a good look, right?" Josiah's hand was hanging over the pew. Benjamin squeezed it.

"I am unnerved by what I just saw," Josiah replied. "She was ethereal. I've only seen one other person in my life who looked like that."

"Who's that?"

"Someone in Venice when I was young."

"Who?" Benjamin tapped him. "Are you okay?"

"I'm tired. When I'm woken in the middle of the night, I find it hard to get back to sleep."

He hugged Benjamin tightly and whispered in his ear. "Perhaps it bothers me that you're growing up so fast. I don't want our special moments to become few and far between."

"That's not going to happen to us. You mean everything to me. You and me against the world. Our motto," he said giving his grandfather an awkward fist bump.

When the team began arriving in the morning, Benjamin went into Josiah's room to wake him up. The old man was achy and said he didn't think he could move out of the bed. Benjamin called for the doctor—the one Josiah liked. An ambulance arrived and took him to the American hospital.

For a week, Benjamin stayed at Josiah's bedside while doctors conducted various tests. They couldn't find anything wrong. But the prescribed drugs were fairly effective, and Josiah began to feel better. He walked the halls, talked to other patients, and ate his favourite Häagen-Dazs chocolate ice cream. When the Turkish doctors advised Benjamin to accompany Josiah home to Toronto, Benjamin began making the flight arrangements.

Cle was in constant touch with Josiah by phone.

The night before their flight, Benjamin had arranged with Cle to return to the church to collect Josiah things, even though Josiah insisted he didn't care about any of them.

When they entered the church, the lights were on. Cle left him alone to pick up Josiah's things, saying she'd return in an hour.

He looked around and peeked down the staircase to the crypt. He walked down a few steps and stopped at the fifth stair to examine the hole leading to the crypt.

Pushing his hand to his face, Benjamin contemplated whether he wanted to go back into the crypt. The workmen had examined it and nothing was there, yet he continued to move towards the hole. When he climbed over the jagged bottom of the hole, he was unnerved by the glow of candlelight.

Looking around the room, he saw a woman leaning on the stairs in front of the sarcophagus, her hands locked in a prayer. It was the woman in purple with the long flowing gown.

That's the last he remembered when Cle tapped him on his shoulder and helped him up from where he was lying on the dirt floor.

"I came into the chapel and she was praying, right here," Benjamin told Cle. "Something supernatural was happening. There was a strange energy. It smelled like incense." He pointed to the front of the sarcophagus. "I stayed behind that column. I didn't want to disturb her. She was praying...in Greek. Or I think it was Greek. Was I sleeping here?" He pointed to the floor.

"I arrived when you instructed me to come. You were not in Josiah's room and I looked all over for you," says Cle. "This was the last place to look and I was apprehensive. But I saw the candle glow. I had a flashlight and almost tripped over you. Do you mind if we go, get out of here?"

Benjamin kept talking as they walked.

"What do you think of all of this? It's all very weird."

"Older buildings have their own character. We've disturbed something. Not everyone approves of our work. We're trying to keep it quiet," says Cle.

As she was opening huge oak outside door, Benjamin grabbed the handle. He paused.

"The woman. The one I saw?"

"Yes."

"I saw her a few nights ago. It was the night I stayed with Josiah, just before we took him to the hospital. I couldn't sleep because Josiah was snoring. It was unbearable. I staggered into the nave and slid into one of the pews."

He slid his phone out of his pocket, flipped through some screens, and turned the screen around so she could see it.

"May I?" She took the phone and placed it up to her eyes.

"It's blurry. I can't make her out. I will instruct the team to close up that sarcophagus. There's no golden book in that church," said Cle.

"Josiah is so desperate to find the book. It could be anywhere. How could an empress who lived in the fourth century have anything to do with the book? Did he share his reasoning?"

"I don't know. Josiah said she could be responsible for the disappearance of the book."

"That's impossible. She would be over 500 years old," said Benjamin.

"Or perhaps she left clues in the book and someone else stole the book or got a hold of it," said Cle.

"Well, it's a moot point. There is no book in that chapel, right? You're fairly certain of that?

"Yes. That woman you saw?"

"Yes."

Cle said, "There could be a simple explanation. She could be living in the church. It happens more than you think."

Benjamin was so cold, weak, and anxious to get back to his hotel and see Josiah.

On the first-class flight back to Toronto, Josiah said they arrested a woman that morning in the chapel.

"No identification and she refused to speak. Of all things, she had your drivers' license and birth certificate on her. Not sure how she got those. Cle will get them back to you. You should check if you are missing anything else. How would she get those?"

It must have happened when I was asleep in the chapel. I can't share any of this with Josiah.

"I'm not sure. Will Cle continue to lead the renovation of the church?"

"She doesn't really like the church. Her health isn't great and she can't be in that dusty and polluted environment. Your story about the woman rattled her."

"I shouldn't have mentioned it?"

"She was afraid we might find her."

"Find her? You mean Paeon?" said Benjamin.

"I don't know. I'm looking for the golden book, not ghosts. Perhaps Cle conjured her up."

"Pardon?"

Josiah's pushed his seat back and placed a huge pillow behind his head. He closed his eyes. The flight attendant gave him another blanket and he barely moved for the remainder of the flight.

She conjured Paeon? I may need therapy after this trip.

When Benjamin arrived home, he realized he'd forgotten his backpack in Istanbul. He contacted the hotel and they searched for days but couldn't find it. It contained some important items: a folder with the research he conducted at the libraries in Istanbul along with a journal that documented the ordeal with Grace Parker. The journal had never been out of his sight. Cle contacted him a few weeks later to tell him she found the backpack in the chapel and it was empty.

Chapter 11

Be not Faithless but Believing

February 27, 2017
Charles De Gaulle Airport, Paris, France

"Cle, come clean with me," says Benjamin. "That woman, the ghostly woman, or the homeless woman, in the church. The one Josiah thought might be Paeon. What do you really know about her?"

"Josiah really had no connection to that woman, who we saw years ago. He never met her. I told him about her, how she was needy, and he financed a few things."

"So, you saw her again, after that morning when she was arrested in the church? How did that happen?"

"Where are you? It's very noisy."

"I'm at Charles de Gaulle, waiting. I have a flight booked to Istanbul. After this phone call, I'll determine if it's worth going. I can't waste time going to places where I'll just spin my heels. You were saying, the woman got arrested."

"I saw her again…many times. She kept bothering me, following me."

"Where did you see her?"

"She isn't someone you'd like to get to know, Benjamin."

"I need to know. Any detail could be helpful in finding Josiah."

"She would appear near the church when I was in a nearby outdoor market. She approached me. She spoke a language I could barely understand. It was Greek, but not modern Greek. She begged me to bring her things like books from the library, books on learning English. She seemed out of this world but she was so alone. I wasn't comfortable around her so I found someone to work with her, to assimilate her, to teach her modern ways, to keep her away from me."

"Did Josiah know anything about this?"

"Yes, he provided financing through a Mannfield program. The name escapes me."

"Breaking the Cycle?"

"That could have been it."

"Who was she? Paeon?"

"A wayward soul, I think."

"Did she share anything about her background?" Benjamin glances up to check the departures board above him. His flight leaves in two hours.

"She could have run away from home. She was young."

"This is a crazy story. Did it not frighten you?"

"No, I have a mystical side to me," says Cle. The people we hired to look after her all said she was so guarded. She had all these ancient gold coins and said they had been in her family for decades. When asked if she'd found them in the tomb, she said she hadn't. But clearly, she must have. Someone helped her find the right collectors. She got a lot of money for them."

"Where is she now?" he asked.

"I don't know. She left Istanbul, quite mysteriously actually, abandoned her apartment we got for her. It was around 2009. I never saw any treasures in the church. Perhaps she had a hiding place. Many antiquities disappear regularly. You know that better than anyone, working at the Louvre."

"I'd like to go back to the church, Cle, and also to see her apartment."

"I don't think it's worth it, Benjamin. The woman may have been a squatter and found all the good stuff and hoarded it. I'm only interested in helping Josiah."

"Where was her apartment?"

"Why do you want to go there?"

"I'd like to see what she has in there. There might be clues to Josiah's whereabouts," he says.

"She didn't know Josiah. Her apartment is empty."

"How do you know that?"

"I have the key. I sold the contents but didn't get permission to sell the apartment."

"Why did Josiah ask about the woman in purple?"

"I don't know. He didn't know her. I just assumed he was having another episode, thinking he knew her because I provided him with updates. There is nothing there. Don't get sucked into her crazy world. She pulled Jenna in and I'm not sure where she ended up."

"Jenna?"

There is a long silence on the phone.

"That's someone I recruited to work with her, do her bidding."

"I need to know details, Cle. It's important. I know someone named Jenna who was interested in *The Immortal*. What was her last name?"

There is another long pause.

"I can't remember. It was a long time ago."

Benjamin is about to ask her if Jenna's last name was Parrish when Cle says, "I shouldn't say anymore."

"What did she look like? Small, blonde? Was she animated? And was she Canadian?"

Another longer pause and loud breathing.

"Benjamin, I should go. I'll meet you in Venice, as we agreed."

Chapter 12

His Nightingale

February 27, 2017
On the Plane to Venice, Italy

Benjamin stares out the airplane window at the French countryside. The trip to Istanbul would have been a waste of time. There are clearly no clues and he'd be going down roads leading nowhere. His father was right. Josiah does pride himself on leaving no breadcrumbs when he doesn't want to be found. Benjamin's hoping Venice, the city that Josiah loved, holds the clues he needs. Cle arranged to join him, but she insisted on going by train, a long journey with stops in Milan and Verona.

While sipping his sparkling water, all he can think of is the woman in purple and her friend Jenna. Could she be his Jenna? The last time he saw her was in Venice.

He received another text this morning from the unknown number.

<Look forward 2 seeing u in Venice.>

That's all it said.

He closes his eyes, hugs the golden book, and digs his head into the white airline pillow. As he is drifting off, his mind wanders back to his apartment, like his body is floating away from his seat, the airplane, back to Paris.

He can see Jenna looking up at him with her beautiful features: upturned nose, voluptuous lips, doe eyes framed by the seductive two coats of mascara he loved to watch her apply. He can see the pink in her cheeks created by the cool breeze, the freckles on her nose, the tiny pearl earrings she loved to wear. He can almost lick her raspberry lip gloss.

Her favourite poem, John Keats's "Ode to a Nightingale," dances in his mind.

> *Darkling I listen; and, for many a time*
> *I have been half in love with easeful Death,*
> *Call'd him soft names in many a mused rhyme,*
> *To take into the air my quiet breath;*
> *Now more than ever seems it rich to die,*
> *To cease upon the midnight with no pain,*
>
> *...*
>
> *Adieu! adieu! thy plaintive anthem fades*
> *Past the near meadows, over the still stream,*
> *Up the hill-side; and now tis buried deep*
> *In the next valley-glades:*
> *Was it a vision, or a waking dream?*
> *Fled is that music:—Do I wake or sleep?"*[3]

He had never believed in love at first sight, and he'd scoffed at friends and relatives when love turned them into googly-eyed crazy people. He couldn't imagine losing his mind like that and preferred a good one-night stand. No commitment, no coffee in the morning. Then he met Jenna in the lobby of the Louvre in February 2015. He was blinded.

She was dilly-dallying in front of the escalator, studying her museum guide, as he was doing a hurried bob in front of her, rushing to get on the escalator to meet an art expert from Venice. He almost fell on her when she stopped to pick up something she'd dropped. He was about to say something rude until she turned her head, ever so slowly and elegantly,

The Immortal's Secret

and looked up at him. He couldn't tear his eyes away. She was pulling him in with her powerful energy. He felt like time had stopped and he had fused with all that was beautiful and good in the world at the exact spot where they were standing—like an angel had walked through him.

She smiled at him and said, "I'm so sorry. My first time here. I'm not sure exactly where the Mona Lisa Room is."

He was speechless for the first time in his life. She was one of the masterpieces that is regularly delivered to the Louvre. Her image reminded him of the delicate face of the beauty in Botticelli's *Madonna of the Book*—a painting he spent ages studying with a flashlight in the Mona Lisa Room when the museum was closed.

She extended her graceful right hand and said, "Hi, I'm Jenna Parrish." She was like a long and lean piece of Greek sculpture come to life. Strength and elegance all rolled into perfect limbs. Her hand was so delicate—an exquisite shade of tan, with no freckles or traces of veins or creases to ruin the flow of perfection.

She wore a jean skirt with a thick knitted cardigan and a light pink T-shirt underneath with a quote from Keats' "Ode to a Nightingale" on the front: *Singest of summer in full-throated ease.* Her blonde hair was twisted into braids and pulled into a ponytail. Ordinarily he would have thought, *Who conducts an introduction in front of an escalator?* But this woman was anything but ordinary. The heat from her hand radiated on his like she had electrocuted him.

He knew that he should have been going up that escalator to start his workday already. Until that moment, he'd developed few deep relationships along his life journey. This didn't bother him at all. He spent no time thinking about it despite continual concern from relatives, especially Josiah and Uncle Ganja—the bona fide hippie in the family with the peace sign tattooed above his pubic hair. Benjamin fancied himself as a ladies' man. In truth, he was the king of the one-night stand. Yet he was also known as a workaholic, a man of purpose, a man who jammed every hour with work, not small talk. His life was books, history, reading, and studying others' lives to distract him from living his own.

His history was studying history and examining dead people, especially beautiful women he could control on his terms, not those who show up unexpectedly to demand any investment in his time. He loved people who resided in the past, not the present. He didn't need a therapist to tell him his life was defined by avoidance. Benjamin's life plan did not include a wife and sharing life's significant moments over morning coffee. He didn't even drink coffee.

When he met Jenna, he was going through a phase. His life consisted of working, reading, eating periodically, and sleeping. Since he had graduated from Oxford with his PhD in art history, he worked for the Louvre, going through periods where he rarely saw sunshine—only the artificial light inside of the museum, conference hall, or library.

He would get his hair cut if someone he respected suggested it was too long. He only dressed well because his mother paid someone to act as a "valet" for him, an infuriating role for the various men who came through the revolving door. His relationship with his mother consisted of a weekly call from her while she was having her pedicure just to make sure he was still alive and watering the plants she bought him. He had always felt like she relished the title of mother but most of the time wasn't interested in any of the meaningful work the job required.

He loved nighttime because the museum emptied of any life, and he could roam the halls going from exhibit to exhibit to analyze the details of the art in silence and disappear into his own world. He once stood in front of Titian's *The Entombment of Christ* for the entire night, taking in every detail. He was captivated by Christ's commitment to his cause and how he was willing to endure so much pain for his faith. Benjamin wondered how anyone could have that level of faith about anything. He knew he was a flawed man.

The morning he bumped into Jenna, he never arrived at his office to meet the esteemed, double PhD language expert from Venice. He ignored the constant text messages on his phone from his assistant. Instead, he spent the day as a truant, touring Jenna through the museum. She said she had to see Sartore's *The Immortal*, see it up close and examine every detail. He was intrigued as to why she thought *The Immortal* was in the Louvre. It had always been in Josiah's private collection.

"Where did you hear of *The Immortal?*" he asked her, staring into her brown eyes. He noticed she wasn't wearing a wedding ring—he checked twice. He never looked for such things, but he did that day.

He was delighted she was doing most of the talking, giving him reason to totally focus on her and examine every detail of her exquisite face.

"I'm interested in Andrea Sartore. I've done research," she said while rummaging in the canvas bag slung around her shoulder.

"How do you know anything about him?"

The Immortal's Secret

"I've gathered information from the archives in Venice about the plagues. I read about the powers of *The Immortal*. She healed so many who were suffering."

"Yes, she had special powers."

Josiah had told him to be on guard if anyone showed any interest in *The Immortal*. Benjamin didn't seem to think Jenna's behaviour was suspicious, proving he was in denial from the first hello. Realistically, how could she be so obsessed with a portrait that was in a private collection?

He didn't care. He guided her to the terrace of Le Café Mollien so he could see her framed by the natural light. She seemed so pure, and her innocence seemed to magnify all his flaws, making him feel hollow, like an outline waiting to be filled in.

When he held up the first photo of *The Immortal* on his phone, she leaned over and pushed the screen to zoom in on the most minute details. She asked if she could take a picture of his screen and she did this on an old phone: a Smithsonian relic. Benjamin was shocked it still functioned. She said she was thinking of writing her master's thesis on Sartore.

She captivated him with her love of art. One thing quickly led to another that day. Before he knew it, they were in the foyer of his apartment, their bodies interlocked as clothes flew off. They made their way past his crowded living room with stacks of current and antique books and finally upstairs to his sumptuous bedroom. They fell on top of his comforter, a lavish, deep purple silk number, a gift from his mother. It was covered in Byzantine crosses that Benjamin always thought looked majestic, like it belonged draped over the shoulders of the flamboyant Louis XIV.

She helped him strip off each piece of his clothing and slid her hands lightly over every part of his body as if she was examining the most exquisite marble. He was worried she would notice his unsightly scar from a random biking accident, but she proclaimed he was perfect as she slowly slipped her hand through his mane of curly chestnut hair. Her running her hands through his hair made him laugh nervously as the pressure mounted in his groin. He rarely paid any attention to or cared about how he looked or what others thought, although he did attract a lot of alluring looks from women when he cared to pay attention.

That night, with her, he felt perfect. He wanted desperately to please her. As she lay beside him on the lavish royal bedspread framed by the moonlight over the terrace, he again noticed her exquisite beauty. She was so comfortably natural as she splayed out beside him completely nude. Her skin was flawless like mocha, not even a mole. She seemed so comfortable and natural in her skin as if clothes were an annoying option. She leaned in to place her lips on his and pulled his body towards her. The man so scared to be human finally felt alive.

Their lovemaking was like a mystical form of CPR for a man who had been hiding in the Louvre for almost a decade running from any emotional connection, surrounding himself with inanimate objects. That night he was no longer recognizable to himself. For the first time since he was in university, he felt young. When he reached orgasm, he felt as if he had just finished the most ecstatic journey of his life.

Afterwards, as he gazed upon Jenna, he felt like he was viewing one of the most famous models of the Venetian masters. He was entranced with her beautiful lines, vibrant colours from her light hair, and soft pink lace teddy that she put back on. She even looked at him like a model in a painting, with her intense brown eyes that seem to follow him without moving her head. He wished he had the hand of an artist so he could capture this moment and immortalize her on canvas. She was innocence meeting deeply erotic pleasure.

She spent most of their first night in front of the terrace window in a chair. His apartment was palatial, with its marble and rich woods and jewel tones. Jenna blended in as if the background was created for her.

He never had conversations with women in bed. He simply inquired about what they liked, where, and for how long. He never made love. It was always a quick fuck. And he never stayed the night. He tiptoed out of their bedrooms and hopped into his clothes in a race to find the door, lest they wake up before he was safely on the other side. There was never a follow-up call unless the woman made it. If the call came, it was always ignored. Jenna was the first woman to be invited into this bed and he didn't want her ever to leave.

Watching her from his bed, he felt that he must be under some mystic spell. He didn't recognize himself.

"Please tell me you're not married," he remembers telling her. "I think I'm in love with you."

Did he just say that? Did that come out of his cold, calculated mouth?

Benjamin jumped off the bed, wondering why he verbalized what he was thinking. He was feeling so vulnerable and embarrassed, two very unfamiliar emotions to him.

The Immortal's Secret

He suddenly realized he was nude. He was about to leap over and reach for his pants when Jenna came over, stroked his face, and peered deep into his eyes.

"Whoever loved that loved not at first sight?" he said, quoting Shakespeare.

She kissed him on the mouth, and they fell back onto the bed.

He cupped her face in his giant hands and said, "I don't think I can ever leave you."

He felt reborn that night, as if his life until that point was a boring portrait that Jenna had just whitewashed and begun painting over, creating a masterpiece of her design. He felt like his nerves had been poked and infused by the most subtle and wonderful narcotic. He thought—he hoped—the feeling would never die. It was a spiritual moment, like he was fusing his body with hers. Their connection wasn't only sexual, although the sex was mind-blowing.

Everything seemed different after that night. He felt pins and needles all over his body. Sounds were louder, taste was deeper, and touch became enjoyable. He never hugged before or ever felt like casually touching someone else.

Now he realized touch could lead to ecstasy, that through touch he could enter a different realm where he was outside of his body floating around. He couldn't stop touching her, examining her, and wanting to blend his body with hers.

They barely left the bedroom for a week. They made love multiple times a day, but they talked in between. Jenna was in Paris because she had been touring Europe. When she arrived, she was floored by the beauty and couldn't bear to leave. She decided to stay for a while and rented a "box" overlooking the Boulevard Saint-Germain.

She was fascinated that Benjamin studied ancient languages, ones he could never dream of speaking with someone else. The purpose of his language studies was to learn more about history whereas her focus was to communicate and connect with people whose culture was different than her own. She loved how the nuances of language helped to deeply bond people.

To Benjamin, Jenna was another species of human, one who wanted to live and experience everything. She would gaze at stars at night, feed the pigeons in the courtyards around the Louvre, and take photos for families visiting the city for the first time. One of her favourite activities was to ride the Ferris wheel in the Place de la Concorde. She could ride it for hours watching the theatre of everyday life from her bird's eye view.

Benjamin had never believed in angels or ever thought about them. But if they did exist, she was one of them. He was inspired by her, yet felt he was incapable of even being a little like her. He had years of privilege ingrained in him. He never wanted for anything and never felt guilty about his life of privilege. He would never have stopped to talk to her if not for her looks, which ended up being her least distinguishing quality.

There were so many details about her he couldn't get to the bottom of despite so much prodding. Jenna divulged only snippets of her life, like her mother was an artist and her name was Maria. When Jenna was a child, they lived hand to mouth. Her mother placed her in foster care when she could no longer look after her.

As time went on, she was putting pressure on Benjamin to take her to Toronto and he found it annoying.

Jenna was very aware of the power of her looks and her presence. She was beautiful and magnetic, and she used those powers, not to manipulate, but to help others and make them feel better about themselves. She had a sense of community and connection that he found foreign.

He didn't understand how she could give so much of her energy to others. He hoarded his energy and focused on his needs and his current works in progress. She made him realize how empty his life had been—that he possessed a leak from which air was slowly seeping.

In August 2015, Jenna started getting calls that she took in private. She told Benjamin they were from her mother. He insisted she tell him about her mother and she showed him a picture that looked like a stock photo used in new picture frames. He was losing patience.

"Who are you? I don't know anything about you."

He instantly regretted what he said and she refused to speak to him. The silent treatment worked. He relented and purchased the tickets to Toronto.

Now he wishes he'd insisted on finding out more about why she was so intent on travelling to Toronto with him and seeing *The Immortal*. The painting was priceless to him and his grandfather. Perhaps he didn't ask because he didn't want to know.

A day before they were scheduled to leave, he was invited to go to Venice to meet a curator at the Gallerie dell'Accademia. The meeting was critical to his work, and he was torn. After trying desperately to get someone to take his place in Venice, work beckoned. He was hardwired to place it before everything.

She capitulated and joined him. Yet she found it hard to take any interest in the ancient beauty of Venice and spent a good part of her day surfing the Internet. Benjamin found this so puzzling since Venice is the city of Sartore.

At the beginning of their second week in Venice, they were preparing for a day trip to Verona, a city she said she was anxious to see. Her phone rang and she excused herself and took it in the bedroom. He could hear her yelling. When she was finished, she came out of the bedroom.

"Can we call off the day trip?" she asked. "I'm exhausted,"

"Is everything alright?"

"I'm fine." Yet she seemed different, like another person had suddenly appeared in front of him.

"Ok. I'm going to pop over to see a colleague from the Gallerie dell'Accademia. I'll keep in touch on my phone."

She gave him the number of a cheap new cell phone. She said she'd lost her old one.

She said a quick goodbye when he left, no kiss. Her voice was even different. He was sure he detected a slight accent—one he couldn't place.

The call she had taken had lasted at least a half an hour. He wishes now he'd asked her what it was about. After he left, he remembered she locked the door behind him, something she never did.

Unfortunately, one hour with his colleague turned into four, with many text messages in between and Benjamin apologizing and promising to meet her at a specific time in St. Mark's Square. He suggested the front of the clock tower beside the basilica because in the flurry of texts, she said she had gone there for mass.

It was nightfall when he dashed over to finally meet her for a late dinner. So excited, he kept scanning the crowd, anxiously looking for her. He was going to make the night special to make up for the botched day.

After waiting and searching for her for two hours, and placing numerous calls to her cell phone, he raced back to the palazzo. He was sure she was just tired and was resting with her phone beside her on mute.

When he entered the palazzo, he tiptoed into the bedroom and walked over to their bed, which he had watched her make that morning. The decorative pillows were placed side by side in front of the bed pillows. The windows were open, and a gentle breeze filled the room with the smells of a Venetian night. A vase of roses was on the window ledge. The room was exactly the way they had left it with one exception.

There were no signs of Jenna. No pink suitcase, no furry slippers, no moisturizer on the bedside table. He flicked the light in the bathroom on and scanned the vanity. No make-up bag, blow-dryer, or round hairbrush.

He stared at the toilet and finally raised the lid to puke.

As he slowly walked down the stairs, he held the banister for fear of falling. His legs felt as wobbly as jelly. The living room was just as they had left it; the art books they were reading the night before were still on the side table.

Then he entered the kitchen and saw the note in the middle of the table. It was her pink notepaper with the Eiffel Tower watermark that she often used. He leapt towards it, almost tripping on the slippery tile floor.

There is a reason for all of this. She's forgotten we were meeting. She's gone out for something, something simple like that.

He anxiously picked up the note and pushed it to his chest. He was going to solve this mystery, scold himself for worrying, and then make himself something to eat. Little did he know, it would be a long time before he fully enjoyed a meal again.

Adieu! adieu! thy plaintive anthem fades

Past the near meadows, over the still stream,

Up the hill-side; and now 'tis buried deep

In the next valley-glades:

Was it a vision, or a waking dream?

Fled is that music:—Do I wake or sleep?[4]

My love, forgive me. I need to return to my life. I will never forget the joy you brought me.

—Jenna

It took fourteen seconds to read the note, fourteen seconds to change his life forever, fourteen seconds to completely slam the door on his faith and any belief in true love. Her sudden departure was the cruelest act, taking his heart and squeezing it so hard he could no longer breathe.

He stared at the note for an hour, his eyes sliding up and down the perfect cursive letters. Without moving an inch from the tile on the floor where he was standing, he just stared at the words like they were hieroglyphs holding a secret meaning.

Finally, he fell hard to the floor. It was August 19, 2015. He didn't move from the floor the rest of that night other than to constantly call her new cell phone number. It just rang and rang. He then desperately placed calls to her old number, which also rang and rang.

In the morning, he rushed to St. Mark's Square and ambushed anyone he could find, searching for information—waiters, priests at St. Mark's Basilica, the people who sweep the square, souvenir sellers, and shopkeepers. When he went to the police to file a report, he could feel their pity with their sad looks and comments about having a single cousin looking for a nice guy. When he returned to his palazzo, he crawled to the office, clicked the lock, and collapsed on the leather sofa Googling the most efficient and painless methods of suicide.

That evening, he blasted "St. Matthew's Passion" on his iPhone, snuggled in the sheets on the bed she made, placed her bottle of Chloe perfume—one of only two items she had left behind—up to his nose. It was the scent that defined her. He lay on the bed breathing it in. He scrolled through his phone, looking at the photos he took of her, enlarging them to examine every detail.

All he ate that day was stale corn flakes with her skim milk, and only when he couldn't stave off hunger any longer.

At the beginning of the second week, on September 3, 2015, there was a commotion outside his window. Someone was hollering in English.

Staggering to the window, he peered down and saw Josiah looking up at him. Josiah was standing in a gondola holding a bullhorn to his lips.

"I am looking for the whereabouts of a Dr. Benjamin Mann," he hollered up towards Benjamin's office window.

Decked out in a pinstripe suit, Wayfarer sunglasses, and a Daniel Boone hat, Josiah was a beacon of hope teetering hazardously in the middle of the gondola, challenging its centre of gravity like Madonna flinging herself around in her "Like a Virgin" music video.

How did he know I was in Venice?

Benjamin never asked or thought about it at the time. He was just so relieved to see his grandfather.

They parked themselves on Benjamin's sofa draining the bottle of Scotch Josiah brought. The conversation is as clear in his mind today as it was that day.

"You will survive," Josiah insisted. "You are descended from frontier people, people who slept beside bears, survived on berries, and were not afraid to drink their own urine if they lacked water. Our family created a billion-dollar company from gold we found jutting out from a rock, exposed by a fire that burnt everything in its path."

"Drinking urine? Pardon?" Benjamin responded.

Choosing to ignore Josiah's pep talks, Benjamin spent the next few hours perched on the edge of the sofa, punching out his exasperating ruminations on why Jenna left him, so thrilled that he had a human to interact with. Finally, Josiah broke, stood up, and dangled Jenna's note on the pink paper.

"Benji, you know I love you."

"Yes, I know. You may be the only one."

"No, I'm not. Let's suspend the self-pity for a few minutes. I cannot listen to your constant soliloquies postulating on every detail related to why she left you. I am a great listener. I know this about myself, but I have limits. Let's examine the facts. She left you a note quoting her favourite poem, 'Ode to a Nightingale.' It's about a guy who hears a bird singing and thinks the bird's immortal," he said watching Benjamin's reactions.

He pointed his finger. "Don't argue, I looked it up. I'm not a poet. Don't care for poetry, other than Bob Dylan. I don't know the inside story on the poem and the both of you. I just know this: she wrote you a note instead of telling you in person. You don't really know anything about her so you can't chase her."

"I know, it appears she is a ghost. We spent a lot of time in bed. You know how it is during the throes of passion. I've never met anyone like her. I was under her spell. You've lived and loved."

"I tend to come up for air and get curious," Josiah said. "I've always been more interested in my paramours than in sharing anything about myself with them."

"She said she was Canadian. From Toronto. Her mother was an artist. Very religious."

"That's it? That's your dossier on her?"

Benjamin stared at him and Josiah stared back.

"What's with you and the judgement, Grandad? It's not like you. I thought we were building a new life together. I liked how she was a blank slate. Family adds complication. I was glad she wasn't close with hers. That is my favourite type of woman. One who travels light."

The Immortal's Secret

"Okay, Mr. Lovestruck. I know what's it like to be guided by love and other parts of your body," Josiah said. Benjamin rolled his eyes. Josiah continued. "I had someone do a little investigating. I care too much about you not to want answers."

"What kind of investigating? For the last two weeks I've scoured this island from top to the bottom. I contacted the police."

"I know a guy. I helped him out. He thinks he owes me. He's always asking if I need something. I thought I'd call him."

"A private eye."

"Yes. It's within the realm of legal. Just," said Josiah.

Pushing his unwashed hair out of his eyes, Benjamin wondered whether he wanted to hear what Josiah was going to say next. He walked over to the picture window and looked out at the canal. Without looking at Josiah he said, "Do I want to hear this?"

"I need to tell you, to protect you."

"Okay," he said as he traced his finger around the design on the marble ledge.

Josiah walked over and touched Benjamin's arm.

"She was back at your apartment in Paris."

"No. I called there. I had the doorman check the apartment."

Benjamin scratched his head and stared at Josiah.

"Grandad, this doesn't seem right at all."

Benjamin continued staring at him while Josiah searched for something on his phone. He tapped back and forth between images and finally turned his phone around to show Benjamin the photo he had been looking for.

Benjamin took the phone and walked back over to the sofa. He poured some Scotch over the melting ice in his glass. He put his glasses up to his face and had trouble getting the arms over his ears. Pushing his fingers on the screen to zoom in, he looked at the photo for what seemed forever until Josiah walked over and sat down slowly.

"Who took this?" Benjamin said. He took a gulp of the Scotch.

"She is sneaking in the back way and placing the key in the door of your apartment."

"It makes no sense."

"Click on the photo details. It shows where it was taken and when. Benji, I don't know exactly what happened between you and Jenna. I am so glad you experienced it. It certainly sounds like it was a lot of fun. The type of sex, well, I can only dream of. Perhaps in another life, if reincarnation exists."

Benjamin held the phone up staring at the photo.

"It makes no sense."

He pressed his finger against his forehead.

"Benji, my guy is pretty positive it's her. She took out a platinum credit card in your name. He checked her credit history, which shows her travel patterns over the past few months, in Paris and Venice with you. He has pictures of her in cafés and designer boutiques in Paris making lavish purchases."

"It's her," Benjamin said.

He pushed his finger into the screen to zoom in on something. He turned the phone to Josiah.

"She's wearing the huge gold necklace she never took off."

Josiah stared at the photo and furrowed his brow.

"It's so hard to disclose this to you."

He slid his phone into his pocket, picked up his crystal whiskey glass, and stirred the ice with his fingers.

"Do you remember the woman who was interested in *The Immoral?*" he continued. "The one who wanted to buy it. She became very aggressive. We had to get a restraining order against her."

"Yes, I remember."

"Her name was Jenna Parrish. I have the report from my guy. I can show you. Apparently, her ID is fake."

"She's the gentlest woman I've ever met. She doesn't have an evil bone in her body."

Josiah took his grandson's hand.

"Benji, let me do some more investigation. Try and figure out what is going on here. See if she's dangerous. I don't want you hurt anymore."

Benjamin didn't move. He filled his glass again and downed it like it was a shot of tequila.

He finally looked up at Josiah and nodded his head in agreement.

He said, "Yes, absolutely," when he was thinking, *Perhaps.*

Benjamin will never forget his fitful sleep that night. Josiah's words kept racing through his mind, a roller coaster fueled by too much Scotch and too little food. He kept thinking how she was a ghost who had appeared out of nowhere. She knew so much about his family yet she divulged nothing about herself. And he didn't probe. There appeared to be absolutely no breadcrumbs to follow in Venice and a scant few in the apartment in Paris.

The next day, Benjamin flew back to Paris with Josiah on his grandfather's private plane (a detour en route to some gold mine in South Africa that Josiah was exploring). There were no signs of Jenna in his apartment. Some of his papers may have been rifled through in his office, but he couldn't be sure. A folder on Sartore that he kept in his office was gone. It was possible he had left it in his office at the Louvre. He was going to check the next day but was forced to visit the emergency department after debilitating, shooting stomach pains awoke him in the middle of the night. While in the waiting room, he passed out on a young woman who was bent over wailing from the pain of a migraine. When he woke, he was in a hospital gown. His new uniform for a year.

Something stuck in Benjamin's mind. How did Josiah know Jenna left him? How could Josiah know so much about a woman he didn't know Benjamin was dating?

Chapter 13

St. Mark's Basilica

February 28, 2017
St. Mark's Basilica, Venice, Italy

Benjamin is enjoying an early morning slow stroll through St. Mark's Square, deftly snaking through the obstacle course of tourists of all sizes, brazen pigeons, and tables and chairs outside the cafés.

He stops in the middle of the square to take in the breathtaking view of St. Mark's Basilica. It's an enormous masterpiece. It remains the most magnificent church he has ever seen. It's St. Peter's Basilica placed on top of the Taj Mahal, placed on top of the Blue Mosque, placed on top of the Louvre, and blended by divine hands. When he looks at it, he's certain all the beauty in the world is captured within its walls.

The basilica is one of the few things on the planet that makes him want to live…that and *The Immortal*, Josiah, and Jenna. In truth, he's not sure about her anymore though. Cle confirmed Josiah's comment about her wanting to get her hands on *The Immortal*.

Still, he tortures himself by staring at a photo on his phone taken days before she left. Is she here in Venice? He wants to confront her.

He approaches the basilica and meets a man named Gianni at the front door, another friend/colleague of Cle's who is more than willing to oblige Benjamin and secure him privacy. He is one of the procurators at St. Mark's Basilica.

"I know your grandfather was instrumental in the restorations of this magnificent place. He is well-respected here. We closed the baptistery to give you privacy."

"Thank you," Benjamin says.

Gianni takes Benjamin to the serene baptistery well out sight of the curious tourists who are constantly looking up, snapping pictures of the ceilings, or both.

Gianni says his guide, a friend of Cle's, will be with Benjamin shortly.

"She brought something for you. It's on the pew. She called it clues," he says, pointing over towards the altar.

Benjamin sits down in one of the pews to take in his beautiful surroundings. Everything around him is framed by the lights hanging from the ceiling. He takes in the smell of the baptistery. It's so thick, like incense was fused into the air, giving it a sweet exotic smell. He closes his eyes, taking deep breaths in and pushing them out, focusing on the way the scent takes him back to his youth, when he had an unwavering devotion to the Catholic faith.

He lifts *The Immortal* out of her protective case along with the golden book and carefully places both beside him on the pew. The box Gianni mentioned is at the other end of the pew.

Benjamin stretches his arm out and slides it closer, rubbing his fingers over the top. The beautiful wood looks like acacia. A memory from his childhood flashes in his mind—a similar chest made of acacia in his mother's bedroom, where she stored blankets.

This box is one foot wide and about five inches deep. It looks like an ancient artifact and smells like the inside of St. Mark's: musty wood baked in incense. There is a note taped on top written in Latin: *Confidential information inside for Dr. Benjamin Mann only. From Josiah Mann regarding Sartore and* The Immortal. The note is on thick paper that looks like it came from an artist's atelier from long ago.

He's hesitant to open the box, so he pauses, studying it while his heart pounds.

Then, with shaking hands, he clicks the latch and opens the box. It smells of the past. The smell is odd but pleasant. There is another piece of paper on top. He unfolds it. It's a letter dated June 2016 written on stationery from the Hotel Danieli, unmistakably in Josiah's hand.

The Immortal's Secret

Dearest Benji,

These are more clues about the golden book. Your grandmother found these in the old Sartore Palace. They are yours now.

Pressure builds up in his eyes as he looks at the floor and taps his feet to compose himself.

He lays the letter on the bench, turns it over, and places his hand on top. With his other hand, he moves through the rest of the contents. There are sketches bound in a leather folder with Latin writing carved into the front that translates to "Portraits of Suffering". He unties the leather strings and fans through the pages. The sketches are all the size of a standard piece of copy paper. The subjects are at various stages of sickness, decay. One man is clearly a nobleman standing proudly, wearing his luxurious attire with sumptuous fabrics falling off his emaciated frame. His face is bursting with pock marks. A monster with a kind smile. A young woman's bulging eyes are staring ahead while she cradles what looks like a baby deformed by bleeding buboes. Hideously beautiful. The sketches are all signed "A. Sartore". The script snakes around the bottom right corner of each page.

Benjamin places them all on the floor in front of him. A grotesque menagerie of human suffering. The horror of disease and the beauty of the humanity struggling for life within bodies decaying from inside out.

Deep penetrating eyes, fragile hands, freckles on a tiny rotting nose. A half smile on a tiny girl holding her mother hands in a grand palazzo, both of them freaks in luxurious velvet dresses. Essays on humanity's suffering.

The last portrait stuns him. He brings it closer to his eyes to examine the details closely. The man is in his twenties, leaning on a parapet, staring ahead with piercing eyes. The background is the baptistery, in front of the baptismal font right where Benjamin is sitting. The man's lips are full, the face chiselled with a deep, cleft chin. Benjamin turns over the portrait and it says in Latin "Self-portrait in St. Mark's, age 24". It's Andrea Sartore.

He sees some fragile scrolls in the box and unravels one. The author, a Father Roberto Sartore, tells the story of how he arrived in the South Sinai Desert.

Alexandra Edmiston

Papyrus Scroll One: The Beginning

Writing a diary is a tradition in the Sartore family to document our family journey. My story begins in AD 380 on an island we called Isola di Speranza in what is now the Venetian lagoon. I landed there with a small handful of Christians along with my cousin Fredrico, my closest family member. My parents had been wiped out by the savages of various names who continually invaded our home in Veneti when I was barely a teenager. The island was pristine and deserted. In time it proved to be a great place to hide from the Germanic tribes prowling the area. The day we arrived we started digging, chopping down trees, and building. The goal was to create an underground church. Although I was totally committed to the Christian faith, I had no desire to be ordained. I left that to Fredrico, who was a man of deeper faith. I was a dreamer who just wanted to know true love. We were living a pleasant pastoral life.

One night, Fredrico and I were returning to the island from a fishing expedition. We were sailing under a full moon. The air was thick and dry. In the waters surrounding the island, we saw the shadowy figures enter our island. Swarms of men were scaling the huge stone wall and gate that surrounded our island. Beads of sweat formed on our skin.

We hid our small boat near the dense forest and followed them towards our underground church and home. We were desperate to be heroic and got ready for battle. We concealed ourselves behind trees, dodging back and forth in the forest, and watched as the savages destroyed everything above ground.

Delicate sculptures of The Blessed Virgin and the Christ Child carefully carved out of alderwood framed the gate. Not far from us, one of the intruders, a dirty beast cloaked in grey, took one of the statues of the young Blessed Virgin, split it in half on his knee, and crushed the pieces into the mud floor. He then grabbed one of the larger pieces, holding it like a dagger, and scrawled something deeply onto the stone wall in a language we didn't understand.

The savages held wooden torches. They set ablaze the beautiful trees and hurled their burning sticks on everything. The flames lit up the passageway as the savages charged towards the home we shared with our fellow holy people.

The Immortal's Secret

When they discovered our underground home, they blasted through the entrance of our sanctuary with such ferocity. We crept over to get a better look. The ball of flame was suffocating. Fredrico demanded we retreat. Somehow, we made our way to the boat and watched our island and the madness of the intruders from the water. When it appeared a rescue was impossible, we set sail on the Adriatic.

After almost a year of travel, we landed in Egypt. Fredrico wanted to be as far away as possible from Veneti. His father had told us one of our uncles joined a community of monks who lived at the foot of Mount Sinai. They were called Desert Fathers.

We undertook a long arduous journey over the sand, which sprawled out into infinity. The hunger and exhaustion were unbearable and we stopped many times to pray for God's help. We were emaciated and near death when we could see the outline of the monastery.

We both found solace in the monastery, and peace for the first time in our lives. I was so very lonely. I never stopped missing home and fantasized about returning. I had pushed ordination off for so long that others assumed I was a holy man. I wore the habit at the monastery because I was as devout as the rest of the monks. In my heart I was not a monk, and I knew one day I would return to what others considered a regular life although I had never known a regular life.

Benjamin picks up the other documents and reads them:

Papyrus Scroll Two: Annacletica

One day, my prayers were answered. I was twenty-four. I was exploring the desert around the monastery, an activity I enjoyed when we weren't in prayer. I found a young wo, to let her stay. She was mysterious and beautiful. Her name was Annacletica.

She had a gentle caring way and I just wanted to look after her. She was a study in perfection. I could not keep my eyes off her. With her pristine mocha complexion and crimson lips, she radiated the energy and emotion of youth. A most exquisite creature, an exotic mixture of statuesque Roman beauty and Greek symmetry, I dared not touch her. I was presenting myself as a monk, and there was no authentic way to tell her I was not. Regardless, we could not have had a relationship in the monastery. It's holy ground. God sees things.

Annacletica seemed drawn to a chasm a short journey from the monastery. I followed her there one day not long after she arrived. She was standing near the edge, and I thought she was going to jump. I tried to leap towards her but there was a force holding me back. I couldn't get near her. Later, I asked her what happened. She was reluctant to share any details.

Fredrico became ill. I was frantic. I was so upset at Annacletica for venturing beyond the monastery. She produced a golden book and said Fredrico should pray on it and ask to be cured. To do so was blasphemous, but I was desperate.

Fredrico touched the book with his weak fingers and made his wish.

The next day there was a change: slight colour appeared in his face, and he experienced hunger pangs. He ate, not much, just a few pieces of bread. But the improvement amazed me.

Papyrus Scroll Three: The Chapel of Hope

We built a chapel so the golden book could help others. I'd found my true calling. The pilgrims flocked to our chapel from all over. It was miraculous. We helped so many. I documented our life in sketches. I created a map for pilgrims to reach the monastery via ship and then land. I was proud of my beautiful works of art.

Document from Venetian Archives—Diary of Andrea Sartore

I performed a ritual I did regularly in the baptistery at St. Mark's Basilica. I softly rubbed a marble image of The Blessed Virgin in the middle of the altar, caressing her exquisite face that smiled up at me. I always said a little prayer. On that magical day for some reason, I did something I'd never done. With my eyes closed, I pushed my hand into her face, overcome with my love for her and the passion of prayer. As I did this, her statue moved towards me, creating a gap in the altar.

I jumped up heartbroken and panicked, feeling I'd damaged the beautiful statue in some way. With the light of my candle, I moved in slowly to examine it in closer detail. I shone the candle over the opening and realized The Blessed Virgin Mary was a hidden door that opened to a secret room. I gently pushed the statue and the door slowly slid wide open. I stood in the door and shone the candle, and I couldn't believe what was in front of my eyes. The sun was rising, and light was streaming into the room.

The interior chapel was masterfully shielded and was identical to the chapel in front of it, the one seen from the outside façade of the basilica. Yet this secret chapel was much more palatial than the one shielding it. Its marble carvings and gold were similar in design to the main rooms in our Sartore Palace. The walls were lined with shelves containing books and scrolls.

I walked up to a beautiful white marble sarcophagus of a man and a woman intertwined as if they were one person. I placed my hand over the marble, touching it, feeling heat on my hand. I climbed onto the sarcophagus and wrapped myself around the sculpture. I am not sure why I did this or how long I remained embracing and caressing the sculpture. At some point I slid down, pushing one of the sides and opening it a crack.

I looked down and smelled lavender, pondering how odd it was to smell something so fresh. I pushed the sarcophagus open a little more, and then a little more, until I could see in. There was a woman, perfectly preserved and beautiful. How could this be? A corpse that refused to decompose.

She was holding a golden book. She was exquisite, with pristine mocha skin and auburn hair. The most beautiful woman I have ever seen. I was overcome and I touched her. She opened her eyes. It was the most extraordinary moment of my life.

She said she had created the golden book. It was a living thing. She said that whoever prayed on it would have their wish granted. I told her about my illness and together we prayed for a cure.

From that moment, I never felt healthier and younger. I became her protector. She wouldn't reveal herself to anyone but me. Her name was Annacletica.

I spent as much time as I could with her in this holy place she called The Secret Sartore Chapel, reading the scrolls and tracing the sketches from Roberto Sartore. I made oil portraits of them. There was a portrait of Annacletica she said was created by an Empress Paeon of the Eastern Roman Empire. I transformed it into an icon, like the stunning examples I had traced in St. Mark's. I couldn't keep my eyes off my portrait. I was so proud of it and called it The Immortal.

Benjamin is stunned. This is a first-person account of *The Immortal*, created in snippets.

What's it all about? Sartore had found Annacletica in a sarcophagus. Could this be true?

And who placed this box here in the baptistery?

He considers calling Cle to ask but she had told him she eschews all modern technology like cell phones and even tvs.

He carefully places everything back in the box, stands up, slips his jacket off, and looks at the altar. It's close to noon and he's getting hungry.

The centrepiece is a spectacular iconostasis stretching the full length of the altar, then climbing almost to the ceiling, anchored by a seven-foot carved gate, framed by a twisting rope of rosettes, hearts, and the letters "A" and "A." Above the gate is an icon of The Virgin Mary, and towering over her is a massive mosaic of a solemn Christ looking down, his features balanced perfectly with the golden background. There's a niche in the middle of the iconostasis. Benjamin places the golden book in it.

He hangs *The Immortal* over the book. It's not a perfect fit, but Benjamin can tell that at one time it was. It creates a beautiful line of sight.

He had brought some candles and frankincense oil with him. He shakes the oil and places the candles on a little ledge around the portrait, lights them, and then looks around at the little shrine he's created. It's so quiet and the lighting from the candles is soothing. The gold, marble, and the mosaics seem to pull him in like they've come to life and want to draw him into a soothing hug. He feels an overwhelming sadness, like everything in this chapel is alive and is crying out in pain.

He wishes he could look down and see a clue that Josiah was here. Some mystic breadcrumbs that lead to him, like his name entwined with Sera's, carved into the gold. Folding his hands in prayer, Benjamin lowers his head and recites this in Latin, a language Josiah taught him:

> *This is a special place. I know great things happened in this chapel. It's a place of worship but also of suffering. My painting and golden book, which I have placed at the altar, have great significance here. They seem to have helped so many people. They are precious. Please bring my grandfather back to me. I need clues. I need to know what happened to him. I am stuck and I cannot move forward without closure.*

The Immortal's Secret

He looks up at *The Immortal* and stares deep into the golden grooves of her eyes. He breathes deeply to inhale the smell of the incense and watches the candlelight flicker and dance around her eyes. As they begin glowing, she looks directly at him. Light pierces his eyes like it did in his office in the Louvre. The shards of light dance like a shower of stars in the darkness, making him feel like he's being electrocuted via every nerve.

His body falls on the cold marble steps leading up to the small altar. He can't move. Feeling so weak, he has no desire to try to push himself up to his feet. He just wants to sink into the marble, become one with this exquisite monument, and meld into a piece of art.

With great effort, he rolls onto his knees, reaches up for the golden book in the niche, and pushes it to his chest like a life jacket.

"Help me. Please tell me where Josiah is."

The energy seems to intensify. He feels like he is floating, examining the details in the mosaics in the dome of the ceiling of Christ and John the Baptist.

This magical moment seems to last forever until he lands softly on the ground, on the beautiful, tessellated marble. He stares at the altar again through groggy eyes and then turns his head and sees that a throng of people have appeared. Unable to move, he watches them.

Sunshine is streaming in through the stained-glass windows, piercing his eyes. He pushes his hands into his eyes. Struggling to see, he can't make out the people in front of him, but he knows they are crushing him and pushing him back towards the altar. Where did they come from? Did Gianni allow a lunchtime tour group into the baptistery?

As the crowd pushes him, he screams, "Hey what are you doing?"

They don't respond.

He reaches out to one of them but he can't extend his arm far enough to touch the person. He shuts his eyes to regain his focus, and when he opens them, his vision adjusts to the light. When he looks at the crowd, he's shocked by the solemn looks on their faces and how anxious they all look, with heavy eyes.

They are all wearing elaborate Renaissance clothing—long flowing gowns and jackets made of the most exquisite fabrics, adorned with rows of precious jewels and pearls. Although their attire is clearly expensive, the colours are muted and the fabrics are worn, as if the people have been living and sleeping in their attire for months.

He feels like he's wearing virtual reality glasses, floating around, fully present in an illusionary environment, watching the action but not being part of it.

The air in this holiest of places should be infused with incense. Instead, it smells like rot: a mélange of putrid decaying flesh, incense, smoke, bodily fluids, and feces. For the first time in days, he wonders about the whereabouts of his green vomit dish. The smell is about to take everything in his stomach and thrust it out violently. He yanks the collar of his jacket over his nose and tries to breathe in through his mouth.

Thank God for my jacket. But why I am wearing it? I took it off and placed it on the pew.

As he ponders this, he also wonders why he is questioning anything that is happening in this strange and beautiful place that smells like a cadaver baking under the blazing sun.

Benjamin thinks the people gathered here must be accustomed to the smell because they aren't shielding their noses. Like mourners at a funeral in various stages of prayer and grief, they are standing solemnly, protecting their place in line to get to his golden book.

The woman first in line is holding her child in front of the altar, pushing her and her child's hands on the golden book. Walking over to the woman, he looks at the altar.

The Immortal is hanging over the book, quite unrecognizable. Almost naked, she is stripped down to a thin gold panel. She's not protected by a frame. Her features are much clearer, with gentle angles.

The most stunning change is the background. He can make out the object in the background. It's a tiny white chapel.

He walks closer to the book. When he touches the woman holding the child, she doesn't flinch. He taps her arm, and she still doesn't move. He raises her hands and places them on her child's shoulder.

What type of crazy illusion is this?

He turns the plates. The book looks the same as his golden book but has the plates numbered VI and VII. They are blank. Pushing his hand inside his pants' pocket, he feels his phone. He carefully photographs the altar, *The Immortal*, and each page of the book.

Deep in prayer, the young woman doesn't react when the flash hits the top of her auburn hair. What is the strange world he's entered? It's like he's a digital intruder inside a hologram of the Renaissance, documenting it with the latest technology.

He turns his head. The crowd of people behind him is recoiling from

The Immortal's Secret

something. Are they finally reacting to his presence? Their actions unnerve him. They are grabbing clothing and handkerchiefs and shielding their mouths and noses.

When he turns around, a woman is standing beside him, dressed in an elaborate gown of layers of rose satin stained with blood and pus. Her skin is so white, she looks like she's been embalmed. She is clutching something and crying like a wounded animal. The object looks like a doll. Benjamin walks over to her and examines what she is holding. The object is—or was—human. The face is bloated, bruised, and punctured with bloody marks.

A young priest runs towards her and freezes when he sees the infected child. Out of the crowd appears an apocalyptic ghoul in black with a long white beak. The crowd cowers to the side to let the creature through but stays in line. The figure walks towards the woman and waves a stick, motioning to the crowd in front of the altar to stay put. Benjamin looks at their frightened eyes and knows they won't be coming near the woman.

"We are doing our best to keep this shrine of God free from the wretched disease, but the sick keep appearing," the masked figure says. "They are desperate like you."

Benjamin thinks how young this plague doctor sounds, how the voice appears almost feminine. Those in line all stare at the figure, their eyes framed by their kerchiefs, their rosaries weaving through their fingers.

As he walks over to the young mother, he sees her head tilt towards the mosaic on the dome. She is chanting something while staring at two angels cradling two babies, swaddled in blankets, bowing towards a merciful Christ.

Benjamin stares at the mother's face, and although he's not an expert, he notices she has none of the telltale signs of the plague. She's doll-like, a baby herself. She's holding a baby rattle that's shaped like an angel. The bird creature appears behind Benjamin and he can smell the lavender and dried roses in the beak—the herbs meant to protect against airborne substances. The creature walks over and extends its delicate, tiny hands, motioning to the woman to hand over the baby.

She looks up at the plague doctor with glassy brown eyes and screams, "No! she's alive!"

The baby is in a pink satin blanket and the young mother is pressing her to her chest. The doctor moves towards the mother with purpose, and Benjamin follows. When he reaches the mother, Benjamin gently slides the satin blanket aside to get a better look at the baby. She is breathing ever so softly through her tiny mouth. She is the size of a newborn, but he's thinking she's probably older. The arm that is exposed is bloated and covered in huge, angry scabs.

A huge, handsome man with piercing blue eyes appears from behind one of the marble pillars and moves towards Benjamin.

"Andrea, don't go near," the priest appeals from the safety of the crowd. The plague doctor moves back to the safety of the marble column and watches the crowd.

"No...I need to help," the large man says without looking over at the priest. He stares at the young mother and holds out his hands, appealing to her to surrender the baby.

"Please...I will carry her for you."

He's a human replica of the self-portrait of Andrea Sartore that was in the box Josiah gave Benjamin. Broad shoulders, deep auburn hair with the funny cowlick, blue eyes, full lips, and a cleft chin.

The mother looks down at her baby and is silent. Suddenly she obliges, slowly placing the tiny human in his arms. The baby's face is drawn, like it is a balloon that is slowly deflating. Andrea touches the mother's hand with the tips of his fingers and guides her over to the altar, towards the golden book, cradling the baby like she's the most precious piece of china.

The woman who was at the altar praying quickly flees to join the crowd, instantly collapsing into the waiting arms of a man. Gently, Andrea motions the mother towards the wooden pew in front of the golden book.

"Please, kneel," he says, as he keeps a strong and caring left hand on the baby while pulling down the kneeler gently with his right hand. It's a selfless move defined by dignity and human kindness.

Benjamin stands right in front of the three of them, listening to Andrea whisper softly to the woman. The baby smells like a basement that is steeped in sewer gas.

"What is your name?"

"Giulia," she says so quietly that Benjamin thought she said "jewelry."

"What is your baby's name?"

"Rosa."

"A beautiful rose," says Andrea.

Giulia smiles and exposes perfectly white teeth, which Benjamin finds so odd when everyone else appears to be prematurely aged.

"Please place both of your hands on the book and recite, 'I appeal to the power of this golden book to….' Then you reveal your wish."

She stares at him with hazel eyes floating in tears.

"Do you understand me?" he asks.

She nods and then kneels and supports her body against the top of the pew. She twists her head towards him and holds out her hands, asking for Rosa.

Andrea gently places the baby back in her arms, and Giulia hugs the child tightly, placing Rosa's infected face up against hers.

Benjamin moves over and sits on the pew with them. He touches Rosa's tiny hand. It's clammy and cool but not ghoulish like a cadaver. The baby reminds him of Grace after she was attacked by the Ewoks and left twisted and battered. She embodies that level of pure innocence, vulnerability, and deformity.

Benjamin spies a huge man behind one of the columns. The man is holding something over his mouth, like a torn blanket, and he is wearing a doublet that appears to be made of armour. He sees Benjamin and glowers back like he wants to slice Benjamin's eyes in two. He's a massive man with a neck that's almost the width of his shoulders; he looks like he could pick Benjamin up and twirl him over his head like a baton.

Feeling uneasy, Benjamin moves out of his line of sight to hide behind another column. When the beast doesn't follow him, Benjamin realizes Andrea is the object of the man's ire.

Disabling the flash, he takes a photo of the man. When he looks at the photo, he can clearly see that the giant is wearing a massive sword and his hands looks like they could flatten small animals with one push.

Andrea gently puts the woman's hand on the book. As he helps her cradle the baby in her lap, he drops the baby's little hand in her mother's other hand.

"Please recite the words for both of you, push your hands into the gold, and recite your favourite Psalm."

She follows his instructions quietly but forcefully, her voice portraying conviction and hope.

They remain at the altar for almost a half an hour praying and reciting Psalm 20 over and over, sometimes powerfully and sometimes gently, trying to force the words through streams of tears.

The LORD hear thee in the day of trouble; the name of the God of Jacob defend thee;

Send thee help from the sanctuary, and strengthen thee out of Zion;

Remember all thy offerings, and accept thy burnt sacrifice; Selah.

Grant thee according to thine own heart, and fulfill all thy counsel.

We will rejoice in thy salvation, and in the name of our God we will set up our banners: the LORD fulfill all thy petitions.

Now know I that the LORD saveth his anointed; he will hear him from his holy heaven with the saving strength of his right hand.

Some trust in chariots, and some in horses: but we will remember the name of the LORD our God.

They are brought down and fallen: but we are risen, and stand upright.

Save, LORD: let the king hear us when we call.

    Benjamin knows the Psalm well. The words were like a warm blanket that enveloped Josiah when his Sera was dying. Josiah asked Benjamin to memorize it, to give him strength and light during his dark moments. He promised he would always be with Benjamin.

    As Giulia recites it like a broken record, Benjamin can see Josiah's face in front of him. The image feels so real. Benjamin focuses on the warmth and the strength of this elderly man, who he loves so much.

    A gurgling sound jolts Benjamin from his meditation.

    It's the baby, he thinks.

    The babbling shocks him back to this reality.

    Giulia is crying and laughing and holding Rosa up to her face. Benjamin rushes over and looks down at Rosa's tiny face. Her eyes are open halfway like little chocolate diamonds and she's looking up at Giulia. She is babbling like she just arrived back in the world and has discovered her stomach. Giulia covers Rosa with the wrap from her beautiful dress, looks down, and fumbles her hands to find her breast to feed her daughter. She stares at Rosa and tries to encourage her, yet nothing seems to happen.

    Then Giulia starts howling and her tears fall on Rosa.

    "She's nursing," she says to Andrea.

The Immortal's Secret

Andrea walks over and caresses the baby's head. He guides Giulia to a pew away from the altar. The mother strokes her baby and rocks her back and forth, chanting "Thank you Lord," over and over.

Benjamin follows them. Moving the wrap, he stares down at the baby, who's deformed with a patchwork of lesions. There is a bit of colour in her tiny cheeks. She is conscious, looking up at her mother, and is nursing. He touches her tiny arm. It's warm.

Has he just witnessed a miracle? He takes in the scene, from the mother and baby to the gentle giant Andrea, to the gasping-for-air crowd.

Has the golden book brought some hope into this dark scene of desperation? Did this actually just happen, or did I imagine it?

He kisses his finger and places it on the baby's forehead.

The plague doctor and the priest have joined Andrea. They stand shoulder to shoulder, each rubbing Andrea's back. Benjamin watches as Andrea grazes his hand over the plague doctor's hand. Benjamin is fixated on it. It's so tiny for a male.

Andrea whispers in the doctor's ear, "Take her home to nurse her baby, cara. I think she is going to live." Benjamin is stunned that Andrea used the feminine Italian word for dear.

He can't stop staring, looking for other clues, as the doctor takes Giulia's hand and whispers, "Come, we want to take you to a safe place to care for your baby."

Giulia stands up with Rosa. The plague doctor guides both to the side of the chapel. The baby's rattle drops, and Benjamin bends down, picks it up, and follows slowly behind them. They turn a corner. When he rounds the corner, they are gone. Like ghosts. He darts his head around to try and find them, but they are nowhere. Benjamin pushes the rattle into his jacket pocket.

Andrea is headed in the opposite direction out of the chapel, towards the Pala d'Oro—the main altar of the basilica—and the front door. As Benjamin runs over to follow him, he thinks about the brute and wonders where he went.

When Andrea opens the doors of the basilica, the sunshine illuminates and frames St. Mark's Square in front of the church like a painting. Running out into the square, Benjamin is excited, expecting to see a familiar sight. He gasps at what appears before his eyes. The majestic building is surrounded by human decay and a fog of smoke created by individual fires burning on every corner.

The fires are everywhere, and people are huddled in front of them. Cadavers are balanced up by the side of the basilica like dominoes. A troll of a man, whose features look like they were molded out of Turkish delight, arrives out of the smoke, pushing a rickety cart piled with cadavers. He is clearly what the Venetians called the pizzigamorti, or the dreaded body collector. Balancing a pipe in his teeth, he grabs some of the bodies with a giant hook and whips them onto the cart as if he's catching a huge fish. A trio of plague doctors rush out of the smoke, like beasts ready to devour the human prey with their giant beaks. One says softly in Latin, "Be careful. Treat them with respect." They help the troll gently hoist the bodies, placing them as securely as they can on the wobbly contraption.

Andrea appears at the cart and places his hand on one of the bodies. It's a small girl, about five, who's twisted in her mother's arms. Benjamin thinks about how they died so tightly wrapped to each other, wanting to be together even in the afterlife. Andrea takes the hand of the mother and the daughter, closes his eyes, and recites, "Dear Lord, we place these two souls in your hands. Protect us from this beast of a disease that wants to destroy our beautiful city and people." The pizzigamorti trundles off, punctuating the quiet with a series of disgusting burps.

While Andrea's eyes are still closed in prayer, a figure appears out of the smoke and moves towards him. She is wearing a long silk black dress and stunning pearls underneath a huge cape that is flapping in the wind. Her face is obscured by a sheer black veil with a silk scarf over her mouth and nose. The veil is secured by a tiny ruby broach. She resembles an elegant woman in mourning. Her eyes are exposed and framed by dark, defined eyebrows. She stops a few feet from Andrea and waits until he opens his eyes.

"Mother." He blinks at her for a few moments and then runs towards her. Raising the palm of her hand up to her face, she beckons him to stop.

Just as he's about to speak again, she says, "You need to come home."

He digs his fingers into his brow like he's heard this refrain one too many times.

"I cannot."

"Look at yourself, Andrea. You are putting yourself at risk, lingering in the heart of this horrible affliction. You will die. You are not going to marry Annacletica. I will not allow it. Who is she? Someone who appeared out of nowhere."

"Mother, I am in love. We are helping others. We are giving the citizens great hope. This is a crisis. You should go back home and stay out of the streets. You will get ill."

"I am going to the Doge. I am going to have her arrested. This is not Catholic. It goes against everything the Sartore family stands for. You are descended from one of the greatest families in Venice. She is a witch. Her golden book is not holy. I am praying for your soul. You are not protecting yourself from this terror from God. You should be with your family."

Pointing to his cheek, he says, "Look at me. I have prayed on the book to make me well. I feel so healthy. You should pray on the book, too."

She is twisting her fingers around a rosary, pushing them into the beads so deeply Benjamin thinks she may crush them.

Andrea looks at her and says, firmly but softly, "If you have her arrested, if you put an end to all of this, you will never see me again. I love you mother, but do not test me." He walks over to her slowly and places his arm around her elegant shoulders like he is a giant caressing a tiny doll. "Let me escort you to your boat to go back home."

She flicks his hand from her shoulder like it's a bug. With a booming voice that doesn't match her body, she says, "Who are you? Who have you become? You…would choose her over me?"

Towering over her like she's his child, he looks down into her eyes. "I love you…but I would, and I will. Let me help you back to your boat."

"No, there are consequences, and you need to make your choice," she shouts while pulling down on her dress.

"My choice is made," he says. "I love you, but my choice is made." Andrea turns his back on her and walks towards the door of the basilica.

"You are testing me, Andrea, and you will be sorry." She throws the rosary onto the ground.

He shouts without turning around, "Do what you must, Vittoria."

The woman watches Andrea as he disappears back inside the basilica. She lets out a monstrous shriek and falls to her knees. Her eyes disappear into a river of tears. Her shoulders thrust up and down like her body is going into a seizure.

Benjamin wants to reach out to her, but a strange energy surrounds her. If he touches her, he's certain he'd turn to ice.

Finally, she rises, stands erect, and takes a few minutes to compose herself, smoothing out her dress. She bends down to pick up her rosary, strings it through her fingers, and kisses it. Floating like a black swan, she walks past the façade of the basilica, pausing for a moment by one of the pillars to take in the horror around her. She pushes a body out of her way with her dainty, pointed, black boots.

Minutes later she walks past the Doge's Palace and finally stops at the foot of St. Mark's Basin, where several boats are moored.

The brute from the basilica walks towards her tentatively with a new companion in tow who is of equal massive stature. They are like twins with features that look like they were punched out of clay by the knuckles of a drunk man.

The woman dabs her eyes gently and says, "Come, please. Join me on my vessel."

They follow her like children, pushing back the netting over the entrance and walking down the stairs into a beautiful boat with ornate carvings of lions, eagles, and bears on the walls. Benjamin follows them down and sits beside the woman on a banquette upholstered in soft brown leather with deep purple velvet cushions embroidered with the same stylized VS in the middle. They don't notice him. The woman removes her cape to reveal a long velvet jacket sculpted to her body, trimmed around the edges with rubies, sapphires, and emeralds.

Benjamin stares at the woman weighed down by expensive jewels, sitting so tall, pushing her neck out like a queen. She's drinking wine from a crystal wine glass and tracing her finger over the rim. She doesn't make eye contact with the two brutes and never refers to them by name. It is clear to Benjamin that she feels they are beneath her.

She keeps her eyes on her glass and says, "I want you to steal the golden book and portrait. I am going to create a frame to hide the book inside. I will help you gain access to the basilica and the chapel after hours. I need you to lock them in a secret room, the one I showed you behind the baptistery, the chapel called The Secret Sartore Chapel. My son discovered the chapel and has been hiding there with that woman, the witch.

"You open the door to the chapel by pushing the head of *The Blessed Virgin Mary*. Bring the golden book and the portrait of her, the golden one over the altar. I will be waiting at The Sartore Palace on the Isola di Speranza.

"That woman has some unholy connection to the book and portrait. They are both a part of her. Make sure you are not seen, or I will deny everything. I will make it very lucrative for you if you succeed."

The Immortal's Secret

They look at her, then at each other, and nod their heads like gruesome bobble dolls.

"Go now. Make sure you are not seen. Do you understand?" They again nod their grotesque faces like puppets, plod up the stairs, and jump from the vessel onto the ground. Benjamin silently looks at her, desperately wanting to give her a good smack over her veiled face.

She raises her thick veil, letting it drape over her head, and dabs the side of her eyes with a white lace handkerchief. It's embroidered with VS.

She is so beautiful: a stunning brunette blessed with exquisite features and luminous skin. He leans closer for a better look. Could she be the women he saw in the chapel in Istanbul? The one who looked like Paeon? The resemblance is uncanny.

As the deckhands start preparing the boat to leave the dock, Benjamin get off the boat and watches the two brutes in the distance stomping along the cobblestones. They are medieval sub-humans, part Neanderthal, part vicious beast. He cannot believe this woman is going to have them trap her gentle son inside a room.

He's so disgusted and he wants to scream out to anyone listening. The one hope for the people of this republic is going to be destroyed by this she-devil in her boat.

The people of the republic are hiding in their homes. Fires are burning everywhere to ward off the disease, carts of dead bodies are being shipped off to who-knows-where. The dead lie in the street decomposing. The smell enters Benjamin's nose and he thinks it's going to singe his insides.

All this is happening around her, and yet she is going to take away all remaining hope and kill her son.

"She has some unholy connection to the book and portrait. They are both a part of her."

Her words ring in his head.

He starts racing back to the basilica to warn Andrea, to save him. Halfway there, he is suddenly out of breath and stops.

What is he doing? This must be a dream, or a hallucination.

Who's he warning? An apparition?

He starts again, walking towards the basilica. When he arrives, the plague doctor is in front of the door blocking his way. Benjamin tries to dodge him since he knows the doctor can't see him. Still, the doctor moves to again block him.

Wait, can *he see me?*

Benjamin decides to try to make contact, to go along with this fascinating hallucination.

"Scusi," he says.

The plague doctor shocks Benjamin by moving to the side but keeps staring at him as if wanting to say something. The doctor's eyes are a deep shade of brown. They are so penetrating, the stare unnerves Benjamin.

As Benjamin turns away and enters the building, the plague doctor follows. Benjamin stops at the altar and turns to face the doctor again. The plague doctor stops beside him, still staring at him.

The doctor's beak rises slowly and Benjamin almost falls over. The doctor is a woman, a stunning woman, glowing with her bright eyes and pristine skin. No signs of any disease or suffering. She resembles *The Immortal*. Not knowing what to do, he doesn't say a word. The two of them just stand still looking at one another.

"Benjamin, Benjamin...."

He keeps hearing his name, but the voice sounds so far away, like he's underwater.

Out of the corner of his eye, he sees someone move in beside him. Everything is blurry and he can't make out if the figure is a man or woman. The voice is so soft.

The person's image is glowing in the sunlight that is streaming through the windows, creating a brilliant halo like an icon floated down from the ceiling. Benjamin is not sure if this person is even human or if he is still hallucinating and this person is a plague sufferer.

"Are you real? Are you one of the pilgrims who've come to pray on the golden book?"

The image moves towards him and places several fingers on his wrist. The fingers squeeze lightly.

"Benjamin, are you okay?"

He looks down at the hand as his eyes begin to focus. The hand is tiny and has a French manicure. He is about to respond when something drops out of his pocket, distracting him. It's something shiny and it falls right beside his shoe on the tessellated tile.

"Hello. Cle sent me to help you," she says. "She and I are friends. I know your grandfather, too."

To check whether he's still hallucinating, he picks the rattle off the floor, holds it in front of the woman, and says, "What is this?"

She leans in to have a close look, bringing with her a whiff of a beautiful garden.

"It looks like a rattle, a baby rattle. It's a little angel."

He collapses onto the marble slab in front of the altar and puts his head in his hands.

Without looking up he says, "It felt so real. Something out of this world. Something so beautiful. Something so evil. Was this a strange hallucination?"

She looks at him and asks softly, "Hallucination?" Benjamin realizes he is talking out loud.

"Do you feel alright? Do you want to go back to your hotel?"

He looks up and finally gets a good look. She is a tiny woman dressed in a light pink sweater with black pants. Her hair is strawberry blonde, extending beyond her shoulders and pulled to one side in an alluring ponytail. Her lips are moist with lip gloss and her skin is light but not exactly porcelain—more like a light pink. The colour of a strawberry milkshake with a dab of cream on top. She has three deep scars on her face: one that starts at the top of her forehead and drops down to the bottom of her chin, one under her mouth, and one that loops around the bottom of her chin. Others might call the scars a deformity, but Benjamin feels she looks a wounded angel. He wishes she were one. He could really use an infusion of goodness.

"Yes, I have to get out of here." He extends his hand. "I'm Benjamin."

"Nice to meet you. I'm Grace."

Chapter 14

The Arrival of Grace

February 28, 2017
Café on Riva degli Schiavoni, Venice, Italy

Benjamin and Grace walk along the Riva degli Schiavoni. The late February sunshine is soothing but chilly and he pushes the collar of his jacket over his ears. They arrive at a café and are guided to a table inside at a front window with a spectacular view of St. Mark's Basin.

He sits still with his head in his hands, trying to steady his breathing. The day's events have been surreal and it's taking him a while to come back to earth.

Grace is quiet and taps him gently on the shoulder when the server arrives. Benjamin orders some lasagna and Grace orders a small Caprese salad. He studies her face. It's fascinating and he's not sure why. Without the scars, she wouldn't be beautiful in the traditional sense, but her features are intriguing. Deep blue eyes, lips the colour of ripe plums, and a long, graceful neck. She radiates goodness. Being with her is calming him, like a meditation session. The cadence of her voice is so gentle, so soothing, so eerily familiar, like Grace Parker's was.

"What happened? When I walked into the chapel, you were at the altar and talking in your sleep," says Grace.

"I was? I thought I was outside of the basilica, standing at the door. I'm confused. Something weird happened to me," says Benjamin. "I'm honestly not sure what happened. I was praying and perhaps I fell asleep. I haven't been sleeping well. How do you know my grandfather?"

"He's a dear friend. It's a long story."

"I love long stories."

She places her hands on the table.

"I reached out to him for a job. I wanted to work for someone like him, someone with integrity. He asked me to look after Cle. She and I have become great friends. She lived at the monastery, the one in the Sinai. Josiah had me conduct research on the golden book and Andrea Sartore. It was like entering a different world."

"Can you please share something that confirms that you worked with Josiah and that you know him well?" He digs into the lasagna and the nourishment makes him feel a lot better.

She rummages in her large tote. It is made of Italian leather but has no designer label. Someone who doesn't want to define herself by a fashion logo. Benjamin likes that.

Out comes a beautiful golden pouch with a big red heart on the front. She unzips it, peers down, and pulls out a photo.

She speaks without looking at him, almost like she's talking to herself.

"This is very special to me. It's a photo of Josiah, Cle, and me at the monastery, taken about five years ago. Josiah was so vibrant, passionate, and full of life. We've always been like family. This was taken just before I started noticing things, little slips of his—forgetting names, going places and getting lost, leaving his keys in the fridge." She stares at the picture and then hands it to him holding the edges.

He says softly, "I noticed that too. It was around 2012. I remember we celebrated my birthday in February but it's in September."

"It's very sad he made that mistake about your birthday. That box, the one you found on the pew?"

"Yes?"

"I placed it there. Josiah wanted you to know the truth about your family and the portrait. He asked me to help organize documents to tell the story of *The Immortal*. We were beginning to prepare them in his studiolo when the police arrived at his home."

"You were there when I was at his house in a coma?"

"Yes. I helped look after you. But you know what happened after that. They arrested him and I heard he went to find the truth. I went back to the monastery with Cle. I was trying to get the documents in order in the studiolo before I left Toronto. Did you see them?"

"Yes."

The Immortal's Secret

"I wanted you to have the box. I brought it here. I wanted you to have privacy and some time to review everything. That's why I came a little bit late today. What did you think of what you saw in the box?"

"Thank you for doing that. I really like the portraits. I never seen any other art by Sartore. The scrolls were interesting, very interesting. I am fascinated by Annacletica."

He watches her eat the salad, holding the fork and knife so elegantly and cutting everything into small pieces before she places them in her mouth. She has a tremor in both of her hands.

Grace says, "The Immortal was trying to help the poor desperate people of this republic. She could no longer hide her secret. The golden book was magical. It granted wishes. She placed it at the altar where you were. This created a stir in the city, near panic. The desperate came from all over, swarming the basilica. Many were cured. It was astounding how many of the desperate Annacletica and Andrea saved."

"Where did you find this information?"

"It's quite sketchy but is compiled from documents Josiah found in the basilica and at The Sartore Palace on the Isola di Speranza. I can take you there tomorrow."

"Your name is Grace?" says Benjamin.

"Yes."

"It is a beautiful name. I knew someone named Grace. She's…"

Benjamin was about to say that his Grace is dead but he's not in the right frame of mind to discuss anything painful.

There is a long pause in the conversation.

Benjamin eats his lasagna and looks out at the crowd on the promenade, so careful and happy. He wishes he was one of them, not a desperate man on a mission that will lead God-knows-where.

She finally breaks the silence.

"You asked me to prove to you that I knew, or I mean know, Josiah."

Jerking his head towards her Benjamin says, "Oh, yes."

"Here's something else."

He notices her hands are trembling heavily as she slides some white fabric towards him. He picks it up.

It's a lace handkerchief with the initials GP on it. He recognizes it. It's the handkerchief Grace Parker was clutching when she was attacked. He could never forget it.

"Where did you get this?"

She lifts her hair to reveal a deep scar hugging her ear. Then she slowly raises her right forearm to reveal a series of angry scars snaking from her wrist to elbow.

"There are also scars on my leg. I won't show you. You can take my word for it."

Sweat is beading up on his brow and he starts nervously wringing his hands. Dabbing his forehead with his napkin, he stands up, looks deep into her eyes, grazes his finger over her face, then walks towards the door.

He walks out of the restaurant, stops at the end of St. Mark's Basin, places his hand over his head, and digs his fingers into his scalp. He's standing on the lip of water like he wants to jump. While examining the lace handkerchief he is still holding, he sees three little brown stains. They are familiar—the stains he tried to remove with soap in the washroom at The Hospital for Sick Children.

Grace joins him outside. He looks up at her, examining her face.

Could she be the same age as me?

"If you are Grace Parker, why have your never contacted me?"

Grace takes his hand, placing her hand on his. He can feel her trembling.

"This is really difficult, and I struggled over whether to tell you. I thought you would feel more comfortable knowing I was here to help. You've known me since childhood, and we clearly have a special bond."

Rubbing his head with his other hand, he stares at the water.

"I was traumatized by that incident. I wanted to kill myself. Everyone thought I was the one who attacked you...you or her."

"Can we go back inside?" She holds out her other hand for him to take it. He clasps her hand and stares at it. It's so tiny and some of the fingers are crooked.

Once back inside, she hands him her glass of wine.

"Please take some?" Without taking his eyes off her, he takes a small sip and hands it back.

"Josiah saved me. This must seem odd. I don't want it to. I always wanted to contact you. I had no idea you were implicated in the attack. I don't even know how that could have happened. I could have cleared your name, and I can't believe it even needed to be cleared. No one ever asked me. My mother didn't know either. She said we were not wanted at the school and took me to BC to live with distant relatives, out in the middle of nowhere, completely off the grid. I was twenty-five when she died and

The Immortal's Secret

I finally felt free to contact Josiah to thank him. He was thrilled to see me and wanted you to meet me but then his decline began."

Benjamin is amazed at how calm she is when talking about such traumatic memories. So grounded and focused as she sips at her wine occasionally.

"I'm so sorry. I wish I could have helped by sharing what happened to me. I've been Googling you and you seemed to have been doing so well until your cancer. I never reached out because I never imagined you'd want to hear from someone like me. But then Cle asked me to come look after you and I wondered if I should bring up the past. I wasn't sure you would remember me because I felt so invisible at that school."

She drinks some more wine, bows her head, and flips her hair to reveal a huge bald spot with a deep scar.

"Can you see the scar?"

Benjamin moves in to have a closer look.

"It is so deep," she continues. "I was very badly injured. I survived. I don't know how. It was a miracle."

She straightens up, flips her hair back, and looks at Benjamin.

"Or Josiah saved me."

She takes his hand.

"Is that proof enough? You know my head hit the bar of the swing. It haunts me to this day. The nightmares have not gone away."

"It haunts me too."

Benjamin squeezes her hand gently. Neither say anything. They just hold hands. Benjamin has never felt so comforted. He closes his eyes.

"I want to help you, go to the places Josiah went before returning to the desert and then to parts unknown. We should start today. Josiah opened up a Pandora's box when your grandmother gave him *The Immortal*. We don't know what others wished for when they prayed on the book. There could be many out there. Some who may not have died."

"You think some people could be immortal?"

"Anything is possible. How can you explain how I was cured? You can't constrain yourself by the limits of this world. You may experience things you can't explain."

Benjamin smiles.

"I'm not sure any acid trips I've had can compare to finding this book. Surreal things have been happening today."

"You seemed so shaken in the chapel. I hope you're okay. Remember, you have the best weapon against evil forces. Now that you have the golden book, it'll protect you. Hold it close to your heart when you're in danger and you can't be harmed. Cle stressed you must always keep it with you or make sure it's hidden. If you can't have it with you…"

She bends down, picks up her purse, puts it on her knee, pulls out a velvet pouch, and places it on the table. She keeps her hands on top of it.

"Cle said you wanted a copy of the golden book that Josiah created. To act as a decoy."

She slides the pouch towards him.

"This one has the seven plates so you can tell the two apart."

Benjamin picks it up, unties the velvet strings, and looks inside the bag. He pulls up his backpack and slips the velvet pouch inside.

"Thank you."

"Use it when you're in danger."

She stares at him, waiting for a reaction that doesn't come.

"It's so nice to see you," she says.

"You've emerged from my nightmare a healthy woman." He moves in to gently touch a deep scar on her face that runs on the left-hand side of her mouth up to her temple. Grace's lips tremble. On anyone else the scar would look horrific. On Grace's porcelain skin it looks like it was blended by an artist.

"I think I should get off to see if Cle has arrived." She takes out a Kleenex, wipes some perspiration from her brow, and then squeezes the Kleenex in her palm. "I am going to say something to you that I've wanted to say for twenty-eight years. Those boys were so evil. I really thought you were my angel, the kindest human I have ever known. Thank you."

Benjamin gazes out the window and his hands start shaking.

Am I equipped to deal with all of this?

She stands up and while she's pushing in her chair, getting ready to walk away, he grazes his fingers over her wrist.

"I am so glad I helped you. It was one of my most heroic moments and I don't have many. I am hoping I can be a hero to Josiah."

His phone beeps on the table beside him. Grace smiles at him and walks away, waving with her fingers. He watches her disappear into the mass of tourists and then looks down at his phone. It's another text.

<See you've arrived. Excited 2 meet up.>

Who is this person? Once thing is certain: it's not Grace.

Chapter 15

The Return of Jenna or Paeon

March 1, 2017
Hotel Danieli, Venice, Italy

Benjamin returns to the Hotel Danieli and twists the "Do not disturb" sign on his suite. He collapses on his king-size bed and stares at the ceiling, listening to his pounding heart rate.

What just happened today?

He rolls over and digs his face into the pillow. His mind is like a movie on fast forward, flipping from one scene to another, whooshing in on the action and whooshing back out.

There is something supernatural about this golden book. He cannot ignore how healthy he is feeling. The first time he dropped acid, he felt like he was floating inside the lava lamp in his living room, and he feels like that now.

There are questions, so many questions. Questions sandwiched between questions. What caused that hallucination this afternoon? He was a curator entering a painting. Did Josiah really have dementia? Or did the experience with Benjamin's grandmother just make him crazy? Is Grace telling the truth? It's impossible to comprehend how anyone could survive such an evil attack. Did Josiah really know about Grace and not tell him?

He can't stop the blobs from floating around when he closes his eyes. One blob is the grotesque baby's face. It freeze-frames and turns into another blob of the young mother nursing, placing such a horrid creature to her breast.

Andrea with his kindness and the gentle touch of his giant hand floats in Benjamin's eyes.

Then, he's in the playground racing to safety with blood dripping on the ground, staring at Grace's face, a slashed Halloween mask, unrecognizable as human.

During the illusion in the chapel with the plague sufferers, Benjamin witnessed a critical moment in Andrea's life. To see Andrea and watch him up close was so surreal. Watch him placing his own life in danger to help others. What a horrific and beautiful sight!

Vittoria Sartore's lips on the wine glass staring out into the distance. Bearing witness to her devious planning was especially haunting. She looked so much like the woman in purple, or did he imagine this?

He wanders into the bathroom, pushes his palms onto the counter, and stares at himself in the mirror. His face is flushed.

What he saw was real. Real to him. His golden book transported him there. Today's events are part of the road he must travel get to Josiah. He has crossed the golden book Rubicon whether he wants to or not.

Throwing some water on his face, he drenches the front of his shirt, then rips his clothes off and whips them onto the counter. Taking some deep breaths, he looks around to see what's causing the horrendous smell assaulting his nose. He places his shirt up to his nose. It reeks. The smell draws him back to the chapel again, the one that smelled like death, like rotting cadavers. He takes off the rest of his clothes and stuffs them into the golden bathroom garbage can.

Did Grace smell that?

The thought that she may feel he has horrendous body odour embarrasses him. Or perhaps he's the only one who can smell it.

He enters the shower and stands under the hottest water he can tolerate. After scrubbing himself clean, he wraps himself in the hotel terry cloth bathrobe and ponders polishing off as much Scotch as he can from the mini-bar. He quickly dismisses the thought. Instead, he throws some pills to the back of his throat, then spits them out into this hand.

No, enough medicating yourself.

He walks back into the bedroom and collapses on the middle of the bed. He stretches his hand out, pulls the golden book towards him, and clutches it to his chest. As per Grace's instructions, he slides himself off the bed to secure it in the safe. He then glides the fake copy out of his backpack, places it where the real one was, falls over onto his pillow, and clutches it. Before he drifts off, he thinks about the rattle on the floor of the chapel back at St. Mark's. In the confusion, he forgot about it.

When he closes his eyes, the parade of images continues accompanied by a soundtrack of constant knocking. He's annoyed someone doesn't answer the door. He turns over and the knocking continues. He can hear someone calling his name.

Not expecting to see anyone because he's sure it's another episode, he staggers to the door. When he looks out of the little keyhole, he cannot believe what he sees.

As he slowly opens the door, his knees almost collapse. It's Jenna or someone who looks like her. The woman is wearing a long red satin outfit. He's not sure if it's a dress or lingerie. She falls into his arms and hugs him tightly as she shoves her tongue into his mouth.

Is this happening? Is this real or another hallucination?

Before he has time to question whether he can even perform the act, they are on his bed. His robe is off and somehow, she has managed to slide out of the red thing. She's on top on him, thrusting forcefully. He stares up at her feeling woozy. She's in her own world, eyes closed, pushing and twirling and twisting like a gymnast on top of him. His body doesn't let him down, but it's not the breathless reunion he had fantasized about. No blood pounding to his heart, no soaring hormones, no giddy reactions. It's like a self-serve fuck, as satisfying as brushing his teeth.

Is she even real?

She continues straddling him and looks down and says, "I missed you, Benjamin."

She's real, he thinks. *She feels real.*

She collapses onto the bed and snuggles up to him. As she places her hand on his cheek, he focuses on how her fingers move gently back and forth. Her caress is so soft and hypnotic. Then he feels a slight prick on his leg but thinks nothing of it.

"I am so sorry I had to leave like that. I didn't want to. You were, you are, everything to me. I had to leave. I had no choice." She sits up and looks out the window at his view of the Grand Canal.

His eyes are heavy; he can hardly keep them open.

"I had to leave to protect you. I didn't want you involved in some things that are dangerous. Things I'm involved in. Things I can't disclose. I need to do this to protect you. The portrait, the one called *The Immortal*. It causes deep suffering to those who own it. It needs to be destroyed."

He notices her accent is no longer Canadian. It's hard to place but there are traces of Italian, particularly in the trilling of her Rs.

Then everything goes blank.

Now he's staring at his room bathed in bright sunlight wondering where he is, where she is. His watch says it's 11 a.m.

Was this experience with her real? The decoy golden book?

He looks on the table where he knows he placed it. It's gone. He stretches his arm over to the side of the bed, pulls himself up, and races to the closet.

He collapses. His legs feel so funny, like they are hollow inside. He pushes his body over the carpet towards the closet. It takes him a while, but after a few tries, he is able to punch in the code and open the special safe the hotel provided him for *The Immortal* and the real golden book. They're both there. He breathes a sigh of relief.

When he returns to the bed, he notices a note on the pillow where she was lying.

Dearest Benjamin,

I told you there are things that can't be explained. Things you don't need to know. I saw you yesterday. You were in the baptistery. I took your precious book so you cannot say no to a meeting with me. Please bring your portrait. Text me.

He crushes the paper in his hand and whips it up against the wall.

How could I love a creature like her so much? What happens to love? Where does it go? What is this strange feeling that takes over your life and then dies? I couldn't live without her, couldn't stop thinking of her, fantasizing about her. Love is blind and I was blinded. I was duped. I was tricked.

He picks up his phone on the bedside table and calls Grace.

"I need to go to The Sartore Palace. Can you accompany me and share what Josiah told you?"

Chapter 16

Isola di Speranza

March 2, 2017
The Sartore Palace, Venice, Italy

Grace is sitting beside the driver of the small power boat with Benjamin seated behind. They are headed for Isola di Speranza.

Benjamin places his hand on her shoulder and says, "I dreamt something last night and the decoy golden book is gone."

She turns around.

"Oh, dear."

"The dream was about a woman I know, or I thought I knew. She's been texting me. She arrived unannounced at my hotel room. The dream felt so real. When she left, the decoy book was gone."

"You had a dream and now the decoy book is gone. Is it really gone?"

He nods his head.

"To answer both of your questions—I have no idea anymore."

"Who was the woman?"

"Her name is Jenna. I trusted her. I had a relationship with her. Then she disappeared. Just said she had to leave and told me to have a nice life. I would have trusted this woman with my life. I loved her deeply and she broke my heart."

Where are these words coming from? They're spewing out of my mouth like each word is releasing some poison I'm trying to purge from my life.

Grace turns around and looks at him intensely.

"Are you still in love with her?"

"I thought I was…in love with her. Past tense."

"Josiah said she left you here in Venice, right? I thought it was just like one of those fleeting things. I am so sorry she hurt you."

"He told you about her?"

She nods.

"Do you remember when he shared that Jenna left?"

She shrugs.

"I don't. I can't remember when it was."

She holds out her hand and he squeezes it tightly, enjoying the warmth of the human connection. He stares at the spider-like scars on her hand and kisses them.

The sun is still blazing as the boat zips towards Isola di Speranza. The breeze is so warm on his arms.

She's wearing a camel-coloured shift dress and is wrapped in a long pink cashmere coat. It's quite the contrast to the demure slacks and sweater shirt she was wearing the day before. He is focused on how her shoulders are moving up and down in a deep rhythm like she's trying to steady her breathing.

The island comes into view. It's lush and green with several buildings in the Venetian Gothic style that Benjamin adores. Although the buildings are in various stages of decay, he can make out the odd pointed arches. The buildings surround a main focal point: a church spire.

The driver is Luigi, someone Grace insists they can trust. He will ensure they are not disturbed. They sail up to a small dock. Luigi says something inaudible to Grace in Italian, pointing his finger towards the long white spire.

"Are you sure you're OK?" she asks Benjamin.

"Yes, thanks for listening."

"We're in this together." She rubs his shoulder with the tips of her fingers. "It's a bit of a hike. This is as close as Luigi can get. We'll lean on each other if it gets to be too much. We have to walk through this path in the forest of cypress trees to make it to the main buildings."

They are greeted by a huge sign that says Private Property. They ignore it and continue towards a huge arched front door. The place where the stairs should be is a pile of small, crushed stones and Benjamin lifts Grace up to the landing. She opens the door. The hallway is a crumbling junkyard of leaning, graffiti-covered walls and caved-in ceilings. Half standing, half punched out, half crumbling.

The Immortal's Secret

She weaves them through piles of assorted junk—wood, white marble, stained glass, bathtubs, boxes, newspapers, plaster, chairs. It's an obstacle course that he can barely negotiate, particularly when they get to where stairs are supposed to be. The stairs are mostly missing in a few spots; only half a stair is attached to the wall. They stop to rest a few times, leaning on walls that are practically floating.

Benjamin secures the straps of his backpack with the golden book securely inside.

"It's a bit crazy, and this is the easiest part. It's The Sartore Palace, or what's left of it. It's quite astounding. Your grandmother discovered this treasure trove that now belongs to you. If I'm right, you now have the deed. This places creep me out and fascinates me in equal measure." She looks at him with huge eyes and he realizes she's shaking.

"Are you OK?" asks Benjamin, squeezing her shoulder.

"I don't really like this place. Our destination is not much farther. I still have a few residual long-term effects from the accident. This smell—this mélange of mustiness, dampness, mold, mildew, and decaying wood—it makes my head vibrate."

"What type of long-term effects?"

"Where do I start?" she says faking a laugh. "Seriously, it's just a few." She slides off her jacket and then holds out her hand with her palm up. It's so elegant. He places his hand in hers; he loves how it fits perfectly in his large hand.

"Please bend down. We have to crawl through this space. It's just a few feet. It's very well hidden."

His bony knees scream out as he follows her for the short distance.

When they can stand again, he leans up against a wall hoping it's solid and doesn't collapse. Grace turns on her flashlight to illuminate a bronze door with deep carvings. He can't make them out and moves in to have a closer look.

Grace watches him and says, "They are of Christ's birth and resurrection, similar to carvings in the baptistery in St Mark's. This place was the inspiration for The Secret Sartore Chapel." She moves past him to place a huge antique key in the door and pushes it open slowly.

She motions for him to walk inside.

"I'll lead the way. We need to go down some stairs."

The smell of incense, ivy, mold, and age is overpowering. He places his hand over his nose.

They enter a little chapel with crumbling pews and an altar constructed of wood and gold speckles.

"Let's have a seat." She motions to a pew that doesn't appear strong enough for use.

They sit together and she strokes his hand softly.

"We can go if you've changed your mind. Luigi is waiting. We can come back another time. It's quite the workout to get to the pièce de resistance."

Benjamin is silent, contemplating whether this crumbling palace could possibly hold any clues to Josiah. Without Grace by his side, he would find it challenging to navigate his way out of this obstacle course.

"No, I'm fine. I'm desperate to look under any rock to find out what happened to Josiah and my family…"

"This structure is built of stone. It was made to last. It's a chapel but it's also a tomb. It was closed for centuries. It's so well hidden. Those iron shutters over there are impenetrable from the outside. It's the only window. I think it was stained glass at one time."

Benjamin says, "Where did you procure the key?"

"Josiah."

"I'm discovering he was a man of many secrets. Did Andrea Sartore live here with Annacletica?"

"I don't think so. This is where Sartore lived with his mother, more like was imprisoned down here. She was engaged in constant prayer with him, trying to cure him of whatever she thought he was suffering from," she replies.

"A medieval version of Munchausen by proxy, perhaps."

"Exactly. Vittoria had issues. I think she would have been at home with the Ewoks."

They laugh and she rubs the top of Benjamin's hand.

"Oh, I brought you something."

She digs into her purse and produces something that Benjamin immediately recognizes. She opens it and says, "I brought you some Fruit Roll-ups. I remember you always ate them in the playground."

They both pull some apart, look at each other, and start laughing. Grace eats some and rubs her fingers with a Kleenex.

"To continue with the story, Andrea fell madly in love with Annacletica. He became obsessed. She had the golden book, your book. Legend has it that Annacletica cured him of his real, or imagined, affliction

The Immortal's Secret

by having him pray on the golden book. When the plague arrived in Venice in the late sixteenth century, they both were driven to help others."

Benjamin swings his backpack in front of him and pushes his hand down on the golden book.

"If you like, I'll show you what your grandmother found—Andrea's former bedroom."

She guides him down a long, stark, dimly-lit stone hallway and Benjamin says, "This is like a bunker or underground cave."

Grace looks at him.

"Yes, I know. This is the original building. The stone came from other ancient buildings in the area. It's an archeological site, really. It's where Andrea lived—all alone. Vittoria didn't want him to go out for fear he'd catch something. She had all the doctors come to him. Vittoria was an evil woman, but she inspired one of greatest artists of the Renaissance."

"The greatest unknown one."

"And you own all his works."

"They belong to Josiah," Benjamin says.

She stops in front of a bronze door.

"Maybe they belong to Josiah or perhaps you. What you're about to see is so well-preserved. It's astounding given the other parts of the buildings are like a cookie waiting to crumble," she says. "It's a fascinating history encased in stone. Thank goodness your grandmother found the key."

Grace places the same big key in the bronze door, decorated with a deep carving that spells out Sartore. The words are encircled by a wreath of laurel leaves.

When the door swings open, Benjamin sees that the room is pitch black. Grace clicks on her flashlight and moves to each corner of the room to illuminate flood lights, revealing a majestic space, as big as a two-car garage. There are marble floors, marble pillars, and porticos.

"These were all painted by Sartore," she says pointing to his signature: A. Sartore.

Grace leads Benjamin to a room off the side of the larger room and illuminates it with the flashlight. A massive dark wooden cabinet with many tiny drawers takes up half the wall. It's not unlike the one in Josiah's studiolo back in Toronto. It sits beside an exquisite bed, which is set apart with its own elaborate alcove, huge pilasters anchoring each side. The bed is covered by a purple silk bedspread and framed by a huge purple ornate headboard, with an oil paint mural in the centre depicting angels holding roses. The ceiling above the bed is a stark fresco of the desert.

Grace walks over to the bed, sits down, crosses her legs, and pushes her hair out of her eyes seductively.

She pulls some candles and incense out of her purse, places them on the table beside the bed, and lights them.

"This incense improves the air in here, particularly frankincense," says Grace just before she pushes her head into her hands and collapses onto the floor.

Benjamin bends down.

"Grace, Grace are you alright? What's wrong?" He grabs her hand and strokes it.

"It's the smell," she says weakly. "It's nauseating. I thought the incense would cover it up a little. I need to lie down."

Ever so gently he picks her up and places her back on the bed, pushing her head on what he thinks is a pillow. He hates the idea of her sleeping on a musty antique bed and bedspread, so he puts his jean jacket over the pillowcase. It would be great if he could carry her out of this obstacle course, but he doesn't want to risk injuring her. He nestles up beside her, rubs her back, and keeps telling her she'll be alright. Being close to her like this, with his body shielding her, is something he's always dreamt of. Her protector is a role he's always wanted to play.

He slides his hand inside his backpack, pulls out the golden book, and clutches it to his chest. He nods off, humming in Grace's ear and listening to her breathe.

Suddenly, he wakes up with one of those strange hypnic jerks that jolt a person when they're moving into deep sleep. Sitting up, he rubs his eyes and is amazed he's feeling quite refreshed.

He looks around and the first thing he notices is the smell has vanished. The room is bathed in bright light and candles. It's like the sun came out and infused everything with energy.

The room also looks completely different, like someone arrived with a huge duster to swipe the cobwebs and dirt. Grace is beside the alcove with her back towards him, rooting around in the wooden cabinets.

"Grace, what are you doing? Are you feeling better? What are you looking for?"

She stops rummaging and stares at something in one of the drawers. She does not respond.

He slides off the bed and begins to walk over to her to tap her shoulder to get her attention, but he can't get near her. She has energy around her that is pushing him away.

He has a clear view of her under a bright electric light.

Where did the light come from? Grace was using a flashlight. Did she not know where the lights were in this place?

Grace seems taller and doesn't appear as curvy from behind.

He watches her as she continues staring at a golden plate. It looks like it could be from his golden book and could snap into place nicely with the other plates like a puzzle. He's about to call out to her again when she places the plate in her large satchel, slides the zipper to close it snugly, and turns around.

It's not Grace.

It's a young woman, barely twenty.

He's conjuring her. She stands still like a statue staring ahead and he thinks she is listening, perhaps waiting for his next move. Then she says, "I better get going before I miss him." He could have waved his hand in front of her face and there would be no reaction.

She is tall, thin, and elegant, with beautiful skin: the colour of the almond milk he loves in his coffee. She's wearing a white knee-length dress with a wide skirt—like the glamorous ones in the 1950s movies—and black, high-heeled patent leather pumps. A white cardigan is draped over her right arm.

Who is this woman? Where did she come from? When Grace unlocked the door, did this person sneak in behind us? Why would anyone choose to mull around this crumbling museum?

When she begins walking out of the room, Benjamin leaps up to follow her. It suddenly occurs to Benjamin that her profile, with her long forehead and long elegant nose, is similar to his father's.

The golden book is warm to the touch. If he drops it, this illusion will probably stop and place him back where he was with Grace. He presses the book closer to his chest like Grace told him to do.

The woman enters the chapel with Benjamin in tow and stops to gently bow down and cross herself at the altar. The chapel is pristine; the obstacle course has vanished. He wants to take in its beauty, but she gets up and begins moving again, walking down a long hall until she enters a massive room splashed in frescos that reach up to the thirty-foot ceiling and massive arched stained-glass windows. When they reach the bottom of a stunning white marble staircase, she grabs the handrail and starts making her way up, her black stiletto heels clicking the marble that is ancient and worn but still beautiful.

Her journey is unencumbered by debris. It's gone, replaced by this room that is still beautiful but would have been sumptuous in its day, probably when Vittoria Sartore was a resident. As she scales the stairs, he looks around at the stately arches and cathedral ceilings anchored by colourful religious mosaics and deep red and blue damask trompe-l'œil wall-papered walls. There are oak tables, carved Tuscan cabinets, gilt wood chandeliers, and in one corner, a harpsichord with extraordinary battle decorations on the soundboard.

The young woman is a sprinter and he must move fast while keeping some distance behind. There is a strange energy preventing him from getting too close, the same one he experienced a few moments ago and in the chapel yesterday.

She opens a massive wooden door, and he follows her as she navigates her way through the forest of cypress trees on a well-worn path. The trees stop at the dock, where a tiny powerboat is secured.

She carefully climbs in and places her satchel on a bench at the back. Leaping in, he sits on the back bench. She ties a scarf around her long, curly, shoulder-length brunette hair. In the sunshine he notices her flawless make-up with dabs of powder on all the right features. She's like one of the delicate women in a Botticelli painting, half woman, half sculpture, with features that appear to be buffed as smooth as the most exquisite marble.

After turning the boat on, she maneuvers it across the lagoon at a good pace. He looks behind at the palace as they're moving away and snaps a photo of it with his phone.

Her satchel is beside him. As she focuses on the water, he leans over and pulls it towards him, clicks it open, and peers down. Inside is a baby-blue wallet, white gloves, a red lipstick case, and a gold compact as well as the golden plate. Slipping out the wallet, he looks inside at her identification and pulls out a large paper. He unfolds it carefully. It's her birth certificate: Serafina Sartore, Born July 25, 1933, Venice, Italy. He is stunned; this is his grandmother, an image or dream version of her.

He wants to take the plate and snap it into the golden book he is still clutching. Instead, he takes her lipstick and smears it on his arm. He wants a souvenir of this mirage.

The Immortal's Secret

She has a hand-written receipt in her satchel for a perfume called Floris Rose Geranium. This must be the superb scent that's dancing with the breeze and tickling his nose. It smells so fresh and natural, like Josiah's exotic garden back home in Toronto. The golden plate is wrapped in a scarf; he's certain it's the same scarf he found covering the single plate in Josiah's secret room, only this one is in pristine condition.

She raises her hand to tug on her scarf, still talking to herself. As he leans in, he can hear her reciting the Hail Mary.

When they cross over St. Mark's Basin to the Riva degli Schivioni, he places her satchel back where he found it and listens to her. The dream is so vivid, he can smell her perfume and he can almost feel the warmth of her skin.

As they arrive at the dock, Benjamin watches a gondolier rush to help her secure the boat. She gathers her belongings, and the man extends his hand to her.

"Buongioro, Signorina Sartore. Come sta?"

"Bene. Grazie, Giorgio."

It's a beautiful morning and there are no crowds at the dock, just workers delivering supplies for the day. She slowly slides off her scarf, places it in her handbag, and pushes some sunglasses onto her face. They are Ray Ban Wayfarers, similar to the ones Benjamin always wears.

St. Mark's Square is also almost empty except for a few older gentlemen picking up the litter from the day before. The only detail that defines this as the 1950s is the different storefronts. She moves with purpose but not so quickly that Benjamin can't keep up.

He thinks about how spectacular this day is—observing his grandmother. He takes a photo of her as she's striding in front of him in the square.

Suddenly she stops at St. Mark's Basilica at one of the porticos, a well-hidden one. Turning her head, she investigates the square, looking at him but not reacting. She moves towards three burgundy Corinthian pillars and pushes a groove in the marble of one of them. A door moves towards her and she enters. As Benjamin rushes in behind her, he finds himself in the middle of a magnificent chapel with the sun beaming. It must be The Secret Sartore Chapel.

Sera rushes towards a woman who is glowing in white beside the altar. They hug and begin talking. Sera provides the woman with the food in her purse.

They are laughing and drinking wine in front of a beautiful white sarcophagus when a man appears, stops, and stares at both of them. The woman in white moves over towards him slowly, and the man begins walking backwards. He falls on something, collapsing onto the marble floor. Benjamin runs over to help. The man is unmistakably Josiah—so youthful, with his rosy cheeks, ginger hair, and over six feet of gangly bones. He looks so innocent and wide-eyed. It shocks Benjamin to see a vision of a younger version of the man he loves more than anyone.

Sera races over to Josiah and pulls her scarf out of her purse. He remains still as she pats at the blood over his eye. She helps him up and guides him to a pew in front of the altar. Benjamin remembers a scar Josiah had over his eyebrow that he said he got on a trip to Europe.

Benjamin walks over to the pew where they are sitting and listens to their conversation in Italian.

"We should get you to hospital," she insists.

"I am fine. It's just a little scratch." Josiah can't stop staring at Sera. "What is your name?"

"Sera Sartore. And yours?"

"Josiah Mann. It's a pleasure to meet you."

"Likewise," she says and pauses...for what seems like forever.

"I'm sorry for intruding. I didn't mean to."

She smiles.

"Apology accepted."

"I've been overseeing the project to help preserve St. Mark's."

"Yes, I know about it."

"You do?"

She nods.

"It's being financed by my father's company." He looks around the chapel and rolls his eyes. "It's quite the challenge. I'm just a titular head, really. I've spent weeks in Venice enthralled by the work of the extraordinary preservation experts. I watch them in fascination as they contort their bodies like acrobats to clean the mosaics. Their hands are so gentle and skilled. It's like watching Michelangelo paint the Sistine Chapel. Vibrant beauty emerges under the dust of centuries.

"I just don't tire of watching them. When I need a break, I retreat to the baptistery to be alone and pray. It's designated by the procurators, who work to protect and preserve the basilica. It's my quiet zone, and a comfortable cot is set up in front of the altar. No one ever disturbs me.

It's where I can come to escape from the pressure of people expecting me to know things.

"I've noticed you in the baptistery praying many times. I wanted to know who you were, but I didn't know how to approach you. A few times, I've watched you disappear, and I wondered where you went. Out of curiosity, I watched you disappear from the baptistery by pushing *The Blessed Virgin Mary*'s head."

"You've been watching me," she says with a sly smile.

"Yes…but just out of innocent curiosity. I thought you were interesting. Who was that woman in white?"

She pauses a long time, then opens her purse and finds some lotion that she dabs on his head.

"We should take you to the hospital."

"I'm fine. It's a scratch. I'm scrawny but I'm tough. I'm descended from people in the Canadian bush who fought black bears. Who was that woman in white?"

"Canada? Hmmm."

"Not a good thing?"

"Very good thing. Far away. I like far away." She stares off into the distance. "If you don't want to get help, would you like to get something to eat? In Italy, all problems are solved by food. If you collapse, it would be easier to call for help in a café rather than in here."

He smiles at her, a wide smile.

"I don't think I'll collapse. Maybe from your beauty," he says. Based on the way Josiah closes his eyes, Benjamin knows he instantly regrets the comment. "The pain is really nothing."

"My beauty? I think I like you already." She strokes his forehead, grazing the tips of her fingers softy on his skin. "I feel I can trust you, but you need to prove it. Tell me a secret."

"A secret? What kind of secret? Why?"

He laughs loudly, the laugh Benjamin loves, like a tight verbal hug.

"I feel like I want to disclose things to you, but I need to be able to trust you."

She continues touching his forehead with the tips of her fingers as he looks up at her.

"I've been watching you for a month, watching you pray. I think I may be suffering from love at first sight, like the great Dante. How's that for a secret?" He blushes and he modulates his voice down painfully in a way

Benjamin has never heard before. "You are my Beatrice, and I hope this will not be our first and last meeting or discussion."

She stares at him, takes her fingers from his forehead, and begins twirling a chunk of her hair between her index finger. She giggles.

"I knew you were watching me…I liked you the moment I saw you too. I would like to get to know you better. When you get to know me better, and you will, you'll discover I'm very direct."

Benjamin starts to laugh. He can't believe he's looking at this vision of a young Josiah, so clearly smitten and eating out of his grandmother's hands. If only he could tap him on the shoulder, and tell him, "You're lovestruck." Who is this Josiah? Not the confident gentle giant he knows. Benjamin laughs so hard tears stream down his face.

Josiah sits up and leans on one of the marble pillars.

"I would like to get to know you better too. You liked me from the moment you saw me? I knew today was going to be a special day. In that book, which is in my memory, on the first page of the chapter that is the day when I first met you, appear the words, 'Here begins a new life.'"

"Dante," she says.

"Yes, Dante." Josiah stares deep in her eyes. So deep. Like his eyes are a camera and he's trying find the right detail to capture. Like he's drugged. He reaches his finger towards her and grazes her cheek ever so slowly with his finger.

"I just wanted to make sure you are real and not a dream. You are so perfect." His lips form into the widest, friendliest smile.

She laughs.

"Today is going to be a special day, but not because I saw you for the first time.… Perhaps I've been watching you too." Before he can respond, she stands and grabs his hand to help him up. "Maybe I wanted to meet you too. Let's go outside." She is able to gently get him on his feet and he towers over her. "This is the first secret." She guides him to the door, holding his hand tightly and watches him intently to ensure he is okay. "This place is called The Secret Sartore Chapel, and it has its own hidden door. Let me show you how it works."

Benjamin notices something as Josiah is inspecting the wall, looking for the hidden door. Sera turns around and looks back. The woman in white is partially obscured by a pillar in front of the sarcophagus. When she sees Sera, she steps out and blows her a kiss. Sera mouths the words, "I will be back."

The Immortal's Secret

The Immortal is part of a wall of portraits hanging above the sarcophagus. They resemble the portraits Josiah gave him in the wooden box. *The Immortal* is stunning, an exotic vision from head to toe.

Absentmindedly, Benjamin moves towards the wall like he's being pulled. He focuses on one portrait to the right of *The Immortal*. It's a young woman and a baby, both dressed in pink. He moves closer to examine it and recognizes the woman he saw in his illusion when he was at St. Mark's, the woman who came in with her baby who was close to death. There are two names at the bottom of the portrait: Giulia Bruno and daughter Rosa.

The young lady he saw. It's her. The same exquisite rose satin dress oozing blood and puss from every fold and crinkle.

He loses his balance recalling the grotesque baby who came to life and started feeding.

Out of his peripheral vision, he can see movement. The woman in white is running over to him like she wants to break his fall. Stopping dead, she suddenly seems to not be able to move, to get close to him. He stares at her, deep into her brown eyes, and she stares back. He wants to say something, but he can't open his mouth. His lips curve into a smile. She smiles back and points towards Sera.

The door is closing and Sera's hair streaks past. Benjamin leaps towards the door and passes through just before it shuts. He's outside in the magnificent bright day following his young grandparents.

When Sera and Josiah are past the pillars and into St. Mark's Square, she slides her sunglasses on and says, "You need something substantial to fill your stomach. I know a special place." She's holding Josiah's hand with the tips of her fingers.

Benjamin follows them through the square, where tourists are feeding pigeons and taking photos. A father of two is dangling a funky Hasselblad box camera. It has the box viewfinder that users peer down into. Everyone is dressed in suits and dresses, a stark contrast to the regular fanny pack/Hawaiian shirt/khaki tourist ensemble he is accustomed to seeing. Sera glides beside Josiah, gracefully, like a dancer. They walk back to the waterfront and Sera guides Josiah into a beautiful building, through a sumptuous lobby, and up a winding staircase that leads to a terrace café.

As they are seated at a table at the front of the patio overlooking the river, Benjamin watches Josiah pull out Sera's chair. They're on the terràzza at the Hotel Danieli, overlooking the splendour of Venice. An exquisite backdrop for his grandmother, framed by the island of San

Giorgio Maggiore and the Basilica di Santa Maria della Salute. He snaps another photo, framing it with Sera and Josiah. He checks the photo. This image from the 1950s is on his 2017 phone. No one notices. In this moment, he is a spectre, dream, or hallucination. He doesn't want this encounter to end.

He can hear Sera insisting Josiah eat something heavier than an Italian breakfast of coffee and pastry.

"Eat meat," he can hear her say. "They will make your Canadian bacon and eggs. If you eat you will feel better. I'm going to have spaghetti."

Benjamin leans up against the railing in front of them at full attention, enjoying this beautiful first "date." His grandmother is frail yet so strong and sure of what she wants. So confident to go after Josiah. She's no demure maiden. It's a look she naturally channels. Sera is so elegant in the way she wraps her fingers around the coffee cup.

Benjamin can tell Josiah is afraid to eat anything. Josiah is sitting on his hands; he's sweating and pivoting back and forth in his chair. He is scrawny but has giant shoulders and is handsome in an old Hollywood movie star way. Not unlike a young Charlton Heston with his chiselled features, dreamily coiffed ginger hair, and tanned skin. Benjamin finds this amusing since Josiah's regular look is now outrageous hair, a bushy beard, and his ratty Daniel Boone hat.

Josiah starts wringing his hands under the table, a habit Benjamin has never seen. Josiah would often reminisce about this day. He said Sera's eyes were like brown garnets that pulled him in until he couldn't look away. He's right.

There are a few facts Benjamin knows based on what Josiah divulged over the years. Sera thought Josiah was the most intriguing man she'd ever met, but then again, she was never around men. He was her first connection with someone outside of her Sartore Palace. She'd never dated anyone; she'd only read up about dating in books, and her father died when she was young. Her knowledge of life was gleaned from art. Her family had an extensive collection of portraits painted by Titian, Tintoretto, and even Raphael. Her mother sold them to save their palace but ended up squandering the money.

Likewise, Josiah thought Sera was the most exquisite woman he'd ever met. He thought of her as if she were a painting come to life; he wanted to examine every brush stroke, every pore, and each nuance, from the deep cheekbones to the lips that curved so smoothly into a smile.

Sera says something that wipes away the romantic haze.

"I am not well."

"Oh no!" Josiah jumps to attention and puts his hand on hers, tentatively leaving it there, hoping she won't pull away. "I am so sorry to hear that. Did this just come on suddenly?"

"No. My illness is serious." She keeps her hand under his and Benjamin can see she is trembling. Josiah squeezes more tightly. "I have a congenital heart problem." Josiah's shoulder collapses, becoming a block of cement pulling his body down. "The doctors have tried everything but I'm getting weaker."

"How could this be? You are so young and you look so healthy!"

She leans in, using her finger to dab his forehead where he was hurt.

"Are you sure you're, okay?"

"I'm fine," he says softly.

He doesn't want to move his hand from hers. Josiah is suddenly silent and stares at his hands. He does this when he's processing things he can't control.

"Do you believe in magic? Things that can't be explained?"

"Pardon?" he says, looking over at her, puzzled.

"Do you believe in things beyond the realm of normal?"

He stares at her for a long time and then says, "How bad is it, your illness? What is the prognosis?"

Digging her other elbow into the table, she leans her chin on her hand.

"Do you believe in magic?"

He finally smiles and says, "Yes."

"In what way?"

"It defines my life," Josiah said softly.

"In what way? I need details."

"I was born on a rock at the edge of a lake in Northern Ontario. My parents retreated to the lake because it was the only place they could go to escape a deadly forest fire."

"Yes, go on," she says pushing down deeper onto her chin.

"At the beginning of the century, my parents, Emma and Noah, and their friends Janet and Daniel were travelling home by train to Northern Ontario from Toronto. It stopped abruptly. They had to get off…immediately. Fire was destroying the trees and flames were shooting to the sky and heating up the tracks. A prospector named Crazy Gus guided them through the blazing forest to a shallow lagoon. The five of them frantically swam out as far as they could, covering their bodies under the water and placing wet clothing over their faces. All traces of the forest vanished in front of them.

"Then the heavens opened. The rain came. When they reached the shore, my mother collapsed on the rock. I was born shortly after. My naked little form was covered with a layer of ash, so my mother says. My birth ushered in rains that put an end to the month-long drought and soaring temperatures. My mother washed me for the first time with her white gloves that had covered her face to protect her from the smoke. They saved her life. When she started nursing me, my father, Noah, saw something shiny between the rocks. It turned out to be a vein of gold. It went miles below the surface. They struck gold in a huge way.

"The sacred patch of land, as they called it, became our home. My father carved out his first family home from the ashes of that devastating fire. It cleared everything in its path: the surrounding towns, families, children, animals, churches. Surviving that summer day gave my father weak lungs and a strong belief that he had a higher purpose. He started his gold company with his friend Daniel, whose last name was Fielding. They called it Mannfield Gold Corporation or MGC."

Sera sits up and exclaims, "Oh! You are a miracle! You must feel so very blessed."

"I guess you could say that."

She leans in.

"No, you must realize how blessed you are. You are young and handsome and have a fascinating job procured by your father. Your family must be well off. I too had a dramatic birth, in a room in our palace, by a mother who refused to have a doctor present. She didn't trust them. But I was not quite as lucky as you. That woman you saw, the women in white…"

"Yes…"

Sera removes her hand from his and twirls some spaghetti. Benjamin notes it's 10:30 in the morning, according to an elegant clock on the wall, and Sera is eating spaghetti. He did not get his weak stomach from her side.

"She is a healer. She cures people of disease. I need a friend I can trust. Can I trust you, Josiah?"

"Yes, you can trust me."

She chews the spaghetti carefully, like she's tasting it for the first time.

She wipes the side of her face elegantly with the corner of her cloth napkin. Grabbing her purse from the floor, she takes out the scarf that's holding the golden plate and places it on the table. Josiah looks at it, then at Sera, and places his hand on top of the plate.

"May I?"

"Yes."

He picks it up.

While he is inspecting it, Sera says, "There was a golden book. A magical golden book that cured those suffering during the bubonic plague epidemic of 1576. The book was found by Andrea Sartore, the artist who created the portraits in The Secret Sartore Chapel. You saw them, yes?"

He looks up, "Yes."

"He prayed on the book, and it may or may not have cured him of a serious heart condition. He set the book up in the altar to help others who were suffering. His mother, Vittoria, thought it was blasphemous and stole the book. It's never been seen again except for this plate. In our palace I found some letters Vittoria wrote along with the plate. Vittoria insisted there was no magic in the plate, but Annacletica, the name of the women in white, says the plate still holds magic and I pushed her for details. She told me if I pray on it, it may cure me."

"How does that work?"

"Magic, or a miracle, or faith, or alchemy," she says.

"How does she know this?"

"She has dedicated her life to finding the book. She has conducted extensive research."

"How did you meet her?"

"Vittoria's letters described The Secret Sartore Chapel and how to enter via the baptistery. I followed her instructions and entered. I met Annacletica there. We were two lost curious souls."

"How did she find The Secret Sartore Chapel?"

"She works at the basilica as a kind of nun, or in a role like a nun. She discovered the chapel like me, by chance."

Josiah responds, "From what I know, no one knows the chapel is there. The first time I saw you disappear I checked my plan of the basilica and couldn't find a chapel there."

"Annacletica disclosed that the basilica was built on the site of a hidden secret chapel. The builders at the time didn't want to destroy it, so they hid it. Annacletica said St. Mark's has many secrets. She spends a lot of time in the chapel, and I've gotten to know her well. I give her food and clothing, things like that."

"So, you want to pray on the plate? Why not consider the traditional route with specialists?"

"I've seen every specialist. I have relatives who are doctors. They can't help. They are shocked that I've lived as long as I have."

"You could come to Canada and see our best specialists. They are…"

"No, Josiah. No. I've done it all. I am at the end of my rope. No more tests. No more probes. Magic is my last hope, or nothing."

"Sera, you have to…"

"No. You have seen me pray every day in the baptistery. I've have appealed for a cure from the depth of my soul. It hasn't worked. I don't have much time…."

Her voice cracks, and she bends her head down and squeezes her fingers into the side of her eyes. The reaction reminds Benjamin of something he does.

"I don't have much time," she repeats. She takes his hands in hers.

"Josiah, I know I have met you formally only today. But I have watched you too, inquired about you to others. I liked you before I even met you. I am so thrilled you came into the chapel. I wanted to meet you but was waiting for the right moment."

Benjamin is staring at Josiah's face. The wide grin and twinkling eyes. This is his day, his most magical day. Life for Josiah would never be more magnificent than it was on this day. Nothing could ever match it. He'd met thousands of women in his life and none of them stirred him the way Sera could with one graze of her finger. This moment was the happiest of Josiah's life…and Sera's.

She leans in again.

"I need your help. Annacetica will never allow me to make my appeal in The Secret Sartore Chapel. I must do it in the baptistery. Could you talk to the procurators to ensure my privacy?"

"If you are sure you want to take this route. If you're sure it's the only option, I can do that…for you. I'd like to be with you," says Josiah.

"I would like that, to have you with me." She squeezes his fingers. "I need another favour?"

She looks over in Benjamin's direction and for a moment, he's certain she can see him. She stares right into his eyes, stimulating every nerve in his body like an electrical storm. He thinks he may collapse.

The Immortal's Secret

Then, as if she senses his shock, she turns away. Benjamin looks behind him to see if she might have been looking at someone else. There is no one, not even a boat on the water.

"Annacetica is a lost soul. She wants to go to the South Sinai Desert. It is her original home. I told her I would help her. If I don't survive, could you take her?"

Benjamin watches Josiah sip his coffee and look out onto the water.

"I would like to help. Let me meet her first, get to know her, to see if I'm the right person to help her."

"I care not where my body may take me as long as my soul is embarked on a meaningful journey."

"Ah, Dante again. You're also a fan?" he says.

"Yes, Dante. You are not the only crazy romantic."

Benjamin stares at her. He rubs his brow, which he hadn't realized was wet.

"Please come. I shall introduce you to Annacletica," says Sera.

Benjamin is back in The Secret Sartore Chapel holding his golden book as Sera darts around with Josiah trailing behind her.

Sera is calling, "Annacletica...Annacletica...where are you?"

Then they are gone. Benjamin looks around but can't find them. The chapel is so quiet, like a tomb. He is standing in the middle of the room and twirls around, taking in the opulence.

His walks over to the portraits and locks his eyes on *The Immortal*. He is mesmerized by her iconic eyes; yet she looks so different, so natural, like a woman who's free of all her make-up and adornments. Her eyes are big, the deepest brown, and seem to look deep inside him. There's no way he can pull his eyes away.

And then the light goes out. Covered in darkness, Benjamin can hear shuffling.

Someone lights a candle. The portrait of *The Immortal* begins to glimmer and shine.

The woman in white is standing next to it, as if she had walked out of the portrait. She parts her lips like she's going to say something. He waits.

"Benjamin. This is all real. I am real. 'Reach hither thy finger and behold my hands; and reach hither thy hand and thrust it into my side: and be not faithless but believing.'" She's quoting John 20:27.

The golden book slides out of his fingers and hits the tessellated tiles on the floor. The sound explodes in his ears like someone fired a gun at close range. He covers his ears with his palms. As the sound vibrates deeper into his head, he collapses onto the marble floor. His body is so weak, like each of his bones suddenly pulled away from one another and he no longer has a form.

He's weeping quietly and he looks over the familiar surroundings.

He's back in the bed beside Grace at The Sartore Palace on the Isola di Speranza.

Chapter 17

Meeting Annacletica

March 2, 2017
St. Mark's Basilica, Venice, Italy

Benjamin stares at Grace sleeping so peacefully, watching her gently breathing, her chest rising then falling. As he traces his finger over her cheek to test if she's real, she moans softly and cuddles up to him.

He thinks about The Immortal and the quote she shared about another portrait that he loves, *The Incredulity of Saint Thomas* by Caravaggio.

He pats his hand over his jacket trying to find his golden book. He can't feel anything. A surge of panic shoots through his body like a missile. He jumps up and paces back and forth like a caged animal. It was in his jacket. How could it be gone?

He rips his jacket off and looks in all the pockets. He takes off his shirt and pulls his undershirt over his head. Off come the pants, which he whips over this head like a lasso. Then his underwear comes flying off until he's standing in the nude. How could he lose his book in an illusion? It must be somewhere. Bobbing up and down, he looks around the bed, in the drawers, behind the three bookshelves.

He looks at Grace and sees that she's staring at him from the corner of her eye.

"Why are you standing in this cold room naked?"

He pulls his clothes back on as fast as he stripped them off. He races over to her and says, "Grace I have to go St. Mark's."

"What...? No. What time is it? How long have I been sleeping?" She sits up with her knees at her chin, trying to get her bearings. "Do you know what time it is?"

"It's 7:30. I need to get to St. Mark's."

"A.m. or p.m.?"

"P.m. I need to get to St. Mark's."

She attempts to get out of the bed but gets tangled in one of the sheets and slides around the bed like she's swimming in them.

"I'm so sorry I dozed off like that. I hope it wasn't very long. I would never have wanted to keep you in this crumbling museum for too long. Would you mind helping me get out of this bed? I can't seem to manage on my own. Did something happen between us? Why were you nude?"

He moves towards her and gently lifts her.

"Grace, I'm out of my mind. I can't find my golden book."

"It must be here somewhere. We didn't leave, or I don't think we left. Unless I'm really out of it."

Benjamin says, "I'm losing my mind, stripping off my clothes in a panic like that."

She walks over to the drawers and starts looking inside. Finding nothing, she dips her head under the bed.

"Your book is safe in here. No one knows this place exists."

He turns back and says, "You have to realize, I am seeing visions."

"What kind of visions?"

"Weird things are happening to me, and I know weird. I've done lots of recreational drugs in my time. I don't know what's reality anymore. It's not a drug flashback or a side effect of cancer. It's otherworldly."

He bends down, digs his hands into his thighs, and takes some deep breaths. Grace runs over and bends down by his head.

"Are you okay? Are you feeling, okay?" she says into his ear.

"I need to go back to the basilica."

"Certainly. Let me guide you out of here." She stands up and extends her arm with her palm up, waiting for him to take it.

The Immortal's Secret

When they arrive back at the basilica, Gianni's on his mobile phone. He keeps raising his index finger to signify he'll only be one moment, but his call goes on forever. The waiting is excruciating, pushing Benjamin deeper into a panic as he keeps thinking about his golden book. His stomach curls up, and then out, like an accordion.

Gianni finally ends the call and lets Benjamin enter. Grace wants to join him but Benjamin insists she go back to her hotel. She is not feeling well and needs to rest. And he needs to do this alone.

He runs towards the baptistery with a flashlight Gianni gave him. He twists the head of *The Blessed Virgin Mary* and when the statue moves, he enters The Secret Sartore Chapel.

Paralyzed by the light in the room, he is bathed in stunning candlelight as the fresh scent of laurel leaves and frankincense swirl around. The room radiates light and love.

Who did this? Who's been here?

Just like in his illusion, a woman is standing in front of him dressed in white, glowing in front of the light like a floating angel. A wave of heat soars through his body and he can't seem to move. He feels like his feet are soldered to the floor.

His eyes lock on the woman and she locks hers on him. She looks exactly like *The Immortal*, only even more beautiful in the soft light hitting off the gold radiating all over the room. Her features are even more flawless in motion.

He wants to move forward and touch her...but he thinks he'd better not. Is this another illusion? He simply has no words. It's like he's reached another level of consciousness, one science has yet to discover. He decides to take a chance and speak. Clearing his throat, he says softly, "Please tell me you are real. That I am not conjuring you."

No response.

He tries to move his legs but he can't. His eyes are transfixed on her as she moves her right hand deep inside her glorious white cotton robe. Her hand makes a hard stop like she's found what she's looking for. Raising her right arm and the sleeve of her robe, she creates a large V. The palm of her elegant hand holds the golden book. She slides it between her hands and walks over to present it to him, bowing her head as she offers him the book.

As he takes it, he feels euphoric. He presses it to his chest, the way he used to hug Josiah, pushing deep into his strong chest, never wanting to pull away. He then kisses the book and circles his fingers over the spot where his lips were. Turning back to the woman, he watches her response; she's staring and smiling. Not a huge grin showing her teeth—a soft smile that radiates warmth.

She moves in beside him and Benjamin feels like all the blood in his body is bubbling up towards his head. When she places her hands on top of his, when their skin touches, when he feels her skin meld into his, he thinks his head may pop. While caressing the book together, he focuses on her hand. It is very cold. The only accurate way to describe it is that it's not entirely human; it's like he's holding a synthetic doll's hand that is carefully fashioned to feel human.

As she looks at him with her brown eyes—a colour so vibrant he wonders if her eyes have pupils—she finally opens her mouth to speak.

After waiting a few moments, as if she's composing her thoughts, she says, "I need to show you the truth. To help you understand, move on, and live a full life." Her voice is so soft, he has to concentrate to pick up every word.

"You have been watching me your whole life. I have been watching over you. We are bonded in ways you cannot imagine. I have been attempting to give you clues, to help you. You weren't ready until now, until you arrived here in this city that defined your family."

He begins to say, "That's not…" Her finger wags slowly in front of his nose.

"No questions. I cannot abide by it. Are you fine with those conditions?"

"I don't understand. Why?" Benjamin is sure this is a dream. It's weird in the way dreams are, bouncing around erratically with odd conversation.

"Are you fine with those conditions?" She says it so softly, not like a question, like she's inquiring about how he is.

"I am," he says obediently, even though he wants to negotiate some terms, like maybe some simple questions that require a yes or no. But he decides against any pushback.

"You have been healed physically but your soul is damaged. I am here to help you live a life full of love."

Her accent is so curious. A beautiful refined international accent, if something like that exists. Familiar, yet not.

The Immortal's Secret

He focuses on her hand and how it feels—like her fingertips are secreting oxytocin and drawing him to her. Looking up at her, he says softly, "Thank you for helping and guiding me."

He so desperately wants to ask her what she is. Is he talking to a ghost, an illusion he conjured? The list ends there. He's not sure what's happening. He has no theory other than the most implausible: the woman walked out of his painting. She was also in his last dream/illusion. He dropped the book after she appeared. Now she's here and has given the book back to him.

She walks towards the portrait and lights more candles, a series of tapers over the portraits that are hanging above the bed. She performs her actions so elegantly and carefully and with such precision, like a priest preparing to deliver the host. When she lights the incense, it goes up his nose and he sneezes.

While fussing with the portrait of *The Immortal* to tilt it at eye level she says, "My name is Annacletica. There is only one Annacletica."

"It is a pleasure to meet you, Annacletica."

In a sudden burst of insight, Benjamin wonders how she got the portrait. He left it back in his hotel room, or he thought he did. Can any of his thoughts be trusted anymore?

Benjamin can hear Annacletica mumbling to herself and he sees her wiping away tears. She seems deeply immersed in the weight of her memories, vacillating between being present with him and retreating into her private reality.

"Please indulge me as we go on a journey," she says. "Look into the eyes of my portrait. Many years ago, I was stranded in the Sinai Desert, sobbing, feeling so very desperate. I had become immortal; I couldn't die. Something happened to me. Something that gave me faith. I'm not sure what it was. A voice…was it real or in my head? It was a voice, I am certain of that.

"Tiny grains of sand began to swirl around my head, dropping on my tears, dancing around my body like a balmy summer breeze, twirling faster and faster. My eyes opened fully, without pain, and I stared at the sand twinkling in the sun as the rhythm picked up and came together as a hypnotic golden vortex of sand, dust, and sun."

She looks at him, her face wet with tears.

"Forgive my tears. The weight of this memory is heavy," she says.

"Some sort of a force was carrying an energy of peace and strength that travelled over my limbs, infusing them with life. I stood up, held out my arms, and spun around in the centre of the vortex as the energy swirled up and down my body until I collapsed with exhaustion. What did the voice say? 'You have two choices: take the golden book back to the sanctuary, let the fumes of the chasm destroy it, and pray for your soul. Or return to the sanctuary and cleanse your soul by making the magic in the book holy and use it to cure others of disease and give them hope.'"

He hates this game where his questions are forbidden. What can he possibly say when someone recounts a memory so profound and mystical? She's talking about his golden book, and he needs to know more.

"Fascinating story. One would wonder how anyone could make such a choice."

She turns her beautiful face to him.

"Yes. I wasn't sure what to do. In hindsight, I wish I'd jumped into the chasm with the book. This happened to me a long time ago. I've stopped counting the years. It's a story about faith. Benjamin, your faith seems to be casual sex. Having sexual intercourse with women who are disposable to you."

Benjamin wants to leap in to object to her accusation, but he holds himself back out of respect.

"You don't really know me. If you knew me, you wouldn't say that."

"I know you. Ignore your body that needs to be healed. Treat your life like it wasn't a blessing from God. Faith is all that matters. When did you lose yours, or did you ever have any to begin with?"

He's wondering if it's within her guidelines for him to answer her questions.

"The golden book will grant your wish. I asked for immortality by carving my image. 'Make the pledge. Carve your image in your golden book in a holy place, light the candles, burn incense, and make a pledge to gain immortality. This is the quintessence that will grant your wish.' These were the instructions from the Pythia from The Gods of the Desert Sanctuary, the place where I did something unholy and asked for immortality. No one chose that path except for a few others…and perhaps your grandmother. Josiah convinced her to carve her name to try and cure her sickness. I was trying to convince her not to. I couldn't bear for her to endure my fate. As much as I loved her, it was her time to go and move on along her journey."

The Immortal's Secret

Benjamin stares at the portrait of Sera—his grandmother—with her stunning light-brown eyes.

"If the eyes are the window to the soul, hers were like a magnificent picture window looking out onto a meadow."

Annacletica walks over and rubs her fingers over Sera's face.

"The face of an angel," she says. "I can't die, and she couldn't live." She stares at Sera's image and Benjamin watches.

"I'd like to take you on one last journey with the golden book." She stares down at the book and says, "May I?"

He hands it to her like it's a piece of delicate glass, and she places her hand on the cover like she's touching a newborn's head. She takes his hand and places it on top of hers, concealing her hand.

She looks him in the eyes and says, "Stare into the eyes of *The Immortal* and breathe deeply. Let the laurel leaves enter your nose and the candles warm your eyes. Immerse yourself. Don't let go of the book. We must stay together."

The book warms under their hands like it's melting. It pulls their fingers into the gold like it's quicksand.

She whispers, "I need to tell you the story of the book and the portrait. There will be things you don't understand. Sometimes there is no explanation. I will tell you everything you need to know."

They concentrate on *The Immortal's* eyes together and he feels himself sinking, like he's sliding out of his body, becoming one with the energy surrounding them.

Suddenly he's back in the present but in another reality. He can feel his feet again. When he can focus his eyes, he realizes he's still in St. Mark's but in the baptistery. It's now dark; night is falling. Annacletica is beside him and they're still clutching the book together, with her hands on one side and his on the other.

A young man dressed in a white shirt and black tunic is on a scaffold. He's straining to touch the mosaics on the ceiling above the altar. They both look up at him, from about six feet away. Benjamin feels so sad, deep down in his stomach. He feels like her emotions have fused with his, touching him on such a profound level. These emotions are foreign to him. He wants to cry when he looks up at the man, so young—maybe eighteen or twenty— and huge, with long arms and long elegant fingers.

"It's 1575. My Andrea is carefully cleaning each piece of stone, each small square that brings the beautiful angel to life. He pushes his cloth into every crevice, rubbing and buffing until he reveals the former grandeur of the angel who sits at the centre of the mosaic. He's rubbing skillfully but softly, in awe of touching something he's certain was commissioned by God."

Benjamin is impressed by the way Andrea is moving, buffing like he is painting each glass square.

Standing in the middle of the nave with the candlelight softly illuminating the art is such an intense feeling when the artwork is viewed in pure silence. The pure golden background of the mosaics wraps around them in the dark.

"Such a dreamer, he wanted to be immortal, to be like the mosaics, to live thousands of years, to have his image on this holy shrine that refuses to refresh with time," Annacletica continues. "To be a symbol for all generations, something that people would always marvel at, stare at for hours, pray before, be inspired by, draw strength from. He never wanted to leave this sanctuary. It was the only time he prayed, saying, 'I just want to have a life.'

"His outlandish goal was to clean and examine every mosaic in The Secret Sartore Chapel. A goal he hoped would extend his fragile hold on life. By tracing these beauties, he wanted to understand their process for interpreting the story of God."

Andrea climbs down from the scaffolding and walks past them without reacting.

"He is going to perform a ritual he does every morning before he leaves. He softly rubs the face of the five-foot marble statue of The Blessed Virgin. It is the focal point of the golden iconostasis that reaches from one end of altar to the next. As he caresses her exquisite face, he always says a prayer:

'Hail Mary, full of grace, the Lord is with thee.

Blessed art thou amongst women,

and blessed is the fruit of thy womb, Jesus.

Holy Mary, Mother of God,

pray for us sinners,

now and at the hour of our death. Amen.'"

The Immortal's Secret

Annacletica guides Benjamin over to Andrea and mirrors his actions.

"This morning he does something he's never done. With his eyes closed, he pushes his hand into The Virgin's face, a reaction to his love for her and the passion of prayer."

They watch as the panel where The Virgin is anchored moves, creating a thin gap in the iconostasis. Andrea opens his eyes. He jumps up.

Observing the look on Andrea's face, Benjamin suspects the young man is heartbroken and panicked, probably thinking he's damaged the beautiful statue. With the light from his candle, Andrea moves in slowly to examine it in closer detail. He shines the candle over the opening and Benjamin notices the gold hinges on the side of the statue. Andrea gently pulls the marble door towards him and light hits Benjamin and Annacletica's eyes. A fiery daybreak is streaming into the secret room.

Andrea walks towards the altar and the white marble sarcophagus adorned with the sculpture of Father Roberto and Annacletica intertwined. It's pure white, not the off-white colour it is in 2017.

As Benjamin and Annacletica follow Andrea, Benjamin brushes his hand over the marble, feeling heat on his hand. He watches Andrea climb onto the sarcophagus and wrap himself around the sculpture, as if he's trying to blend his body into the marble to become part of the sculpture. After a bit of a struggle, he slips down. As he's trying to maintain his balance, he grabs the side of the sarcophagus and it opens it a crack.

"He pushes the sarcophagus open a little more, and then a little more, until he sees me lying in the sarcophagus, clutching the golden book to my chest. He touches me and I open my eyes.

"I had wanted to sleep forever. I wasn't dead but I could sleep. I was surviving in the crypt as a living cadaver. So began our journey of doomed love and healing. My portrait was his first work of art, a beautiful portrait created on top of another portrait of me, one I didn't care for. His was an attempt to capture what he thought was a perfect woman. When I opened my eyes, it was the moment he says he fell in love."

She collapses. Benjamin reaches to her, almost hitting his head on hers in a desperate attempt not to take his hand off the book.

"Stay with me, Annacletica," he says.

Still holding his hand, she slowly creeps over and touches Andrea.

"Look at me. Look, I'm here, my love." She grazes the side of his face, but he doesn't react.

Benjamin is enthralled with her mirror image in the sarcophagus. Two beautiful immortals up close. He's watching the artist examine his subject.

A glorious moment of first love. Two people setting eyes on each other for the first time. The present and future fusing. Two different dimensions colliding.

Annacletica is watching herself, knowing how the story is going to end courtesy of the book they're holding onto. The scene in front of Benjamin is like a guidepost…a view into horrors of the past that perhaps should remain buried there.

Annacletica is sobbing quietly and Benjamin strokes her hair with his left hand to comfort her. It's like her brain is connected to his. He can feel her heartache and he wants to collapse into her arms to ease the pain.

Bowing his head, he closes his eyes to block out the pain, and he can feel her body freeze.

It's suddenly so quiet. He looks up and they are in The Sartore Palace on Isola di Speranza in one of the large palatial rooms Benjamin visited with Grace. Annacletica and Andrea are at a large ornate table, surrounded by plates piled high with meats, vegetables, and cheese.

Vittoria is at the head of the table, resplendent in a red satin dress, sitting up straight, deep in conversation with the other two, waving her hands elegantly. They are drinking wine from elegant crystal wine goblets branded with a huge S on the side. Annacletica is stunning in a purple velvet dress with a high collar, her face framed by her auburn hair—an exotic creature more beautiful than the stunning palace.

"I did not want to go to her palace. I did not want to go!" she screams. "I implored Andrea to not go, saying, 'This is a trap of some kind.'"

"He told me, 'Cara, she needs to know we are in love.' In this vision, he is telling Vittoria how deep his love for me is. How healthy he is feeling. How he wants to focus on his art. How he wants to help others. Vittoria focused her life on making him feel weak and dependent on her. I don't think he was ever ill. She knew how to get her way and she wanted rid of me. When she started probing about the golden book, I became nervous.

"Another pitcher of wine appeared. I told her I'd had enough but she insisted we toast to our marriage. With one small sip, I could tell it was off. When she turned away, I poured mine into her empty water glass.

"She poured me more. I sipped some, and she insisted I drink more. Then her voice began to wane in and out. My head throbbed and my stomach contracted. I looked over at Andrea and saw his head had collapsed on the table in a pool of wine. I saw her walk over to me, as if in slow motion, and my head tilted. Then everything went blank."

Benjamin watches as the two brutes appear, the ones he witnessed in his vision. One throws Andrea over his shoulder and stumbles towards the door. The other one scoops up Annacletica underneath his arms, as if she is an item he's hauling around in a warehouse.

Benjamin realizes the brutes are carrying out the plan Vittoria discussed with them on her boat.

"I was fading in and out of consciousness. It was painful to stay alert. They threw us into the back of Vittoria's boat and I twisted my arm. I groped around for Andrea and touched his leg but he didn't respond. I was so frightened he was gone.

"When we arrived back at the foot of St. Mark's Basin in Venice, they dragged us to the basilica in a cart under blankets that reeked like mold and wine. They knew people could enter The Secret Sartore Chapel by pushing the head of *The Blessed Virgin*, and they trampled through the holy chapel like they were drunks in a crowded tavern. They pushed the sarcophagus open and threw both of us in, right on top of one another, like we were sacks of trash. I tried to revive Andrea but his hands were clammy and cold.

"They didn't close the lid completely and I was listening intently. I thought Vittoria had stayed on the island, but I suddenly heard her deep voice. It was definitely her. The sick and desperate were always in the chapel night and day, praying on the book. She said, 'Go into the chapel. Create a commotion. Get them to throw you out. I'll arrive and secure the golden book and that revolting portrait.' I heard screaming and was sure it was because the devout had discovered the book was gone. I went out the secret door and ran to where the boat had been docked. It was gone.

"I stumbled to the sarcophagus, completely defeated, and closed the lid tightly. Andrea was so cold and stiff. I wrapped myself around him and appealed to him, 'Darling, don't leave me. I cannot live in this world without you.' I couldn't accept he was gone. It was easy to open the sarcophagus. Father Roberto had created a latch on the inside to open it. I put on my plague doctor costume and went into the baptistery desperate for help, to save Andrea. But no one could help me. I felt so alone."

Benjamin and Annacletica are standing in front of the golden iconostasis in the baptistery. They are in front of the same plague sufferers again, the dirty people searching for hope. The people who have sunk to the lowest level of suffering. They are like living cadavers, refined zombies. People are swarming in, bumping into each other, screaming, crying, moaning. They are all pointing to the altar.

Suddenly the familiar aroma of death goes right up Benjamin's nose and stays there. He's having trouble breathing. He looks at Annacletica. She's silent.

Then she looks at him and says, "She stole the golden book; she stole my portrait. It was all over. I went back to the crypt and closed it. I was hoping to die beside my beloved. Time ceases to mean anything when you're immortal. You fall asleep and when you wake up, you have no idea how long you were asleep. Andrea only wanted to help others. He believed in hope. Like the golden book, he was destined to help others. He didn't want to live a life of being used and destroyed. I was saved by your grandmother. The beautiful Sera...Serafina. My heavenly winged angel."

They are cloaked in darkness and silence. When light appears, Benjamin sees he is beside his grandmother, who is collapsed on top of the carving of Annacletica entwined with Roberto Sartore on the sarcophagus.

Benjamin tries to reach out his hand to touch her, but the more he stretches, the more she seems to move away.

Sera is clutching one of the golden plates, and *The Immortal* is leaning against the side of the marble wall. Sera chants something softly, like a prayer, one Benjamin can't make out. Then she calls out, "Annacletica." Her weight slides the lid of the crypt open an inch or two and she stands up looking startled. She then peers down tentatively.

"I was looking up at her. I don't think she was sure how to respond. She appeared scared and excited. I smiled at her and she smiled back. She eventually helped me out of the sarcophagus and we sat together silently on the marble steps of the sarcophagus. Finally, she divulged that she knew my story. Someone had stashed away one of the plates from the golden book and *The Immortal* in a room in The Sartore Palace. But the golden book was not there. She insisted that she searched the palace and was never able to find it. She saved me and she became my best friend and protector. She started coming to see me every day.

"I watched her die. I was so helpless. She prayed on the plate and it made her better...for a while. She wanted to carve her name into it but I told her I couldn't allow her to endure my fate. I'm not sure if she ended up appealing for immortality. I couldn't bear to ask for clarification."

Benjamin follows her eyes towards a bed with a golden bedspread. Sera is there with Josiah beside her. Annacletica is cradling a baby, Benjamin's father. Sera's face is drawn, her eyes hollowed out and her skin grey. She is nestled in Josiah's arms with her emaciated arms on top of her nightgown, which is soaking wet and sticking to her body. There is no resemblance to the women he saw previously.

He watches her cough like she is choking, then struggle to take a breath. She thrusts her chest up and doesn't exhale. Silence. She is gone.

Josiah howls, a long doleful sound that makes tears well up in Benjamin's eyes. Josiah squeezes her so hard Benjamin thinks he may crack her bones.

"We went to the Sinai Desert, to the monastery. I looked after your father, Duncan, when he was a baby. Josiah's father, Noah, was pressuring him to come home. When Josiah recovered, he went back to Toronto, a broken man. I couldn't go. I couldn't leave. This was not of my time, not my time in history. I have always sought out places where I can live quietly out of sight, like the monastery."

She takes Benjamin's hand off the book and places it on top of his other hand. He can't stop crying. He is a mess. Such sadness.

"One question?" he says. "Just one question?"

"Yes."

"How can any of this be real? Are you real?"

She stares at him and wants to say something, but she just blows out the candles. She opens one of the ornate drawers in the chapel and takes out a red wig, T-shirt, and pink furry purse, and he asks a second question.

"Why do you have Cle's outfit?"

Chapter 18

Reckoning

March 3, 2017
The Secret Sartore Chapel, Venice, Italy

"You are Cle. I don't understand."

Benjamin is standing near the sarcophagus. Annacletica guides him to the bench beside the altar and they both sit down.

She dabs sweat from his brow with the sleeve of her robe.

"I told you. I knew your grandmother."

"You're the woman in my portrait. It can't be. You'd be over 2000 years old."

Benjamin slides down off the bench to the floor.

"Benjamin!" shouts Cle as she tries to lift him to his feet. They fall together onto the floor. "Are you okay?"

"I'm okay." His skin is flushed and he's sweating. He pulls up his T-shirt and wipes his face.

"I'm okay. None of this makes any sense."

"You've discovered something that perhaps you shouldn't. Isn't that why you're a curator? To find that exclusive piece of art? Discover the elusive one?"

"Yes, but usually the subject in the painting doesn't walk out and start talking to me. It's a bit challenging to get my head around."

She looks over at him and smiles.

"What a story!" he says. "I'm wondering how my illusions transformed into my new reality, Cle. Or should I call you Annacletica?"

"No, Cle is fine."

"Okay, absolutely."

They had just experienced something phantasmic together. She relived part of her life—part of Josiah's life—and Benjamin relived it with her. He knows it wasn't a dream or drug-induced hallucination. It was real. No one gets to experience anything like that. Some wouldn't survive the pain of seeing those you love but knowing you cannot stay with them.

Annacletica stands up beside him, staring ahead like a delicate little statue, shivering. He rises from the floor as well, takes his jacket off, and puts it over her shoulders.

What the fuck is happening to me?

Sliding her hand in his, he whispers, "I am your friend. You can trust me. Let me help you." Her hand is so tiny and he doesn't want to press in case he hurts her.

He looks down and sees her face is moist with tears. When she looks up at him, she's as gentle as a child. Her stare seems to last forever.

Just as he's about to say something, she slides back to the ground. He assumes she's fainted but when he puts his hand on her shoulders, she looks up at him. He grabs her and holds her tightly, and she whispers something he cannot make out.

"Annacletica, what are you trying to say? I can't hear you."

"Seeing him again was too much," she says.

The room is so beautiful. It feels like they are both in a womb, like the world is beyond them and they are in an in-between reality where no one can touch them.

Benjamin starts to weep too. The sensation is so cathartic. He feels like he's releasing all the stress he's held in for the past year.

"I'm sorry my journey to find Josiah has made you dredge up so many feelings, so much history. I've always wanted to do good. You are guiding me in how to figure out how to do that," says Benjamin.

He holds her and whispers in her ear.

"When I was an altar boy at St. Michael's Cathedral, I used to watch our priest give his sermons. The altar was my favourite place to be. I felt I was blessed because I was chosen, everyone else was so far away. I didn't have much of a family and the church made me feel like I belonged to something. It filled a hole. Looking into the face of *The Immortal* made me feel the same. Then I witnessed Grace being attacked and I couldn't believe in anything for a long time. I need to go back to my faith. Seeing my family made me realize pure love and happiness is possible. I need to believe. Your book has made me want to believe again."

They hold hands and they stare at the altar. She moves her hand on top of his.

"You're a good person who is descended from great people, people who wanted to achieve extraordinary things to help others. You must honour their legacy and make it your legacy. Benjamin, you can start by helping me. I need to go to the Sinai. You know your grandmother helped me get there last time. We need to go together. We have to leave as soon as possible."

"Sure, I'll make the plans."

"I need some drugs. You seem to have a closet full."

"You want me to drug you?"

"Yes."

They stare at one another and neither pulls away. They start laughing.

"I can't do that to you."

"It's the only way. I can't fly. I'm terrified. Aviation is not of my time."

"It's of my time but I'm not keen on it either."

She stares at him with such tired eyes but she doesn't blink.

He folds his hands in prayer and looks up at the altar.

"Benjamin?"

"I'll check out my stash and find you something."

"These people you have connected with here in Venice?"

"Yes?"

"Josiah had a lot of strange characters following him. I need to find the last plate, Benjamin. This Paeon, the woman in purple, or the Jenna woman you know, may have one of them. I am praying she has one."

"Why do you think that? How would we possibly find it?"

"Can you meet with the woman and look for it?"

"I could do that if I knew where she was, which I don't."

"I need you to help, Benjamin. Please. I am desperate. I know Vittoria Sartore took a plate out of the book because your grandmother found one of them."

Benjamin stares at the altar as they remain quiet, alone with their thoughts. Benjamin thinks about a necklace Jenna used to wear with various delicate chains of gold, a huge one that she never took off. She said it was a gift from her grandmother.

"I might know where it could be...it's a long shot."

Annacletica looks up at him. Her eyes are wet.

"You've seen it?"

"Maybe," he says while leaning in to wipe a tear from her cheek with his pinkie.

"When I spent time with Jenna, she wore a necklace. A thick one. It could have been the same yellow gold from the book. It's hard to say. I'm going from memory but it's coming back to me. I remember it made her skin very warm when I touched it."

She holds out her trembling hand. He takes it and begins massaging her fingers.

"Let me get you back to your hotel. Shall I carry you?"

Annacletica stands up and he gently picks her up to make the short journey through St. Mark's Square to the Hotel Danieli.

Annacletica is sleeping and curled up in a ball when he leaves her hotel room. Stripped of the crazy red hair and getup, she looks like an angel that rolled out of a picture frame. She looks so tiny as she squeezes the edge of the pillow with her black hair framing her gentle face. He takes a picture of her with his phone.

Chapter 19

Moment of Truth

March 4, 2017
Terrace at the Hotel Danieli, Venice, Italy

Benjamin sits on the spectacular terrace at the Hotel Danieli with a bottle of wine and one glass. The bottle is half full. He stares over at the Basilica di Santa Maria della Salute, the church that was built for those who died from the plague of 1630. A monument to all who suffered.

Benjamin can't stop thinking about the people he saw at the altar, those who placed so much hope in an inanimate golden object. It was all they had.

He has placed his faith in the book too. He is a believer. Yet somehow he has now become the one who must destroy it. Why could it not serve its purpose as an object of faith and hope for others? Why does good always attract evil? He thinks of a quote from Marcus Aurelius: "Life is neither good or evil, but only a place for good and evil."

He's terribly shaken and overjoyed in equal measure and needs to talk to someone he trusts. He calls Grace and leaves a message asking if she'd like to join him.

He flips through the photos on his phone, replaying his adventures. He's never been one for family photos. Perhaps it's because there weren't many opportunities to take any, or perhaps it's because he's never been nostalgic about his own life. He'd prefer to spend his time staring at great works of art, getting lost in their history, and exploring the moment they were captured in paint. The photos he took of Josiah and Sera are like precious works of art to him: pictures of the man who means the world to him and the woman Josiah loved. He emails the pictures to himself so he has duplicates to prove the scene was real.

Josiah loved regaling the story of meeting Sera; now Benjamin's experienced it himself. He witnessed one of the poignant moments that defined his grandparents' lives.

Did any of this happen?

It did. It's not something he will ever question. The book has given him special powers and he feels blessed that it is taking him to a supernatural place. Every day at the Louvre, he was trying to transport himself back in time. Now the golden book is providing him access.

He dials his father.

"Hi, Dad," says Benjamin, staring out at the water.

"How are you feeling?" says Duncan. "We have been so worried."

"I'm okay. I'm sorry I've haven't called."

"Are you in the Sinai?"

"No, Venice. I've been doing some research on Josiah. I found some photos of your parents. Do you want to see them? I can email them."

As Benjamin waits for Duncan to respond, he finishes up his glass of wine and pours more. The pause is so long Benjamin thinks they may have lost the connection.

"I thought no photos survived of both of them, not even a wedding photo," says Duncan. "Where did you find them?"

"They were in some archives that I found, Sartore private archives. What did Josiah share about her?"

Duncan is silent. Benjamin hates lying to his father but what can he do? He wants to share his experience with his father, who never knew his mother. Benjamin isn't crazy about his mother but at least he has one.

"Dad, are you still there?" The silence is painful.

Just when Benjamin is sure they've lost the connection, Duncan speaks up.

"Your grandfather kept her perfume. He said she smelled like roses."

Benjamin thinks about the receipt he saw in Sera's purse.

"Like the ones in Josiah's garden?"

"Yes."

"And gardenias?"

"That's right. I love that smell more than anything in the world. She was so beautiful. Glamourous. Josiah said she was a lot like you. Are you sure you're okay? We've heard nothing."

"I just need this time. I need to find out what happened to Josiah. To bring closure," says Benjamin.

"Have you found any new clues?"

"Not yet. I'm going to the Sinai. There are people I've met who think he could be there...throwing everyone off of his scent."

"Benji, you know he is probably gone."

"Yes, I know. I'm prepared for that reality. But I need to turn every stone before I can get closure. You know what I'm like."

"The detectives couldn't find any details. Those monks weren't helpful at all. They said he wandered off and they've stuck to that story."

Benjamin watches a gondola on the water. It makes him think of Jenna, who loved to jump in on a whim and sail the canal.

"The pictures I'm sending you of our family make me feel so much closer to you. Your mother looked like you."

"She also looked like you. Those eyes." Duncan's voice is cracking and Benjamin finds it unsettling but not as unnerving as what Duncan says next.

"Benji?"

"Yes."

There is a long silence.

"I...love you."

Benjamin is not sure how to respond. This is the first time those words have crossed his father's lips.

"Love you." he says quickly as he hangs up the phone.

That as good as it gets. He's going to work on "I love you." This quick utterance is a start. Things are changing. He feels happy.

Suddenly he hears someone whisper in his ear.

"This place is so gorgeous."

When he turns around, he can't believe what he sees. Grace is standing in front of him in a black jacket and matching dress, her strawberry blonde hair falling on her shoulders. She's wearing black high-heeled pumps. She looks magnificent.

She slides into the chair across from him and adjusts her sunglasses.

"How are you?"

"Much better now that you're here. All of this, this look," he says while swinging his hands in front of her. "The only word I can think of is luminous."

"Thank you," she says. She is turning bright red. He suddenly remembers she would blush in school when the teacher would call on her, drawing all the attention in the room towards her.

"How's Cle?"

"Resting," he says. "We had some very emotional moments together. She's adamant she wants to go back to the desert. She has one last task she needs to do. She needs the last plate from the book. Not a small task."

"That's for certain. How on earth could you find it?"

"She feels Jenna Parrish or Paeon could have it. The plate may have been melted down into a necklace that Jenna wears all the time. Honestly, I think it's a long shot."

"Really?"

"It's a thick piece of gold. I asked her about it, and she always insisted it was a family heirloom. She never took it off. One night, she wasn't feeling well and I carried her to our bed…I mean the bed. I was able to release the clasp and place it on her night table. The next morning, she lost it on me, swearing and saying words I'd never heard come out of her mouth. She made me promise never to do that again. It was our only fight. I was thinking about this incident recently. I remember when I was taking the necklace off her neck, it was warm. When I went to bed that night, I had a horrible dream. I had forgotten about this."

"What kind of dream?"

"It was like I was dreaming with her. It shook me up. I was in some kind of palace with her. She was agitated and trying to pack her things."

"I'm happy you are suspending your disbelief, prepared to believe she or the woman in purple could be a woman from the Renaissance still roaming Venice. That's what Annacletica believes, or thinks she believes."

"What do you believe, Grace?"

"Life is a mystery. What happens to us when we die? That question used to make my head go funny. The idea of not being here anymore and perhaps being gone. Like what happens when you go to sleep. You wake up and wonder where you were. Is that what happens when you die? You just go to sleep, like they say. I was seeing a psychic not long after my mother died."

She twirls a silver ring on her finger.

"This woman told me things she could never have known. It was like I had a pipeline to my mother. It gave me such a sense of calm, that everything is going to be fine once we make that final journey."

"Do you think you have a connection to the golden book?"

"I was granted a miracle. I was cured, there's no doubt about it. I was in such a bad way. Connection to the book? Not sure. My scars remind me how close I was to death. I've learned to love them. They're a part of me. They're a testament to how tenuous life is. How it can be over in a second."

"I know. I thought about death a lot when I was ill. The chemo was so debilitating. I was sleeping most of the time, trapped in an endless stream of bad dreams. I was pulled into so many dreams about you, on that day, how helpless I felt as I tried to help you. I've never really recovered from that trauma and now I'm here with you. Josiah was always by my side."

Grace extends her hand and puts it on top of his.

"I'm choosing to not give up hope. Josiah wanted you to explore Venice but we now need to get to the Sinai. There is this matter of the necklace. How do we get it? Or maybe the best way to look at it is, how do we try to get it?"

"The necklace could be in the palazzo where I lived with Jenna. I've tried to sell the palazzo. Truth be told, I wanted to hang on to it. It was my only reminder of her. Now I don't care. I'm going to head over there after I get the key from my friend who's managing the palazzo for me."

"We're dealing with a needle in a haystack. If we can't find that plate, let's move on. Cle is ready to take her next step. Whatever she's been searching for all her life, I think she's done. She can no longer endure whatever she's been enduring."

He sips some wine and looks out onto the water.

"If Jenna asked you to come back, would you?"

"Grace, where did that come from? No, no, not at all. I just want to maintain my focus on getting the necklace with no surprise guests. I'm dealing with some intense emotions. Jenna is not who she said she was. I am still feeling the chemistry, the pull of her. I'm fighting it. We all do crazy things for love. I used to wonder how anyone could be so blinded by love. I used to wonder what was wrong with them. Have you ever felt like that?"

"Yes." There is a long silence as she stares at her drink.

She looks out over at the water and says nothing as a gondola passes by. There is a young couple in the gondola holding wine glasses and kissing. The silence lasts for a few minutes. Grace is clasping her hands together pushing in her fingers.

He finally says, "I'm sorry if I was intruding. I didn't mean to."

"I have always loved just one person. No one could ever live up to him. He's perfect in my eyes."

"Lucky guy," he says feeling quite jealous. This is a woman he had a huge crush on as a child. He can't keep his eyes off her as she radiates in the midday light.

"Who is he? If you don't mind me asking."

Her eyes move back to the water and the gondolas, then turn back to him. Her hands are clutching the side of the table and they are shaking. She lifts her glass and takes a drink of red wine. Some trickles down her chin and she wipes it off with her finger.

"You don't have to tell me."

"No, I want to. I need to confess." She downs half a glass of wine and looks into his eyes. "You don't know?"

Just before he says no, something pops into his head. Could she be talking about him? It's his turn to stare at the water.

When he turns his attention back to her, he's certain she is talking about him. Her eyes are floating in tears that then move down her face onto her beautiful black dress.

Staring her right in the eyes he leans forward and says, "When we were in school together, I had such a crush on you. I was always looking out for you. I would walk behind you to make sure no one bothered you. That's why I was watching you on the playground that day. Tragically, I was too late."

Grace's eyes get big like blue saucers. In an instant her sad eyes are glowing and her sadness turns to joy. She starts laughing and dabs her eyes with her napkin.

He slides his hand over towards her and places it on top of hers, loving the sensation of her skin on his. Ever since he saw her in the baptistery, he's been fighting the desire to touch her. She is so gentle and caring. He wants to be filled with her goodness. She represents the familiar. She is someone he knows, someone authentic, someone who doesn't want anything but to help.

"I can't believe you had a crush on me," she says. She keeps pushing her fingers to her nose to cover her face.

"I used to dream of buying you nice things with my allowance. I could tell you were so beautiful," says Benjamin. "I knew your beauty was

The Immortal's Secret

hidden under the hand-me-down clothes. I was right. You are stunning. When you were walking over to the table, I was praying you made the effort for me."

Before she has a chance to say anything, he leans forward on the table and pushes his lips softly onto hers.

Her breathing changes. She begins hyperventilating; he can hear her making wheezing noises.

When she controls her breathing, she says slowly, "I have loved you from the moment I saw you. I couldn't wait to go to school to see you." She pauses to catch her breath. "Those boys were so evil but the other students, the rest of us who didn't belong, clung together. I felt you never noticed me. If you had told me you had a crush on me, I would have thought you were just teasing me. I was safer when you were just a fantasy. I was on death's door after that accident. Knowing you were the one who saved me gave me hope."

She opens her purse, takes out a small gold folder covered with hearts, and places it and several other items on the table: a small Valentine's Day card, a page from a notebook, their class photo, a Polaroid photo of Benjamin playing soccer, a magazine feature of Josiah from "Toronto Life" magazine with a photo of Benjamin standing in front of the Louvre after his appointment as director.

"This is my little shrine to you. I have never stopped thinking of you. When I reconnected with Josiah after my mother passed on, I was hoping, praying I would see you again but I dared not share this with Josiah."

Benjamin picks up the Valentine's Day card.

"My mother bought them for me. I only gave one to you. Remember the girl who used to wear pink dresses?"

"Yes, Jessica."

"I liked how she sat up straight in class and knew all the answers. I'm sure she's a lawyer now."

"I heard she wasn't doing well. Two divorces led to alcoholism."

"Really?" Benjamin asks.

"Do you remember Jason Arlette? He was one of the projects?"

"Yes, I think I do. Strawberry blonde hair. Always wore Toronto Maple Leafs swag."

"Yes, that's right. He's a lawyer. He saw her in court."

"Sad."

Grace nods.

"What you see on the outside often doesn't always mirror someone's inner world," says Grace. "Yet we judge. I sent Jessica some money to help her. I didn't sign the card. She was kind to me and I wanted to return the favour."

"Why didn't you sign it? I think she would have loved to hear from you and know the money was from you."

"I wanted her to know someone cares. I didn't have to identify myself. I just wanted to help her get back on her feet."

Benjamin says, "It's a dream come true for me to see you again. You have haunted me my whole life."

He stands up, moves over to the other side of the table next to her, and slides his arm around her shoulder. As they watch the water together, he digs his head into her hair, takes her hand, and plays with her fingers.

"I have been so tortured since the day of your accident. It had a profound impact on me. I thought you were dead. I didn't want to believe in anything. I couldn't understand how a loving God could allow those evil monsters to attack you like that."

"My mother told me to look at everything a different way. She said those boys were envious of me and my gifts to the world—that they had to cut down anyone who was good. She said they were trying to do the same to you."

He kisses her and runs his fingers through her hair.

"It is a miracle you are here," says Benjamin.

"It's a miracle *you* are here. Cle said you prayed on the book to be healed."

"I did. She did it with me," says Benjamin. "I feel like I used to, healthy and energetic. It's quite extraordinary. We have to help Cle achieve what she feels she needs to do."

"Thank you for helping Cle and helping Josiah," Grace says.

"What are your thoughts on Jenna, the Vittoria Sartore connection? She does resemble Vittoria, or pictures I've seen of her."

"I don't know, Benjamin. Since I met Cle, I've witnessed very strange things. Odd people trying to get near her. Maybe Jenna is an art fraudster obsessed with Sartore and his mother? Or maybe she's a kook? Or maybe she is from another time. I've suspended my belief."

He looks at his watch.

"I don't want to go but I should head out."

They kiss again, pressing their lips together. No passionate French kissing. Just simple touching that feels unbelievable to Benjamin, exploring each other gently.

Grace walks down the stairs with him. He heads to the main door to leave the Danieli, stops before he walks through revolving door, and watches her until she disappears into the hotel elevator.

Chapter 20

Settling the Score

March 4, 2017
Benjamin's Palazzo, Venice, Italy

Benjamin walks into his palazzo and enters the portico. The dining room table is filled with an Italian feast of lasagna, Caprese salad, fresh bread, and olive oil, along with some nice touches like fresh flowers, fine linen. The room smells like lilac perfume, the one he used to buy Jenna from the elegant store called The Merchant of Venice.

What the heck?

His home has been locked up for ages and it never occurred to him someone might take advantage. Clearly there is an intruder. Benjamin starts looking around to see if anything else is off.

Then he hears a noise coming from the huge antique front door. The lock is twisting. He stretches his arms behind him and places his hands on the top of the back of the velvet sofa.

A woman walks in and makes an abrupt stop. When she spots him, she turns around, leaves, and closes the door abruptly. Before he can decide what to do, the door opens again. She re-enters and stands still.

She is dressed head to toe in a purple velvet dress. A fur shawl draped around her shoulders is fastened with a ruby pin, and a red velvet cap covers her hair. Her face is obscured by an elaborate Venetian mask with golden lips and milky white skin that curves around the back of her head. Benjamin notices something gold under the shawl. Could it be the necklace?

He stares quietly while she fiddles with her black lace gloves and doesn't look up.

"May I enter?" She has an accent he can't place.

When she starts walking towards him, Benjamin steps forward.

"Do I know you?" he asks.

"Yes."

"Who are you?"

"I am Jenna."

"You're not Jenna."

She walks over and wraps her arms around him. He places his hands on her shoulders and pushes her.

"Let's go into the bedroom," she insists.

Oh my God, this woman is delusional. What do I say to distract her?

He raises his hands, palms up, and motions towards the table.

"Did you prepare this food?"

Taking her hand, he guides her to the kitchen. She slides a bottle of wine out of her large purple tote. The bottle has a cork, making it impossible for her to get up to any poisoning trickery. He takes a corkscrew from the counter drawer, twists off the cork, walks to the cupboards, and pulls out two wine glasses.

"Could we think about reuniting? Put the past behind us?" she says.

He goes along with the lame toast and clicks her glass.

"Please, let's sit," he says, pointing to the sofa.

As she follows him, all he can think of is the day Jenna left him. His face burns thinking about the details and he wonders if she notices.

I slept on this sofa because of Jenna, the conniving bitch. I could barely function as she went out on the hunt for whatever she was after.

She sits down, leans back, and tucks her legs into her side. She is silent, and her eyes stare intensely through the purple mask.

"Who are you? Be honest with me for once," he says.

"I am not Jenna."

Lifting his glass to the sky Benjamin says, "Thank you for being honest with me. Where is she?"

"I'm not sure." She takes a straw out of her tote and drinks the wine through it.

Weird. Should I insist she take the mask off? No, I don't care.

"How do you know her?" he asks.

The Immortal's Secret

"We met in Istanbul. She lived in my building. She was a student when I met her, so good and sweet. I didn't understand anything about this world. I was so lost. I modelled myself on her. She was there for me. Many kind people came to my assistance as well as opportunists who would do anything for money. I had money."

"Where did you get the money?"

"I sold things."

"What kind of things."

"Valuable things that I'd rather not say. When you are in my situation, you are trying to survive. Money can buy you anything. Just like in my time. Some things never change."

"Are you the woman I saw in the church in Istanbul?" says Benjamin.

"Yes, when I saw you, I instantly had a connection to you. I can't explain it. I think it's the golden book."

"What do you mean?"

"There are many things I can't explain, Benjamin. The book is mysterious. Annacletica didn't even understand it. Just recently, I had a vision that you were in a chapel with the plague sufferers. I've been having similar visions since that first day Annacletica gave me a plate from the book and told me to pray on it. It's like I'm connected to some of the people who prayed on the book," she says.

"When was that?"

"A very long time ago. Your grandfather released me from my sarcophagus, my solution to this torture of being immortal. I had to take on a new identify because no one would believe who I am."

"I saw you in my hallucination. You resembled Andrea Sartore's mother, Vittoria."

She says, "People look like people. She resembled me. She wasn't me. I know nothing about her. I did not get out of the sarcophagus until your grandfather opened it. My goal has always been to find the golden book and pray on it again. End this constant life. I took the book from you but I was going to give it back. I had one moment with Annacletica that cursed my life. I cannot forgive her. You are searching for Josiah, yes?"

"Yes, how did you know that?" says Benjamin.

"He is at the monastery. One of the monks told me."

"How can I be sure you're telling the truth?"

"This was taken by one of the monks."

She shows him a photo of Josiah in a tiny bed with grey blankets. It's from a phone and is date stamped.

"At some point, I didn't want to live a life of wandering. My sisters placed me in the sarcophagus with my husband, Marcian. I thought it would kill me. I awoke when Josiah opened the chapel."

Benjamin looks at his own phone and sees he doesn't have a lot of time before he has to meet Cle to catch their plane to the Sinai. He wants to get this woman into a vulnerable state. He stands up and starts shedding his clothes, beginning with his shirt, to entice her to follow his lead. He has a surprise in his pocket for her. He throws his shirt on the sofa and begins unzipping his jeans.

"Right here?" she says.

He says, "Okay, this is good a place as any."

She begins extending her arms behind her back to unzip her purple dress and he says, "Let me help you." He slips a syringe out of his pants pocket, one he brought just in case. It's time for him to turn the table on doing the drugging. He shimmies the dress down and when it slides down to her thigh, he jabs the syringe into her skin like a dagger.

"Benjamin, whaaaat are you dooooing?"

With one big flop, the top half of her body is splayed on the sofa and her legs are on the floor. He looks at her perfectly-applied make-up and toned body.

He lifts her legs onto the sofa and places her head on the furry orange pillow that Jenna purchased. He picks up her wine glass and places the straw on the coffee table as he slides down on the leather chair across from her and takes a swig from her glass. He can't believe what he sees. It's the necklace—ten strands of thin gold. She is wearing it. It is twisted and has fallen over her right shoulder.

If one plate were melted down, would it only create a necklace?

The clasp is small and he fiddles to open it. Frustrated, he twists the clasp with his teeth and pulls the necklace off her neck.

She moans. He pushes her over and sits at the edge of the sofa beside her. Lifting the necklace to the light, he examines it like it's an exquisite jewel under a loupe.

Could this have come from the plate?

Benjamin feels she must have created other items with the plate.

Who hid the golden book in the portrait? If she did it, why? Was she hiding it from the authorities? How did she lose the portrait?

The Immortal's Secret

So many questions, and he's not sure he needs or wants to know the answers. Could Josiah be hiding at the monastery? Call it instinct but he feels she's telling the truth. He just wants to help Cle and to find his grandfather.

He yanks Paeon's purse towards him by looping his leather shoe through the long handle. There is a stack of Euros on top and he fans it. There must be 3000 Euros. Under the bills is a paper folder with a stack of news clippings about Josiah.

He snaps open her wallet. She has a Canadian birth certificate that says Jenna Parrish. Born February 25, 1979. There is another piece of ID. It's an Italian birth certificate that says Maria Branzino born July 3, 1982.

The purse also contains a curio with a photo of a young man who looks like Sartore. Inside a side pocket he finds the fake golden book. Surprisingly he finds a smartphone. A clunky flip phone was Jenna's device of choice when she was with him. He stares at the home screen of the phone. It's a photo of him and Jenna at the summit of the Eiffel Tower. Why would Paeon have photos of them?

There's another folder on the phone, this one labelled "Benjamin". It contains hundreds of emails.

Why would Paeon have a smart phone, and why would she have my emails?

It looks like every email he sent Jenna is there. Paeon must know all about their affair. For a moment, he considers deleting them all. Removing all traces of him. Yet, at the same time, he can't fool himself that he isn't a little elated that she kept all of their emails. It's a sentiment that he likes.

Maybe I made a mark—got under her skin. Interesting... or just plain weird?

He unzips the pocket at the side of her purse. Inside is a small notebook with Jenna's name and phone number on the front page. The notebook documents their time together. There are sketches of him sleeping, receipts from times they spent together, photos, poems, and a pregnancy test. It is negative.

Maybe she stole Jenna's purse?

He stares at her like she one of his favourite portraits in the Louvre. Such a perfect silhouette sprawled out on the sofa. Like Giorgione's Sleeping Venus. She is sleeping so peacefully.

He places his hand on Paeon's chest and concentrates on her breathing. He jumps when she moans.

He put her down on the floor and gives her a little more medication. When she is breathing softly, he picks her up from the floor and walks up the stairs to the bedroom.

His plan: when he leaves, he'll lock Paeon in the room and he'll have his friend Tomas, who manages the palazzo, let her out. Once he and Grace are thousands of miles away in the Sinai, she is no threat.

He places Paeon on the king-size bed and surrounds her with Jenna's round, velvet, pastel throw pillows.

Has anyone been on this bed since I left a few years ago?

As he's about to leave, he looks over at Paeon covered by her elaborate mask and is tempted to have one last look at her exquisite face.

He sits beside her and examines her. Such a tiny woman who is breathing so deeply with her chest pushing up to get air in. He brushes her hair away from her face and begins unwrapping the mask. It's stuck in her hair with hairspray but he's able to pull it away easily from her ears.

He steps back, shocked by who is lying in front of him.

He falls and lands on a few of the pillows he threw on the floor. He can't believe it and moves closer to examine her face. It's her, no doubt in his mind. He traces his fingers over her face. She's back in the room where he saw her last, so vulnerable and helpless. He kisses her and sits with her examining every detail of the women or fantasy that he loved.

This makes no sense but I don't care. I'm moving forward.

He pulls out his phone from his pocket and dials Tomas's number.

"Could you come over to my place? Jenna has returned and won't go. Could you stay with her until she's ready to leave?"

He gets up, turns off the lights, and locks the bedroom door. Standing beside the door, he feels incapable of moving. He wants to go back and kiss her again. No, he must keep his promise to Cle and find his grandfather.

Chapter 21

The Chapel of Hope

March 5, 2017
The South Sinai, Egypt

Benjamin and Cle are sitting together on the bed in Cle's room. Cle eats a cookie with some cold mint tea. She hasn't eaten anything else and couldn't be tempted to eat the bread and cheeses he brought for her from the feast that somehow arrived in his palazzo. He is dreading the long journey and wishes she would share how she's feeling.

"Did you get the plate or necklace or whatever Paeon created?"

"I did. She makes me nervous, Cle. She is an unhinged woman. Was she one of the first people you tried to cure?"

"That day at the chasm I met her. She was desperate. I helped her. Evil forces wanted to steal my book. Mai and I had to escape. Whatever she says about me is fabricated. Grace probably told you about people she paid who were trying to find the book."

"She did."

"Benjamin we've got to put an end to all of this."

He squeezes her hand.

In a few hours, they're flying to Sharm el-Sheikh in Egypt in a chartered plane arranged by one of Josiah's business colleagues. From there, they'll travel the last seventy-five kilometers through the desert in a private car the colleague ordered to drive them to The Sacred Sinai Desert Monastery. The Chapel of Hope is a five-minute drive from the monastery, according to Cle. In his carry-on Benjamin packed two long, white robes suggested by Cle and procured online.

"You'll thank me when we get there," Cle had said the night before, when the robes arrived wrapped in white tissue paper and plastic.

The golden book and the items from Jenna's purse are also in his carry-on. *The Immortal* is in a special case.

Now, he's staring at Cle as she's sitting with her eyes closed, rubbing her hands together.

"How are you feeling?"

"I'm getting tired," she says without opening her eyes.

"No, I mean how are you feeling about the journey...about the reason you're going? Do we need to do this?"

"Yes, I have to, Benjamin."

"What if I hide the golden book so you can't?"

She opens her eyes. "I must, Benjamin. I've run out of options. Promise me you will help me do this. You've saved me and I have to put an end to this."

He doesn't say anything.

"I promise," he says. He leans in and kisses her softly on the cheek.

She traces her finger over where he touched her.

"What a surprise."

"Was that okay? Should I not have done that?"

"No, it was lovely. Thank you. You're a good person, Benjamin. You just need to convince yourself of that. We should go." She stands up, tips back onto the bed, slides down the bed spread, and lands on the floor. The cookie Benjamin had spiked was kicking in.

Benjamin joins her on the floor. She mumbles something and digs her head into a pillow that fell on the floor.

I could abort all of this. No, it's unthinkable. For once, I have to put someone's needs before mine and help someone.

He misses Grace already. They had agreed it was best for her to remain in Venice for a day or two on the off chance Josiah returns.

He lifts Cle up and gently sits her on the side of the bed.

The Immortal's Secret

"Cle, do you think you can walk to the dock to get the water taxi?"

"I can walk."

She stands up, staggers to the door, and pushes her face into the door frame. He leaps towards her and grabs her purple backpack, swinging it around his shoulder. Just as she is about to grab his luggage, he notices an 8.5X10-inch manila envelope that was hidden underneath her backpack. On the front of the envelope is written on a Post-it, "Benjamin, please don't read this until I'm fast asleep." He stares at the words that are exquisitely written in a quill pen. He tucks the envelope into the backpack in between Cle's belongings.

When they're sitting in the departure lounge, with her head leaning on his shoulder and strands of her hair grazing his lips, he unzips her backpack. He twists open the clasp of the manila envelope. Inside is another Post-it on top of about ten 8.5X10-inch sheets of lined paper. The writing on the Post-it says, "I felt compelled to share my history with you Benjamin. Let me tell you my story of how our golden book was created so you understand my life."

He turns over the first page. The text is written in her elegant hand.

The year was AD 590. I first rode into the monastery on a donkey behind Father Roberto Sartore. He found me in the desert, almost dead. I heard his voice as he lifted me from the sand onto his donkey.

When we arrived, the monks peered at me through their hoods. A woman had never stepped on their holy ground and my presence created a slight commotion in a place where commotion was not welcome. Their rules relating to hosting visitors only applied to men. What to do with me required hours of anxious negotiation with Abbot Fredrico and Father Roberto as I waited in a small ossuary chapel beside the monastery gates.

For five hours, I lay in pain in front of the altar on a wooden bench. The spectacular golden iconostasis burnt like fire under the afternoon sun stretching out across the tiny altar, a five-foot screen of gold climbing almost to the ceiling. Yet I was oblivious to the beauty surrounding me.

My eyes were fixated on a glass case full of human skulls. Hundreds of them. It was the monastery's ossuary but I didn't know that yet. I had no idea that bodies couldn't be properly buried in desert sand. It made perfect sense, but death was not something I ever dwelled on. My terror of the skulls made me forget my pain and the stream of blood dribbling down my leg.

Slightly before midnight, Father Roberto arrived and sat down beside me on the bench. His face had a golden glow under the candlelight but his eyes were red and heavy. Slowly taking out a small loaf of bread from under his cloak, he ripped off a piece and placed it in my hand. I bit into it. It was the most delicious bread I'd ever eaten.

I sat up and the pain returned like hundreds of daggers pricking my skin. With his finger, he tipped my chin towards him. A wave of my auburn hair tumbled out of my hood and I pushed it away from my face.

"I made a pledge to keep you far away from the monks," he told me. "I will be your protector. My brothers are not comfortable in the presence of women, particularly a young woman and especially one of immense beauty. We must follow the rules, Annacletica, or they will cast both of us away."

My mind was focusing on the word protector. I had wandered for years, moving from town to town in Egypt, making no deep connections with anyone. Now I had a protector. It was the most wondrous word.

Father Roberto guided me down a long dark quiet corridor to the guest wing of the monastery. It was furnished with a straw bed, a table, a vase of dry desert flowers, a chair, a wash basin, a Bible, and some blankets neatly stacked in the corner. It was the most beautiful room I'd ever seen. It had precious walls that were going to protect me. And they did for hundreds of years. I was clearly the only guest.

Neither of us said a word as he cleaned and bound my wounds.

"Sleep well, my desert angel," he told me with such a precious smile as he lit the small candle on the table and walked out with his candelabra.

I was alone. Surrounded by silence, darkness, and the eerily mesmerizing sounds of night in the desert. I snuggled into the blankets and caressed my golden book. Everything else I owned was packed in a small bag that was lost in the last desert storm. All I had left was what was hidden in my robe: the golden book and my signet wedding ring from Mai.

When the sun rose, I walked over to the window and was greeted by the most spectacular view of Mount Sinai. On those first few mornings, I sat at the window and watched the sun crest over its highest point while listening to the joyful sound of streaked scrub warblers. I started waking up early so I could stretch out this extraordinary moment. The only word I could think to describe it was holy, which is not a word I'd ever used.

After convalescing in my room for a week, I felt more energetic and much more hopeful than I had in years, all due to the kindness of Father Roberto, who delivered me broth every day, bread he made himself, and some delicious hard candies that I wondered where he had procured in the desert. When I felt well enough to explore, I started accompanying Father Roberto on his daily one-hour walk as he wandered in the desert to gather wood and anything edible he could find. He guided me on a geriatric donkey while he rode an even older one. My donkey's name was Job and his was Bildad.

An exceptionally strong and masculine man, Father Roberto was eager to surrender to my whims, like a father fascinated by his child. It amused me since he was not much older than I looked. He loved the hours he spent in the open every day, exploring the barren desert terrain, picking up rocks with his large hands, and examining them like they were gold. He was from a place called Veneti in the Roman Empire on the Adriatic Sea. He missed the water and was always in search of some elusive well. He could not be convinced one was not beyond the next hill.

We spent so much time together, yet that was all he divulged about his former life. He never probed into my background to inquire why I was in the desert alone.

The monks adhered to a strict schedule. They only spoke at certain times during the day and never to me. If they communicated at other times, it was by hand signals, like touching hands or a tap on the shoulder. Some of them refused to communicate at all.

They prayed every three hours: Matins (nighttime), Lauds (early morning), Prime (first hour of daylight), Terce (third hour), Sext (noon), Nones (ninth hour), Vespers (sunset evening) and Compline (end of day). Their singing and chanting filled the air and made my skin tingle like the heavens had flung wide open.

Between prayers, I liked to sneak into their Church of the Transformation, lay down on the marble floor, and stare at the golden ceiling and the icons representing the story of Christ's birth. They fascinated me. The icons and the monks' practices were so different from my pagan rituals in Egypt.

When I wasn't in the chapel, I spent time in a hidden area of the library reading the most coveted Bible in the collection. It had arrived many years before me, delivered by a holy man whose name was never recorded. I spent hours studying the passages, pondering what I read when I lay down at night, surrounded by the darkness, and caressed by the desert air and the silence. On our walks, Father Roberto tested my knowledge of this Psalm, or that verse or passage.

This was my beautiful journey to Christianity. The miracle of the scripture was developing my mind. Silence was going to transform me. It defined life at the monastery. It was the shroud that hung over the monastery separating it from the outside world. It was their shield. I had never noticed silence before. During my first weeks at the monastery, it had become like a wild beast that followed me everywhere.

At first, I rejected the silence. It made me anxious. I wanted no part of silence. The sound of my voice was my only lifeline to my former life. Eventually I realized I must try to conform, but it was torturous. It was like I had become possessed by the regular noises of my daily life as they charged through my mind, trying to fight the silence, demanding an outlet. I talked to myself and danced and sang to the birds, to the sky. When the silence became unbearable, I ran into the desert and screamed until I couldn't talk.

One day I woke up from this constant exhaustion, watched my sunrise, and disappeared into the sounds of nature. Everything was different. I felt at one with the sounds of the desert that were amplified from heaven. They caressed my soul. I felt their splendour.

When one is forced to break down the noise of regular life, a whole new life opens up. I noticed everything: sounds, smells, touch. The wind became like beautiful music, and rustling leaves were like a mother's soothing voice. I felt a part of nature, like I was one with the ground I was walking on. Silence became a huge part of my life. It was fascinating and soothing, like a drug; it was my new friend, a gentle lover.

It delivered immense clarity of thought, like a strong wind arrived and sent all the clutter flying from my mind. My favourite pastime was sitting in the small garden near my room, where I concentrated on nature and watched the rhythms of natural life, like a spider crawling on a rock or a Sinai baton blue butterfly flitting around me like a graceful dancer.

I was at peace, but not entirely. Some thoughts were not purged. They only became clearer. The need to make my decision was one of them. When Father Roberto found me in the desert, I was there for one reason: to make an appeal to God, similar to what I am doing now.

In July of AD 590, lying in the desert sand, feeling like death but unable to die, I lifted my head and rolled onto my side to gently slide my golden book out from the secret pocket I created in my white robe.

That day, a voice said, "Take the book back to the sanctuary, let the fumes of the chasm destroy it, and pray for your soul. Or return to the sanctuary and The Gods of the Desert and cleanse your soul by making the magic in the book holy and use it to cure others of disease and give them hope."

I knew where there was a Chapel of Hope. It was so close to the monastery. I had gone there with my husband, Mai, hundreds of years before. It was where the golden book was infused with its magic.

When I reached my second month at the monastery, I knew I had to find this Chapel of Hope and make my choice. Sext was the busiest time in the monastery, and I knew I could sneak out when Father Roberto was busy leading prayers. Holding my golden book to my chest, every day I searched for the chapel until one day I finally spied the tiny spire. I was back.

I was frightened to move closer to The Chapel of Hope; it held so many powerful memories. But it also housed a mystic energy. It pulled me. I staggered over on legs weakened from heat and stress.

The Chapel of Hope was badly weather worn, much different than I remembered. It was stripped of all its carvings created from the exquisite gold and silver from all around the world that visitors would offer the Gods as gifts. I stood on what used to be The Chapel of Hope steps, now a mound of dust and rocks.

Treading carefully until I reached the front of the entrance, holding onto the door, my fingers shaking, I scanned what was left. The Chapel of Hope was packed with so many people the day long ago when I arrived with Mai. The stone benches where we once sat were still there. They were quite worn from use but were well-protected from the elements outside. I remember we were holding hands so tightly.

I sat down and examined what used to be called The Gold Altar but it really wasn't an altar; it was more like a pagan abattoir. Every visitor was required to burn a live sacrifice at the altar and offer it to the Gods. Mai and I burnt something, but I can't remember what it was. The altar was now crumbling stone with speckles of gold.

I raced out of The Chapel of Hope because I couldn't bear to think of that day, which changed my life and turned me into a modern-day Tithonus. I staggered down the slate stairs leading from The Chapel of Hope to the chasm and sanctuary, holding my golden book securely.

When I got to the bottom, I could see the chasm and the steam rising. I pushed the golden book to my chest. My fingers started to tingle and the sensation began zigzagging through my body in waves, I wondered if it was the heat. I collapsed onto the ground and stared at the rising steam. It had a hypnotic effect.

Memories of my life started skipping around in my mind, a collage of images floating in and out. I was there for hours just thinking.

I thought about that day when we travelled to Mount Sinai, to the chapel and the sanctuary, with our golden book to consult The Gods of the Desert. Our interpreter, the Pythia, offered the promise of unanswered questions. Family legend said relatives travelled there and had success.

I was practicing how I would pose the question to the Pythia as she sat perched at the side of the chasm, her body washed in the steam. When it was my turn, I blurted out ineloquently, "How do I achieve the quintessence—attain immortality—with our golden book, slip off the path of life that leads to a final destination, and join one that is beautiful, circular, endless?"

The Immortal's Secret

The silence was long. It hurt. Mai squeezed my hand. The Pythia finally spoke: "Make the pledge. Carve your image in your golden book in a holy place, light the candles, burn the incense, and make a wish to have immortality. This is the quintessence."

That was it.

We went back up to The Chapel of Hope and I did as instructed. Paeon and her husband Marcian were there that day with the Pythia also seeking help. Paeon was ill. They watched me make the pledge. After making it, I felt so different but we weren't entirely sure if it worked. Mai wanted to wait until we were home in Alexandria to carve his image in the book.

Evil forces were watching us that day. We had to escape or risk death and we were powerless to help Paeon and Marcian. I gave them one of the plates.

When we returned home after infusing the book with the magic, a strange sickness gripped Alexandria. Confusion was everywhere. Bodies were piling up on the streets. We were horrified by the people we saw, like monsters with huge growths called buboes on their skin. My parents confined themselves to their luxurious home. One morning when I awoke, my mother was examining my father's skin. He had suppurating sores on his groin. The same strange sores that terrified everyone. My mother placed salve on them and tried to drain them. I tried to get him to make the pledge but he was too weak and delirious. In three days, he was gone. My mother was inconsolable, and she died not long after.

I insisted Mai make the pledge. It was too late. He collapsed lifeless in my arms, in our sprawling garden near his favourite tree, a sycamore fig. I refused to contact anyone. I was prepared to die beside him.

Days passed; my mother-in-law arrived and uncurled my fingers from his. I was so very thin and she made me eat meat and fowl for months until the risk of the strange sickness was over in our community. Separation from Mai was out of the question. He would not be buried. I would not allow it. I would use the golden book to bring him back. He was decomposing and I was oblivious.

Mai's mother insisted on following custom and mummifying him and placing him in the family tomb. I protested, erupting in emotion, and collapsed. They took his mummy to the funeral; I refused to attend. It was nightfall and I snuck off into the desert intent on never being found.

Why, upon my return to The Chapel of Hope, was I thinking of this horrendous moment? My vision was blurry from my tears and the vapours from the chasm were rising into my nose. I stood up and peered down but I couldn't see anything through the mist. I was so tempted to keep walking forward. I would be free…I thought. I was never sure if I could die and was too afraid to test this possibility out.

The fumes were rising and enveloping me. They were like a wonderful narcotic, soothing me, lifting me up. As I contemplated this fate, I heard a voice. It was as clear as a bell. It sounded like the Pythia.

"Annacletica, you are back here at The Gods of the Desert Sanctuary. You now have two choices: are you going to let the fumes of this chasm destroy your unholy book and pray for your soul? Or are you going to cleanse your soul by making the magic in the book holy by placing it at The Chapel of Hope and giving those who suffer one wish, their heart's desire: hope?"

I felt something touch me. I thought it was another vision. A large hand was around my waist. I was moving; the hand was dragging me onto the ground, safely away from the edge of the chasm. I fell onto the soft soil and looked up. Father Roberto was beside me, out of breath, his eyes drowning in tears. I wondered if he was real and then he spoke.

"I thought you were going to jump. You terrified me."

I waited a while before speaking, to familiarize myself with reality again.

"I am so sorry I frightened you. I wasn't going to jump. I was curious."

I touched his hand. I had never seen him so upset and it hurt me so. I wanted to collapse in his arms. My feelings confused me. I wasn't sure if it was romantic love or like the love for a father.

"You are alright?" he said struggling to form words. He stared at me.

"I am fine."

He placed his hand on mine and my body reacted in a way that could only be described as sexual.

"Please don't come here again. It's dangerous. I was looking for you. Abbot Fredrico has taken ill. We feel death may be near."

I stood up and placed both of my hands to my mouth.

"I am so sorry to hear this. We need to get back."

We walked back swiftly to the monastery in silence. When we arrived, he guided me to my room and held the door open. I thought he was gone when he came back into the room, startling me.

"Annacletica, what were you doing at that chasm?"

I told him, "I don't know. I wandered there when I was walking. I think I got confused about the way back."

He stared at his hands folded in front of him, waiting for me to say more. He grabbed his hair and scrunched it with his fingers.

"Alright. Please stay here. I must leave to help the other brothers."

I lay down on the bed and pressed my golden book to my chest.

I closed my eyes and whispered, "I will do what you instructed. I will do good with this book."

When I opened my eyes, Father Roberto was standing in front of me bathed in sweat. He sat on the bed with me and stared at the wall. Finally, he spoke.

"What happened today?" he said softly, turning to look me in the eyes. "You are different. You have a radiant aura like our Abbot Fredrico has after fasting and praying for days."

"I was just exploring, like I explained," *I said.*

"I followed you down. I saw you on the edge. I thought you were going to jump." *There was a slight quiver in his voice. I noticed that the large hands of my protector were shaking.* "I called your name and leapt towards you, but I couldn't get near you. It was like something was holding me back. I heard a voice talking to you. Something happened to you down there."

I stared at this kind man and questioned myself for holding back since he believed in me so deeply. I trusted him completely. My emotions were confusing me.

"Who are you, Annacletica? You never told me what you were doing alone in the desert when I found you."

"I got lost in the desert. There isn't anything to tell. It was that simple." *In desperation I was hoping he wouldn't ask for elaboration. He opened his lips to say something, and I closed his lips gently with my finger.*

"Father Roberto, is Abbot Fredrico really dying?"

"Yes, we feel he is on his deathbed. A deep sickness has overtaken him. I really must get back to pray with the other brothers."

"Could I take my golden book and have him pray with us? I think I could help him."

"Why on earth do you think that?"

"If he's close to death, I would like to try and help. I will stay in the background so he can't see me."

Father Roberto paused, stood up, and stared at the ground while he dug his shoes into the wooden floor.

"That day you found me in the desert, I had a vision. A voice told me I must reform my soul by making the book's quintessence holy and using it to help others. Today that voice spoke to me again. Let me do this. Please. For you."

Father Roberto walked to the door and held the handle like he'd forgotten how to open it.

"Why is the book magic? Is it part of a pagan ritual?"

"No, I created it and I need to make it holy. My soul is lost."

"You created it? Were you trying to do something unholy?"

"No, I created it out of love. My husband and I were misguided. We didn't believe in Egyptian immortality. We wanted to create our own immortality and die together so we would never be apart. I now realize immortality is a curse."

Without turning around, he said, "Follow me, Annacletica, but don't let anyone see you."

Abbot Fredrico's chambers were dimly lit from a few small candles. The room smelled like lavender oil. Wearing a monk's habit, I slipped into the room, pulled the hood down over my face, and hid beside the large wooden door. Abbot Fredrico's bed was circled by at least ten monks, all deep in prayer. Despite laboured breathing, he was sleeping.

Father Roberto walked up as I instructed and took Abbot Fredrico's hand. He whispered something in Abbot Fredrico's ear and placed the Abbot's hand on the book. Barely conscience, the Abbot attempted to look up at Father Roberto as he recited Psalm 20 as I suggested. It was one he had been reciting to give me strength during these confusing days.

Abbot Fredrico was weak; he was only able to hold his head up slightly and recite only a few of the lines slowly in unison with Father Roberto:

> The LORD hear thee in the day of trouble; the name of the God of Jacob defend thee;

> Send thee help from the sanctuary, and strengthen thee out of Zion;

> Remember all thy offerings, and accept thy burnt sacrifice; Selah.

> Grant thee according to thine own heart, and fulfill all thy counsel.

> We will rejoice in thy salvation, and in the name of our God we will set up our banners: the LORD fulfill all thy petitions.

> Now know I that the LORD saveth his anointed; he will hear him from his holy heaven with the saving strength of his right hand.

> Some trust in chariots, and some in horses: but we will remember the name of the LORD our God.

They are brought down and fallen: but we are risen, and stand upright.

Save, LORD: let the king hear us when we call.

When they reached the last lines, the rest of the monks raised their heads from their quiet prayers and joined in. When they were finished, Father Roberto kissed the Abbot's forehead and rested his hand on top of the Abbot's hand on the book. He stayed all night, surrounded by the other monks, while I slept quietly in the corner out of view.

When I woke in the morning, Abbot Fredrico took some drops of water from Father Roberto's fingers. Each day forward brought some hope: some colour in his cheeks, a smile, a deep laugh, a small meal, until he fully recovered exactly one month later.

Father Roberto told Abbot Fredrico what had happened and the Abbot insisted the monks suspend their spiritual duties to focus on restoring the chapel. They donated the iconostasis from the ossuary chapel to create the focal point of the improved chapel, and they took some of the gold from The Church of the Transformation and fashioned gold leaf for the roof. The chapel was expanded to create a small living quarter in the back for me.

When their work was finished, I was dazzled by how it looked. More beautiful than the original. We conducted a mass, christened it the new Chapel of Hope, and placed the book at the altar. I prayed the needy would come so I could fulfill my mission. The monks were so devoted to me and set up a schedule to bring me food and water daily.

Pilgrims trickled in from the surrounding area and eventually from further afield, each one suffering from various levels of sickness. I sat with them, prayed with them, and pressed their hands to the book. Word spread about the miracle chapel and my reputation grew as a Desert Mother who could provide hope to the needy.

One sunny day, a creature arrived in regal glory in a procession of chariots that lit up the desert sand like an overflowing treasure chest. The procession stopped not far from the chapel and I could not take my eyes off the magnificent camel chariot at the front, with a canopy made of thick gold cloth. An army of servants swarmed the chariot to help the occupants. Three elegant ladies-in-waiting draped in silk opened the golden flap and took the hand of an emaciated creature floating in gorgeous purple vestments. The creature's face was covered in a veil.

The sight was most astonishing, as her giant male servants carried the ghoulish human towards us. The body looked like a decomposing corpse.

I have always been guided by my instinct and I knew these visitors did not come in peace. The peculiar visitors spoke Greek to one another, a language I had not spoken in many years. Even when I did speak it, I didn't speak it well.

Father Roberto moved forward to help carry the ghoul, and the biggest guard raised his large hand to warn Father to keep his distance. The guard looked straight at me and said in Egyptian, "We have heard you are a woman with special powers to heal. This is Empress Paeon of the Eastern Roman Empire. God is calling her. You must help. Her people need her. She is their pious and giving angel."

I felt I was looking in a mirror. Another human ravaged by the desert, the sand, and the storms of this gentle yet brutal landscape. This empress had transformed into the same bashed up shell that I had become. Both of us had been drawn to this terrain in pursuit of hope, which was now years ago for me. She reminded me of Paeon, who would be a relation.

I guided them gently to the chapel and the guard placed the empress on the altar.

Once she was positioned, I moved forward and asked her, "May I take your hand and we can pray together, your Imperial Majesty?"

The large brute moved in, grabbed my tiny hand, and screamed, "You cannot touch our empress!"

Paeon scolded him softly, "No...step back."

I told the empress that Father Roberto was the holy man of this chapel and must be present for the healing to be successful. After I gave her thugs a look, they instantly relented. Father Roberto came to the front to stand beside me and the empress.

She turned to me, nodded her head slowly like it was a dead weight, and stared at me with eyes that looked like they'd been hollowed out. I gently lifted up her claw of a hand and placed her fingers through mine. Father

Roberto burnt the incense and lit the candles to create the environment we needed for healing.

"Your Imperial Majesty please say, 'I appeal to the quintessence in this golden book to heal me.'" She did as I instructed and smiled at me.

Everyone watched in silence. The chapel was so still and quiet. Nothing happened. Father Roberto coughed. I recited Psalm 20 aloud.

As the empress tumbled over onto the altar, I attempted to hold her up. The brutes leapt in like savages to push me aside.

"She must be healed. Heal her," they ordered me. I stared at them and my body turned cold, stone cold in a matter of seconds. Father Roberto raced over to shield me from them with his giant arms. As the rest of the empress's entourage charged in, Father Roberto carried me down the side aisle to the back of the chapel to avoid them.

Someone yelled, "The empress is fading! Her pulse is so weak, and I think she is gone."

Everyone watched in horror as one of the smaller and shorter brutes snatched the book from the altar, separating it from the thicker back plate, creating a horrible cracking sound. Pushing the throng aside, he ran out of the chapel.

Father Roberto and I raced after him as he flew down the slate stairs at the side of the chapel, skillfully taking them two at a time. When the brute arrived at the edge of huge chasm, he looked over and paused to catch his breath. He spotted me and said, while shaking the book like it was as thin as a pamphlet, "You must heal our empress or I will throw this work of trickery into this chasm."

Tiptoeing towards him, I said softly, "I am trying to help your blessed empress. The healing does not happen immediately."

He countered, "We were told from those who came here that it does. You are lying."

Father Roberto appealed to him. "Sir, please give me the book. You cannot destroy it. I beg to you to stop. It has helped so many desperate sick people."

The Immortal's Secret

The other brute appeared from behind me and thrust his huge hands inches from my tiny neck. "Heal her now! Heal her now!" he screeched.

The eruption triggered a crackling sound at the side of the chasm and the walls started crumbling. The opening sucked both brutes downwards, pulling them into the mist with my golden book. Horrified, I moved forward and stopped as soon as I realized the side wall was vanishing like quicksand.

Father Roberto followed me and said, "Annacletica, no!" He grabbed me gently. When I was safe, he bound me in his arms. There was a gurgling noise. The mist became so thick it created a shroud over the entire opening. I dove to my knees, started to weep, and put my hands together to pray. Just as I did this, my book came floating up like a beautiful bird, billowing above the opening of the chasm. It landed gently at my feet.

Father Roberto picked it up and handed it to me. I took it and pressed it to my chest like a newborn as I wept on the cover and struggled to catch my breath.

Father Roberto tapped me and pointed. As we both stood up and looked down into the chasm, the mist started to dissipate. The side of the chasm where the two men were pulled down seemed to fall back into place like nothing had ever happened. It was extraordinary.

We stared at one another and then hugged tightly.

"Annacletica, I am afraid. These people are dangerous. They are courting danger. We almost lost your healing book. They must leave."

"We have to heal her."

When we arrived back at the chapel, one of the empress's ladies-in-waiting was holding the empress's talon of a hand up to where the golden book had been before the brutes snapped it off the wall. The lady was praying with the empress softly in her language and the empress was following along. I moved over to them and said, "Shall I place the healing prayer book back in its place?"

For three days, the ladies remained glued to the altar, praying continually, working through Psalm 20, reciting it quietly and then loudly, trying every tone to make their plea. On the third day, the empress rose and her ladies began wailing. They held her up, babbling to her in their own language, and wobbled over with her to one of the pews. There, they all sat staring at the door.

They were singing and chanting and saying prayers so jubilantly. The empress pushed her hands on the front of the pew and her ladies leapt towards her. She motioned for them to stop. With everyone watching, she stood slowly, holding the pew, and staggered to the door with her holy man, the Patriarch of Constantinople, following behind, ready with his hands up to provide protection.

When she arrived at the door, she stopped and raised her hands in prayer. Father Roberto and I came up behind her and I heard her say, "I am healed. My child Annacletica has healed me."

She turned around, saw me, and extended her hand for me to join her.

"I thank you, dear woman. The people of Constantinople thank you."

Her hand was so cold, like a tiny block of ice. I placed both of my hands on top of it and rubbed it gently. Everyone watched, waiting for the empress's reaction. She bent down and everyone lunged forward but she s firm. Her lips landed on my hand, and she kissed it ever so gently.

I guided her to the back of the chapel, where tiny opulent living quarters for guests were located. Everything was decorated in gold and silver—gifts the pilgrims brought over the five years since we built it. Father Roberto and I lived in our separate rooms beside them. Our rooms here were as humble as our rooms at the monastery with a bed, chair, and small window looking towards the stairs and leading to the chasm.

The ladies-in-waiting placed the empress gently on the bed with a purple and gold velvet cover and fussed until she was comfortable. I made them some mint tea, which was the most opulent gift I could present. Father Roberto grew the mint in my little garden beside the chapel.

With every day, she got a little better, eating a bit more of the food Father Roberto prepared in the monastery. More people arrived in golden carriages, turning the chapel into a palace with a small court. There were more brutes, bigger ones who guarded the chapel.

The Immortal's Secret

Early one morning, Father Roberto and I came into the chapel. The Patriarch of Constantinople was about to begin a service and motioned to us to take seats at the front of the altar. Something was at the front of the room covered in a golden cloth. The patriarch lifted the gold cloth to reveal a portrait of a woman. Father Roberto squeezed my hand.

It was me. Benjamin, your portrait was created by them. The artist is unknown. Their original was perfected by Andrea. He turned it into his own version.

The empress stood, looking healthy with pink cheeks, shockingly beautiful. The transformation was astounding. She was dressed in a long silk crimson dress. I'd met her before.

The empress said, "I created an icon to venerate you, blessed holy lady." The patriarch placed the portrait at her feet and she said, "You saved my life, and this is my glorious gift to you, to immortalize you. We melted some of your gold from your book for your face. We are bringing you to Constantinople, where you will be revered as my holy woman.

"Do you not remember me? I met you in this sanctuary many years ago. You gave me one of the golden plates, and it made me immortal but I continued to age. You have saved me."

I nodded my head and extended my thanks to her and her people. Father Roberto watched me. I didn't know what to say. If this was the Paon she would have been hundreds of years old.

When Father Roberto and I were finally outside of the chapel away from the court, I fell down and wept with my head in the sand. I kept saying, "They melted some of the gold. They did something they should not have done. I know her, Roberto. I met her long ago, right here."

Father Roberto said, "I am concerned, dear Annacletica. There have been many whispered conversations amongst the men who accompanied her. I feel they mean to steal your golden book and use it for their own purposes. I am certain of it. We must stay in the chapel to guard it."

That night, while they were asleep, Father Roberto and I bolted the door to the empress's living quarters. We quietly awoke two of the camels with some food. A vile dull growl coming from one of them startled us but didn't appear to wake anyone. I secured the golden book and portrait from the chapel, gathered them with the few things we both owned, and carefully packed them in a cloth bag. Father Roberto helped me mount my camel.

We rode into the vast expanse of dark with the ominous sounds of adventure and danger embracing us. Our plan was to ride, far away from our home, with no thoughts of where the road would lead us. Father Roberto told me he had always chosen Veneti as our destination. He longed to go back to his home and recreate our chapel there. As we rode, he confessed he had never been ordained. The monks assumed he had when he arrived years ago and never questioned him. A wanderer again, I was thrilled this time to have Father Roberto at my side.

We made it to Veneti and then the marshland, which eventually became Venice. We created our new chapel of hope. It was hidden in the bones years later when they build St. Mark's Basilica. I was so deeply in love with Roberto that I would have stayed forever by his side in my sarcophagus if Andrea had not awoken me. Andrea was an exquisitely talented artist. He improved on the portrait the empress's artist created for me. He called it The Immortal. *He carefully cut down the size of each plate.*

The Immortal *is made from a little piece of all the plates. There's no way to separate it from the book. It must be destroyed. Your multi-million-dollar portrait must be destroyed.*

I must do this, Benjamin. There is no other peace for me. I need to finally have peace. I am counting on your kindness to help me destroy the portrait and the golden book.

Chapter 22

Reaching The Chapel of Hope

March 7, 2017
The Gods of the Desert Sanctuary, The South Sinai, Egypt

Benjamin clutches the paper and stares at Cle. Such a long fascinating journey her life has been. It's now going to end with his help. His is travelling with a portrait and the subject who has come to life, and now both are going to be destroyed.

Cle drifts in and out of her sleep in the private car they are riding in. They are getting close to the monastery. It's so dark. The driver doesn't want to run down the battery by using the headlights. It's therapeutic to look out the window and see nothing. Benjamin feels like he is travelling from one reality to another.

The map to the monastery was drawn out by Cle. But they're bypassing the monastery to go straight to the chasm.

As the sun comes up, Cle sits up and starts nibbling on an energy bar Benjamin bought her in Marco Polo Airport before they left Venice.

"Is this the right direction?" the driver says. He's has been asking this since they left St. Katherine-Nuweibaa Road, the main road, as Benjamin and Cle bounce around in their seats.

"Yes," Cle says. "Can you see the tiny spire?"

He's such a disagreeable man and smells like Polo After Shave and peppermint gum. He's sweated right through his white T-shirt, leaving no traces of dry fabric. He told them his name, but Benjamin instantly forgot it. He keeps taking his eyes off the path to check his cell reception, mumbling something under his breath in his own language. There isn't a bump on the path that he hasn't hit.

Benjamin is so thrilled by how healthy he's feeling. His stomach hasn't reacted to the bumps and he's cruised through the eighteen-hour journey that brought them from Venice to this bumpy path without any nausea, weakness, or pain.

He sees it as they ride over a sand dune: a structure peaking though the sand dust. The chapel from the background of *The Immortal*. It's circled by beautiful huge sand waves that make it look like it's floating.

"This the place?" the driver asks, stopping the vehicle.

"Yes," says Cle as she opens the door. The driver can't whip their bags out of the vehicle fast enough and get back behind the wheel.

"I wait, or you good?" he asks from his window while the car moves away from them.

"We're fine," says Cle looking over at him before Benjamin has a chance to say anything.

Once the car has disappeared, they stand side by side, their belongings surrounding them. They stare at the chapel. Benjamin has never been here before, but this place is familiar. He knows it from his dreams.

In his dreams, the chapel was a small, exquisite building no larger than a garden shed, made of pink granite stones, each one carefully cut as if by the most talented artisan hands.

This chapel is a crumbly block of stone that's been beaten and whipped by sand into a dingy grey colour. There are golden specks on the stone door. The pattern is a Rorschach test except for one area on the top of the door where the golden specs are deeper. Cle says they spell out the word "Hope" in hieroglyphs.

They spy a cross in front of the arched stone door. It's a Roman cross speckled with gold. It's lying vertically, blocking their way like a sentinel. They have to move it to pull the door towards themselves.

"That's ominous," says Cle. "It used to be on top of the spire." She examines it. There is a huge gouge out of the bottom courtesy of the steep drop. "The cross came from the monastery, in their chapel. You should take it back."

"*We* should take it back.

"Probably best you take it back. I don't think anyone will get it back on top of the spire. Someone has to climb up. Most of the monks are elderly. You'll see when you meet them. It's too dangerous now."

The Immortal's Secret

Cle smiles and drags the cross over to him. He backs up and places it inside the case protecting *The Immortal* and the golden book.

"Pull on the door and let's see what we find," says Cle.

Benjamin pulls at a groove carved into the giant stone slab.

They stand in the chapel and Benjamin wipes the sweat from his face with a clean white handkerchief Cle hands him.

Everything in the chapel is beaten down by the years and the air that has slowly seeped in from outside. The scene makes Benjamin think back to the rooms in The Sartore Palace on the island back in Venice. It's so quiet and he can smell faint traces of oleander and frankincense.

"You read my letter, the one in the envelope that I left for you?" Cle asks him.

"Yes," he says.

"Did it answer your questions?"

"It did."

"Did you secure the necklace?"

"I did." He snakes it out of his bag. "Do you think she fashioned the necklace out of the rest of the plate you gave her?"

She takes it from him. "I don't know. I have no choice but to go on blind faith. Can you help me put it on?"

"Certainly." It takes Benjamin a few tries with his huge fingers.

"I hate wearing anything that belonged to her but this is essential. I am ready to make my journey wherever it takes me."

"I'm happy to help you carry on with your journey. There will be no surprises on my end," he says.

They sit on a worn stone pew and share the food Benjamin purchased in Sharm el-Sheikh: shawarma, aish baladi, and a bottle of wine that Benjamin felt was critical given the circumstances. Annacletica eats everything Benjamin puts on her plate and then starts sipping some of the wine he pours into a Styrofoam cup.

"When I was here as a young woman, sitting on these pews with Mai, we were so full of hope. I don't know why we decided to create a golden book to make us immortal. We truly wanted to be together forever. Our heads were full of so many romantic notions. In the Egypt of our time, everyone was always dreaming of the afterlife. We wanted to live life to the fullest in this lifetime."

"What has your life been like?"

"Not unlike anyone else's, I suppose. It's just been long. Moments of sheer joy and sheer pain. I spent a lot of time in deep sleep. When your body doesn't die, there is a desire to fall into a deep sleep. You wake up feeling refreshed at a level that is incomprehensible, but it doesn't last. You're cold and then you're hot. Your heart starts beating alarmingly slow and you think you might not make it through the night. In the morning, you are back to normal. Your skin turns blue then returns to its normal colour. It's like you're continually dying and then being revived.

"What is my legacy for being blessed with this long life? What have I done? Caused a lot of pain. Yet, I have also reduced suffering. It wasn't a natural cure, but it helped a lot of people. Most of them, I never saw again. I heard their stories through others. I think I...." She doesn't say anything for a long time. She just stares ahead.

"When Paeon came to our chapel in the desert when I was with Roberto, she had to be over 200 years old. She wanted the golden book. For what purpose? Perhaps to keep praying on it and gain riches. She has a connection to Vittoria Sartore. Are they the same person? Who knows. I'm certain she has masqueraded as many people. Maybe people you know, people Josiah knew. She was always coming to the desert but the monks protected me. This necklace may have given her more power when it was on her skin, close to her heart...."

Benjamin's eyes are locked on Annacletica as she suddenly stops mid-sentence and begins moving around, surveying the chapel, studying everything, touching various items, lost in her thoughts. She is clutching the golden book to her chest.

He doesn't move from the stone pew. He savours his wine and watches her as his mind drifts off too.

What's happened to him over the past few months? It's been so profound. He could write it off as a glorious drug trip or too much mixing of prescription meds. He doesn't want Annacletica to complete her mission. He wants to leave with her. He is certain he could help her another way. But this is what she wants. For once, he is going to place someone else's needs squarely before his own.

Cle walks over to him, pulling him back to the present. Peering down at him, she pauses, glances at the golden book, looks up, and says carefully, "When we are done here, go find Josiah at the monastery. I am not certain he is alive but recent discussions with some of the monks have given me hope. There are rooms carved into the Sinai, into the rock. They are used as a small hospital. He could be in one of them. Grace will show you." She picks up the golden book and presses it to her chest.

Benjamin feels his stomach tingle. The way it does when he's happy. He wants to run to the monastery. But no, he needs to be here. To stay with Cle, to be with her until the end.

Taking her small hands in his, he asks, "How are you feeling?"

Touching his face with the tips of her fingers, she smiles.

"Content. Very content. And blessed. I am here with you. I was alone last time I came back to the desert and made my appeal. You don't realize it, Benjamin, but I have had many angels who have helped me throughout my lifetime. You are my last angel. You are going to help me move on."

She lets go of his hands and moves to sit down behind him on one of the pews.

"We are both exhausted from the journey. You must be delighted that you brought the robe."

He laughs.

"Yes, it's great travel attire, like walking around in my pajamas." Staring at her, deep in thought, he says, "Cle, I need you to give me a sign. To let me know that you're okay once you have passed."

She looks down and touches her ring, the signet one Mai gave her.

"You have to twirl the ring," she says.

"Yes."

"Do it when you think of me."

She places the ring on his finger and twirls it.

"Okay." He kisses the ring, looks up, places his hand on his heart, and says, "Thank you."

Using his huge backpack as a pillow, he sits and leans back on the pew behind her. It's so uncomfortable. Josiah's wooden box had to be jammed in the backpack; he pulls it out carefully and places it on the dirt floor. Benjamin is looking forward to discussing the paintings with Josiah if he gets to see him.

"Benjamin, one last request."

Without looking at her he says, "Yes, I can't say no to you."

When she doesn't say anything, he sits up and looks over at her. She is holding up half a cookie in the palm of her hand.

"You didn't eat it all?"

"No. It's too powerful for me. The cookie worked its magic. I was able to get here without too much anxiety from flying for the first time. I saved this for you. I'd like you to eat it. I've got to carry out my mission. No interference. Please."

She outstretches her hand and gives him the remainder of the cookie. He picks it up gently with the tips of his middle fingers like it's delicate china. Cle lies down on the pew on her back and places her head on her backpack. She drifts off quickly.

Suddenly it's eerily quiet.

She looks so peaceful and luminous. Benjamin wants to wake her up. He wants to talk to her, to share, to hear more about her deepest thoughts. Were those the last words they will share? She's in a deep sleep and he's out in the middle of the Sinai somewhere, not sure exactly where. There is no phone reception. Without her, he is truly alone.

Why does she have to go now? Can't we wait? Can't we support one another? Fill a hole in my life?

He feels intensely lonely. The feeling is overpowering, like a beast has crept into the room and is squeezing his chest until he cannot breathe. He stands up, places the cookie on the pew, and goes over to Cle.

He drags the case holding *The Immortal* towards him and pulls her out. Placing her up against the wall in front of where Cle is resting, he then uncurls Cle's tiny fingers clutching the golden book and brings the book over to his pew. He wants to make sure she wakes him before she leaps into the chasm.

Placing the cookie back in his palm, Benjamin lies on his back on the pew and slides the golden book onto his stomach. With his hand on the book, he stares at *The Immortal*. His childhood fantasy has come to life. Tears flow down his eyes as he realizes he's saying goodbye to one of his grandfather's most precious possessions. He bites off small pieces of the cookie, one then another, and then spits them out.

Nope, I won't be sleeping through this.

With heavy, tired eyes, he fumbles for his phone in his backpack, pulls it out, and sits up so he can see Cle in front of him. He snaps one last photo: *The Immortal* and Cle together.

Chapter 23

The Chasm

March 8, 2017
The Gods of the Desert Sanctuary, The South Sinai, Egypt

Benjamin wakes up with a pain shooting up his spine. Rubbing his back, he flicks a sharp stone that was digging into him. He was sleeping in front of the rubble where the altar used to be. Did he crawl there? Sleepwalk? While rubbing his back, he looks around.

Oh no, Cle…the golden book…*The Immortal*…where are they?

Panicked, he jumps up, still quite groggy, and looks around the crumbling chapel. He walks over to the pew where they both were. She and *The Immortal* are gone.

How much time has passed?

He flies outside, jerks his head around looking for her, and calls out, "Cle, Cle, CLE, WHERE ARE YOU?"

He races around the perimeter of the chapel, bending up and down, poking under things, like a dog sniffing for a ball. Then he sees them.

The slate steps. He knows them. He's certain if she's still alive, she'll be at the bottom. It's all strangely familiar. He's seen it before: he's walked them or floated over them in dreams many times.

He flies down the steps, and when he's at the bottom he's gazing over the ridge of a massive chasm.

How could something like this exist? It's like a mini Grand Canyon in the middle of the desert. It's awe-inspiring, horrifying, and dizzying.

There she stands, poised at the brink, a vision of tranquility amidst the rugged terrain. Dressed in a magnificent brown satin gown with a fur stole, crowned with a matching jewelled headpiece, she appears ethereal, a queen amidst the starkness of the landscape. Like a portrait in the Doge's Palace or someone of the royal house in ancient Egypt. Benjamin feels her look has been carefully chosen for this moment, not the climate. Perhaps she is hoping to finally find a place where she truly belongs.

He moves towards her stealthily walking the stone perimeter, keeping his eyes on her. His goal is to try to get to her and grab her.

Suddenly, a blanket of mist and fog moves in, and he can no longer see the edge of the chasm.

He inches close to her, feeling his way with his hand. Just when he's about to stretch out his arm, pushing it to its full length, he feels her arm but he cannot see her clearly. He sees only a blob of brown.

"Benjamin, I need to destroy the book and your portrait. Immortality is unholy. The only immortality is living a good life and leaving one's mark on this important world. Enjoy being mortal. Not knowing when your life will end gives it meaning. The mystery is beautiful. I will watch over you."

Before he can reach for her, she plunges into the fog with the book and portrait.

"Cle, Cle don't!" he screams. "Please don't!"

He leaps, loses his balance, and falls on the edge. A huge surge of air pushes him back onto safe ground. A bubbling sound fills his ears until they hurt and he places his hands on his ears. The thick mist and fog bubble, boil, and rise like a funnel cloud in front of him.

Suddenly his body is hurled violently backwards. His robe is ripped. That's the last thing he remembers. The ferocious eruption created by Cle's last act causes him to lose consciousness.

Benjamin tastes sand in his mouth. It's gritty like the tasteless laxative cookies the nurses forced him to eat in the hospital. He is groggy and tries to focus. He can't move his legs, or arms…nothing below his head. His body is encased in sand except for his head.

How long was I out?

Before he has a chance to panic, he cranes his head and spies what he's hoping is an image in the distance. He's praying it's not one of his visions.

It looks like a donkey with a woman on top. She has light hair and is dressed in a beautiful pink robe. As she gets closer, he can make out a face. Delicate features. Her eyes shine like jewels in the sunlight.

Is she real?

She gently dismounts. The donkey shrieks as she walks towards Benjamin tentatively as if she's trying to figure out what's happening in front of her. He can see now that she's trailing another donkey.

When she drops the second donkey's reins, the animal drops his head and lies down. The woman races over to Benjamin, takes his face in her hands, and kisses his cheek. Tears well up in his tired eyes. It's Grace.

He watches her as she starts digging him out, piling the sand behind him. It's not long before she has released one hand, then an arm. With a little freedom, he's able to help push himself up.

When he can finally stand on solid ground, he feels chilly and realizes he's naked. He doesn't feel uncomfortable in front of her but covers himself with his hands. She hands him a robe.

"The temperature is warming up. Nineteen degrees Celsius but still chilly in my estimation for late March. Modesty doesn't suit you. I'm learning you have a penchant for parading around naked. You recall I saw you nude in The Sartore Palace when you were darting around looking for something."

He smiles and puts him arm through one of the robe's arm holes.

"I really am quite shy."

She twists open a canteen and holds it while he drinks some water. It's still cold and tastes heavenly as it hits his tongue.

He looks at her and doesn't say anything.

Dropping the canteen and wrapping her body around him, she whispers into his ear.

"I've gotten my chance to repay you for your kindness. Now I've saved you," she says.

They bend down and fall back onto the sand, curling their bodies together. He hugs her tightly and wishes their bodies could fuse together so they would never be separated. He lifts his head to look at her and remains silent. He strokes her face and she moves in to kiss him. This is what he's dreamt of for years.

Sliding the top of her robe aside, he pushes his fingers gently into her shoulder, stroking it slowly with the tips of his fingers. Gliding upward to her neck, he moves her face gently towards him, rubbing his fingers slowly back and forth circling her lips.

She kisses his fingers, takes them in her hand, and pulls him closer. He kisses her on the lips gently like he's done before but this time he pushes deeper to open her mouth, enjoying the deep movements over and around her tongue. Sliding his hand back down to her shoulder, he moves the fabric further down. He notices her scar. It's deep like a rope. His hand slides over the curve of her back, pushing himself closer to her, disappearing into how she feels in his arms—the way her soft fragrance delights his nose, the way her hair feels so soft on his arm, and the way her heart is beating loudly in his ear.

He slides his hand in further towards the rise of her breast to feel it in his hand for the first time, to explore a pristine place on her body.

As they lie side by side facing one another, she moves towards him and glides her finger slowly over his cheek. His hand rests on her back on top of the zipper of her white dress. With each subtle movement, he slowly slides the zipper down.

He wants to see her, every curve of her body, up close. He wants to remember this forever: to capture a painting in his mind, this one moment when everything comes together. The desert, the silence, the sunlight beaming down on the sand, the silky touch of her bare skin—to create perfection, something that could never be recreated the same way again.

As he unclips her bra, she raises her arms, allowing him to slide it off her body. She moves onto her back, and her breasts splay naturally to the side. His hands slide over her stomach and up towards her left breast. He, holds it in his hand, pressing it between his fingers.

He circles the tips of his fingers down her stomach, a perfect colour of light creamy coffee. They kiss again but their movements are stronger, their breathing deeper, and their bodies warmer.

Crawling on top of her, he continues kissing her, moving, up and down, slowly, then faster and faster. The ecstasy is hypnotic. He slides inside of her, surrounded by the warmth, pleasure, and the rhythm of moving towards a perfect climax.

After he rolls over beside her, he reaches over and holds her. Their breathing is perfectly synchronized. Their chests move flawlessly up and down as they quietly share this perfect moment.

The Immortal's Secret

As she remains still, topless, and vulnerable, framed by the sand, he places his hand on her shoulders and gently pulls her towards him. They stay tangled in each other arms laughing and weeping together.

"She's gone," he whispers in her ear. She burrows deeper into his shoulder. "I hope I helped her."

"She wanted to go, Benjamin. You helped her on her way like no one else could. It was what she wanted."

"I wanted to save her."

He strokes her face, starting with her forehead and moving his finger clockwise over her cheek and her nose, finally resting his finger on her chin. He tilts his forehead onto hers.

"She jumped. I tried to save her. It was so hard, Grace. Cle took the book and the portrait."

"This is what she wanted, Benjamin. She didn't want you to save her. It was time. She experienced a lot of happiness, but she was a lost soul. You found the golden book and saved her. You were her hero."

He twirls the signet ring Cle gave him and a tear falls onto his hand. Grace touches his shoulder and massages her fingers into the muscle.

"I discovered the most amazing news."

"Oh yeah?" he asks as he grabs her hand.

She pauses and looks at her hands as tears well up in her eyes.

"Josiah is here, at the monastery. He came back and never disclosed where he had been. He asked the monks for a hiding place, one where he would never be disturbed. They told him of a series of tiny rooms, like shelves, built into the mountain—a place where they go when they want to be alone for quiet contemplation. He insisted they take him there. He has made himself so very ill, but he's still alive. I saw him briefly."

Benjamin slowly untangles his arms and legs from her, kneels in the sand, and says, "This is the most spectacular news." He drops his head in the sand and quietly weeps while Grace massages his shoulders.

Benjamin rides on his donkey behind Grace on hers as they approach the area where Benjamin is certain The Chapel of Hope was, or should be, located. He climbs off of the donkey to inspect the area. Grace stops her donkey, dismounts, and walks over to stand behind him, slowly rubbing her hands together nervously. There is a massive sand mound in front of them.

Like a dog, Benjamin digs into the mound with his fingers, a futile attempt to find the door. He races over to where he thinks the stairs might be. There is a drop, but it descends into even more sand like a ski hill made of sand.

"What is this place?" says Grace. She takes his hand to try and get him to stop.

"You've never been here before? Cle never brought you here?"

"I've never really wandered far from the monastery, other than today. Before you left with Cle to come to the desert, she asked me to join both of you as soon as I could. She said you would need me and gave me directions that were not easy to follow. She asked me to bring the donkeys. She said you would be at the chasm and I should head there."

Benjamin stares at her, brushes some sand out of his hair, then returns his gaze to the sand mound.

She moves over, kisses him on the lips, and pulls him towards the two donkeys.

"We should get to the monastery so you can be reunited with Josiah."

"Just one more minute, please?" he asks, smiling at her. "This was the last place I saw her," he says, his voice quivering.

Grace walks back over to the donkeys and turns her head away from Benjamin.

Benjamin picks up some sand from the mound where the chapel was. There is no question he is in the right place. He places his foot on a ledge in the sand and tries to climb up, but it's like quicksand and he falls over. Something sharp digs into his back. Digging it out with his hands, he holds up the object. It's warm in his hands.

It's the cross that fell from the top of the spire. The one he placed in the backpack containing *The Immortal* and the book. He hugs it to his chest and says, "Take thee beautiful soul and deliver thee to even more beauty where the Gods will be waiting to guide you in the next journey." Cle's mother's prayer.

He buries the cross under the sand. It would be too painful for him to take it back to the monastery. He hopes Cle is at peace at last and thinks of the image of her on the pew in front of *The Immortal*. The image will be embedded in his mind forever. He twirls his ring and thinks, *Is this all I have? The only piece of evidence that any of this happened?* Grace is the only witness

The Immortal's Secret

to prove he isn't crazy.

He walks over to the donkeys.

"Are you okay? Why is this place so important?" Grace said.

He thinks about responding but feels it doesn't matter. Cle's gone and he's trying to get his head around what happened.

"I am so glad you're here with me," he finally replies.

"So am I," she says and moves over to kiss him on the lips.

"That's all that matters now. I can't prove anything about Cle's existence. I've lost so much evidence. It's under the sand over there."

"Who do you need to prove it to?" says Grace. "As you said, all that matters is me and you."

Chapter 24

Finding Josiah

March 8, 2017
The Gods of the Desert Sanctuary, The South Sinai, Egypt

Benjamin quietly rides on his donkey to the monastery. For the first part of the journey Grace was riding beside him, but now she's in front. She told him that she wanted some quiet time. This was her beautiful way of providing him time to reflect on all that has happened.

She had shared that Josiah is weak. Benjamin is bracing himself for what he is going to find. It's the moment he's waited for. His pursuit may be over. He wanted to find Josiah alive, and it appears his wish is about to be granted. He never planned beyond that and never thought about what he would find. How would he react to seeing Josiah? His emotions are exploding, but he fights back tears by clenching his teeth.

They stop in front of the monastery—a massive mud-coloured structure that resembles a castle with huge walls that blend into the desert landscape. Grace kicks her donkey into motion and guides Benjamin to the back of the monastery, which hugs the Sinai Mountain.

The old donkeys climb about 200 feet up the rough terrain of the mountain. Grace dismounts on a patch of level desert sand and secures her donkey's rope under a massive rock.

Benjamin pulls on his donkey and stops behind her. She turns to look at him and points to a rock shelf in the mountain with a few squares that act as crude entrances. Grace extends her hand. He walks over and places his hand in hers.

She whispers, "Josiah is over there." They walk towards the cave and then stop. Together they stand at the opening of his cave carved into the landscape.

"Are you ready?"

Unable to speak, Benjamin nods his head slowly. Grace leads the way inside.

His legs shake so badly that he needs to hold the dirt wall beside the entrance. The cave is small, at most 10 feet wide by 10 feet high.

Josiah is lying on a small bed covered by a grey blanket, barely taking up half of the bed. He looks like a mummy, with his gaunt face, cracked lips, deep cheekbones, dry skin, and mottled arms. The only feature that looks familiar to Benjamin is his luscious hair, now fully grey and falling over his eyes. He's asleep and his teeny head is so deep in the large pillow, it looks like the pillow could suffocate him.

Beside him is a table with photos of Benjamin—one of Josiah holding him as a baby, one when he was graduating from grade school, and one Benjamin doesn't remember being taken. It shows him in the middle of St. Mark's Square, all alone.

A simple wooden cross hangs over Josiah's bed. The cave smells faintly like lilac, a scent Grace probably sprayed.

Benjamin whispers, "How long has he been here?"

"I don't know. Retreating to this cave is a recent development. He wanted to throw us all off his scent. Perhaps this was intentional, perhaps it was his condition. When he came back here, he swore the monks to secrecy. This is what he insisted and you know he gets what he wants. This is how he wanted to spend his last days. He is a tough man. He's still drinking but not eating. The cave is warm but thankfully not as hot as it can get outside. It's like he wants to punish himself. I need to feed him, and you."

"I don't think I can eat."

"You need to have something, at least drink something. I'll get you a few things to wear since I don't think you have anything other than the robe."

"No, I don't. I lost a lot of valuable things."

"Here in the desert, they don't place much value on material items."

She places her hand into a sack she's been carrying over her shoulder.

"This is Josiah's phone. You should take it. The password is BenjiM or 236546."

He takes it from Grace and cradles it with both hands. When he pushes the home button, he's looking back at himself. He's the screensaver, a photo taken in Josiah's backyard in his hidden garden when Benjamin was in his twenties.

"I'll be back," Grace says. She points. "You can sit there if you like."

He looks over at a dark wooden chair beside Josiah's bed. It's as solid as a couple of sticks tied together with string.

He stands like a statue watching Josiah. He can barely look at his grandfather. The image is too shocking. It's like someone took the giant man and squeezed him until he was under 100 pounds. His dirt room is like a tomb—so sparse for a man who has everything.

Josiah retreated to this barren landscape, so far from home, with little more than the things in this room.

Benjamin wonders, *Am I to blame for pushing Josiah here?*

The thought makes his knees collapse and he drops onto the dirt floor landing on his butt.

He crawls to the rickety wooden chair beside Josiah's bed, sits down, and composes himself with several deep breaths. He rubs Josiah's brow with the back of his hand.

The old man is cold even though the room is warm. Leaning in, Benjamin softly kisses his grandfather's cheek and says, "I'm here, Grandad. It's Benji."

His voice quivers on "Benji". There's no reaction from Josiah.

Sitting in the quiet room, Benjamin holds Josiah's hand and watches him breathe. Josiah's breath is steady but weak, the rising and falling of his chest barely making a movement on the blanket. Benjamin counts the number of seconds between each breath. It remains steady at ten.

He finds Bach's "St. Matthew's Passion" on Josiah's phone and plays it softly. The reception is perfect in the desert. The luck of Josiah. Things like that happen to him.

Even though he's thirsty, Benjamin doesn't want to drink. There is a huge heavy ball of emotion in his chest. It keeps getting bigger and he feels like it could suffocate him. He tries to ignore this reaction from his body. He thinks of something funny: Favreau's moon face, Josiah's Daniel Boone hat, and Cle's silly pink purse.

The tears start. They run down his face and he can feel them cover his cheeks. His shoulders start to convulse. He wants to crawl in the bed and die with Josiah.

Just then, Josiah's hand tumbles out of the bed. Benjamin strokes the fingers and rubs his hand against his grandfather's face. It's warm and it's trembling. Just slightly.

Is this what he wanted?

Benjamin is with his beloved Josiah, but they cannot communicate. Josiah is alive but he may as well be dead. *Is this what he was searching for?*

Benjamin stands up, walks outside, kicks some stones, and pounds the dirt wall. More tears flow from his face.

Josiah had so much. He spent his life chasing a dream for his Sera. Practicing alchemy, travelling the world to search for clues, advocating for others, running a business, trying to find meaning. Was this a life worthy of his vast talents? Did he achieve his full potential? But who is Benjamin to judge?

He had it all except what he really wanted. Perhaps immortality to Josiah is doing one honourable deed during his finite time here on Earth. Perhaps reducing his life to this spare existence was his noble way of trying to find the real meaning of life.

Benjamin returns to the cave and an hour later Grace returns with some bread. They both nibble without saying a word. She rubs Benjamin's shoulder with her tiny hands. When she finishes eating, she kisses Josiah's hand, then kisses Benjamin on his nose and whispers softly in his ear, "I will leave you alone and I'll keep checking."

The room is suffocating. Benjamin stands up and drops the phone on his foot. The rush of pain is excruciating. He runs outside and lets out a massive scream, followed by tears that cover his face. Putting his hand up to his face, he wipes his cheeks.

It's dusk. He looks out onto the desert sky—a mélange of gold and orange rising from the horizon. Standing in this white robe that belongs to God-knows-who, beside a cave dug into the Sinai Desert that overlooks a monastery that's hundreds of years old, he is stripped of all of his wealthy comforts. So is Josiah.

He sits on a rock to massage his toe. Is this what he was searching for? To see his grandfather like this? He kicks some stones with his good foot and starts hurling others off the mountain to see how far they will go, to see how far he could run right now. He pushes more tears from his cheeks with the tips of his hands.

Bending his head down, he puts his hands together in prayer. It's the first time he's done this since he was a child.

The Immortal's Secret

Something tumbles out from his robe. He picks it up. It's a rosary. Sliding his fingers over the beads, he begins to pray, "Please Lord, give me one last moment before you take him to heaven to be with you and Sera. I need one last moment to let him know he did not kill me. To let him know how much I love him and let him know he's a good man who lived a moral life."

He closes his eyes and places his hands on the side of the mountain, pushing his palms deep into the dirt.

Benjamin concentrates on the silence. It's pure silence, as if everything around him has stopped to mourn with him.

After a few minutes the beautiful silence is broken by a slight coughing noise that is so subtle he doesn't notice it at first. It happens again.

Turning his focus towards the cave, he hears it again. He kisses the rosary, twists it around his wrist, and turns his right ear towards the cave. The coughing starts again as he slowly walks back to the cave. Tentatively, he pokes his head back in. The air seems cleaner.

Josiah is trying to sit up. Benjamin races over and places his hands gently on his grandfather's shoulders to help him. Josiah looks up at Benjamin, staring at him with his piercing blue eyes. The look is what Benjamin has dreamt of for months.

Josiah coughs again and Benjamin grabs a tissue from the table. Josiah again looks up at Benjamin and makes a noise but isn't able to speak. Benjamin hugs him gently and breaths in his scent. The woodsy scent that defines him. Josiah makes another strange noise.

"It's okay, it's okay. It's me. I'm alive."

The old man stares at his grandson. He digs his fingers into Benjamin's cheeks and kneads them like dough.

"Benji?"

Finally, something is familiar. His voice is the same, only weaker. Removing one of Josiah's hands from his cheek, Benjamin kisses it. "Yes. I've been searching for you."

Benjamin watches the tears form in Josiah's blue eyes.

"I recovered with your help," says Benjamin. "I was searching for you and found the golden book inside the frame of *The Immortal*, the book you were searching for."

He stares at Josiah. Benjamin wonders if he understands, if he's lucid.

As Benjamin carefully slides Josiah's head back onto the pillow, he closes his grandfather's eyes gently with the tips of his fingers. Josiah takes a deep breath and Benjamin counts his grandfather's breaths again until their breathing starts to sync.

He whispers to himself, "I helped Annacletica on her way."

Josiah opens his eyes and their eyes lock. He curls his middle finger, pointing at a bottle of water. Benjamin twists the cap off and slides the bottle over to Josiah, who picks it up. Benjamin cradles his grandfather's head in his other hand and places the water bottle up to his mouth. Josiah drinks some and coughs, spewing the water on Benjamin's shirt. Benjamin cleans up the water with some tissues.

"Benji?" Josiah says in a whisper.

He touches Benjamin's face and pushes his finger into his grandson's cheeks again.

"Yes, it's me," Benjamin says laughing. "Grandad. I am alive."

He kisses the old man on the forehead and pulls him to his chest. As they hug tightly, Benjamin does not want to let go. This is the feeling he values most in this world.

Benjamin takes Josiah's face in his hands.

"You didn't kill me. It's heartbreaking to watch you punish yourself like this by living in this dirt box. You are the most important person in my life."

Taking Josiah's hands in his, he gently squeezes.

"I need to get you into the monastery to safety, to heal you. I cannot leave you here in this place."

Josiah stares at his grandson.

"I'll carry you if I have to," Benjamin says as his voice cracks on the last two words.

Josiah nods.

Benjamin gently helps Josiah from the bed by sliding his body to the side and guiding him to stand by placing one foot on the ground followed by the next. Surprisingly, Josiah is somewhat steady on his feet.

Benjamin guides him to the door with his hand around Josiah's waist, holding him tightly as Josiah negotiates one wobbly step at a time. They arrive outside in the sun and Josiah slides out of Benjamin's grip onto the dirt. Benjamin picks him up and carries him ever so carefully down the sandy and rocky hill towards the monastery. He's amazed how light his grandfather is, like a twig in his arms.

Josiah points to a wooden gate and Benjamin follows his directions. As they reach the gate, he sees a young monk tending to a little vegetable

The Immortal's Secret

garden. The monk looks up, moves out from behind a tree, and walks towards them.

He looks at Benjamin and says, "Let me give you a hand. I'm Father Paolo. I can take one arm and you take another."

They enter a quiet courtyard. A throng of monks is gathering, probably headed to prayer. One looks over, then another, and the throng rushes towards them. Before Benjamin can take in his surroundings, the men are carrying Josiah gently towards a door. It leads to a dark corridor that seems to go on forever. They enter a windowed room with a tiny bed and table. The monks exit the room with perfect synchronicity and appear again with pillows and soft blankets. Others push in various crude medical machines.

They make the bed, covering it with brown blankets and three pillows. With the help of the monk who greeted Benjamin outside, they place Josiah on the bed and attach him to an intravenous drip.

One of the monks arrives to check him over. He tells Benjamin he's going to give Josiah medication for pain and to give him energy.

"You convinced him to come back to enjoy some comforts. We call this our hospital. We'll get him food and anything else he requires," one of the monks says. "We'll get you a bed so you can stay with him. Our beloved Grace says you are his Benji."

Another monk brings in broth in a wooden bowl and gently holds up Josiah's head as he sips a little of the soup. Benjamin watches and when Josiah has had enough, he turns around and looks at the doorway. Grace is standing at the door and walks over.

She whispers in Benjamin's ear as her perfume fills his nose.

"There's no longer a golden book to heal him. It's got to be done the natural way."

They sit together, holding hands with Josiah. Benjamin's never felt more connected to Josiah and Grace.

This comfort and nourishment lasts for five nights. Josiah is eating and drinking. Not a lot, but he's getting stronger.

Benjamin procures a laptop from one of the monks and is able to sign into his account to see the pictures he sent to his email account to ensure he didn't lose them. When he shows Josiah the picture of his lunch with Sera at the Danieli, Josiah won't take his hand off the screen, as if he's touching something real. Benjamin leaves the laptop with him to flip through all of the photos until the battery dies.

When Josiah is stronger, they walk around the monastery together arm in arm. They go to The Church of Transformation together and pray, Benjamin following Josiah's lead since he knows every line in the daily mass. They eat hamburgers that the monks grill in the oven, they kick a soccer ball around awkwardly and slowly, and they take in the surroundings in a dilapidated 1970 jeep jalopy that the monks procured from who-knows-where.

One morning as they are sitting on a hill overlooking the monastery, Josiah takes Benjamin's hand and says, "This is the way we should live life, with no distractions. It provides time to focus on what matters: the people you love. I just wanted to be surrounded by the people I love but I kept losing them. I have focused on one thing to keep a promise. I could have given so much more. Life is for the living and I have dwelled in the past. It was a romantic notion but not a path to follow. Your grandmother would have wanted more, would have wanted you to live your life. Do you think I've been a selfish man?"

As Benjamin is about to respond Josiah says, "You know Cle's story?"

"Yes."

The old man pauses for a long time.

"I need you to believe...you experienced something profound. You are linked to the other side. What happened to Cle may be real or a reality of her making. I don't care. I choose to believe. What we shared with Cle, with each other, it transcends this world. It's the one thing that remains eternal. The only immortality is love."

Benjamin listens intently, feeling the weight of Josiah's words settle in his chest. He reaches out to touch his grandfather's hand.

"I have been following Annacletica, or Cle to all of us, for years as well as Paeon, a fraud who only seeks money," Josiah continues. "I tried to keep Paeon away but she somehow engaged your Jenna. She did extensive research to make Jenna irresistible to you. I was convinced,

The Immortal's Secret

almost certain, Jenna did something to you to make you so sick. I felt it was my fault. Did she have an opportunity to do anything, to hurt you?"

Benjamin thinks before answering.

"Does it really matter? We're together again. For now, I'm thrilled to be reunited with you. It's all I wanted. I'm savouring these moments."

Josiah stares at him and touches his nose, an affectionate habit Benjamin loves.

"Can you do something for me?" Josiah asks his grandson.

"Certainly."

"You're not even going to ask what it is?" He winks.

"Anything."

Josiah sits in silence, his gaze fixed on the horizon as if searching for something beyond the vast expanse of the desert. When he finally speaks, his voice trembles with emotion.

"I want to see Cle's resting place. The three of us—you, me, and Grace. He produces a small bag from inside his light jacket and cradles it in his lap.

"What is that?" Benjamin asks.

"I'll show you when we get there."

"Everything is a secret," Benjamin says laughing.

"I'm not secretive. I just like the element of surprise."

Josiah, Benjamin, and Grace stuff themselves into the jeep. Grace takes the wheel and negotiates the bumpy dirt roads and sand dunes. Benjamin is trying to direct her but his directions are confusing. Guiding her is no easy task when he's only been to the location once and he's staring at a vast expanse of sand with few landmarks. In the distance Father Paolo and a few other monks follow along on donkeys.

After Grace barely negotiates a huge sand dune, she stops the jeep. Benjamin jerks his neck around. He's pretty sure they've arrived at their destination because he sees something poking out of the sand. He steps out of the jeep and falls over onto the sand.

He digs the cross out of the sand. It's the one he left behind a few days ago.

"This is where it was." Waving his arm he says, "The chapel was around here and the chasm was over there." Benjamin is pointing anywhere because he's not sure of the exact locations, but they are in the vicinity. Josiah needs to know. Benjamin is giving him what he needs.

The two men sit down together on a rock. Grace had brought a scarf and now places it over their heads to protect them from the heat, which is warm but not intolerable. Benjamin and Grace put their hands on top of Josiah's. The old man's hands are stone cold and the other two rub them to warm him up.

"This is the last plate from the golden book," Josiah says as he pulls his hands away and slides a plate out of his bag. It's a basic white porcelain plate, one of the ones the monks use to serve food to Josiah. Benjamin sneaks a look at Grace and she raises her eyebrows.

They listen to Josiah as he slowly says, "Paeon, or whoever she is, had this plate. Our brothers the monks told me they found it in her room. They gave it to me. We have all been impacted by the golden book, prayed on it, seeking its power. How different are we than Cle or my Sera? We need to cleanse our souls. Ask for redemption. Let's all pray quietly from Psalm 51. Place your hand on the plate with me. Benjamin, can you share the Psalm?"

Benjamin nods and he recites the words slowly by heart with his eyes closed. He wants to let himself be carried away by the moment, by the overwhelming presence of love.

> *Have mercy upon me, O God, according to thy lovingkindness: according unto the multitude of thy tender mercies blot out my transgressions.*
>
> *Wash me thoroughly from mine iniquity, and cleanse me from my sin.*
>
> *For I acknowledge my transgressions: and my sin is ever before me.*
>
> *Against thee, thee only, have I sinned, and done this evil in thy sight: that thou mightest be justified when thou speakest, and be clear when thou judgest. (v.1-4)*
>
> *Deliver me from bloodguiltiness, O God, thou God of my salvation: and my tongue shall sing aloud of thy righteousness. (v.14)*

Josiah squeezes Benjamin's hand and Benjamin squeezes back. The moment is so peaceful: three people holding onto one another, listening to their hearts beat. The power of touch.

Josiah closes his eyes, leans on Benjamin's shoulder, and says, "I love you and I will always love you."

"I love you too."

Josiah cradles Benjamin's head against his chest. They all sit still alone with their own thoughts.

Suddenly, Benjamin looks up, his stomach in a knot. He places his ear on Josiah's chest, then places his finger on his grandfather's neck checking his pulse.

Benjamin looks at Grace and whispers, "He is gone."

Benjamin and Grace hold each other. It's completely silent. Benjamin feels the emotion start at the bottom of his throat, and the pressure rises up. He emits a moaning sound and she grabs his arm.

As Benjamin is leaning on her, he thinks about how Josiah was one of the only humans he has truly loved. He's praying Grace will want to take Josiah's place as the most important person in his life.

He whispers in her ear, "Love is weak when there is more doubt than there is trust, but love is most strong when you learn to trust even with all the doubts. If a thing loves, it is infinite."

She says, "That is beautiful."

"It's a saying Josiah believed in. From Willian Blake. Love is immortal. Come sit with me. Let's pray."

Benjamin takes Josiah hands and says softly with his voice breaking, "Take this beautiful soul and deliver him to even more beauty where the Gods will be waiting to guide him in the next journey."

They caress Josiah until the monks arrive with a stretcher. As the monks carry Josiah towards the jeep, Benjamin observes his grandfather's face. He is smiling, the smile Benjamin loves.

Maybe this is a sign that he's reunited with Sera.

Grace is focused on Josiah and making sure the monks place him gently into the jeep. When Benjamin enters the jeep and sits beside Josiah, he his hears someone call his name.

He jerks his neck to look behind him. The voice is so clearly Josiah's but it's in Benjamin's head, which makes no sense. The voice is saying something, but it's all jumbled words that sound like the speaker is scrolling through radio channels trying to land on something. Benjamin is trying carefully to decipher what the voice is saying when the words finally settle down into one clear line that Josiah keeps repeating:

"Everything is going to be okay."

Chapter 25

The Funeral

March 17, 2017
The Church of the Transformation & The Sacred Sinai Desert Monastery, The South Sinai, Egypt

The monks hold a Catholic mass of sorts for Josiah and Cle in the monastery in The Church of the Transformation. It is officiated by Father Paolo. In attendance: ten of the other monks, Grace, and Benjamin.

It is Father Paolo's first Roman Catholic mass, and he nervously practiced ensuring the details were authentic, as per Josiah's request. Always one to be steadfastly different, Josiah couldn't have an orthodox ceremony in an orthodox church.

When Benjamin walks up for the host, he is given fresh bread made by the monks and the finest French wine, which was what Josiah wanted.

Benjamin lets the bread dissolve on his tongue as he looks at Josiah. His body has been carefully placed in a modest pine box on a table at the altar. He looks so peaceful in a plain blue suit—no tailoring for Josiah. His Daniel Boone hat is large on his shrunken head. The monks had taken great care to place it evenly on his head with the racoon tail snaking around his neck to frame his face. Benjamin imagines him, the consummate explorer, as a handsome lovestruck man, finally united with his Sera again. Josiah insisted he be cremated by funeral pyre in the desert and Benjamin is going to take his ashes to Venice and place the urn on top of Sera's sarcophagus.

The Immortal's Secret

Cle is represented by a golden icon of The Virgin Mary, one of the most precious from the monastery's rare collection. They've placed a little sign under the icon with her name written in calligraphy: Annacletica Bernice.

The chapel is quiet when the service is over. It is as if the monks control nature. Benjamin can't even hear a bird. He can't move and Grace remains still like a statue beside him.

Father Paolo whispers to Benjamin, "Please take as long as you like. We will wait outside."

Humanity shows its beautiful side when someone dies.

Josiah always used to say that. The gentle tone in Father Paolo's voice is comforting and reduces Benjamin from the pillar of strength he was attempting to be.

Benjamin remains still with his eyes closed, squeezing the pine box, thinking how a man as wealthy as Josiah was reduced to something so modest. But this is what Josiah wanted, spelled out in a two-page will that he wrote a few months ago.

"What should we do?" Grace says.

"I need a moment to collect myself," Benjamin says without opening his eyes, afraid that if he opens them tears will cover his face. He squeezes her hand, and she squeezes back.

She is silent for a long while and then finally says, "No, I mean what should we do without them? I'm feeling desperate. I can't imagine a life without them. They were my anchors in life."

When Benjamin is sure he has composed himself, he opens his eyes and looks at her. The deep scars on her face fascinate him and he's delighted to keep discovering more on her nose, forehead, cheeks. His favourite is the one that begins at the top of her forehead and like a thick pink snake, reaches down to the bottom of her chin. The snake branches off into two faint lines that curve to the side of her face. They create a shape not unlike a dove, a beautiful symbol of peace, love, and renewal. The patchwork of scars is a solemn reminder of how precious life is. He traces the dove gently with his finger and whispers, "You are so perfect."

They sit in the chapel. Two of the most influential people in Benjamin's life are gone. Thankfully he still has Grace. Benjamin slides her tiny hand in his and stares at how elegant it is with her polished red nails and a delicate bracelet of tiny pearls. He whispers slowly and softly, "Please don't ever leave me."

She cups his face in her hands. He isn't embarrassed by how vulnerable he is, with his cheeks soaked in tears and his skin on fire from this foreign emotion.

"I won't," she says.

They get up and walk out of the chapel holding hands. As they emerge, the light of the new day settles upon them. Moving away from the church, they sit on a short brick wall that encloses and protects the chapel. Kissing the back of Grace's hand, Benjamin stares up at Mount Sinai, where Josiah was hiding in the cave.

"Tell me about you and Cle. Were you close?"

"She was my best friend. She confessed she was very ill and wanted to die on her own terms. I told her not to tell me how she was going to do it. I couldn't bear to know. She and Josiah were also close. I didn't ask much, and they didn't disclose. Those were always the terms."

"What do you know about her past?" he asks while playing with her fingers.

"She lived here at the monastery since she was a young woman. Josiah said she was like me, someone kind of lost, without much family. He brought me here to look after her and teach her about life. She lived a reclusive life at the monastery. She liked learning about life through me."

"That's all you know?"

"That's all I needed to know. We both agreed the past didn't define us. We were like sisters. I taught her English, and she picked it up fast, including slang, colloquial phrases, that type of thing."

"Who was Sister Annacletica?"

"It was a name she used. I'm not sure why. She always referred to herself that way. I think she enjoyed it. Annacletica was her real name. She was so very pious and good. It fit her."

Benjamin stares ahead and doesn't say anything. Wiping his face with the back of his hand he says, "I need to go to Venice. To fulfill a promise...to her."

"Sure, absolutely. You definitely have to go." They kiss and she touches his hair. It's come back, a few centimetres of chestnut hair. Not a shock like he used to have, but it's hair. "I am so sorry you had to suffer with this cancer. I wanted to be with you, to meet with you, but it was complicated."

"I would never have wanted you to see me like that," he says.

"I hope you will allow me to make it up now."

"Just stay with me. That's all you have to do. Help me live a better life. Cle inspired me. She wanted me to live a different life. One of faith, faith in something," says Benjamin while looking down and tapping his feet nervously.

"When are you going to go to Venice?"

"I thought *we* could go to Venice."

"I accept your invitation. What are *we* doing there?"

"I have to do something important. Close the loop on so many things. Then I can move forward with you, no distractions, forever."

As he's kissing her and pushing his fingers gently through her hair, he sees an image coming towards them. He stops kissing Grace and looks at the image. It's a living cadaver, a zombie, a survivor of a nuclear blast. It is shuffling along slowly and staring right at him with hollowed out eyes.

Wrapping his arms around Grace, he pushes her head away, but she screams and falls off the ledge. He tries to catch her, but he misses and she drops onto the dirt.

He gently lifts Grace, keeping her head away from what's coming towards them while keeping one eye on the ghoul as it keeps getting closer. When it's a few feet away, it reaches out its hand. The skin is peeling off, revealing the angry red underside. The face is melting, melting like its features are made of wax.

Benjamin digs his face into Grace's hair.

"This has to be another illusion," he says.

Grace is sweating and shaking uncontrollably.

Something staggers out from the side of the ghoul. A companion who is also wearing a hooded robe. The ghoul plunges to the ground, and the companion struggles to get on its feet as the ghoul's skin melts in front of their eyes, blending with its insides to create a pool of gruesome liquid that quickly evaporates into the sand. The companion drops to its knees and tips over, overcome with grief, pushing its face into a white robe.

Benjamin and Grace walk backwards, their steps mirroring one another.

"Let's get back to the chapel," says Benjamin.

While moving, Benjamin looks at the ground where the remains of the ghoul are melting, creating steam on the sand and a putrid blend of sickly and sweet smells. The stench hangs heavy in the air. Whoever the person was is quickly evaporating into the desert sands.

The ghoul's companion starts moving towards them. Its hands are covered in the sticky remains. Benjamin's eyes are locked on it and he's ready to pounce if it makes a move for Grace. He looks at the sun and then back at the ghoul's companion as it raises its head and slowly pushes its hood down. Charging over, it grabs his hand and says, "Benjamin."

He steps back and pushes its hand from his. He looks down at his hands; they are covered in the pinkish remains. He looks up at the creature and cannot believe what he sees.

"Benjamin," it says again. "Benjamin."

"Jenna?"

Pushing her away with his large hands, he moves backwards towards Grace and grabs her hand with his clean hand. He wants to run from the scene with her, but Jenna is clearly in distress. As much as he now despises her, he cannot leave her.

He kisses Grace's forehead and says, "Are you okay?"

"I think so," she says, wiping her eyes.

He whispers to her, "I have to see if I can help her. I know her. It's Jenna." He points to the chapel. "Could you go back and wait for me inside where you'll be safe? I won't be long."

"Benjamin, are you sure?"

"I don't know. I can't leave her. I'll be fine. Will you?"

"I'll be okay. I'll wait inside the church at the door."

As Grace retreats to the chapel, Benjamin takes Jenna's hand and guides her to a stone fence surrounding the chapel where they can sit. He gently helps her sit down and takes a seat a foot away to leave a comfortable distance between them. Her face is a blend of red blotches from the crying. He pulls a package of Kleenex out of his pocket and hands it to her.

After she composes herself and her breathing settles, he says, "What did we just witness?"

"It was Paeon. She was fine but over the last few days she became progressively ill. It started with vomiting and nausea and progressed to problems breathing and talking."

Benjamin is thinking Paeon's deterioration could be connected to Cle's departure and Paeon's connection with the portrait and book.

"I'm so sorry this happened. I'm not sure what it was. You should let the monks handle retrieving her remains. Why do both of you keep following me?"

The Immortal's Secret

"She wanted to find the golden book. She knew you were headed here. She knows people at this monastery."

"The book was destroyed along with the portrait. Did that woman pray on the book?"

"Yes, that was Paeon. You know she had been searching for it."

"I didn't recognize her. I've never seen something so horrifying happen to a human."

Jenna falls to the ground crying. "All hope is lost for her."

"Jenna, we need to get you help. Come with me and we'll find someone at the monastery. They have a small hospital and can help you."

"No, please. I want to stay with you."

Benjamin is amazed at how different she looks. Her robe is far too big for her small frame. She looks like she hasn't removed her make-up or bathed since he last saw her a few weeks ago. Her nail polish looks like it's been scraped off by an animal and her robe has symbols written all over it in blue pen. One of them is the Eye of Horus.

"No please. Let me explain my actions."

"It doesn't matter. We need to get you help." Truth is, he doesn't want to hear what she has to say. He can fill in the blanks on his own.

"Please, I am begging you. Allow me to explain myself finally."

Benjamin doesn't say anything and she sits breathing in and out. He looks behind and sees Grace watching at the side of the chapel with Father Paolo. Jenna launches into her explanation.

"I love you. Like no one I've ever loved before. I had to leave you. She needed me. She felt you were no longer useful. That's harsh and I'm so very sorry. She wanted to immobilize you so she could bribe Josiah. I wouldn't go along with it. She pushed me and I gave you some of the poison. I put it in your milk. I am so sorry it made you ill and perhaps gave you cancer. I have to live with that."

She wipes her nose on her robe and starts sucking the wool like a child. Her voice changes and she sounds like a caged animal.

"You have to understand. She was desperate and had no one. She said she would be lost forever if we didn't get the book. She would roam the world forever."

She grabs the sleeve of his jacket lovingly and he pulls away.

"You poisoned me and duped me." Benjamin feels his anger rising.

He stands up and starts walking backwards, staring at her while he retreats. He feels odd, like he might throw up or collapse.

Father Paolo walks over tentatively with Grace close behind. Benjamin shifts direction and moves towards Jenna. He puts his hands on her shoulder, gently pulls her up, and guides her towards Father Paolo.

"Can you help her? She is in distress."

Father Paolo walks over and whispers to him, "What happened outside the church? There are ashes that have stained the sand."

"I don't know. This woman is Jenna. She might be able to shed light on that. She accompanied the other woman here. I think you know her. Her name is Paeon."

Father Paolo puts his hands on his heart.

Benjamin takes the Father's hand and says, "I have to leave and I thank you for your kindness and support."

He receives an email from Father Paolo the next morning. Jenna spent the rest of the previous day in the monastery hospital, but when Father Paolo checked on her late in the day, she was gone. They searched the monastery and surrounding areas but couldn't find her. He said he'd keep Benjamin posted.

Chapter 26

Returning Home

March 24, 2017
St. Mark's Basilica, Venice, Italy

It's a beautiful sunny day with a cool wind when Benjamin and Grace arrive at St. Mark's Basin in a water taxi. Benjamin gets off the boat first and takes Grace's hand to guide her. Slinging their backpacks around his shoulder, he pauses to gaze up at the terrace at the Hotel Danieli, where he saw the vision of his grandmother and Josiah. The image will be embedded in his mind until the day he dies: an image of pure love and joy, one he hopes his new life with Grace will mirror.

As they walk hand in hand past the Doge's Palace towards St Mark's Basilica, Benjamin says, "Do you want to go back to the palazzo and get settled in? I just need to deal with something in the basilica. Some unfinished business."

"Shall I take your backpack?"

"No, I'll be fine."

He's still wearing the white robe but he's now paired it with a black cape that Father Paolo gave him. The ensemble is definitely not something he would have worn before, but he's a different man with hair on his head and some lean meat on his bones. It feels right for this mission.

"Please call me if you need me. I won't be long," he says.

She blows him a kiss, and he watches her walk away past the clock tower, kitty-corner to St. Mark's Basilica.

When he enters the basilica, he sees Gianni surrounded by the wide line of tourists packing the aisles, all of whom are pointing to the stunning golden mosaics on the ceiling. Their eyes are glued upwards.

He walks over to Gianni.

"I need to go to the baptistery. You'll ensure I am not disturbed?"

"Yes, I got your call. I am happy to be of assistance." Gianni looks at Benjamin. "What's with your outfit?"

Benjamin just keeping walking with purpose.

Gianni hollers out, "What is with the new look?"

"Do I look different?" Benjamin yells back as he steps up his walking to get to the baptistery and The Secret Sartore Chapel.

His hands are shaking, and he folds them together to calm himself. There are a few people milling around outside the baptistery and he pushes past them to enter via the large ornate wooden carved door. No one is inside.

He stands in front of the altar, dominated by the massive golden iconostasis, and thinks about the day when he placed *The Immortal* on the niche with the golden book. The plague sufferers were swarming around him, desperate and tragic yet full of hope because of an inanimate object. They were desperate to touch the golden book, their only hope during the plague, courtesy of Annecletica. She was an angel. Their angel.

He bends down on the marble floor in front of the five-foot statue of The Virgin Mary, puts his hands together, and prays:

The LORD hear thee in the day of trouble; the name of the God of Jacob defend thee;

Send thee help from the sanctuary, and strengthen thee out of Zion;

Remember all thy offerings, and accept thy burnt sacrifice; Selah.

Grant thee according to thine own heart, and fulfill all thy counsel.

We will rejoice in thy salvation, and in the name of our God we will set up our banners: the LORD fulfill all thy petitions.

Some trust in chariots, and some in horses: but we will remember the name of the LORD our God.

They are brought down and fallen: but we are risen, and stand upright.

Save, LORD: let the king hear us when we call.

The Immortal's Secret

Psalm 20. For Josiah and his grandmother. It was Josiah's favourite, his emotional panacea for every challenging moment in life. It will now become Benjamin's.

As he rises to his feet, his shoe clips something that almost sends him onto the marble floor. Looking down, he sees something familiar. It makes him smile. He picks it up and stares at it. It's the rattle belonging to Rosa, the baby with the plague. The little angel with the golden hair.

As he's examining it, he thinks, *Another piece of evidence that the illusions may not have been illusions*, not that he needs proof. *I will treasure you for the rest of my life along with the ring Cle gave me. My two souvenirs of the other side.*

He places the rattle securely in the pocket of his cape.

When he's sure no one is looking, he walks over to the statue of The Virgin Mary and pushes her delicate face in gently, then more forcefully, and the statue moves towards him. He slips inside via the narrow opening.

He walks into the centre of The Secret Sartore Chapel and stares at the muted light beaming in from the blackened windows. He looks for the paintings of the plague sufferers, the ones over the golden altar. There's nothing there, not even any clue anything was ever there. He looks around thinking perhaps Grace took them down and placed them somewhere but there is no sign of them.

He walks over to the sarcophagus and traces his finger over the carved names Roberto and Annacletica Sartore. He wants to push the lip of the sarcophagus open like Andrea had done. Perhaps find Annacletica inside beside him, sleeping peacefully, looking glorious, clutching the golden book. Placing his hand on the marble, he wills his hand to push but he can't do it. What if she were inside? What if, somehow, he had imagined her on the edge the chasm? If she had travelled back to Venice? The thought excites him but frightens him too.

No, it's all over. He must accept this. No more illusions. Only reality, no matter how stark.

Opening his backpack, he places frankincense oil, candles, and a small cross on the top of the sarcophagus, arranging them neatly in the middle. Bending down and leaning on a pew in front, he folds his hand in prayer.

"Please bless this place. A glorious woman who cared deeply about humanity lay here. She created a golden book that alleviated suffering for so many people of this great world. Treasure her soul."

He breaths in the scent of frankincense and falls onto the top of the sarcophagus and begins to weep. There is no more magic. Just his faith.

"I'm going to follow your path to help others. You have changed me, Annacletica."

As he's rubbing his tears with his sleeve, he looks over at the marble wall directly in front of the sarcophagus and sees a portrait leaning up against it. Walking over slowly, he bends down to look at it carefully and then picks it up to examine it more closely.

It is clearly *The Immortal*. He rubs his finger over the gold of her face and then her eyes, which are modestly looking off into the distance. This is *The Immortal*. It's her; it's definitely Annacletica. But it's not his portrait. It's the same portrait, but everything is muted and soft. She is floating in a gold background with no painted background anchoring her, no Chapel of Hope. She is much more beautiful in a delicate, sparse way, more like a Byzantine icon, like the famous Hodegetria icon that has been copied numerous times.

In this version her features are still so delicate and lifelike, cast in the gold like it was poured onto her face. She is a perfect woman, but this is not an exact replica of *The Immortal*. This is the version that will hang in the Louvre for all to see, bequeathed by Benjamin and Grace. Art experts who saw the original just might deem this version more exquisite.

As he's placing the portrait back down on the floor, he notices something on the back. It's an envelope; his name is written on the front.

He pushes his finger into the flap to open it. Unfolding the piece of paper, he recognizes the flawless cursive script. It's from Annacletica.

Dear Benjamin,

You have your painting to take back to the Louvre. Andrea created many portraits of me. This is one of them. It has no special gold. It's just a gesture of love from him to me.

And you have my ring. I want you to cherish it. Twirl it and think of me.

I will continue to watch over you as I have always done.

Leaning over towards the wall, he slides down and lands on the cold tile. He places the new portrait on his lap and studies it. This is all he has left of her and Josiah.

He stares at her and fantasizes about slithering into the sarcophagus and becoming part of the history of the golden book, staying with everyone who was changed in this beautiful chapel, everyone who was touched by the book.

He's the only one left. All the secrets are now his to keep. And keeping them is a burden he must bear.

As Benjamin rubs his eyes on his sleeve, he stands up, takes a deep breath, blows out the candles, slings the backpack around his shoulder, and gently picks up the painting.

He walks towards the secret door that leads to the spectacular St. Mark's Square. He pauses before pushing it in and walking back into reality and the stunning day. The full extent of his emotions pushes down on him and he holds the wall to keep himself from falling. As he is standing in the quiet composing himself, he feels a bit of tingling from his baby finger. Looking down, he stares at Cle's ring. It's so small that it only fits on his baby finger. It's the only personal reminder of her. She's wearing it in the new painting, on her wedding finger. Now he's connected to this painting, connected to her through the ring. The little elf with the funny clothes changed his life, and this artifact will remind him of her until he dies.

At a table at one of the cafés in the square, he has shed the cape and is comfortably ensconced in one of the red basket chairs. He orders a plate of cicchetti and ómbra.

When was the last time I did this? he thinks.

The new *Immortal* has her own chair and her back is to the crowd. He's quite pleased that he's getting a few glances from women rushing by him flanked by their fellow vacationers. He's again someone who gets a second glance although he doesn't want one. It's a nice validation that perhaps he's officially in remission. Was it the drugs or was it the golden book? He'll never know. One thing is clear. He's in love. Deeply in love. As Grace said, they both get to drown in the depths of true love.

He scratches his wrist and takes off his Rolex, which keeps catching the fabric on his robe. The watch is one of his favourite possessions, a precious gift from Josiah. It's engraved on the back with his name along with a quote that defines how he's feeling about his future on this glorious day. It's from Friedrich Nietzsche:

"He who has a why to live for can bare almost any how."

Although he doesn't need evidence, he is acutely aware that anything that would validate his fantastical adventure is quickly disappearing. He takes inventory:

1. The portrait. It's not the original but it's just as magnificent. This one has no background. She's no longer holding a golden book. She's captured in her golden background all alone, calm, and blessed. Home at last.
2. His personal effects, including his phone and the many photos he took, are buried beside The Chapel of Hope, submerged under sand where the chasm was. The only photos that survived are the ones he emailed to himself.
3. The secret room in the crumbling Sartore Palace on the Isola di Speranza holds all the beautiful artwork created by Sartore.
4. The Secret Sartore Chapel in St. Mark's exists, and he knows how to access it. The gorgeous basilica has been the centre of something so profound and beautiful. With the exception of the painting beside him, Sartore's portraits are hidden in the jewel box. With permission, he could lead a search and get experts to look more thoroughly for more treasure.
5. Jenna disappeared without a trace and he's praying she doesn't reappear.

Are the ring, the rattle, and a few photos all he has left to prove any of this happened? He pulls out the rattle and shakes it, listening to the soft sound the balls inside make. It smells like the desperate mourners in the baptistery who swarmed around him yearning to get a chance to touch the golden book. He twists the ring on his finger.

While watching the tourists line up at St. Mark's for tours, he pulls of his backpack the new phone he bought earlier that day and dials a number.

"Boniface, it's Benjamin. How are you?"

He waits until Boniface replies.

"Good, very good. Remember my painting, *The Immortal*?...Yes, the one that belonged to my grandfather. I'm on my way to Paris and I'm donating it to the Louvre."

He continues watching the tourists snap photos and join the queue for tours.

"What happened to me? That's a good question Boniface. It's a long story. I was on a bit of a journey but I'm ready to come home."

Benjamin nods his head, "Yes, yes, totally. I'm about to propose to my girlfriend." He nods again and smiles at the portrait. "I'm turning over a new leaf. A new Benjamin. Thank you for your patience and support during my illness and my latest adventure. I will see you soon. Oh…are you still there?"

He drinks some ómbra. "Great. I have some other paintings that belonged to my grandfather. Sartore masterpieces. They're in a palazzo I didn't know existed, on an island in the lagoon. I'd like to donate them. Let's chat when we meet."

As he's staring ahead at the tourists feeding pigeons in the square, he concentrates on what Boniface is saying.

"Yes, I'm looking forward to seeing you. The donation is my pleasure. My family's pleasure. Ciao."

After he ends the call, he watches everyone in the square interacting with people who are so important to them. Sharing special moments in this glorious place. The only immortality he wants is this painting and the basilica…and love. He's choosing to live like a mortal and accept that no other option exists, even though he may be the only one remaining who knows it does.

He absent-mindedly twists the ring and stares into *The Immortal*'s brown eyes. He feels like they are pulling him in as a hypnotist would do. It unnerves him a little, but he can't turn away.

As he continues to twirl, the brown eyes become crystal clear, like a mirror, and he can see an image. It's Annacletica walking in the desert with The Chapel of Hope behind her.

Wearing a white robe with a hood, she walks, her long auburn hair blowing with abandon in the wind. She's walking with someone. A man. His back is to Benjamin and he doesn't recognize him.

Suddenly she turns around and stares right at Benjamin. His stomach tingles. His lips form into the biggest smile as she folds her hands in prayer and raises them to the heavens.

About the Author

Alexandra (Alix) Edmiston is a Toronto-based storyteller whose debut book, *Confessions from the Cubicle: Women Talk about Surviving in Today's Work Force*, received rave reviews from CTV in Montreal and Toronto, TVO, and CBC Radio. It delved into the unique challenges young women face adapting to the corporate world.

A versatile writer, Alix effortlessly weaves between fiction and non-fiction. She enjoys exploring magical realism and reflecting on the complexities of contemporary life through her writing. Inspired by cinematic storytelling, Alix is in her element when immersed in film during the Toronto International Film Festival.

Beyond her literary pursuits, Alix is a former journalist and internationally accredited corporate communicator (ABC) who works with leaders to hone their unique stories to place them at the centre of the conversation.

Fascinated by all things digital, Alix earned A+ in the digital marketing management program at the University of Toronto. She is also a graduate of Ryerson's journalism program for university graduates (JRAD), holds a degree in psychology from the University of Windsor, and earned a self-employment development certificate from Centennial College's Centre for Entrepreneurship.

Alix cares deeply for her community and is passionate about empowering others. A graduate of the prestigious Yale School of Management Women in Executive Leadership program, she tirelessly works to bridge gaps, shatter stereotypes, and build a more inclusive world for all.

She is known for her passion for Paris, London, Venice, and Istanbul, and for her signature red lipstick.

Notes

[1] Hermes Trismegistus, *Emerald Tablet of Hermes*, Accessed May 8, 2024 from universalfreemasonry.org/en/library/emerald-tablet-of-hermes/jabir-ibn-hayyan-translation-of-the-emerald-tablet-of-hermes.

[2] John 20:27, accessed May 12, 2024 from biblegateway.com/passage/?search=john+20%3A27&version=KJV.

[3] John Keats, "Ode to a Nightingale," Accessed May 14, 2024 from poetryfoundation.org/poems/44479/ode-to-a-nightingale.

[4] Ibid.